VAGABOND

VAGABOND HOLES

DAVID McCOMB AND THE TRIFFIDS

❋

EDITED BY

CHRIS COUGHRAN
& NIALL LUCY

FREMANTLE PRESS

For the kids — Dylan, Hannah, Jakeb, Joaby and Thomas

Contents

Preface

Chris Coughran

Some births are worse than murders ... The present volume, a labour of love for all concerned, was conceived via transcontinental email in the early part of May 2006. Inevitably, no doubt, its gestation and delivery were fraught with complications. Most unexpected was a concurrent surge of interest in the legacy of The Triffids, buoyed by a raft of admirable initiatives: a reissued back catalogue replete with detailed liner notes and perfect-bound booklets; a series of retrospective concerts in Belgium and the Netherlands; a television documentary and plans for a feature-length film; the Sydney (and subsequently Perth) Festival showcase, *A Secret in the Shape of a Song*; and the band's induction by St Nick into the ARIA (Australian Recording Industry Association) Hall of Fame. As the misbegotten, poorer cousin of the bunch, floundering like a retard in the backwash of such illustrious forebears, this book could hardly be expected — indeed, was never intended — to be 'the last word' on David McComb and The Triffids. Even so, it is with a sense of tremendous pride and more than a little relief, that we sever at last the umbilical cord and unleash our little monster — in all its polymorphous perversity, and bearing several aspects that even a mother would be hard pressed to love — upon an unsuspecting world of noble aesthetes.

This book owes its existence, first and foremost, to the generosity and forbearance of its contributors, to whom we humbly express our gratitude. We are especially thankful for the cordial encouragement shown to us by the surviving members of The Triffids — Jill Birt, Martyn P. Casey, Graham Lee, Alsy MacDonald and Rob McComb — and for services rendered along the way by various others. Maria Barnas, Emily Bitto, Ruth Blair, Robert Briggs, Sally Collins, Maryanne Doyle, Trevor

Hogan, Sascha Jenkins, Steve Keene, Braden King, Toby Martin, Steve Mickler, Julian Miller, Negeen Nichols, Elizabeth Pippett, Max Richter, Margaret Sankey, Douglas Sheerer (Galerie Düsseldorf), Samantha Stevenson, Darren Tofts, Steven Vandervelden (STUK), Brian Waldron, McKenzie Wark and Sarah Wilson provided much-needed moral support, indulging the editors' many whims, facilitating often importunate solicitations, and countenancing all manner of recherché requests. For service above and beyond the call of duty, Georgia Richter, our consultant editor at Fremantle Press, deserves special mention. We should also like to thank Curtin University of Technology, for contributing towards travel costs associated with the book.

Finally, it would be remiss of us not to offer, in the spirit of The Triffids' album liner notes, a parting gesture acknowledging certain adversarial powers, whether real or imaginary. *No thanks*, therefore, *to you know very well who you are.*

Introduction

Niall Lucy

I am a loose strand
You may never tie nor mend
—David McComb, 'Keep Your Eyes on the Hole'

This book is not a rock biography. It doesn't feign to tell the story of David McComb's life, or to explain his music as an expression of that story. It doesn't seek to psychologize McComb by construing some eventful moment in his childhood as the talismanic source of meaning in his songs. While several pieces here are clearly biographical or historical in nature, these are no more imperative than other — fictional, poetic, speculative, critical or variously visual — inclusions.

For us, McComb's work is more than capable of sustaining — indeed, clearly warrants — such wide-ranging and varied discussion. We didn't want that discussion, therefore, to settle into a familiar style or be constrained by a single point of view. While welcoming the insights of those who knew McComb — friends and fellow musicians alike — we were equally interested in other ways of looking at the topic, which, once collected, would constitute less a work than a work in progress: loose strands 'bound', in a certain sense, but still untied. An *Exile on Main St* of a book. A vagabond collection, full of holes.

The devil here is in the mix. Why this piece, alongside that one? Why this photograph, and not another? In most but not all cases our response would be that, where possible, we've sought to avoid familiar, obvious or predictable associations. We didn't want the visual pieces, for example, to serve merely as 'illustrations,' marking them as supplementary to the primacy of words. We didn't want the more speculative or theoretical pieces grouped together, marking them as different for being 'academic' and therefore out of place in a music book. This is not to say that, as editors, we are in full control of the book's possible meanings, uses and effects, or that the order in which we've assembled the pieces is sacrosanct. Far from it. Readers who, for whatever reason or none at all, elect to shuffle back and forth among the book's contents will hardly have violated our intentions by doing so. The vagabond, after all, the very figure of aimless wandering, may assume any number of forms but inevitably travels an idiosyncratic route, often beating an inscrutable path to who knows where.

When it came to assembling this eclectic 'mix tape' of a book, we loosely arranged the various fragments under three headings that could easily be mistaken for a beginning, middle and end. The first of these, 'Suburban Stories', is perhaps in little need of explanation, comprising pieces either set in suburbia or which have something to say about the suburban experience. Jon Stratton's essay, for example, tells the story of a serial killer who, in 1962, the year McComb was born, terrorized the good citizens of Perth, Western Australia, with the perverse effect of 'modernizing' that city. In Richard Gunning's painting *Crucifixion*, encroaching shadows darken a sun-scorched suburban tableau, deserted but for the dominating Christ-figure who hangs suspended, if unbloodied, from what appears to be one of three inexplicably wireless electricity poles. (As a kind of companion piece, the Thomas Hoareau painting in section two, *Lovers (Business as Usual)*, positions an imagined statue outside of Perth Railway Station at night, the coldness of the scene ironically warmed by the intimacy of the lifeless figures' embrace.) It was in the suburbs, too, that a young boy won a Divinity prize at school and later, in an apparent act of renunciation, became a martyr of Perth punk, a tale recounted here by Andrew McGowan.

Section two, 'Temporary Monuments', turns to questions of legacy, inheritance and commemoration. McComb himself, after all, was no less a *fan* than a composer of music, and often sought to explain the sound or atmosphere of his own songs with reference to records by his favourite artists (Springsteen, Van Morrison, Tom Waits … the list was long). He also wore his literary influences on his sleeve, along with his taste in movies and other cultural forms. 'Didn't McComb's fiery energy,' Jean Bernard Koeman asks here, 'spring from his self-pro-claimed adoration of Dylan and Leadbelly and the poets Les Murray and Marina Tsevetaeva?' To these could be added, among countless others, musicians as diverse as Kraftwerk, The Velvet Underground and Laura Nyro, and the writers F. Scott Fitzgerald, Flannery O'Connor and T.S. Eliot. Accordingly, Koeman continues, isn't McComb's music imbued not only with grand, ahistorical themes and sentiments ('loss, rage, the empty landscape'), but also with 'the dustbowls of Woody Guthrie, the melodies of The Byrds and The Stooges, the poetic voice of Joseph Brodsky, the agitated, inventive energy of the "Post" Wave?'

In a sense — in what might be called a postmodern sense — McComb made music from materials to hand, and not sim-ply from the depths of his 'soul.' Borrowing a line or an image from Murray or Fitzgerald here, a musical phrase from Van Morrison or Television there, McComb's is an art of assemblage: piratical, nomadic, vagabond. But … as if there were any other way, as if an art could be the pure, unmediated expression of an artist's 'interiority.' Art doesn't express; it invents. It invents new possible ways of imagining a world and of relating to it: *art* does this, and not artists. *Art* invents, and we fail to respond to that invention when we see art purely as the prod-uct of an artist's self-expression. To the extent, then, that McComb's music is a pastiche of sonorous and verbal elements and larger narra-tive and thematic structures that are not in themselves unprecedented or unique, it is not essentially different from the art of Chuck Berry or Elvis. Its distinctiveness lies not in the naïve assertion of an abso-lute originality, but in its own peculiar borrowings and combinatory styles. James Paterson refers to some of these in his piece (in section one) on collaborating with McComb, while something of the eclecti-cism of McComb's musical taste is revealed in Nick Cave's commemo-ration of a drunken sing-along between the two.

From a different perspective, written as a kind of diary entry on his experience of singing with The Triffids at the 2008 Sydney Festival, Steve Kilbey underscores the necessity of sonority (hitting the right notes) in the production of rock's most valued effect, sincerity: a 'sin-cere' performance rests on the manipulation of a certain *technique*, the peculiar 'grain' or sonic characteristics of the voice notwithstanding.

This explains why McComb, like every singer before or since, recorded several versions of a song before settling on a particular vocal performance, just as John Lennon is famously supposed to have achieved the right cut for 'Revolution' by lying supine on the floor of Abbey Road Studios while he sang. The romantic quest for a kind of sublime monumentality is always tinged, in other words, with a sense of that quest's futility, since all art is inseparable from the historical, material, cultural and other forms of contingency surrounding and infusing its possible meanings, uses and effects. Yet still we feel compelled, as here in the Sean Whelan poem, 'How to Climb Inside a Song and Disappear Completely', to celebrate what moves us, however fleetingly, if only in the recollection of 'a stage adorned with electric tulips' at a Triffids' gig at The Old Greek Theatre in Melbourne, one night long ago … or of a few boozy days spent with The Triffids, as Gavin Martin recalls (albeit from Bangor, Northern Ireland), in the Perth summer of 1989.

In the final section, 'Unmarked Tracks', which takes its name from one of McComb's alternative titles for *Born Sandy Devotional*, we detour off the wide, open road through secret, bonus pathways. As always, our guiding star in these parting perambulations (or, indeed, depending on where you came in, these initial forays) is the aimless wanderer, and like the chance meanderings of the vagabond or that figure's well-heeled equivalent, the *flaneur*, the point is not to have one. The point is not to arrive at a destination or a *telos* but to affirm the heterogeneous and supplementary pleasures of meandering for the sake of it, without contriving an outcome. Here, then, we go circuitously back to a time when letters and phone calls were the only means of keeping in touch with loved ones far away (Megan Heyward); forward, to a bathroom in Singapore and recollections of youthful nights in London pubs spent listening to The Triffids in the 1980s (John Dyer); and elsewhere, to a way of thinking about The Triffids as an occasion or inspiration for a 'people to come' (Claire Colebrook). All of which gets us somewhere past the middle, but nowhere near anything as definitive as an end.

Endings, even sudden deaths, are never as final as they seem. A book no more ends at a last word than a song ends on a conclusive note. When something intrigues us — a life, a work of art — it goes on intriguing us, long past the point at which it might officially be said to have passed away. There are always loose strands, or else only neat packages; mysteries, or else only facts.

This is art's elusive essence: to remind us, dear reader, to keep our eyes on the hole.

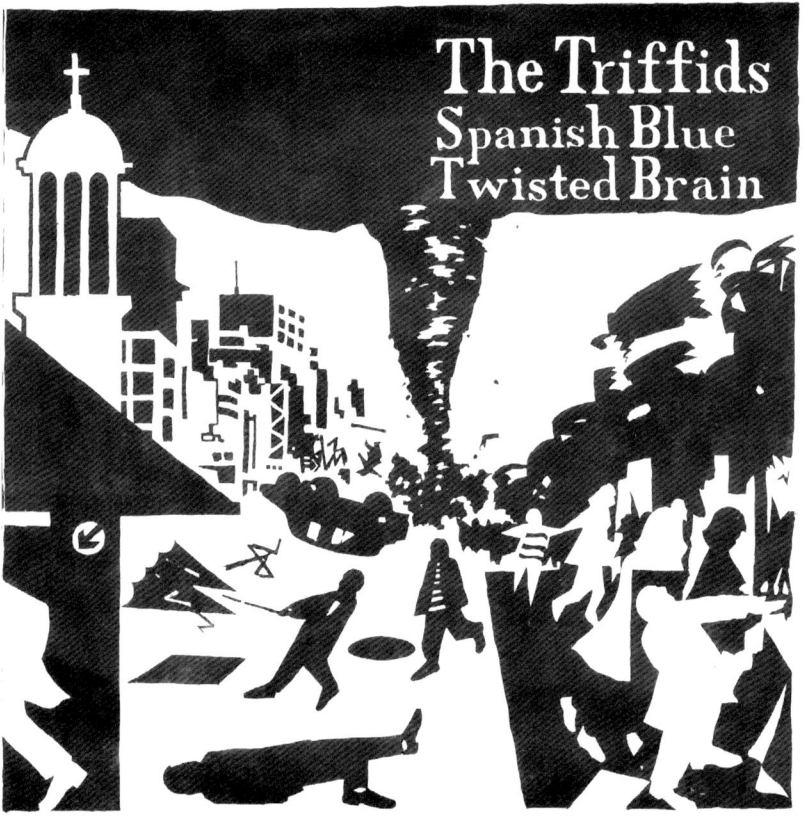

Two faces of
suburbia: 'Spanish
Blue' backed with
'Twisted Brain'
(1982). Artwork by
Thomas Hoareau.

Suburban Stories

Alsy MacDonald
and David
McComb, near
Devil's Elbow,
Peppermint
Grove, c. 1979.

1969

Alsy MacDonald

I was not brought up in a religious family. My family never went to church or observed any religious rituals, except for the familiar, commercially driven ones at Christmas and Easter. The McCombs did go to church, although I wouldn't have described Harold and Athel, Dave's parents, as overtly religious.

If I stayed the night at Dave's house on a Saturday, which I did every few weeks, he and I would have to go to church with his family on Sunday morning. Of the children, only Dave, and possibly Rob, was required to go. John had been let off the hook by this stage and I think Peter had moved out of home.

We were both seven years old. Maybe I had already turned eight. As Dave got older, and bolder, he would eventually succeed in getting out of having to go, but at that time, we just accepted it. Anyway, leaving us behind was not an option.

So, at around nine o'clock, we would drive in Harold's Holden HR Premier to an unassuming, neo-gothic, Presbyterian church in Kingsway, Nedlands. Nedlands, where I grew up, was, and is, a conservative suburb that seemed to exist more in the 1930s than the 1960s. This was still the era of horn-rimmed spectacles, hair nets, and shorts worn with long socks, and all were usually present in abundance. Upon arrival, and after pleasantries, we would take our place amongst the faithful.

Dave and I would pretend to sing the hymns, although I had no idea how the tunes went, and wondered how everyone else knew them. At some point, the minister would stop the service, and the children were 'invited' to attend Sunday school, which was conducted in an added-on area at the back of the church. The children then filed out and were led down to the Sunday school. The school was conducted by two or three 'young adults,' friendly and casually dressed. They were probably older kids who had volunteered to be teachers so they could get out of having to sit through the whole service, but I can't really say.

Activities included drawing scenes from the Bible, listening to fables, and discussing the deeds of Jesus and his disciples. Nothing wrong with that, I suppose, except that Dave and I were not exactly the most conscientious of students. I remember an occasion when both of us drew a depiction of the crusades, broadswords hacking into limbs, viscera spilling out of gaping wounds, and shields smeared with blood. We knew it was probably not what the teachers had in mind but it made the whole thing bearable for us.

It was on one of these Sunday mornings that something happened to make me realize that not only did Dave regard society and its conventions in quite a different way to most other people — which I already knew — but that he wasn't afraid to say so, even at such a tender age.

We were asked by a teacher, a young woman, who had a sixties-student look about her, to sit in a circle on the floor. She told us she was going to ask us some questions on a Bible-related topic, I can't remember what. She then produced a portable reel-to-reel tape recorder and placed it in the middle of the circle. Perhaps she was doing some research. Whatever her background, everyone was impressed with the technology.

The teacher went around the group of kids, all about our age, getting them to speak into the microphone. I vaguely remember Dave and I discussing what we might say or do when it was our turn. We had been joking around a bit, so a mood of subversion was building up like static electricity. When the teacher got to us, she placed the microphone in front of our faces, and asked a question about Jesus. There was a brief pause.

'Mary's a bitch.'

Dave uttered the statement directly into the microphone, without hesitation or aggression. He then looked at me with a grin, and we both started laughing. I can't remember what the teacher said or if she asked us any more questions. I doubt it. No amount of lay psychology would have assisted her. She didn't tell us off, but I'm sure she moved on to someone more compliant. Of course, we didn't tell Athel or

Harold about it, and, as far as I'm aware, nothing was reported back to them. On the other hand, it got our day off to a great start.

This episode represents my earliest appreciation of Dave's adherence to non-conformity as a guiding principle, fashioned through a keen sense of the profane. I shared his view of things (most of the time), and we urged each other on. I knew that he hadn't set out to deliberately cause offence as an end in itself, although maybe there was an element of that. And I don't think it had anything really to do with Jesus or Mary or religion. I doubt Dave had seriously formed a view about such things at that stage. He was simply making the point that he didn't have to go along with, or like, what everyone else was doing, a notion he was driven to express many times again.

It was an aspect of Dave's character that others came to experience in the years to come, not always to their advantage. His assessment of other people's opinions and motives could be cruel and unfair. Ironically, it was New Age mysticism, not mainstream religion, that Dave came to loathe. Back then, however, he was just finding out how easy it was to get a reaction.

Country
Gentleman: David
McComb with
newly acquired
(vintage) Gretsch
guitar, 1981.

Three Songs

Robert Forster

What a lucky city Sydney was on this pale blue morning to see two tall charismatic young men such as David McComb and myself walking towards each other. I had been back in town for under a week, returning with my band The Go-Betweens from our current home in London to start a tour to promote our latest album. It was the early eighties and both David and I were walking the fresh morning streets of Darlinghurst alone—he coming down the hill on one side, me going up the hill on the other, when I saw him.

We knew each other of course. The Go-Betweens and The Triffids had played gigs together before we'd gone to London and, through this and the crossover of certain people we had in common, both bands had become friends. We also shared the fate of being outsider musicians from far-off places, Brisbane and Perth, and that meant both of us had already done some travelling and were going to have to do a whole lot more to fulfil the ambitions of our respective bands.

We talked on the street and I told him that I had just heard the latest recordings that The Triffids had done; that in my rambling about Sydney over the previous days someone had played me their new record and that I had liked it a great deal—especially a song called 'Red Pony'. What I didn't tell him but felt in my bones was that it was a breakthrough song and that if a songwriter can write one great song then they will certainly write more. This seemed a little too much to say and phrase without sounding condescending. But I praised 'Red Pony' heavily. I also said to him that if he had a spare moment over the next days and he was around, could he possibly show me how to play the song on guitar. He smiled, said he would, and we parted.

I must explain why I asked David this. I'm not a natural musician (David was) and music had always been a mystery to me. It was hard to decode. I learnt other people's songs primarily from song-books. Very basic songs I could work out from records — Ramones songs say. But anything more complicated I didn't trust or believe in myself enough to learn. I remember someone playing me a song from Television's *Marquee Moon* once, and it seemed wondrous and impossible that I was seeing someone's hands move on a guitar and a Television song come to life. So when I asked David to show me 'Red Pony' I wasn't being cute. It was because I thought 'Red Pony' was a great song and I wanted to know great songs and it just popped into my head at that particular moment to ask him.

Two days later I was in Darlinghurst in a friend's house. I was alone and there was a sudden knock at the door and I wondered if I should answer it. I did and standing in the doorway with a big semi-acous-tic guitar in his hand was David. I invited him in and walked him through to the back of this small workers' cottage where there was a tiny kitchen with a wooden table and chairs. We sat down, he settled himself, and then he began to play me 'Red Pony'. My eyes burnt on his fingers. The song started in A-minor and I watched the chords descend, holding as they did, the beautiful melody he'd created and now sang. His voice was strong and dignified over the metallic clang of the guitar. When the song ended I thanked him for finding me and playing me the song, and I offered him the only thing I had in return, a cup of tea, which he accepted.

The second song happened two years later. This was a very dif-ferent scene. It was at a party in London, in a flat The Triffids rented near the centre of the city. Everyone was there — Triffids, Moodists, Go-Betweens, photographers, journalists, girlfriends, boyfriends, London friends, Perth people, all cramped into a couple of rooms drinking and smoking and yakking. Parties of this time had a par-ticular pitch. It was brought on by the fact that it was impossible to buy alcohol in London after eleven o'clock at night and that all public transport closed down soon after. Friends who seldom saw each other, locked as they were into lives in a foreign city, drank and talked at a pace quicker than usual. Everything had to be said and done within three hours. I was happily weaving my way through the party when I came across David in the kitchen. 'Wide Open Road' had just come out and after some initial conversation I asked him if he would play me the song sometime. He looked at me with an indulgent smile. I was helpless for a second and then he surprised me by saying he'd play it to me now.

The guitar he held was the same from Sydney, a big Gretsch semi-acoustic. David sat on the edge of his bed and I sat on my haunches on the floor. He started to play. My eyes burnt on his fingers again. 'Wide Open Road' started in G-major. I watched him peel off the chords. They were simple and majestic. It was a classic song and I followed it round as he played. His voice was similar to the way it had been in Sydney, perhaps a little grander, because the song was a little bigger. When it was over the volume of the party rose up again. I looked out the window of his room and there was a railway track, ghostlike and quiet. I thanked him and we both stepped out of this world back into the bright lights of the party.

The final song happens ten years later. The Triffids and The Go-Betweens are no more and I am performing a solo acoustic show at The Continental in Melbourne. I am backstage in the large dressing room with waiter service that the venue provides to its performers. I am going on in twenty minutes and there is the fear in the pit of the stomach that only really hits hard when performing alone. I am pacing the room doing what I always do before such shows — thinking of passably witty or informative things to say between songs. These few sentences are especially needed when the only thing between yourself and the audience is an acoustic guitar.

David is at The Continental too. He is out in the room deejaying — entertaining people and establishing a mood for me to walk out into. I am just about to go on, at the curtain, when I hear the familiar opening strains of 'Mississippi' by John Phillips. This is a song that I know. John Phillips was in The Mamas & the Papas. He wrote 'California Dreamin'', 'Monday, Monday' and most of the band's other hits. He also recorded a solo album in 1970 called *The Wolf King of LA* which has a small cult following among singer-songwriters such as David and I. So at this particular moment when I am about to step out on stage I know David is sending a message to me through this song. It is support. It is good luck. It is a pat on the back as I walk out to the microphone.

After the show the crowd slowly thins and as I pack up to leave there seems to be just two other people around — David collecting up his records, and Jo his long-time partner and friend standing by the door. I'm asking the owners of the club to get me a cab when David and Jo offer to drive me to my hotel in town. We walk out of the club to the car and we drive into town. The hotel is up at the far end of the city centre near Parliament House and the theatres. We pull up there. I'm in the back seat and I thank them for the lift and tell them I can get my suitcase and guitar from the boot of the car by myself. I open my car door and walk around to the back. David is suddenly standing there. It is after midnight and no one else is on the streets. I get my stuff from the car and look at him. We are the same height. He smiles at me the way he always did, with the sides of his mouth curled. What do I read into it? Patience, a lingering suspicion he may have of me, and a lot of affection. It is a warm goodbye. He gets back into the car and they drive off. It's the last time I will see him.

Soon after I move to Regensburg, Germany with my wife and we start a family. I am cut off from the immediate music world and the Australian scene in particular. In 1999, in the middle of the five years I will spend there, I hear that David has died. It is distant news but brought into sharp relief through encounters and times with him. I think of the meeting on the Darlinghurst street, 'Red Pony', the London party and sitting low to hear 'Wide Open Road', the farewell in Melbourne — and other moments too. I also weigh these encounters trying to find a ledger in my heart and mind of what he gave to me and what I gave in return. You do this when people die. And I find myself in debt to David.

Rent

Steve Miller

By 1986, The Moodists had been living in London for a while and were an empty shell. Nothing was happening or going to happen. No one wanted to know. Chris Walsh had gone home to Melbourne; Dave Graney and Clare Moore were a tight unit and planning their escape; my girlfriend had had enough and left. Our guitars had been stolen. We were fucked. I had shingles in my left eye. The dream was over. Might as well stick around until the money runs out and limp home to Melbourne, to God knows what. It was hopeless.

I'd visit The Triffids' houses, always around dinnertime, cadge a meal and have a few beers. Dave rang me to come for dinner one night, on my birthday as it turned out. Not that anyone knew it was my birthday, I supposed. But Dave had arranged a surprise party in my honour, and asked everyone to do a cartoon of me. I was stunned. The guy on the front cover of the *NME* was blowing up balloons for a scumbag from The Moodists.

Dave seemed to know I needed a break and he gave me one. He gave me the thrill of being part of something again. Then I got a phone call from The Go-Betweens' manager: 'When are you coming in to start working on the tour?' 'What tour?' I asked. The Go-Betweens had taken literally an off-hand remark I'd made at a party, about tour managing 'Handsome Steve'-style. So I went in and I became their Tour Manager. I didn't even have a bomber jacket or a metal briefcase. PAs? Forget it. I didn't know how to calculate the VAT. Stage technician Duggie Guthrie saved my arse there. But I took a keen interest in the rider because I thought if the talent was fed and had plenty to drink, things would go okay. And they did.

The day after I got back from The Go-Betweens tour I got a call from The Triffids to go on tour for them. I was with them for a year or so. It was a very happy time, everyone looked after each other. Victor Van Vugt, Peter Mackay and Duggie Guthrie (I nicked him from The Go-Betweens) took care of production and I was food and beverage manager.

In early 1987 The Triffids toured Australia and I hated the way they were treated. Horrible promoters, the clubs were awful, the club managers thought bands were 'part of the problem.' At the end of the tour I had to return a van from Sydney to Melbourne and Dave suddenly jumped into the van for the drive. Ten hours on the Hume Highway … why would you do that? To keep me company?

Years later I leased a little pub (The Standard in Fitzroy, Melbourne) with another guy, and Dave and Jo came to stay. They'd just returned from London, I think. My business partner, who was going on holiday, agreed to let them stay as long as they paid rent. Just about every Tuesday night at the pub Dave did 'Trick of the Light' with Graham Lee and his band, The Paradise Vendors, and the place stopped.

When my partner got back from holiday he asked for the rent. I said I couldn't charge Dave rent. My business partner said I was piss-weak. He was probably right. He just had no idea, no idea at all.

Dave played his last gig at that same little pub, which I'd sold a year before, on New Year's Eve, 1998. He'd certainly paid his rent by then.

'Handsome' Steve Miller in 1970, as pictured by David McComb in 1986.

1970

D. McL.

Dave & Alsy at The
Triffids' house on
Brunswick Street,
Fitzroy, Melbourne,
late 1982.

Dutch Courage

Judith Lucy

The last time I saw David McComb was at the 3RRR community radio station ball. I made a point of telling him something that had been true for over a decade: I had a massive crush on him.

My older brother, Niall, took me to my first ever concert at the age of fifteen. It was Adam and the Ants and I don't know that a sibling has ever made a bigger sacrifice for their little sister. I was close to passing out with excitement but within about fifteen minutes had to admit that while I wanted to marry Adam, he couldn't really hold a tune. Fortunately, he removed his dandy highwayman shirt at some stage and I was in heaven; strangely it did not have the same effect on my brother. Niall, after I badgered him for his opinion, told me that he thought the band had been 'as weak as piss.' I was shocked by such criticism of Mr Ant, but when he later took me to gigs by Simple Minds and New Order I had to admit that neither of those outfits had to rely on their nipples to entertain a crowd.

I believe the next band he took me to see was a local one called The Triffids. I had been pretty excited at the other gigs but this one was different, my brother *knew* these people. I got to meet them. Well, I was a fifteen-year-old girl who was years away from being the floozy I am now, so would have been standing in a corner clutching a Fanta and behaving a little like a twelve-year-old but — wow! — I was backstage and thought Dave McComb was one of the best-looking men I had ever seen. I thought he was just so fucking cool.

I wound up being (and still am) a huge Triffids fan in my own right. I simply cannot think of my home town of Perth without also thinking of their music. I remember a particularly packed gig one summer afternoon where much of the exhausted crowd was sitting on the filthy floor of the venue and nothing could have echoed our thoughts more aptly than Dave's lyrics: 'it's too hot to move and it's too hot to think.'

One Christmas holidays I worked for the FTI cinema in Fremantle where we were supposedly hosting a 'cutting edge' collection of Australian music clips — we're talking videos that make The Buggles' 'Video Killed the Radio Star' look like *The Fifth Element*. My mind-numbing job was to walk around this room all day to make sure nothing was stolen (were people going to smuggle a television out in their sleeve?) but I would always time it so that I never missed The Triffids' 'Wide Open Road'. Unlike the other clips, this one was about my home.

When I was still relatively young I went and visited my brother who had by then moved to Sydney. We went and saw The Triffids and once backstage, no doubt trying to impress the object of my affections, I made one of my first and most pathetic attempts at smoking. My brother's girlfriend told me off in front of the whole band — in front of *Dave*. He'd never sleep with me now.

I got older and while my adolescent crush for this tall, eloquent man had been replaced by a much more realistic one on George Clooney, every year as soon as it grew hot in my new home of Melbourne, I would drag out my Triffids vinyl. For me no other band captures summer in Australia, particularly WA, like The Triffids.

Occasionally I would see Dave around. His health by now was poor, and certainly he did not cut quite the same figure he once had, but I found him no less intimidating. I would say hello but generally that was all I could muster. At the 3RRR ball, Dutch courage enabled me to actually sit down next to him and make my confession. His reply was gracious and I suspect not true, but the fact that he was talking to me at all was more than enough.

Suburban Stories: Dave McComb and the Perth Experience

Jon Stratton

While much of Dave McComb's lyrical output for The Triffids uses imagery drawn from the bush, the organizing structure of such lyrics is based on a mythic understanding of Perth as experienced by the inhabitants of that city. This understanding is infused with the idea that living in Perth is a suburban idyll. Consequently, any major crime in the city is experienced as excessive and transgressive — a Gothic eruption into the utopian everyday. In other large cities, a major crime is seen as an unfortunate element in the experience of everyday life; in Perth it is considered a threat to the idyllic community and a marker of the city's decline.

In 1962, the year McComb was born, Perth was embroiled in a crime wave perpetrated by Eric Edgar Cooke, who was apprehended in 1963 and hanged for murder the following year. The effect of Cooke's criminal acts on the people of Perth is summarized on the flyleaf of journalist Estelle Blackburn's chronicle of the Cooke case, *Broken Lives* (1998): 'The end of Estelle Blackburn's childhood saw the end of innocence for her safe little home city, all because of one man.' Construed as a Gothic bogeyman, Cooke was held responsible for various changes, such as loss of community, more often associated with urban expansion.

In 1986, three years after The Triffids had left Perth, Catherine and David Birnie commenced serially abducting, raping, and murdering girls. They were both given life sentences in 1987. The reaction in Perth was similar to that experienced in the aftermath of the Cooke case, as an ABC news report on David Birnie's prison suicide, in 2005, makes clear: 'Graeme Scott, a retired Supreme Court judge who also prosecuted the Birnies, says the case changed Western Australia. "I think it's probably the first time in Western Australia's history, apart from Eric Edgar Cook[e], where I think the public were justifiably in a general sense [as] apprehensive … as they are now about terrorist bombings," he said.'[1] Here, again, we have the idea of a set of crimes transforming the way residents of Perth experience their city. Again, the sense is of the loss of the suburban idyll.

McComb grew up in Perth when the rhetoric of a loss of innocence, a loss of suburban utopian community as a consequence of awful acts constructed in Gothic terms — of Cooke's actions specifically, and of the constant apprehension, to use Scott's word, that something similar might happen again — were the dominant ways of thinking about living in the city. Through what is generally regarded as the highpoint of the Triffids' corpus, however, McComb wrote very little about Perth and suburbia as such. Rather, the bulk of his lyrics concerned the male experience of female rejection, in other words thwarted or failed relationships. In these songs the man is left desolate, unsure of his identity, unable to move on, and at times, suicidal. I want to suggest that this pattern, too, is a function of the social order of suburbia.

Of course, suburbia is not unique to Perth. As a form of spatial organization it can be traced back to the expansion of eighteenth-century London and contemporaneous developments in the middle-class way of life, such as the establishment of the privatized nuclear family as the norm. However, Perth — along with Los Angeles — is one of the rare cities in which the suburban spatial form has become dominant to the almost complete elimination of a central business district.[2] Although recently an attempt has been made to increase the population density of the inner city in order to slow suburban sprawl up and down the coast, during the 1960s and 1970s — when McComb was growing up in the riverside suburb of Peppermint Grove, midway between Perth and the port city of Fremantle — the suburban dream was much vaunted and widely celebrated.

In Perth, the cultivation of suburbia coincided with what Veronica Brady describes as 'the Arcadian strain in Western Australian writing.' This tendency, Brady notes, is in keeping with 'a society founded by English gentlefolk in search of the "good old days" which, it seemed, would not come again in England.' For Brady, the Perth experience precipitates the kind of 'passionate need' that continues to drive denizens to the beach in summer, 'something more than the heat and a hankering for unlimited water,' which Katharine Susannah Prichard wrote about in *Intimate Strangers* (1937). According to Brady, this need 'arises from the pressures of place and history or rather, the lack of history. On the one hand the sheer distance which separates the West Australian from the rest of the world, and on the other the uneventfulness of life leads to the sense of *ennui*, the classical *accidie*.'[3] The beach is the one place where the utopian elements of the Arcadian and the suburban come together. In Perth it is the most generally accepted site of pleasure.

In McComb's corpus of lyrics, indulgence in relaxation — a kind of laid-back hedonism — brackets the Gothic mid-period albums. Thus, in 'Spanish Blue', an early single: 'Nothing happens here/Nothing gets done/But you get to like it/You get to like the beating of the sun/The washing of the sun/In Spanish Blue.' The sentiment is reworked almost verbatim in 'Bottle of Love' on *The Black Swan*, The Triffids' final studio album: 'Well nothing happens here/And not too much gets done/But you get to like it/You get to like the drinking and the swimming around/Oh, passing around the bottle of love.' This is the easygoing hedonism of suburban, utopian, idyllic Perth.

Summer is the time when this hedonism is most apparent. In Perth, summer offers clear skies and almost unrelenting sunshine. As befits the city's Arcadian mythologizing, the natural world provides a context for the hedonistic experience. Thus, in 'Spanish Blue': 'you get to like the beating of the sun,' etc. But as McComb's lyrics shift to a more Gothic perspective — as on *Treeless Plain* — sun and summer begin to assume a threatening aspect: 'It's been a hell of a summer to be lying so low/Dogs and cats dropping down in the street' ('Hell of a Summer'). This is a summer where the natural world is not in harmony with human — for which, read: suburban — pleasures. Now the sun is *too* hot; pets can't handle it. Friendly relations have soured, becoming toxic: 'Every word of kindness tastes like bile.' In this hellish scenario we find an echo of Eric Edgar Cooke and Perth's anxious preoccupation with murder: 'What you cannot have, sir, you must kill.' This summer is the opposite — if you like, the Gothic, excessive and transgressive inverse — of that suburban, sybaritic idyll: 'And I say to you/It's been hell'; not, McComb emphasizes, the idyllic summertime pleasures that the people of Perth like to imagine for themselves, but the hellish experience of constant fear and anxiety as when, for example, a serial killer such as Eric Edgar Cooke is at large.

Writing in the same issue of *Westerly* as Veronica Brady, poet Dorothy Hewett repudiates Perth's utopian image, and the commonplace notion of Western Australia as 'a wonderful place to bring up kids.' In her experience, 'Western Australia was mostly innocent, but … naïve, self-congratulatory and deeply conservative, a perfect field for corruption.' The corruption of Western Australia, Hewett writes, 'is partly hidden, the worm in the bud is secretive, and mainly bears only a silent witness.'[4]

Since awful things do not happen in Utopia, they have to be thought of in terms of that 'excess' which I have been describing as 'Gothic.'[5] It is not merely coincidental that Gothic, as a generic form of literature, developed in the same historical period that saw the invention of the suburb. The writing of Western Australia abounds with salient examples of the genre, from Peter Cowan's collection of short stories *The Empty Street* (1965), to Philip Masel's neglected novel *In a Glass Prison* (1937). Dorothy Hewett's poem 'Sanctuary', from her collection *Rapunzel in Suburbia* (1975), 'presents Perth as a place of quiet … desperation where suicide seems the chief option for wild spirits.'[6] And forms of violent or unnatural death, such as murder and suicide, offer a crucial challenge to the construction of Perth in terms of a bourgeois utopia.

Conversely, 'the terrors and horrors of transgression in Gothic writing [can] become … a powerful means to reassert the values of society, virtue and propriety.'[7] The crimes of Eric Edgar Cooke were constructed, in both the media and the courts, in Gothic terms; Cooke was transformed into a bogeyman figure, and for a generation after the case was closed mothers would tell their children to make sure all the windows and doors were locked 'in case Cookie comes.' The account published by Blackburn in 1998, thirty-four years after Cooke's execution, is structured along the lines of the Gothic doppelgänger, the 'double' characterized in Robert Louis Stevenson's *Strange Case of Dr Jekyll and Mr Hyde* (1886). Dr Jekyll is convinced that human beings are an amalgam of good and evil. He conducts experiments to try to find a way of separating these two components of human nature. Hyde was the evil aspect of Jekyll. By the same token, in Blackburn's account, Cooke 'was married with seven children, but these nights were his own, when he could give vent to his dark, evil side.'[8] Further on she writes:

> Clumsy and accident-prone as he was at his job, late at night he turned into the most skilful cat-burglar who could creep through houses and steal even while the people were at home. On the prowl at night he was a completely different person. People who knew him during the day could never guess the other side of him.[9]

The motif runs right through the book until, near the end, we are told that 'those who knew Cooke were stunned that this charming, helpful man could have such an evil side to him.'[10] Harelip and cleft palate notwithstanding, Cooke is construed as a good suburban family man by day who becomes an evil predator at night, dispensing with middle-class morality and 'going native' as David Punter suggests of Jekyll/Hyde.[11] Blackburn credits Cooke — an evil, malevolent force emerging, like the Birnies, from a perpetually obscure working-class background — with single-handedly transforming Perth into a typical Western city. She writes that after Cooke was caught,

> the people of Perth were getting over their shock and settling back into the normal life of a city — though a vastly changed one. Perth would never be the same again. Never again would doors be left unlocked and keys left in cars. No longer would people enjoy the safety of a big country town where everyone could be trusted. Perth had grown up to become a city of suspicion and locked doors.[12]

In Peter Cowan's story 'The Empty Street', an apparent recension of the Cooke case, it is the failure of the marriage bond that transforms Michael, the frustrated middle-class husband, into a serial killer of women. Readers have observed that Michael and his wife Leila 'communicate on the most superficial level, confining themselves to bickering over minor domestic issues, without any hope of ever understanding or resolving their incompatibility' and that Cowan develops these 'underground tensions until the explosions of violence and murder seem inevitable.'[13] The apparent cause of that Gothic excess and transgression, then, is the failure of the marital relationship that functions as a cornerstone of 'the utopian fantasy, the suburban dream.'[14]

In McComb's lyrics the couple never get as far as being married. Nevertheless, on albums such as *Born Sandy Devotional* and *Calenture*, the theme of failed love as a source of excess and transgression serves as an implicit acknowledgement of the centrality of that relationship in the suburban social order. From its cover, a nostalgic image from a photograph taken in 1961 of Perth's southernmost coastal suburb of Mandurah — a small town whose local population is made up mostly of retirees and British immigrants, swollen by holidaymakers in the summer — *Born Sandy Devotional* projects itself as an album located in the Perth experience. The theme of the album, as McComb himself wrote, is 'unrequited love.'[15] This thwarted love proves disastrous for the album's various narrative personae. As Wilson Neate observes on the *All Music Guide* website, *Born Sandy Devotional* 'is dark, its lyrics replete with death, psychological turmoil and despair.'[16]

In 'Lonely Stretch', driving through the Western Australian bush serves as a metaphor for the emptiness and despair that comes from a failed relationship. At one point, the narrator sings: 'Sha La, Sha La La' — McComb giving us an echo of 1960s girl groups.[17] 'Sha La, Sha La La' sounds like the backing chorus on The Shirelles' version of 'Baby It's You', released in 1961; a version also appears on The Beatles' *Please, Please Me* album of 1963. Written by Burt Bacharach, Mack David and Luther Dixon, 'Baby It's You' is characteristic of the songs written by the Brill Building composers in the late 1950s and early 1960s.[18] These articulated the ideology of romantic love as it existed prior to any groundswell of disillusionment with suburbia in the United States. For a later era, disillusioned both with suburbia and the distractions offered by post-war consumerism, the songs of these girl groups offer a nostalgic fantasy of a time when true love was permanent and provided the foundation for married life in a utopian suburban existence. For McComb in the 1980s — as for Perth in the wake of the Cooke murders — both aspects of this fantasy were tarnished.

In early 1978, the band that David McComb and Alsy MacDonald formed was renamed The Triffids after the predatory, carnivorous plants in John Wyndham's novel *The Day of the Triffids* (1951), a book that had been incorporated into the Western Australian school curriculum just a few years earlier. Wyndham's novel speculates on the ways in which middle-class English suburbanites behave when they are — suddenly, violently — no longer able to lead the life to which they have become accustomed. The book can be read as an acknowledgement of the instability that threatens the seeming certainties and solidity of suburban life. The carnivorous plants establish a motif combining aspects of science-fiction and Gothic writing; throughout *The Day of the Triffids*, the invaders' threat to suburban life remains paramount.

At a time when the utopian Perth idyll had been disrupted by the Cooke murders, the very name 'The Triffids' underscores the threat of strangeness and violent excess attending that disruption (though of course the name was not necessarily chosen self-consciously with such an effect in mind). In an unrecorded juvenile lyric, 'Take Me to Your Leader', McComb envisions a spaceship visiting Perth:

> You think I'm a fool? Listen what I say:
> I was walking home from school,
> It was a Wednesday.
> A spaceship came down from the sky
> It landed on the ground, that's no lie
> Take me to your leader, tell her we
> Need her, we've all got the fever now

In the next verse we are told that 'little green men' emerge from the spaceship. This highly conventional image drawn from the kind of pre-WWII science fiction that Wyndham had mimicked becomes a vehicle for the latent threat of disturbance to mundane, suburban experience.

Perth's Gothic anxieties are clearly exposed in another early McComb song, 'Nervous Side of Town', released on The Triffids' 5th cassette, recorded in 1980. 'Nervous Side of Town' couples an almost jaunty, sing-along tune with lyrics suggestive of a darker, more problematic aspect of cultural life. The lyrics themselves, especially in the second verse, suggest the personal suburban neurosis that Jonathan Richman mined in his first album, *The Modern Lovers* (1976). 'Nervous Side of Town' starts as a suburban love song — 'If I took a turn at the next traffic lights/I could be at your door by the end of the night/

The effort required is less than small/To lift the receiver and place a call' — but the song's chorus effectively transports the listener to a territory much less safe, 'To the nervous side of town/Where you jump at every little sound/And you wear a nervous frown/And you sink helpless into the ground.'

We are never told *why* the narrator's girlfriend is nervous. Hers remains a nameless, incipiently Gothic anxiety (McComb uses the same sense of nameless horror in 'Hanging Shed', on *Treeless Plain*).[19] The girl's anxiety in 'Nervous Side of Town' is so great that she collapses, not just onto the ground but into it. We might read this, together with the unnamed horror in 'Hanging Shed', as a resonance of deep-seated anxieties among Perth residents. Indeed, apropos of 'Nervous Side of Town', it was younger women that Cooke mainly attacked.

In later songs, McComb's acknowledgement of suburbia as a disturbing place to live gives way to an engagement with a more conventional theme, that of failed love. Occasionally, both themes intertwine, as in 'Hometown Farewell Kiss' on *Calenture*. As the narrator's home town burns in an excessive, Gothic conflagration, McComb sings: 'Erase my name from your lips as we kiss.' For those who know Perth the fire imagery conjures up the long hot summer weather when, without rain which falls mostly in winter, bushfires are a constant hazard in the districts around the city. At the same time, the image of a burning city carries Old Testament connotations of God's fiery destruction of Sodom and Gomorrah for their evil practices. Elsewhere I have discussed the influence of McComb's Presbyterian upbringing on his lyrics.[20] Here, certainly, there is a moral subtext. It would seem that the failure of the marital order on which suburbia is built was, for McComb, a moral failure interpreted first through his religious upbringing and then through the Perth mythology of the loss of the utopian idyll. Indeed, in 'Hometown Farewell Kiss' McComb revisits 'The Nervous Side of Town' with more malevolent motives: 'Now I drive familiar smoky streets/I know this town, I know where to turn/ All the while I kept a roadmap in my head/I just came back to see the people and their houses burn.'

Elsewhere on *Calenture*, as Michael Sutton suggests, McComb's lyrics 'detail … the anger of romantic rejection with unflinching bitterness'; even the up-beat 'Trick of the Light' articulates 'the tortured confessions of a man obsessed with his ex-lover.'[21] In McComb's lyrics the male characters are lost, stranded. Their lives lack purpose when they are not in a relationship.

What we can see in these songs of unrequited love and despairing male self-destruction is the consequence of men adrift without the moral anchor provided by the love of a woman. As I have argued, in suburbia this romantic love leads to the marriage that underpins, and gives meaning to, the utopian suburban life. McComb grew up in Perth when the people of that city were recovering from the crimes of Eric Edgar Cooke which were construed in the excessive and transgressive categories of Gothic horror. McComb's lyrics express this horror and, like the stories of Peter Cowan, seek its origin in the failure of the love relationship that underpins the marital order of the nuclear family on which suburban society is built. In general terms this is the structure of what has become known as 'suburban Gothic' — the horror that lurks beneath the banal and benign surface of middle-class, suburban life. McComb's lyrics start by acknowledging that a horror lurks beneath the utopian fantasy of suburban life, and move on to explore this in terms of what happens for men when romantic love fails. Writing in the genre of the love song that is so typical of popular music, McComb's lyrics can be read as a metaphor for the experience of a lost utopia that continues to haunt the cultural life of Perth.

the triffids in May.

San Miguel –
Wed 4 . Wed 11
Trade Union Club.
Sat 7.

The Triffids played their first 'special covers night' at The Red Parrot nightclub in inner-city Perth, in 1982. At that time the local scene was dominated by cover bands, performing mostly 'white' Top 40 hits to huge crowds in suburban beer barns. As an ironic gesture of capitulation to the status quo, and for the sheer pleasure of indulging themselves, The Triffids organized what was intended to be a one-off covers night of some of their favourite records by the likes of Dylan, The Stooges, The Velvet Underground, The Ronettes and The Stones. In case anyone mistook the evening for a cloyingly reverential affair, the set included 'covers' of The Triffids' own singles (beginning with 'Farmers' and performed in sequence) and a spirited rendition of the theme song from *Gilligan's Island* by Alsy MacDonald. The band had so much fun that occasional covers nights became a much-loved feature of their live dates.

the Triffids

Appearing at:

Melbourne:
The Club 21, 22, 23* March.

Adelaide:
The Tivoli 27, 28, 29* March.

*Special Covers Nights!

Hear tasteless renditions of Massive Hits by Elvis, the Stones, Velvet Underground, Johnny Cash, Atlanta Rythm Section and many more performed by Perth's **most** unoriginal band.

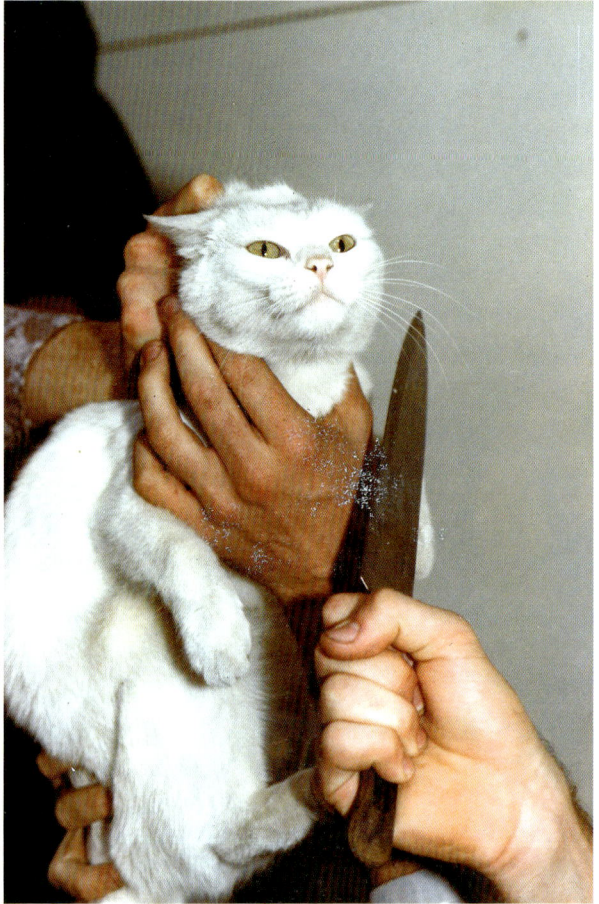

David McComb
(holding knife)
with mock-
sacrificial victim,
late 1982.

Hell of a Summer

David Cavanagh

The scar crosses the upper side of my right wrist like a diagonal watch, and in moments of tension and fear I aggravate it. It's one of the principal symptoms of Endogenous Panophobic Psoriasis — 'Eppy' to its international legions of malingerers — and it means, to swathe through science for a moment, that I'm afraid of all kinds of shit I can't put my finger on. It's very groovy. In hot weather, or in panic, or in supermarkets, I scrape at my legs and my arms and they itch for weeks. One of my few ambitions is to someday rip my own head off.

The wrist-maiming tragedy happened to me at a Monochrome Set gig early in 1984. The Monochrome Set were by no means a happening scene and would soon pack it in for a while, unloved and unable to translate their upper-class toilet humour into acceptable cash-flow or even mild controversy. Back in '84 they would gig intermittently at college venues. It was all very childish. The students would smirk knowingly as the singer, Bid, spooned contempt and derision upon us; it was a bedamned ritual that left neither party particularly thrilled. At one particular under-attended Monochromes symposium at the LSE, I had been shoved out to the right and into the PA, ripping my arm.

Nice one, but ... how to extract the full mileage? Squeezing my wrist to make it bleed more, I pushed back through the crowd, wiping my white T-shirt repeatedly to give the impression of having been brutally stabbed in the heart. My eyes stared deep into strangers' faces and my mouth lolled open.

'There's been an ... accident,' I whispered.

At the porter's office I was given a strip of plaster, which, in a spirit of fun, I replaced the following day with a cumbersome shag-pile bandage that encased my arm from elbow to thumb. I refused to talk of the horrors beneath, preferring instead to wince meaningfully and affect ashen. 'You have good days,' I would explain with a sigh. 'And you have … bad days.'

At the University — my detestable day-job — my reputation was, I was sure, thoroughly clear-cut. Weirdo; ill; won't make it to thirty; inchoate mutterings mask voluminous hidden agenda of angst. I wasn't conning myself. I knew I was a neurotic and a hypochondriac. The thing was, I also knew that I was suffering from several mysterious terminal illnesses. It made concentrating on the job in hand difficult.

Each morning, I passed the Scientologists' office in Tottenham Court Road. 'Would you like a free personality test?' a well-balanced young canvasser would venture neutrally. Each morning, with a theatrical gesture, I would demur. I didn't realize they asked everybody.

A perpetually drunk, uncool nineteen-year-old, I swivelled up and down the echoing stairs of Senate House ('fear of lifts,' I would explain shakily) and in and out of the University's local pub, ludicrously named The Friend at Hand. For a change of scene, I would patronize my college's own subterranean bar in Russell Square, where exciting foreign vodkas with names like Bok and Vax were sold for ten pence. Here I would sit, imaginary handkerchief clasped tight to my mouth, knocking back the Vax and looking like I was really getting into *Vanity of Duluoz* by Jack Kerouac.

My heroes were, as far as I was concerned, secrets, and I worshipped them through a private fug. Representing the jazz world I had Miles Davis, whom I was convinced no one had ever heard of. He was one of my cool discoveries, like the fact that you fall over if you don't sleep very often. Idolizing Davis (a white kid like me would never have called him Miles; it would be like calling your father 'geezer') usually indicates an otherwise shallow and superficial knowledge of jazz. Too bad. I loved all his albums, particularly *In a Silent Way*, and kept Ian Carr's biography of him within browsing distance. Lester Bangs' massive *NME* piece, printed posthumously (for Bangs, that is) in 1983, was actually up on my bedroom wall, its amazingly daring conclusion ('… all that's left is the universe') following me around the room like a pair of paranoid eyes.

My other heroes were the equally obscure Beatles, Captain Beefheart, Syd Barrett, The Byrds, Tom Verlaine, Can and a weird Canadian actor named Alexis Kanner who, at fifteen, had lied about his age to land a role in *Softly Softly* in the mid-sixties, and had subsequently acted his arse off in the last three episodes of *The Prisoner.*

Kanner had a hell of a vision. In 1984 I saw a film he'd directed, called *Kings and Desperate Men,* which was edited like a Tango advert but provided me with an important catchphrase: 'Mr Lucas has a grievance.' This you were supposed to say in a curiously high-pitched Shakespearian screech. I do recall it was a bastard trying to manoeuvre it into conversation.

I listened to practically no contemporary music. I had abstained from the 1980s. They were evil. Even their best stuff was rancid and poxy. Their politics, their films, their music, their weather, their football, their eerie emphasis on cash and muscle … I knew that if I was foolish enough to mix it with the eighties they would fucking bury me. I sort of hibernated.

But, I needed a role model for this one, otherwise I couldn't proceed. I found him in a 1958 British film called *The Man Upstairs.* Richard Attenborough, my main man, played a mousy little lodger who goes mad because society is really evil. He barricades himself in his upstairs room. As the police circle the house (I can't remember why; perhaps he'd murdered a few people) and shout at him to come down, he suddenly throws open the window and screams — really loudly for Attenborough — my all-time favourite cinema line: 'I am not available!' Unavailability was my big thing in 1984. It all got a bit stupid. Then one day in October, looking through *Time Out* for the week's afternoon showings at The Gate, Bloomsbury, I observed that The Monochrome Set had yet another LSE gig pencilled in for that week, supported by a bunch of what the capital's hard-pushed listings directory confidently termed 'quirky, B-52's-influenced Aussies' called The Triffids. The name rang a vague bell. *Melody Maker* had reviewed them the previous week, supporting The Mint Juleps. The *MM* man had made an off-colour reference to Triffids organist Jill (misspelt Gill) Birt and impending blindness. But his gist was that The Triffids were very good, so I went along. By now I was alone in London. I had been left behind by the evacuees.

During my university end-of-term party the previous Easter, a ridiculous altercation over some pâté had finished up with me waving a knife around and being punched into some chairs. It was a small disagreement, soon forgotten, except by me.

In the three or four weeks it took me to calm down, gazing up at my mantra, which, you'll recall, read, ' … all that's left is the universe,' my understanding of the knifing incident subtly changed. The role of the pâté, particularly, underwent a complete restructuring, shrinking in relevance from its one-time key role as a sinister, liver-based catalyst or agent, until, like eighty percent of Dennis Hopper's part in *Apocalypse Now*, it wound up on the cutting room floor.

In my mind, all that was left was a hard frost, halfway between waking dream and horrified recollection, that spelled out my imminent downfall in big scary footprints. I had attempted the cold-blooded murder of a fellow student.

It was laughable and stupid and implausible and it all made perfect sense. My guilt established, it became difficult to look him in the eye without immediately visualizing him as a corpse. *Ach! That wretched pallor. Those horrible dead eyes!*

There was no way we could carry on as normal. Previously, I had always sat next to him in tutorials. *God! That pestilent stench! That fetid aroma!*

Presently, with a murderer's cunning, I began to arrive for tutorials somewhat on the late side. I would apologize in a faint, some might say distracted, whisper. All the seats being taken, I would offer to 'go and get another chair,' which I would ruthlessly position on the opposite side of the room. Then, with a groovy catatonic stare based on Storm Thorgeson's memories of Syd Barrett in Rick Sanders' book *The Pink Floyd*, I would gaze out of the window, looking penitent and full of self-loathing.

'I know you've said Tolstoy was … (*shakes head sadly*) immature and glib, David, but perhaps on your next visit to Earth you could drop in and comment on the principal disparities *Anna Karenina* experiences between Levin and Vronsky?'

I would let four seconds elapse, then snap to attention with an expertly panicked double-take.

'No! I, uh, didn't say he was, uh, immature, I just said he (*voice gets indistinct, eyes start to wander*) … didn't go far enough.'

'Yes. (*Sigh.*) Well, one tends to find this complaint of Tolstoy, doesn't one, cropping up in most of the major biographies. That somehow he just didn't go far enough.'

Irony is wasted on the insane. They just hear the words, not the tone of voice. In the far right-hand corner of my field of vision I could discern the impassive face of my victim. *O putrefying lips, O disjunct brow.* And in my fever, I saw myself standing over him with bloody blade, turning in horror to greet the shadow in the doorway.

'*Porfiry Petrovich, it is you …*'

'*My dear fellow, of course it is I. Cannot an official of the Criminal Investigation Department of the Spasskaya District Police Office pop in on his old friend for an informal drink when he wants to? But my dear old chum, you look agitated!*' (*His eyes drop to the carpet, positively liquid with fresh blood.*)

'*Look, I don't want you getting the wrong idea here, Porfiry Petrovich. This has never happened before.*'

'*Hmm. "All that is left is the universe." The phrase intrigues me. Is it yours?*'

I'd read *Crime and Punishment* and I knew a slippery slope when I saw one. Then they sent for me. I knew they would.

As a student of Russian, I was up for the big holiday. The second year of the course was traditionally, almost obligatorily, spent in the Soviet Union. The young holidaymakers, if everything went to plan, would return to Britain fluent in the language of Pushkin, or at least Chernenko, and aflame with a craving for zealous learning. Qualified thus, and provided you were prepared to vote Tory, a job at GCHQ [Government Communications Headquarters] was as good as in the bag.

There were three choices. For those who sensed they might respond well to a life of sub-zero penury and Rugby Unionesque male bonding, the university offered a year in Minsk.

Failing that, the travel agents could heartily recommend five months in Leningrad. The advantages of Leningrad were that the tourist came home seven months earlier and was near a useful-looking river, the Neva.

Finally, for the profoundly timid, there was the three-month bucketshop calling at no stations to Voronezh, with no buffet car. Very few people bothered to read the literature on Voronezh, but I did. It was a sobering brochure. Three months in Voronezh would have been extremely similar to three months in the Russell Square bar with no heat and no nearby cashpoint machine. Voronezh, while admittedly being situated in the Soviet Union, had no Soviet people living in it whatsoever. It was a student village. Soviets never went there. Why should they? They didn't need to learn how to speak their own language. The only people the student would meet would be other students.

I wanted to go to Leningrad, and nobody was going to stop me. However, in the light of the murder attempt, the whole tawdry affair became wrapped up in politics and I was expressly told by the Head of Department that I was not yet felt to be ready for serious foreign travel. They offered me Voronezh and I turned it down flat.

In the event, one guy who got a Leningrad place was later arrested on a train, after attempting to hold it up armed with a home-made wooden rifle and a false Cossack beard. When accosted, he was heard to shout, 'Look, my friends, I happen to know this is the Lupin Express.' Meanwhile, a girl from Nottingham was almost instantly raped in Minsk and had to come home eleven months and two weeks early. And two girls from Hull University cried themselves to sleep every night in Voronezh, wrapped in each other's arms and convulsing in unhappy spasm until sleep and their comforting redbrick dreams gently prised them apart.

I stayed in London and was forklifted out of the abyss by five Australians called The Triffids.

To silence, they walked onstage at the LSE in Houghton Street and picked up their guitars, all except for a tiny girl, whom I shrewdly took to be Jill Birt, who held aloft a single drumstick and positioned herself in front of the drum-kit. Not behind it; they already had a drummer. She stood by one of the cymbals. It looked odd.

They were all youngish, probably a bit older than me, and hand-some. But the singer, who had wild black eyes, a complexion like scuffed pink tarmac and a black leather jacket, was a frowning, prowl-ing vision of the uncomfortable. He didn't bother with introductions. At the back of the stage, by his amp, he suddenly banged out a one-chord reveille, the same frenzied chord over and over, fast and angry. Then he paced menacingly towards his microphone, at which point the rest of the band exploded into a leering, upwardly swooping riff that practically re-booted my aimless existence there and then.

It stuttered and exploded, again and again. As the drummer slashed at his snare and hi-hat, Jill Birt nonchalantly tapped at the crash cym-bal, holding down a kind of swinging jazz beat. The singer swung into the lyric — about having no family, friends or life — with a demeanour of totally convincing psychosis. I wasn't to know it, but what they were playing was the most inflammable reconstruction of a Bob Dylan song since Jimi Hendrix poured petrol over 'All Along the Watchtower'. 'I am a Lonesome Hobo', or at least a weedy blueprint thereof, appears on side two of Dylan's *John Wesley Harding*, and only the most black-eyed, agile minds approaching the end of a feverishly intense bout of sleep deprivation could have re-wired it as recklessly as The Triffids did that night.

As soon as it finished I moved to the front of the stage and stood, tensed and thrilled, as they tore through one magnificent song after another. The next one was a Triffids original, I presumed, that chopped and scythed like a non-cartoonish Birthday Party. The one after that, a rowdy rockabilly thing, made an instant star out of the lead guitarist, whose violent string-bending was totally at odds with his nonchalant appearance.

Four points were buzzing round my mind. One: how could these people look so calm — apart from the singer, who was hospitaliz-ing himself a little more dramatically by the minute — when they were playing explosive, exciting rock music on a par with The Velvet Underground?

Two: they were so tight, so together, so new and fantastic: they pissed all over every other band I'd ever seen live.

Three: did the rest of the band know that the singer had a mon-strous drug problem, and, if so, did that mean that they all did too?

Even the girl, who had now moved to organ, which she wrenched at like a sluggish iron?

And four: did they have any albums out? They didn't look like the kind of band who would make helpful announcements about this.

When the lead guitarist took up a violin and they played a slow, gorgeous waltz, I was convinced I was hearing the loveliest song ever written. Which one of them wrote the songs? Clearly not the singer. He didn't look like he could be trusted with a pencil. Was it the lead guitarist/violinist? Was it Jill Birt?

Then she sang a song. It was a fragile, aching thing which she sang like a child, eyes wide and alive, not imploring or beguiling like all the other girl singers in all the other bands. She sang not like Nico, but like Deerfrance, the mysteriously named girl who had sung 'Only Time Will Tell' on John Cale's *Sabotage* live album in 1979. Now I was thinking furiously. My impression of Deerfrance had always been of a limpid little ingénue, kidnapped by the mad Cale and his band, and forced to sing her song under duress, after which she would be flung back into her dungeon, mewling pitifully, until the next gig. Was this the case with The Triffids? No band could possibly include that black-eyed singer and that girl, other than by the most nefarious of devices. What would conversations between them be like? Could I overhear one someday?

As she finished singing, the forbidding features of the front-man softened and he spoke his first words. 'Jill Birt,' he said, grinning at the crowd and clapping his hands. She got a round of applause. It was the coolest thing I'd ever seen in my life.

They did a song called 'Hell of a Summer', a title which was destined to become a new catchphrase in my life. Whatever happened to me between 1984 and 1985, I would shake my head sadly and repeat, 'It's been a hell of a summer.' It was perfect. And it didn't even have to be summer. It just had to have *been* summer, at some point previously. People who had previously said, 'Shit happens,' or 'God moves in mysterious ways,' well, they all thought, boy, his catchphrase is much better than ours, and started ripping me off.

Meanwhile, the singer was talking about a Triffids album, but I only caught a few words, two of which were 'Rough Trade.' In an instant, I saw the cover: a blurred garage, and monochrome musicians in movement, with just the leads from their guitars in focus. The song titles written in red on the back cover. To finish, they played an endless song which had patterns of The Doors both in Jill Birt's organ playing and in the evangelist-style hollering which the singer employed to get over his message. Even now, as the melody collapsed and they drilled their way through to the heart of all musical chaos, not a flicker of emotion could be detected on the faces of the lead guitarist or the bassist. They just did it. By the time they left the stage, I was absolutely assured that I had discovered the best band in the world. I wanted to talk to them, quickly.

Stupidly, I deliberated too long. I watched too much of The Monochrome Set's feeble performance, and when I collared an LSE doorman he told me The Triffids had left.

'Oh, wow, for Australia?'

He looked at me oddly.

I walked down The Strand to Trafalgar Square and caught a bus. Those songs were making my wrist itch. No junk food for me. I couldn't get my brain out of waltz time.

October at the School of Slavonic and East European Studies was like a quiet day at a snowed-in hotel with Jack Nicholson and Shelley Duvall presiding. Tutorials-for-one were not uncommon. There was a war vibe on. My fellow non-evacuees were either ill or old. We were the infirm; the guys out in Minsk and Voronezh were fighting the real war. Had I done the right thing in staying? It didn't look like it.

Time Out served me well. It told me where this week's obligatory screenings of *Darling* and *The Return of the Secaucus Seven* were happening, and, about a week after the LSE gig, it told me where I might next track down The Triffids. It was at the Rock Garden. Here, wherever the hell it was, I would meet them. I hadn't prepared an introduction, but it was going to be something slavering and epic.

After a quite staggeringly dreadful support band, who used backing tapes of — they claimed — their girlfriends having orgasms, The Triffids singer strolled on stage, dropped to his knees and started fiddling around with leads. I went up to him and suggested non-committedly that his band's gig at the LSE had been the best thing to happen to music in my lifetime, and that all their songs were, as far as genius went, absolutely off the scale.

'Outside of music business people, you know, you're our first real fan,' he grinned charmingly.

His name turned out to be David, too, David McComb. Still in his songwriting infancy, he would later be hailed as one of the great masters of the songwriting art, a visionary, a poet. I bought him a drink and grilled him for information.

They hailed from Perth in Western Australia. Unable to progress there, they had invested all their money in a trip to England and were now living here, just as fellow Australians The Saints, The Birthday Party and The Go-Betweens had before. Money was so tight they had borrowed a drum-kit off Clare Moore from The Moodists. They loved music, it was just a case of getting the English to find out about them.

Yes, yes. And the waltz song?

Embarrassingly, I had to get him to repeat the title three times. I just could not make sense of his accent. Rare *what*? Rare Pining?

Just as he was about to write it down, I twigged it. 'Red Pony'. My favourite song was called 'Red Pony'. How beautiful. Would they do it tonight? Sure. They did it every night. It was, after all, one of their songs. The endless evangelist's song, it transpired, was called 'Field of Glass' and had only recently been added to the set. Jill's song was 'Raining Pleasure'. The rockabilly one was 'Branded'. He listed three or four others: 'Jesus Calling', 'Property is Condemned', 'Bright Lights Big City' and 'Monkey on My Back'. And the album? What was the title of the album? This needed about five or six efforts. I couldn't get it at all. Patiently, he kept saying it, over and over, until eventually … Oh! *Treeless Plain.* Did he mean like a plain that didn't have trees on it?

'Er … yeah,' he said. 'I guess so.'

Well, if *Treeless Plain* wasn't the best title for an album I had ever heard, I didn't know what was. He told me they had another album, too, called *Raining Pleasure.* Next big point: were they available?

'They're coming out over here on Rough Trade Distribution,' he explained. What the fuck did that mean? Did that mean I could have them tomorrow? He looked amused at my excitement. These were songs The Triffids had been playing live for two years (hence their tightness) and some guy was asking him to say all their names five times. After arranging to go backstage and meet the others when the gig was over (thus showing unbelievable naïvety: you don't have to arrange to go backstage at the Rock Garden, you just go), I retreated about four feet into the small audience.

Now I was ready for all the songs. I recognized each one instantly, noted a new one called 'Embedded', watched every musician in turn, picked out phrases and waited for 'Red Pony'. I learned that my catchphrase had a bit more to it. 'It's been a hell of a summer to be lying so low.' Wow! I thought I knew just the occasion for that one. When they played 'Red Pony' I felt privileged to be there. It was that autumn's big moment. Hearing them play it was the only thing that could make me stop thinking of Voronezh and all my absent friends and I never wanted it to finish.

My brief chat with McComb hadn't enlightened me much on what other music they liked, other than to confirm that the support band, apart from being truly appalling, were also dickheads of galactic expanse. But when The Triffids came back for an encore, we were given a clue.

The lead guitarist took over on drums and the drummer picked up a guitar. They sang Elvis Presley's 'Can't Help Falling in Love' and McComb and the drummer harmonized like dissolute Everly Brothers. In 1984, Elvis to me was just a big fat dead person, but they sang his song with total commitment and no irony. They sang it with love, basically. Although most of my memories of that era relate to the weather — it was cold, it was colder, it was coldest — those three minutes at the Rock Garden will always be a warm place. It wasn't as complicated an emotion as the one 'Red Pony' triggered off in me. It was a simple, pleasing, womb-like warmth and it had nothing to do with any of the music I ordinarily listened to.

It was, for instance, the precise musical opposite of *Stimmung*, a wintry, nullifying piece of choral experimentation by Stockhausen, which I had taped off Radio 3 and listened to every morning on my Walkman. Fuck knows why. In fact, now that I thought of it, all my favourite music completely alienated me from the people who made it. The idea of following a band was ridiculous, like following a lorry purely because it was on the move. The Triffids were the first band who made me come closer. I clambered across the Rock Garden's stage, downwards and in.

If meeting one of them was tricky, coming face to face with all five was petrifying. In the space of two gigs, these people had turned my life around. Unversed in backstage protocol (rule one: no excessive use of metaphor), I yammered tentative greetings and waxed perilously solemn, manfully struggling to keep the abyss out of it. David McComb wasn't a drug addict or anything of the kind. He didn't even smoke. He was simply an excellent, vivid performer of his own songs. Yes, the songs were his. The lead guitarist was Rob, his brother. At twenty-seven, Rob was the oldest Triffid, an easy-going Bohemian guy who helpfully answered each question as though it were completely fascinating, which, believe me, it wasn't.

The others were about twenty-two or twenty-three. The drummer was Alsy MacDonald, a thoroughly excellent fellow with a dry wit. The bassist, Martyn Casey, seemed even drier, quiet and unfailingly polite. Jill Birt wanted to know if I could understand their accents. I wanted to know if I could move in with them.

Helping them load their van up, I was delighted to be offered a place on the guest list at Dingwalls, their next gig. But again, when, with abundant overuse of adverbs, I brusquely demanded information about their two albums, they shrugged and said they would probably be released in a few weeks, through Rough Trade Distribution. I really hated Rough Trade Distribution now. I hoped they knew what misery they were putting me through. In the following days, I seethed my way through chilly Stockhausen bus rides, affected catalepsy and muteness in tutorials and waited for darkness. Then it got dark.

Ever since I had moved in, I had known I was living in a street with a curse on it. Up around the bend of the L-shaped St James Lane, just where the hill reared up in near-vertical abruptness to connect with the elevated Muswell Hill Broadway, there was a pub. It was called The Royal Oak. The big murder case of the previous year had introduced the world to Dennis Nielsen, his evil fridge, and his rapidly dwindling cache of neck-ties. In a murdering spree going back some years,

Nielsen had picked up young homosexuals, brought them home — at first to Cricklewood, then subsequently to 23 Cranley Gardens, Muswell Hill — where he would drug them, strangle them with one of his many ties, dissect their bodies and dispose of them in instalments via the lavatory system.

An unsatisfactory arrangement at the best of times, the lethargy of his U-bend led inevitably to blocked drains, saucepans cluttered up with bits of torso, and a ferocious odour that stirred plaintive feelings in his neighbours. It was this odour that finally led the police to his door.

What was not widely reported at the time was that one of my fellow students at the School of Slavonic and East European Studies had been a lucky escapee from the dreaded house of Nielsen. Indeed, he had awakened from his drug-induced stupor just in time to monitor the downward momentum of the tie with his name on it. I knew this. I also knew, from my flatmates, that The Royal Oak had been Nielsen's local. He used to sit in there, on his own, drinking 'steadily.'

One of my flatmates, Brendan, reckoned he could speak for the population at large when he said The Royal Oak had a horrible feeling about it. I gave it the full-on swerve. When Brendan left, he was replaced, first by a girl called Heather, then by a guy called Neil, whom I perfunctorily auditioned one afternoon and more or less okayed. He was older than we were — about thirty — and because socializing with my flatmates was way out of my range, Neil began to go for an evening pint in The Royal Oak without checking it over with me. It is quite possible that he sat on his own on these occasions, and it is by no means out of the question that he drank 'steadily.' All I knew about him at this stage was that he came from Tring and he didn't arrive home on certain nights.

Around that time, as if through a thick fog, my subconscious began to take note of a sequence of worrying news stories in the *Evening Standard*. These concerned a highly dangerous criminal nicknamed The Fox, who operated in the Bedfordshire, Hertfordshire and Greater London manors. The reason he was known as The Fox was because he would break into people's houses while they were not there, then, while waiting for their return, he would construct a kind of den, or lair, from pieces of furniture. These he would arrange around the living room's most comfortable armchair and, settled in, he would watch TV and eat beans.

Like a lot of people, I felt uneasy about the beans. Mention of beans can only mean bad news. The beans invariably appeared early on in each Fox-related story in the *Standard,* even before the bit about the lair. It would go: The Fox, struck again, beans, lair, latest ghastly crime, police warn residents. Because when the people returned, The Fox would put the beans down and he would become extremely scary. He raped women. He defiled them. He stripped them of all their dignity. Once, when a married couple returned to find him there, he forced them to have sex while he watched. Then he had sex with her, while the man watched, and the man couldn't do anything about it. The Fox permeated my inner discussions quite listlessly and randomly, rather like the King of Spain had once troubled Poprishchin in Gogol's *Diary of a Madman.*

You could learn a lot from the *Evening Standard* in the autumn of 1984. You could find jobs. You could find out which West Ham players were receiving treatment for hamstring injuries. You could learn that The Fox was now thought by the police to hail from the Tring area.

Further down, and maybe you would be shaking a little now, you could learn that the police urged people to contact them if they knew of a man, about thirty, who was a bit of a loner and who didn't come home on certain nights.

What I did next says a lot about me. I ran to the kitchen and looked in Neil's cupboard for signs of beans. I tell you this, I badly wanted to know what the beans situation was, regarding old Neil. To my fantastic shaking relief, there were no beans.

Ohhh … I started to laugh uncontrollably and went back to my room. Whoa! Boy! Beans scare over. What a hell of a summer that had been. Then I got very scared again. I had made a dangerous error. I had been looking at it the wrong way round. Of course there weren't any beans! We'd already established that he liked beans! He'd eaten all the beans! He couldn't get enough of the fucking things.

I flew back out to the kitchen and emptied out the black bin-liner. Kicking through the rubbish, I now kept an eye open for beans-like debris. Tins, labels, even sardines in tomato sauce might qualify. I didn't need to sift for long. There, grinning up at me, was an empty tin of Sainsbury's beans. Neil was The Fox. I was alone in the house. Madly, I decided to search his room. I was delirious. Just then I decided not to search his room. Fortunately.

'What do you think you're doing?'

'Oh, hello, The Fox! Ha ha ha ha. Listen, you're not going to believe this. Ha ha ha. Only, I heard a noise and I thought you were a burglar coming to steal your Heinz. (Pause.) Your stereo. *So I thought I'd hide in your room behind the beans. The* door. *And kind of pounce, you know, sort of pounce and, and, and, oh God, don't rape me, The Fox, don't rape me.'*

Instead, I called my parents and relayed the worrying developments. Wisely, I kept the beans out of it.

'Are you sure it's him?'

'Absolutely. The Tring connection was the thing that convinced me.'

'You don't know for certain that The Fox is from Tring.'

'Of course I do. The police said so.'

'Maybe you ought to call the police, then.'

'Yes, but what if he isn't The Fox? It would be terrible. I have to make an important decision here.'

It was okay, in a way. All that was left was the universe.

Every lunchtime, just before slapping on some of that *Stimmung* and getting the 134 bus home, I would visit the Virgin Megastore, looking for the two Triffids albums. They were never there. 'Possibly they're in your Antipodean section?' I once suggested to the man at the Information Desk.

Then, one afternoon, things started to happen very fast. Neil left the house, owing a lot of bills. And The Triffids albums arrived in the Megastore. Neither of the records looked like I had imagined. *Treeless Plain* was green, for a start, which really threw me. *Raining Pleasure* was yellow. *Treeless Plain* started with 'Red Pony'. That seemed wrong.

I wanted those albums to be perfect and, for a while, they were. The sound was softer than their live shows. There was even a fruity country number or two. *Treeless Plain* ended with a song sung by Alsy, called 'Nothing Can Take Your Place'. It was sweet and happy, very un-Triffids. It wasn't long before the three music weeklies started raving about the band. Lynden Barber from the *Melody Maker* interviewed David McComb for a full-page feature, which ran under the inevitable headline 'Day of The Triffids'. I read it downstairs in the Wimpy in Tottenham Court Road. The big news was that McComb hated everything. Absolutely detested everything. Nothing about the 1984 music scene brought him any pleasure whatsoever. I munched my hamburger thoughtfully. He and The Triffids were even angrier than I had bargained for.

At my third Triffids gig I began subtly to befriend them for real. Cruising into Dingwalls for the first time ever (come 1988, I would spend every Monday night there for an entire year), I approached them all in turn and got them to sign my *Treeless Plain* lyric sheet. They knew I was Irish so, cutely, Martyn Casey signed his name Martyn O'Casey. At the bottom, one of them wrote the band's communal telephone number in West Kensington.

Yet again, they played magnificently. The stage of Dingwalls was small, with a big pillar in the middle, and they stood cramped, all squeezed together. They looked electrifying. I loved their name. I loved their songs. I loved the way there were five of them.

'Why do you only play for fifty minutes?' I asked David afterwards. 'You should play for two hours — more.'

I was getting pretty cocky. I was now leaving my coat backstage during gigs. Watching the headlining band — I can't remember who — with Casey, I informed him in the most officious voice ever that his bassline on 'Red Pony' was a stroke of Godlike ingenuity. It was. But there are occasions, as a bass player, when you don't need the hassle.

The bills came to about £50. It was obvious what had happened. Neil, sensing that I was on to him, had split for Tring, where he would fling a few possessions into a rucksack — shirts, socks, beans — and go on the run. My other flatmate, Kerry, didn't know about the Fox business. She knew him as Neil, just as Son of Sam was once plain old 'Sam's lad' to his drinking companions. Once or twice she had even stepped into The Royal Oak with Neil for a spot of 'steady' drinking herself. Although this scared me, I didn't want to freak her out.

'Kerry, something really problematic's occurred with Neil,' I explained one night. 'He's left. And there's lots of bills which I've taken care of and now I'm incredibly in debt.'

'Oh no, what a bastard.'

'Yeah, I know. What shall we do?'

I got the job of phoning Neil's father in Tring. I explained who I was, making sure I called his son Neil rather than by, say, a vulpine-style nickname.

'If I see him I'll tell him, mate,' he promised.

The chances of you seeing your son again are pretty remote, you deluded fool, I thought as I disconnected. He's done a moonlight. He's had it away on his toes.

I saw The Triffids play at the Jackson's Lane Community Centre in Archway. Jill Birt was swaying in the bar. She and Alsy told me about Perth. 'It's just like Houston,' Alsy revealed. They had been drinking all day. We painstakingly went through the formalities of establishing that they would play 'Red Pony'. I saw them play upstairs at The Manor House pub, headlining above yet more Australians, The Scientists and a band called, what else, Purple Onion. Martyn's strap broke at the beginning of their newly introduced Otis Redding cover, 'You Don't Miss Your Water', and he had to go back to the dressing room, where, let us not kid ourselves, I had once again left my coat. He arrived back on stage just in time to hit the song's last note.

The best part of that gig was the first airing of McComb's new Triffids song. David had told me about it and I latched on quickly.

'So does this mean you'll be playing for longer tonight?'

'No, we'll just drop one of the old ones.'

O bitter night, O palsied moon!

It was called 'Lonely Stretch'. For what seemed like about nineteen minutes, but was probably nearer six, McComb reared up over the microphone and bellowed one scintillating metaphor of doom and panic after another:

I took a wrong turn off of an unmarked track,
I did seven miles and couldn't find my way back,
Hit a lonely stretch.
Must be losing my touch
I was out of my depth …
Fingering my silver St Christopher
and saving my empty shells for her.

I could not believe that this man was not revered throughout the world. These were the best words to a rock song I had yet encountered. I had to let him know, just in case he didn't realize. And unfortunately for Casey, his bassline was tremendous too, which I planned to tell him all about in a head-on effusive backstage tryst.

'Well, I suppose I did write it, yeah, if you can write a bassline. Er …?'

That gig had been pleasingly full. The reviews were nothing less than a thrill to peruse. The *NME* called them 'the best band in the country,' which showed real class. I wanted to work for the music press and write things like that too.

In the meantime, they had recorded a session for John Peel. I rang David before it went out, after it went out and, in all probability, while it was going out. 'It's still going out!' he'd helpfully confirm.

On 13 November it went out. I knew in advance what they had recorded: 'Bright Lights Big City', 'Monkey on My Back' and 'Field of Glass'. The evil three. 'You've only done three?' I remarked, crestfallen. 'But you could have done four. Normally, bands do four.'

'Well, "Field of Glass" is really long.'

In an instant, I was revitalized. 'Really long.' That could mean anything. That could mean endless. An aural picture formed in my mind, of Peel bidding his listeners goodnight at 11.27: 'Well, that's it for tonight I'll leave you with the last number from The Triffids, who, as the *NME* so rightly said, are the best band in the country. If only they'd play for two hours, though. Incidentally, this last song is the most incredible piece of music you will ever hear.'

Alone in the house, alone in London, already over-familiar with *Treeless Plain* and *Raining Pleasure*, I tuned into Peel and finally heard

The Triffids as they were meant to sound. 'Bright Lights Big City' was awesomely loud and scary. It also gave me my new pet catchphrase.

The only reason I'd moved to Muswell Hill in the first place was to live within crawling distance of a girl at college whom I adored, but she immediately panicked and fled to Clapham. Hurt, I examined the situation for plus points. Let's see: Muswell Hill, *aaarggh*, Clapham. No, it didn't look too good. There was no chance of getting hold of the wrong end of the stick with that one. It looked quite clear-cut. And yet I needed proof. This, I felt, would only be forthcoming if I were to move to Clapham and she were to commit suicide.

Symbiotically, on 'Bright Lights Big City', McComb screeched the words: 'I followed her round like a lapdog.' This became my tragic new catchphrase, and I had no one to say it to. When 'Monkey on My Back' finished, with a resounding slam, Peel said, 'That was fantastic.' At that precise instant, I felt for Peel a rich, quivering, sexual longing.

'Field of Glass' lasted about ten minutes, which I had to reluctantly admit was quite fair. The chaos bit in the middle sounded shaky and unconvincing — there was a line that went 'What would your little doggie say' that I wished McComb would remove — but the last two minutes ate up the airwaves like a Pacman. The Triffids had done wonders.

'Oh, thanks, Dave,' McComb retorted bashfully.

'No, really, it's absolutely imperative that you appreciate how brilliant it was right now.'

Meanwhile, a letter arrived from Neil. Oh God, would this beast perpetually torment us? Frightened, I ripped it open, expecting a folded-up Heinz label and a card reading, 'There are some areas in which The Triffids cannot help you. Regds, The Fox.' It was a cheque for £50. Reimbursed and light-headed, I headed back to my lair.

My twentieth birthday was scheduled for 7 December, but since my friends were scattered across the Soviet Union, I thought I'd invite The Triffids out for a drink.

'Yeah, come round,' said McComb.

They lived in a block of flats called Welbeck Court, opposite Olympia. There was a pub on the corner called The Hand and Flower, which has since been renamed Harvey Floorbanger's Hammersmith Charivari. It's nowhere near Hammersmith.

I walked down the sedate little residential turning, looking for lonely stretches. It amazed me that David McComb had written a whole song in this sleepy West Kensington side-road. A tiny lift scraped me up to their floor. It was much nicer than the house I lived in — warm, friendly, full of beer and life. There was a settee that beckoned softly to me. They were listening to side two of *Pet Sounds*. It was paradise.

The plan was to eat at a nearby Italian restaurant. I didn't eat much in those days — mad people like to stay thin — but reckoned I could handle this. Again, the restaurant was lovely and warm inside. My cold life rubbed up against the heat and enjoyed the sensation. When you're as hopeless a case as I was, straightforward acts of friendliness seem uncommonly beautiful and harsh words crush you effortlessly. I remember two things about the meal, one of each.

Firstly, they paid, which genuinely threw me. As far as I knew, they had even less money than I had. 'It's your birthday, Dave,' Casey said kindly.

Secondly, David asked me what other bands I liked. 'I really like R.E.M.,' I said. 'Do you?'

'I don't listen to Byrds rip-off bands,' he shot back, cutting me dead. I said nothing for the rest of the meal. This would have worried me all night if he hadn't later given me a birthday present back at Welbeck Court. It was an Australian 7" single of 'Beautiful Waste', one of their prettiest songs, with 'Property is Condemned' on the B-side. The cover was silver and shiny and there, at last, I had my song-titles in red letters.

Later, at home, I studied my gift. 'Beautiful waste,' David sang over perfect drum tattoos and peals of trumpet. 'Terrible fever of love/ Stupid feeling, making fools out of us.' I looked up from my map of the Clapham area. Did he know?

Dingwalls was fuller this time, and The Triffids were headlining. Bill Black in *Sounds* had belatedly reviewed *Treeless Plain* and written that 'Red Pony' had the best string arrangement he'd heard in his life.

I wanted to know about that life. It sounded like Bill Black could help me. The support band at Dingwalls was Bush Telegraph, led by Kevin Armstrong, later David Bowie's guitarist, and I listened to them at the bar with David McComb. He was saying how frustrated he was by having to play the same set, in the same order, night after night. Already outgrowing their old songs, he was listening to more and more country music. A Triffids set held no more secrets for him.

All I did was suggest they start with 'Monkey on My Back' rather than 'I am a Lonesome Hobo'. I had always been amazed at the ferocity of the roar in his voice as he sang the first lines of Monkey, 'I have this monkey on my back/I dare not even mention his name.' It was his big demon moment and he always rose to the occasion.

'Do it first,' I said. 'You'll scare the shit out of people.'

'Where would we put "Lonesome Hobo"?'

'After "Field of Glass". You know when it's all chaotic at the end, all white noise and feedback? Just start banging out the chords.'

'Yeah! I could do that, actually. They're both in A.'

I tried to look like I had known that all along, then gave up. He was really happy. He went back to tell the others. Being totally naïve about rock bands, I didn't know that musicians change their sex more regularly than they change their set. It's a very big deal. It's their agenda. It's their life-force, as The La's later proved when they played the same set for four years running. When I went backstage to park my coat, Martyn Casey looked up and said these magical words: 'Looks like we're playing the Dave set tonight.'

I have to be honest, it didn't work as well as I'd intended. McComb's microphone wasn't working when he roared the first lines of 'Monkey'. And the first chords of 'Lonesome Hobo' didn't sound nearly powerful enough after the chaos of 'Field of Glass'. But they tried it. For one night only, they tried it. That was the closest I got to them.

At Christmas I returned to Ireland for a while, and The Triffids moved back to Perth, their London stint complete. They had done everything they could have. Maybe, leaving Heathrow, they experienced some kind of professional satisfaction. Maybe, like The Birthday Party before them, they took their exit with a sackful of stinking contempt.

I wrote to McComb in Perth, wished him a happy Christmas and asked him to recommend me a country album, as a first-time buyer. He wrote back suggesting *Grievous Angel* by Gram Parsons. 'It's just perfect,' he wrote, and he was right. The New Year began with me in scared limbo and The Triffids on the cover of the *NME*.

Back to London came the inmates from Voronezh, but we were too estranged to be proper friends again. They had seen things I hadn't.

The Triffids came over to play the University of London Union in the spring. It was a prestige show for them. Martyn Casey spotted me in the bar before the gig and took me backstage; this required official passes and it was obvious that The Triffids were on a new, elevated level. Also, they had added a sixth musician, 'Evil' Graham Lee, on pedal steel. They now had organ, violin, raging drums and pedal steel. The sound they made was thrilling. But afterwards, in an overcrowded dressing room, McComb looked weary and irritated to see me. I said I'd catch him soon, and left for home. *You'll get over it*, a pragmatic inner voice counselled me, *you little loser. Stop snivelling and set to work. It's the beginning of your life.* I couldn't help but agree with this voice wholeheartedly, beating out a familiar waltz on my pockets and thinking furiously as I ate up the miles.

David McComb, 1983.

Light and shade: Jill Birt
and David McComb in
Sydney, 1983.

Memories

Rob Snarski

The Cat and the Fiddle tavern on the corner of Beaufort and Chelmsford Streets in Mount Lawley, Western Australia, was the first place I found myself among so many obviously alternative types — skinheads, punks and mods, plus the occasional rockabilly. It was as if *Quadrophenia* had been chewed up and then spat out and brought back to life in inner-city Perth, on the other side of the planet.

'The Cat', as everyone called it, was the first place I heard Tony Thewlis (The Scientists) play guitar, or Brian Hooper (Beasts of Bourbon) bash out a Public Image cover. It was also the first venue at which I saw and heard The Triffids. In a way they looked more alternative than the alternatives. I seem to remember a lot of chequered shirts on stage, a kind of anti-fashion statement. The support act on the night was called The Real Dreamers, with Phil Kakulas on guitar, Byron Sinclair playing a Rickenbacker bass, and Alsy MacDonald on drums. They did a cover of 'Hey Bulldog', The Beatles' tune. I'm not quite sure what I made of them or The Triffids that evening. They just struck me as being outsiders, not really belonging.

Months later (this was around 1982), The Triffids left for the eastern states. I remember reading a list of David McComb's heroes in a fanzine, possibly *Distant Violins*, picked up from Dada Records in Perth. Dave had listed, among others, Billie Holiday and Richard Hell; at the time I thought Billie was a guy. Some time later I remember reading another fanzine article written by Dave, on Melbourne band The Moodists, warning readers that the crown of James Osterberg (aka Iggy Pop) was about to be toppled by The Moodists' charismatic, wise-cracking singer, Dave Graney.

By 1983, my brother Mark and I had formed our first band, Chad's Tree. One night we were performing at The Shaftesbury Hotel on the outskirts of the city with our friends, And An A, possibly the only electro-art band to exist in Perth at the time. And An A were like nothing else in Perth back then, listing Pere Ubu, Elvis Presley and Cabaret Voltaire as their influences. Somehow David McComb, who was back in town for a brief visit, appeared backstage after the show and berated us in a friendly fashion. He thought Mark and I 'sang like The Walker Brothers'; he was extremely generous. I remember him popping back to my place one night with Margaret (my friend and his beau at the time) where we started playing a few old singles, 'Sittin' on the Dock of the Bay', 'Here Comes the Night', 'To Sir, with Love'. He mentioned that Sydney band The Lighthouse Keepers played 'To Sir, with Love' as their encore, and said that he missed not having a copy of Big Star's *Sister Lovers* or Van Morrison's *Astral Weeks* with him in Perth.

I remember the little and not-so-little things, the gracious and the ugly: Dave on stage at The Subiaco Hotel outside of Perth in the early days, giving the bar staff grief over the mic for charging patrons for tap water … Dave helping me to his car after I had fallen — literally — flat on my face on the landing of The Prince of Wales Hotel in St Kilda after one of The Susans' failed shows and far too much rider, poor Dave nursing my battered ego all the way home … Dave being in an extremely difficult mood when we travelled to Lake Mountain ski resort for the *All Souls Alive* photo shoot with Bleddyn Butcher … sneaking us into a London studio on his time and with his recording advance to record The Susans' *Depends on What You Mean by Love* … watching *Basket Case* with The Triffids at Julian Wu's family home in the exclusive surrounds of Melbourne's Toorak … sitting around Dave & Jo's kitchen table in Ladbroke Grove, London, with Kenny Davis Jnr,[1] listening to Dylan sing 'Spanish is the Loving Tongue' — three grown men close to tears … Dave on stage with The Susans at The Cherry Tree Hotel in Melbourne, holding the mic directly into the foldback wedge, causing deafening feedback as a not-so-silent protest directed at the band.

Then the memories of struggling in the studio and there'd be Dave's words of encouragement and/or frustration: *Sing the song … Deliver the words.* I kinda got the feeling that with Dave, the song came first.

CLOCKWISE, from left: David McComb, Martyn P. Casey, and The Triffids live at The Shaftesbury Hotel, Perth, 1983.

Outside The Cliffe,
Peppermint Grove,
3 February 1983.

1982

Dom Mariani

It was sometime in 1982 when I first became aware of The Triffids. 'Spanish Blue' was getting regular airplay on one of the local public radio stations, 6UVS-FM, which we all listened to for the alternative stuff … and at first my power-pop sensibilities weren't exactly taken by the low-key production. But after hearing it several times, the song stayed with me and I was compelled to go to Mills Records in Fremantle to buy a copy. Marshall Martin, who managed Mills back then and also did some shows on 6UVS, was a huge Triffids fan and set about filling me in and singing their praises. (Both on air and in the shop, Marshall was a tremendous source of information when it came to new releases and older records alike.) When I took the single home and played it, I quickly fell in love with the song. Those opening lines perfectly expressed the way I was feeling about Perth at the time.

I only saw the Triffids play live on a few occasions that year — The Broadway Tavern in Nedlands and Adrians nightclub in Northbridge, on the outskirts of the city, come to mind. The next time would have been in March '84 when my band The Stems played their debut gig with a line-up that included The Triffids and a few other bands supporting The Saints, and on another occasion The Stems and The Triffids shared a bill with Ed Kuepper in Melbourne.

But I never really got to know Dave or the others beyond a friendly back-stage hello, given that the different crowds our bands attracted meant that we rarely played the same venues and so our paths seldom crossed. It wasn't until early '87 — on a break from a recording session for the first Stems' album at Planet Studios in Perth — that I saw The Triffids play again. Having scored a free pass, I walked across to Subiaco Oval where the *Australian Made* concert was taking place. I got there just as The Triffids were playing and the crowd was still building, so I was able to get up fairly close. It was an impressive set from a band that was clearly in command of its material, and Dave McComb looked very comfortable on the big stage.

They'd come a long way from 'Spanish Blue' and, musically, would travel further still, but to this day I think there's something about the sound and feel of that early single which captures a moment in time, a moment belonging to a particular place. There aren't many records you can say that about.

In a sense you had to be there, but for me when I listen to 'Spanish Blue' I'm taken back to Perth summers of the early 1980s. Somehow, and this is its great mystery, the song doesn't play in real time. It plays forever in 1982.

WAIT film and television studio, 24 January 1983.

Wow and Flutter

David Nichols

'…and at least six self-produced {++}s from this Perth band'[1]

The Triffids' first six cassette albums, recorded and released in Perth over a two-year period between May 1978 and April 1980, comprise an unusual and interesting archive that not only allows the enthusiast to track the development of a unique group but also provides clues to the design and direction of The Triffids' subsequent career. In addition, the seventy-nine recordings on these six albums — titled simply *Triffids 1st* (with the alternative title *Logic*) through *Triffids 6th* — allow a considered and textured understanding of the group and of David McComb's development as a songwriter. Here I want to identify the local and wider musical context of the creation of these cassette albums, together with some of the threads that run through the songs, the lyrical and musical ideas within them.

I was privileged to be lent copies of these tapes by David McComb in 1983, along with lyric sheets. A great fan of The Triffids as they then existed, I was amazed and delighted to hear where they had 'come from' in the previous five years of their existence back in Perth, a place I would not visit until the mid-1990s. Their own mythology of place, and the loyalty they held to Western Australia in a variety of ways, already intrigued me. These six cassette albums and the three that followed in the 1980s (*Dungeon Tape*, *Son of Dungeon Tape* and *Jack Brabham*), formed a parallel universe of diverse and clever songs by a group of great dexterity and temerity.

The Perth incubator and other influences

The term 'influence' is bandied about in music criticism and history, often as if particular groups or songwriters were the sum total of their record collections; the trick as a critic being merely to identify the extent of particular 'influences.' This is easy (some might say lazy) historical analysis and, unsurprisingly, more than a little problematic.

In his adult life, David McComb was content to represent the early Triffids in the same way Australian eastern seaboard, and then British, journalists represented them: as the sum of their musical influences, isolated in backward, hot, sterile Perth. This is an example of the value of exercising caution when taking on an artist's own estimation of his or her creative development. As it transpires, the group's cassette albums complicate the notion that the band was simply an extension of its influences. For one thing, many of the cassette albums' compact, witty guitar-pop songs are very *good*: crafted, clever, tuneful. Indeed, McComb's 1980s work was much more genre-based than his output in the 1970s. McComb always took an ethnographic approach to the wider musical world, and as well as being a highly creative and driven individual, his output in the 1980s sometimes saw him craft songs and even albums as an imaginative DJ might (or as, for instance, The Who did with *The Who Sell Out*). He was to do this in the eighties with swampy-gothic songs in the mould of The Birthday Party, such as 'Dead Wind' and 'Twisted Brain', and the Moodists-styled 'Field of Glass', and *The Black Swan* album, which runs a gamut of musical styles. Such appropriations serve both as a guide to McComb's own interests and a commentary on contemporary taste and cultural preferences.

While the teenage McComb's lyrics were by and large less sophisticated than they would later become and more likely to manifest on the cassette albums as in-joke ditties, self-deprecating and fantastic, he was also much less inclined to drift towards the adoption of specific generic styles. In their earliest incarnation, The Triffids, a 'straight', new wave pop/rock band, were not overtly referencing any specific groups or musical modes, even though the kinds of groups McComb later claimed as influences — The Velvet Underground, The Stooges, or Television — are not particularly difficult to imitate, should one be inclined towards replicating song structures, vocal cadences, or lyrical subject matter and style. McComb was never this kind of a performer (and The Triffids were not that kind of a group, even if their live renditions of The Stooges' 'No Fun', or The Velvet Underground's

'Femme Fatale' were empathic readings of songs they much admired). It appears that, from the beginnings of the band, they did compile an armoury of well-chosen and well-arranged covers for their live shows. The cassette albums, however, feature only band originals, with McComb taking a leading role in composition and Kakulas and MacDonald contributing occasionally.

Perth, David McComb told Clinton Walker in the early 1980s, is 'a bit like being in an incubator, being bottled somewhere.'[2] One might imagine at first glance that this is a negative summation, but McComb and the other Triffids were almost always positive about their home town, where McComb claimed people 'at least … have a bit of spirit and personality.'[3] Jon Stratton has recently offered a novel examination of The Triffids' 'sense of a place'; in this instance, a deep and formative connection to the largely middle-class suburbia from Mosman Park to Nedlands. Using elements of the group members' biographies alongside urban theory, Stratton discusses the ways in which 'the cultural experience of Perth permeated the band's music … regardless of where they were actually living.'[4] There was, says Stratton, no genuine inner city in Perth as the young Triffids knew it; therefore, David McComb and his cohorts 'did not turn their back on the suburbia which is so central to Perth's existence, but, ideally, wanted to find ways of making it more habitable, to return suburbia to the mythic utopian state from which Western Australians believe it has fallen.'[5] The Triffids' only recording forays in Perth were their first two 7" records ('Stand Up'/'Farmers Never Visit Nightclubs' and the *Reverie* EP) and, of course, the cassette albums *1st* through *6th*.

Stratton perhaps too quickly avoids the work of imagination in The Triffids' worldview: like any intelligent Australians, they were participants in and critics of contemporary Western culture as much as they were residents of Perth. Stratton is also, apparently, unaware of McComb's flippant summary of suburbia as 'obviously much the same anywhere.'[6] Since Stratton completed his article, statements by Alsy MacDonald would seem to challenge a central plank of his surmise. According to MacDonald, The Triffids played 'inner-city venues' in Perth and would have been 'lucky to escape' with their lives had they played in the suburbs, albeit the notion of an inner city in the context of Perth's suburban sprawl does not have the meaning it does in, say, Sydney or Melbourne.[7] Stratton is correct, then, to insist on the necessity of a suburban Perth viewpoint in any assessment of The Triffids' work, and to identify that viewpoint as largely positive. The film clips the group made for its singles 'Spanish Blue' (1981) and 'Beautiful Waste' (1984), which both parody and celebrate Perth life, are the best examples of this, and the cassette albums are its genesis and foundation.

The creative partnership of David McComb and Alsy MacDonald was central to the Triffids — even during the brief period in 1980–81 when MacDonald was absent from the group. The 'group' that can be seen as forerunner to The Triffids was formed when both were schoolboys. Called Dalsy, it initially recorded on 27 November 1976. This led directly to the 'tinny and quirky' Blök Musik, featuring Phil Kakulas, a group that recorded a cassette which McComb humorously referred to as 'the famous Blök Musik tape.'[8] McComb would later describe seeing The Sex Pistols on the TV show *Weekend Magazine* as a formative experience which eliminated the idea that one had to be Eric Clapton to play guitar, though the evidence of Dalsy's early foray (whatever it may have sounded like) suggests that he and MacDonald were already creating music in a 'DIY' sense prior to that motivating experience.[9]

McComb's handwritten and gently parodic memoir of his early music career records that Blök Musik played shows such as the 'Febuary [sic] 18 Garage Concert and at other parties … In April they played at the Leederville Town Hall Punk Fest … as usual, no-one danced.'[10] The group changed their name briefly to Logic, and then to The Triffids; there is evidence in McComb's scrapbooks that Logic's first album was to be named *The Triffids* and that, just as the Sydney group Flowers would do two years later, the band simply swapped their album's title for their band's name. Whether *Triffids 1st* was made commercially available in any degree is unclear, but certainly its successors were. McComb recalled that 'Nineteen stereo copies of the 2nd and third Triffids tapes were made' and that these were sold at the record shops 'Mark's and Dixie's for $3 each, along with 7 page lyric sheets.'[11] These lyric sheet booklets were foolscap-sized and stapled. The Triffids — still schoolboys — were emerging.

The age of the fun cassette

Recording — and most particularly the cassette as a distribution medium — was clearly core to The Triffids' ethos from the beginning of their existence under that name. It is useful to briefly consider the importance of this technology in the 1970s, and the ways in which it could be implemented by a young band like The Triffids to foster a local fan base. Pre-recorded cassettes, made available as an alternative to vinyl LPs since the 1960s, had some currency at this time and there was acceptance in the late 1970s for the notion that 'local' bands might produce albums solely on cassette. Releasing a vinyl record was prohibitively expensive for many. More importantly in the case of The Triffids' cassette albums, the 'throwaway' aspect (or mere tape-over-ability) of the medium meant that the home-made and experimental nature of the material within might be more acceptable: it need not be regarded as a definitive statement.

Cassettes were coming to be seen as adaptable. In 1980 Malcolm McLaren launched what was intended to be a snook cocked at the record industry with the cassette-oriented releases of the group Bow Wow Wow. This aside, the best-known cassette-only production from this time, at least in Australia, was Melbourne's *Fast Forward*, a bimonthly magazine on audio cassette edited by Bruce Milne and Andrew Maine alongside designer Michael Trudgeon. *Fast Forward* ran to thirteen issues between November 1980 and October 1982 (there was discussion at the time about a forerunner, Bill Furlong's *Audio Arts*).[12] Milne and Maine had planned a conventional magazine with a flexidisc, before they heard of EMI's standard procedure for unsold pre-recorded cassettes: they would be bulk erased and sold on. The early *Fast Forwards* had new labels stuck over reused pre-recorded cassettes, and the temporary or makeshift nature of them was part of the appeal. Milne told Australian *Rolling Stone*'s Andrea Jones in 1981 that the music on *Fast Forward* was not 'a permanent document like a record. We hope that people will hear the tape and then go out and see the bands.'[13]

The Triffids' six cassette albums pre-dated *Fast Forward* but can perhaps be seen in the same light: as well as being properly edited, sequenced albums, they are also bulletins and updates of the group's progress, 'serious' songs interspersed with more whimsical and parodic tunes. 'On every tape there'd be at least a couple of good conventional songs,' mused David McComb in 1986, 'and then there'd be the weirder, more quirky songs.'[14] 'Quirky' is an insufficient description for these ruminations on the late-1970s Perth 'scene', friends (and enemies) of the group, and the wider world. Yet it is important to keep in mind the complex nature of these releases: they are transient by virtue of their format, yet importantly, the fact that they are numbered adds an air of monumentality commensurate with David McComb's self-conscious tracking, tabulating and documenting of his career, which was evident even at this early stage. It is worth remembering also that McComb was not, unlike many of his contemporaries, embarrassed by these early forays — as much as he came to subtly misrepresent them — and was happy to facilitate their dispersal among friends and fans as late as the mid-1980s.

Martyrs of Perth punk

There remains an endemic tendency, both within and without Australia, to pigeonhole cultural movements with reference to international developments. Through this process, innovation of any stripe is ignored and local developments are shoehorned to appear derivative. In Western Australia, Dave Warner's early-seventies band Opus — later known as Pus — are reputed to have had the shock value, and intellectual challenge, of the best punk music; Warner claimed in 1977 that he 'preceded' The Sex Pistols by five years.[15] Another Perth band, The Cheap Nasties (featuring Kim Salmon), formed in 1976; they performed their first show in front of a backdrop featuring a drawing of Nana Mouskouri, which they slashed as a finale.[16] In 1977, The Geeks were rehearsing in a scout hall in the Perth suburb of Wembley, but their drummer, James Baker, had already had experience drumming in local groups such as the (reputedly campy and aggressive — they antagonized audiences with extended versions of 'Louie Louie') Slick City Boys.

Perth's punk movement was celebrated at the Leederville Punk Festival in 1978, at which Blök Musik played. Yet in 1979, the student newspaper *Pelican* could reveal an absurd ignorance of the city's own very recent musical history by publishing the statement that 'Perth, as always, follows behind European trends. Punk really hit Britain a couple of years ago. It is only just starting here.'[17] On the same page as that statement, the putatively punk group The Manikins could claim 'to a great extent, we've actually set the trends. Most probably, the developments in Perth have mirrored the Eastern states and overseas trends, but this wasn't a conscious thing on our part … What happened basically was that the movement diffused itself and got rid of the crap, a lot of stuff on the lowest level.'[18] The hindsight required in assembling anything close to a retrospective canon was yet to fully emerge, and in many respects has yet to do so.

I have already suggested that I do not see The Triffids' early work as derivative, confined by the parameters of unpretentious, guitar- and drums-oriented rock/pop. Yet the putative influence of American punk/new wave on the early Triffids has often been cited. In Tracee Hutchison's 1992 book *Your Name's on the Door* McComb puts forward a case for The Triffids' international roots:

> We felt a strong bonding with the New York bands that came out at the end of the '70s, people like Television and Talking Heads, who played guitar music in a totally 'un' rock and roll way. They just went about things as though the whole history of rock music hadn't existed, so they could do songs about buildings on fire and doing their cleaning, or whatever. We did a song about farmers not being socially accepted at nightclubs.[19]

'Farmers Never Visit Nightclubs' was the B-side of The Triffids' first vinyl release; an earlier version appears as track three of *Triffids 5th*. However, there is little overt evidence in the recordings that any Triffid had been listening intently to Television or Talking Heads on any of the songs (including 'Farmers').

McComb and MacDonald's musical forays coincided with the rise of punk internationally. The Triffids' song 'Martyrs' on *Triffids 1st* is one of many songs on the cassette albums that satirizes both the group and its environment, in which McComb proclaims that the group are 'martyrs of Perth punk.' Other songs, such as 'Mark' ('from White Rider,' a local import record shop) compares its protagonist not only to a spider but to Florian Schneider, of Kraftwerk. While this group had enjoyed a Top 40 hit in Australia in 1975, it took a certain 'new wave' sensibility to know the names of any of its members, and the name-check provides a nifty piece of culture-cueing which fits the good-natured and provocative humour of the song. McComb claimed in 1983 that The Triffids were rebels inasmuch as they 'rebelled initially against just the usual things … boring rock music which we heard all around us, a complete lack of feeling or frailty of humanity in music.'[20] The Triffids' involvement in 'punk' was, seemingly, a knowing and wry nod to the movement, rather than a strong identification with it.

In 1979 Australian *Rolling Stone* appeared comfortable in putting forward the notion that international multi-million dollar concerns such as A&M and United Artists were examples of independent record labels.[21] There had been a genuine independent music scene — or, at least, individual independent music producers and distributors — operating, however precariously, across Australia for some time by the late 1970s. The Triffids tapes were not released under the guise of any label, and distribution was limited to Perth record stores and friends of the band. Some covers, such as that for *4th*, were hand-drawn and some or all were hand-coloured. Incidentally, and for reasons that are not obvious, a selection of these included representations of Ludwig Bemelman's children's book character Madeline, who served as a basis for a song on the first vinyl album *Treeless Plain*.[22]

Triffids 1st was recorded, according to technical details on the cover, on a Revox A77; though there are no details on later releases, it is likely that the subsequent five tapes were recorded on the same machine. Editing between songs is jagged, and often slight snatches of dialogue and ambience are captured. Whether this was deliberate — for quality, the master may have been created by splicing tape — or otherwise, the cassettes can be said to capture a certain 'messthetics' (a 'visionary fusion of ethics with lo-fi aesthetics' as expounded by Britain's Rough Trade label in the late 1970s).[23] One song, 'Human Interest' on *Triffids 4th*, features a false start with McComb apologizing to the band for an error; this was retained, surely, to make a point.

They may have been independently produced, but the sound quality of the cassettes is largely impressive. The A77, used for the first album and some or all of the others, came in two- and four-track models, and it may be that there was overdubbing and mixing, or perhaps (more likely) the group merely experimented with group-microphone configurations to find a way to best record live, and then selected the best takes. Notably on 5th and 6th, the overall sound of the group is sometimes muffled relative to the keyboard of new recruit Margaret Gillard.

The things themselves and 'the thing itself'

While recognizing the futility of attempting to find a strong narrative of progress within any 'dense text' such as the six cassette albums, there are some connections that appear to emerge and to give a clear picture of David McComb's, and the group's, development. In 1985, McComb told Toby Creswell of Australian *Rolling Stone*:

> I guess lots of people feel, especially in adolescence, that emotions are false and that people just live out charades. I used to wonder how you aim for a true emotion, and one way is to have a detached narrator. I generally don't like writing confessional lyrics that are supposed to be completely honest, because I don't think you usually are very honest to yourself. However you can't go on forever dealing in images of something; eventually you have to make music that touches the thing itself.[24]

One form of the 'detached narrator', of course, could be McComb 'himself' — his self-deprecation, whether natural or cultivated, being deeper and more revealing, perhaps, than even he was aware. So, for example, the self-satirizing 'Martyrs' is joined on 2nd by 'I'm Not Losing Sleep', another statement of lackadaisical contempt for the 'cool' world, while 'I'm Sincere', a song in which he similarly ridicules himself and everyone else ('you may laugh and you may sneer … you may fart and you may jeer but I'm sincere') appears on 3rd. Broader social comment is also prominent: 'What Would the Martians Think', the very first Triffids song, imagines the world of 1979 as perceived by aliens. Local culture is similarly canvassed, in for instance the rather strained ballad 'Nedlands by Night', or in such flippant references as appear in 'Jeremy Joy', a catchy piece appearing on both 3rd and 4th (it is the only song to be repeated among cassettes) in which, for no apparent reason, the hero 'wakes up in Perth/the greatest place on Earth.' Other songs are in-jokes, such as 'The Frontier' on 3rd, describing then bass player Byron Sinclair as a brave cowboy.

An important development around this time is the departure of Phil Kakulas, and his replacement by Robert McComb, between 3rd

and 4th. Robert McComb's voice is intriguingly similar in many ways to MacDonald's. As the older brother, he was presumably being teased by being given a composition by David, 'Kids These Days', to sing on 4th; it includes lines such as 'what is this thing called "raging?" ' The 4th also features two openly self-conscious experiments in craftsman-like songwriting: 'Actress' (presaged by David McComb's spoken explanation that it is about 'a certain type of person') and 'Artist.' If there is anything on the cassette albums that demonstrates McComb's narrative experimentation, it is these. Coincidentally this emerges hand-in-hand with a late-blooming streak of jocular 'gay' songwriting from both McComb and MacDonald (the former's contribution is 'Surfer Boy in Leather', the latter's, 'I Can't Wait to See Your Gun'). These were, presumably, taunts to those who might have perceived The Triffids as foppish, or as other than iconically 'masculine.'

In 1986, McComb mused that The Triffids had 'made records where the tone isn't consistent all the way through, losing the whole atmosphere as we plunge into songs of completely different styles and atmosphere.'[25] Yet, with releases such as April 1980's 5th, the band made a strongly cohesive album (though closer to pastiche than most of their recordings released on vinyl), presumably inspired in great part by the evocative and 'retro' possibilities of Gillard's keyboards. On 5th, The Triffids enter into a pop terrain that endures through marvels such as 'Reverie' and 'Spanish Blue', their first vinyl album, *Treeless Plain* (their ninth album overall), and particularly songs like 'Rosevel'. The Triffids, and McComb as principal songwriter, are embarking here on experiments in jaunty, organ-driven beat pop. 'Tuscan Street Retirement Village' and 'In the Tropicana Lounge' are good examples of this, along with a forerunner, the parodic but effective instrumental 'Everyone Likes to Disco', on 4th.

In further experiments, the first four songs of 6th — 'Somewhere in the Shadows', 'You Can Spend', 'The Marrying Kind'[26] and 'A Place in the Sun' — are seemingly interconnected, dwelling as they do on the plight of a lonely stoic from different narrative perspectives.

McComb is also, throughout the cassette albums, honing a craft in wordplay which appears to derive initially from his fondness for satire. Titles such as 'Spring in the Fall' (on 2nd) and lines such as 'there's a six-car pileup on Memory Lane' ('Pile-Up', on 5th) are, essentially, clever lines developed into whole songs, an approach that would culminate in songs like 'Falling Over You' on *The Black Swan*. Indeed, the cassette albums serve another purpose — as McComb's notebook — with certain elements, lines and ideas being recycled in later songs: the song 'Little Voices' on *4th* would end up reworked as 'My Baby Thinks She's a Train' on *Treeless Plain*, and lines such as 'these are the cracks where the splinters belong,' from *5th*'s 'The Nervous Side of Town', would be detached for reuse in 'Plaything', also on *Treeless Plain*.

From time to time throughout the eighties, The Triffids would return to their pop roots in the cassette albums. In 1983, McComb wrote that The Triffids 'used to secretly hope/suspect that we could have commercial success, 'cos we wrote pop songs; and we presumed they would be played on radio, TV, sung along to, etc.'[27] Those expectations, he claimed, had dissipated, but in fact it would be only a few short years before they were revived with, for instance, the use of 'Bury Me Deep in Love' as Harold and Madge's wedding theme from *Neighbours*. Employing an unusual metaphor, McComb regarded his old recordings 'with some amusement and some admiration, like fossilized dog turds.'[28] Yet he found he was able to plunder the cassette albums for pop material: the early songs 'On the Street where You Live', 'Digging a Hole' and 'Too Hot to Move' (from *5th*, *6th*, and *Dungeon Tape* respectively), the last being reworked for *The Black Swan*, would feature in the ABC-TV musical comedy/drama series, *Sweet and Sour*.

The Triffids' *6th* cassette album overlapped with the group's first vinyl release, the single 'Stand Up'/'Farmers Never Visit Nightclubs', in retrospect an unfortunate choice of songs as it represented the group as slight (McComb later blamed 'Perth's jingle studios' for the 'ultra-bubblegum' nature of these songs, a rare departure for one so prone to self-deprecation).[29] Both tracks were re-recordings of songs from *5th* and *6th*, and the four songs of the 1981 *Reverie* EP featured two songs from *6th*, the title track and the aforementioned 'A Place in the Sun'.

After moving to the eastern seaboard — first to Melbourne, then Sydney — in 1981, The Triffids continued to produce cassettes, with *Dungeon Tape* (Blök Musik had recorded a *Loft Tape*) and its more readily available sequel, *Son of Dungeon Tape*, which featured six of the same songs. These were named for a rehearsal space, the Dungeon, where some of the songs were recorded. McComb claimed in 1983 that the group 'survive by playing live, selling tapes.'[30] Alongside the *Dungeon* tapes there was one more cassette release from the early 1980s: *The Triffids* contained the songs from the *Reverie* EP on one side and other tracks including the subsequent A-side 'Spanish Blue' in 'an eye catching vinyl pouch … plus an information sheet and sticker.'[31] This was, it is to be assumed, more of a promotional tool than a genuine release, though it was reviewed enthusiastically as legitimate product in the music magazine *Roadrunner.* The group was changing, however, and its market broadening: *Son of Dungeon Tape* can be regarded as the template for *Treeless Plain.* One final official Triffids tape emerged in 1988: *Jack Brabham,* created in an edition of fifty, combined numerous 1980s' recordings, demos and covers, and the hitherto lost pop classic 'Lanallu', the last song on the final of the original six cassette albums.

It could be argued that the *In the Pines* album, recorded exactly six years after *6ᵗʰ* and originally titled *The Woolshed Tape*, was an attempt by The Triffids to revive the spirit of those earlier recordings, both in sound and ambience (David McComb for instance requested that his brother's 'sorry' before the song 'Blinder by the Hour' should be retained on the album, evoking his own apology before 'Human Interest').[32] As early as 1986, David McComb was discussing a compilation derived from the original six cassette albums, claiming that Robert McComb in particular was keen to see them issued in some form. 'Unfortunately, my dilemma comes down to this,' he said, 'I couldn't choose the more conventional songs and put them on a compilation tape, 'cos I actually find the quirky ones very good.'[33] Late in life, David McComb also prepared a possible tracklisting for a compilation of songs from these tapes. He would seemingly come to regard his own prolific teenage output with some awe, and it is rumoured that he harboured ambitions of reworking many of his 1970s songs, a project he did not carry through.

The Triffids' progress 1978–80, and beyond

Typical of so many documentary films, Larry Meltzer and Toby Creswell's 2007 television documentary of 'the story behind the album' *Born Sandy Devotional* glosses over complexities, compacting historical origins into a narrow and easily digestible précis. A video for the

1983 song 'Bad Timing' is enlisted to illustrate the band in their early days; at one point, the sound on this video is distorted as if the video tape has been pushed through the player head carelessly, creating an impression that the group in its early days was slapdash and incompetent. Nevertheless, some core messages get through from the film's interviewees, most notably Robert McComb's suggestion that The Triffids in the late 1970s, prior to his involvement, had 'more power and creativity than anything else around'; other Triffids, such as Alsy MacDonald, suggest that the group was a 'small but electrifying' band.

As indicated, I would refute the suggestion that the key to David McComb's, or The Triffids', development as musicians or creative individuals can be tracked on the cassette albums like a fossilized record of ancestral progenitors (or, for that matter, dog turds). Indeed, the cassette albums are possibly most important in this regard for what they show the group were not: they are not a catalogue of attempted rewrites of other people's songs, and nor are they awkward or angst-ridden teen confessionals. The tapes are sprightly, containing sometimes amusing or in some cases throwaway, guitar-pop songs with little connection to Top 40 pop or 'progressive' rock, but otherwise well-arranged and melodic tunes sung with spirit and played with energy.

Perhaps what is most important are the clues the cassette albums give to The Triffids' suburban, middle-class origins. These origins are not addressed directly within the songs, yet an educated and detached objectivity is inherent in almost every one. In these cassette albums we see David McComb forging an identity for himself as a narrative songwriter or commentator focusing on his craft as a writer and his skill as a performer. He would continue to play with this identity throughout his music career, but it was moulded most strongly on these earliest recordings.

The Tape

David McComb

In front of me here
is a ninety minute, low-noise
cassette tape.
I put it in a little electric box
and though it isn't as romantic
as my reel-to-reel tapes
I can speak into it
and then, a minute later,
or a decade later
I can hear just what I had to say.
I think.

c. 1976

Hooked on McComb

James Paterson

I

I first heard about The Triffids a short while after I moved to Sydney with my band JFK and the Cuban Crisis in the autumn of 1982. Jonathan ('Ike') Lickliter, bassist for The End, another Brisbane band which had made the move southwards at the same time, told me they were 'kind of like The Go-Betweens but poppier.' This sounded like a good recommendation, so a few days later I went to see them play at the Southern Cross Hotel (near Central Station), where they had scored a Wednesday-night residency. The first time I entered the bandroom, they were playing shambolic covers of old American hits like 'Marie's the Name'. I wasn't impressed and retreated to join a friend at the bar.

David McComb enjoyed hearing the story of my first encounter with The Triffids, and several times urged me to try to remember the name of the song they'd been playing when I first laid eyes on them (I now think it was 'Nervous Breakdown'). For some perverse reason, he delighted in hearing more about the negative impression they'd made on me at that moment than about the more positive impression that followed shortly afterwards. As it happens, I decided to take one more look before I left. As I entered the bandroom, it was encore time and Robert McComb was striking up the first notes of 'Place in the Sun', the twelfth-fret harmonics, on his brown Fender Telecaster Thinline. Halfway through the song, I came to the conclusion that they probably had something to offer after all. I stayed to the end and heard them play a couple more originals.

After they had finished a second encore, audience members began calling out for a song called 'Reverie'. The band ostentatiously (albeit good-humouredly) indicated they had no intention of playing it. The calls for 'Reverie' kept coming even after the lights had come back on and the band were packing up their gear. I was intrigued. What kind of band refuses to play what was clearly one of its most popular songs?

I've never been able to abide a mystery, and it was probably a desire to plumb The Case of the Strange Refusal to Play 'Reverie' that made me a regular member of the audience on Wednesday nights. Perhaps I thought that eventually The Triffids would cave in to the requests and I could hear the damned song after all. Although the requests persisted for some time, they never did capitulate, and I found myself left pondering the deeper mystery of a band that, without even being famous, was refusing to indulge its own audience simply by playing the lead track from what was, I subsequently learned, its most recently released record. Didn't they want to be 'successful'?

The fact that even without 'Reverie' the Triffids had plenty of good material kept me returning to see them time and time again. After witnessing another four or five performances with mounting enthusiasm, I took the plunge and invested in a copy of the band's recently recorded cassette album, the *Dungeon Tape*. I bought it for a few dollars from Robert McComb, the band member to whom fell the duty of manning The Triffids' merchandise table during set breaks.

Over the next few weeks, I grew familiar with the tape's contents. The first few times I played it I decided that the first song, 'Too Hot to Move, Too Hot to Think', was very, very good and that all the rest were simply okay. Then, a few days later, I decided that the second song was also very, very good. A few days later it dawned on me that the third song was also very, very good. The process of discovery went on in this manner, until within perhaps a month I found myself contemplating the unthinkable: at a time when it seemed to me that it was impossible to find any new songwriters anywhere in the world with more than a handful of decent songs to their credit — the art of songwriting was to my way of thinking virtually extinct by the early eighties — David McComb, who was only nineteen when the tape was recorded, had already written seventeen very good ones. An ambitious songwriter myself, I was eaten up with envy.

The achievement of the *Dungeon Tape* lay not solely in the relative abundance on offer, but the fact that the songs were not remotely derivative. Although they were (mostly) more or less traditional pop songs, they did not resemble the works of Elvis Costello, who was at that time regarded by many people as the consummate 'pop' song-writer. I could not think of anyone else they sounded like: they certainly did not sound like The Go-Betweens to me, although that had already become established among inner-city cognoscenti as the closest reference point, while the lyrics, which were much better than anything I had heard in a long time, betrayed a unique sensibility.

The cliché runs that it's darkest just before the dawn, and it seemed remarkable to me that precisely at a moment when I despaired of the death of songwriting, a great songwriter seemed to have sprung up in my own backyard. Meanwhile, it had become the height of my ambition to write something that would have sat comfortably alongside the tracks on the *Dungeon Tape*. For months I tried — and failed — to write a song consistent with the tape's spirit. It was a source of immense frustration to me that while David McComb seemed to be in the process of reinventing pop, I didn't seem able to tap into the process myself. By the end of the year I was well on the way to developing writer's block, as I discarded one song after another because it failed to pass the *Dungeon Tape* litmus test.

By the end of 1982, I had acquired all other available Triffids recordings — the first single, 'Stand Up', and the *Reverie* EP — and The Triffids had become my staple listening fodder. I played the tape and the records incessantly and attended each and every gig. One day I was playing the *Reverie* EP when I went out the front of my house to check the mailbox; there I saw a tall figure walking slowly down the footpath in the hot sun. It was *him*, David McComb himself, black suit, sunglasses, pretty much the way he always dressed. I wanted very much to speak to him, to tell him how highly I regarded his talent, but my fear of appearing gauche got in the way. Fortunately, I was able to open a channel to Dave through Denise Corrigan, a girl from Perth who was sharing a house with JFK's singer, John Kennedy. Denise, who already knew them, passed the word on to David and Alsy Macdonald that I wanted to meet them.

In early 1983, I ran into Dave and Alsy pushing a shopping trolley down the aisle of the supermarket at Redfern Mall. They invited me over for dinner the next night at their house in Marlborough Street,

Surry Hills. To my surprise, I soon found myself on friendly terms with someone three years younger than myself who I felt deserved to be regarded as the best songwriter in Australia, if not the world. To my great surprise, I learned from Dave and Alsy that he had already written, according to his own estimate, between one hundred and 120 songs. The *Dungeon Tape* was in fact the The Triffids' seventh tape. David loaned me the earlier six — one at a time, to forestall the possibility of them all being lost in some unanticipated catastrophe. I found that by the fifth tape he'd reached a standard of songwriting comparable to many of the better albums that were around. There were three or four standout tracks, a couple of other good ones and a few fillers. The sixth and seventh tapes, on the other hand, were packed with exceptional compositions.

A large part of my motivation for wanting to meet David was to find out more about the person who had written the songs on the *Dungeon Tape*, which continued to impress me every time I listened to it. But the David McComb I was to meet proved little interested in discussing his past output, no matter how recent. To him, the twenty-odd songs he'd written only a year before were already ancient history. The reason, I soon learned, was that in January 1982 — in other words, around the same time the *Dungeon Tape* had been recorded — David had seen The Birthday Party perform, an event that he described to me as a huge watershed in his musical development. To a considerable extent, the influence of The Birthday Party, which had already been registered on two tracks that appeared on the *Dungeon Tape* ('Twisted Brain' and 'Dead Wind'), truncated his autonomous line of development and sent him scrambling in a quite different direction.

Within a few weeks of meeting, David and Alsy had taken to doing their laundry at my place in Chippendale. While the clothes were thrashed about in the backyard shed, Dave, Alsy and I would chat. Alsy was the easier of the two to talk to, as he took more of an interest in politics than Dave, who seemed to get bored once a conversation veered too far from music or the music business. The Hawke government having recently been elected, there was much to talk about. On one of these occasions, I handed Dave a guitar and suggested that we try writing a song together. After lodging the guitar on his knees, he strummed a few chords at random and looked more helpless than I was to ever see him. Finally, he said, 'I'm sorry but I've got no inspiration. I just don't have any ideas right now.' Having already pegged Dave in my mind as a kind of songwriting machine, I was taken aback to discover that he didn't seem to have a clue how to go about writing a new song. The awkwardness of the situation led me to resolve never to talk about writing songs together again. But what Dave didn't say on this occasion, perhaps because he hadn't yet realized it himself, was that he already had a highly evolved modus operandi for writing songs and it didn't involve trying to pluck them out of thin air.

Insight into one of Dave's songwriting strategies first arrived one afternoon when, lounging on the sofa at Dave and Alsy's terrace house in Surry Hills, Dave suddenly came towards me brandishing a page of lyrics and an acoustic guitar. He handed them both to me, mumbling something about the possibility that I could find some music to go with the words. After glancing quickly at the lines, which seemed considerably stranger than anything I'd tried to set to music before (for example, 'I hope I die by spontaneous combustion in a scorching blaze of heat'), I tentatively strummed a few major chords and hummed a bit of a tune along to them. Dave looked at me rather indulgently, and explained, 'We can't really use that. You see, everything has to be in a minor key now.' This was my introduction to the fact that, in the aftermath of 'The Birthday Party revolution,' Dave had decided that all new Triffids songs were to be in minor keys.

Duly compliant, I strummed a sequence of chords starting on A-minor — based on a song I'd written when I was sixteen — and tried to get the somewhat verbose lyric to fit. 'That's it!' exclaimed Dave, who duly began writing the chords down on his copy of the lyrics. Although I was gratified to have come up with something that he liked, I also assumed that Dave wouldn't remember the song fragment and that the whole exercise would amount to nothing in the end. Yet when the record that featured the song, the *Raining Pleasure* mini-album, came out a few months later, I had no trouble recognizing it as the same piece of music that had been assembled in a few minutes in his living room. For one of the many remarkable things about David was his uncanny ability to remember pieces of music after hearing them only once — an ability he erroneously assumed that I, and perhaps everybody else, also had.

Only many years later did I figure out that Dave would have written the words with another tune in mind, probably Dylan's 'Quinn the Eskimo (The Mighty Quinn)'. One day we were walking along the street when he suddenly asked, 'Do you ever write new words to a favourite song and then later, when you've forgotten what the original music was, use them to write a new song?' I said that I had, although in fact I think I'd only done that once and the music I'd tried to write had borne too great a resemblance to the original song for it to be worth persevering with. I have reasons now to suspect that on that occasion Dave was sharing with me his peculiar modus operandi.[1] If you listen to 'Everybody Has to Eat' it has some telltale resemblances to 'The Mighty Quinn'. Both songs for instance, use the phrase 'cup of meat'. I'd suggest that he asked me to come up with something because he knew that, since I didn't know the original tune, I would inevitably send the song off in a completely different direction. I have a feeling this is what also happened with 'Save What You Can' and 'Go Home Eddie'. I can't prove that this was his regular way of writing, but I can say that almost invariably the words were written first and the music was worked up later. I'd be very surprised if there were many cases of him writing words to pre-existing melodies. The only case of which I'm aware is 'Holy Water', whose melody, he told me, came to him while he was sleeping and remained hanging around in his head after he'd woken up.

II

When I first met David, I was somewhat dismayed to find that, like so many musicians I'd met earlier in Brisbane, his taste in music conformed rigidly to what I tend to refer to as alternative music orthodoxy. As I went through his record collection and was exposed to his opinions about music, I was simply staggered to discover that someone who demonstrated immensely more songwriting talent and greater depth of musical expression than most musicians was beholden to much the same circumscribed alternative pantheon as the average inner-city musician of the time, one that consisted almost entirely of American artists who were perceived to have passed the 'cred' test like Lou Reed, Neil Young and Leonard Cohen. For, despite the passage of the punk era, there remained a marked preoccupation with 'credibility' — which term meant, if it meant anything at all, that such artists possessed the imprimatur of a few music critics whose views were considered 'authoritative.'

At the time I was rapidly losing interest in contemporary music and becoming something of a collector of Merseybeat and so-called 'British invasion' bands. David, by contrast, didn't seem to have a British rock or pop record in his collection. The only British album I recall seeing there was The Sex Pistols' *Never Mind the Bollocks*, which periodically came up in conversation and which I think he regarded as one of the best albums ever made. However, he must have had a few David Bowie and Elvis Costello records as well (I recall that he hated Bowie's latest album at the time, *Let's Dance*, which he dismissed as a 'sellout' record). As a fan of British rock, I was stunned to learn during one of our first encounters that he had never listened to a Rolling Stones record. I urged to him to listen at least to the Stones' *Let It Bleed* album, which I assured him was very good. 'I won't,' he replied. I asked him why not. Somewhat testily, he retorted that he 'couldn't see the point.'

It was therefore with a growing sense of discomfort that I watched David work his way systematically through my record collection one day when Alsy and I were lounging around my living room discussing Australia's newly elected prime minister, Bob Hawke. Dave didn't comment on my collection at the time, but it can hardly have escaped his keen eye that I seemed to have every album The Kinks had ever released. In those days, with The Triffids playing shows only once or twice a week, there was plenty of time for the two of us to sit and chew the fat. We talked a good deal about songwriting, and my impression was that he enjoyed having someone to talk to who shared his more or less traditional approach to songwriting and was interested in it as a craft. During such conversations, Ray Davies of The Kinks emerged as one of my major reference points. Dave professed not to understand what I saw in him.

Ironically, the day Dave and I went to ABC studios to record demos for subsequent use in the forthcoming *Sweet and Sour* television series, the recording engineer remarked that he liked Dave's voice, which reminded him of Ray Davies. That comment seems to have set something off in Dave's mind, and he would take more seriously my routine invocations of Ray Davies as one of rock's greatest songwriters and 'Waterloo Sunset' as one of its greatest songs. Finally, some weeks after the band had gone to England for the first time, I received a post-card from him in which he explained the conclusion he had finally reached:

> I've realized that what I like above all in a song is a sense of Mystery (not the modern dictionary meaning — more a kind of inaccessible truth, an unresolved core of strange beauty). Are you with me? This to me is why 'Would you lay with me in a Field of Stone' is a greater song than 'Waterloo Sunset'. To me, Ray Davies has no grasp of Mystery. Still, let's not quibble. (10 November 1984)

I had to see his point, although, if I had been allowed to quibble, I would have replied that quite a few of his own best songs — 'Too Hot to Move', 'Spanish Blue' — would not have passed the Mystery test either. For all that, mystery — a quality I would ascribe above almost any other song to the Gram Parsons classic, '$1000 Wedding' — was obviously something to aim for, and I think there's little doubt that many of Dave's best songs, including 'The Seabirds', contain 'an unre-solved core of strange beauty' that has ensured that they continue to resonate with listeners even after every note has been assimilated a hundred times.

III

Twenty-five years on, I still think that 'Waterloo Sunset' is a consider-ably better song than 'Would You Lay with Me (In a Field of Stone)', whose melody I find barely memorable. For what it's worth, 'Waterloo Sunset' is number forty-two on *Rolling Stone*'s list of the 500 Greatest Songs of All Time, while 'Field of Stone' isn't on the list at all. Dave's preference for the latter song I would attribute to the primacy he assigned words over music. One of the striking facts about David McComb — particularly when one takes stock of how very many won-derful melodies he actually wrote — is that the heart of a song was, for him, undoubtedly the lyrics. The music he seemed to regard simply as the setting for the words. This trait was evident in his response to my own songs and song fragments. Dave's tendency to fasten on the lyrics when confronted by a new song almost always disconcerted me.

Hardly a nuance in the words escaped him, and he would immediately hone in on both the most inspired and the most flawed lines in a song, doling out praise and criticism in almost equal portions. Yet while a dodgy line seemed to him almost unforgivable, a rather ordinary piece of music — say, a predictable or monotonous melody — was acceptable, provided it functioned to carry the lyrics.

Of course, I don't wish to give the impression that Dave didn't care at all about melody, and one role I did end up playing for him in those years was that of helping him decide whether a new song that he had written had enough of a tune to be worth persisting with. Nonetheless, the primacy of the lyrics helps explain why he was riveted by a record like Bruce Springsteen's *Nebraska*, whose starkness rather bored me after a few listens. My predilection for melody (and corresponding tolerance for dodgy lyrics) was, I think, something new and unusual to him and even baffled him slightly. I remember one afternoon how he was determined to explore the subject of our different approaches to music at great length. In an exhausting conversation that must have lasted two hours, Dave interrogated me long enough to finally reach the conclusion that he and I differed fundamentally in our beliefs about what music was for. In hindsight, it would be of considerable interest to know what Dave said he thought music was for; unfortunately, I simply don't remember.

IV

After The Triffids left for England in late '84, Dave and I didn't often find ourselves in the same city at the same time. Dave and The Triffids spent most of their time from that point onwards either in Europe or at home in Perth, and on the two major occasions he returned to Sydney for a stay of some length I happened to be travelling overseas. My hopes that our relationship would evolve into a serious songwriting partnership were therefore sabotaged by the geographical factor, although this was at least partly my own fault — Dave's letters from England contained numerous solicitations to join up with him in London. JFK and the Cuban Crisis having disbanded in relatively unpleasant circumstances, I had no desire to get involved with another band quite so soon, nor did I wish to impose upon myself a life of expatriate muso poverty in Thatcher's ugly England.

As a result of the relative infrequency of our subsequent meetings, most of our songwriting sessions were little more than troubleshooting exercises. Typically, Dave would arrive at my place in a taxi, black briefcase in hand. After a few minutes' chat, Dave would often be keen to set to work and his briefcase would disgorge cassettes and astonishingly thick wads of lyric sheets.

On most occasions, Dave would work through the songs systematically, carefully managing the time so that each song or song fragment was accorded its due share of attention. He would only play me the songs he was having difficulty with, in the hope that I would be able to fix a problem or add that special something that would make a song work. As he once wrote to me on the back of a postcard:

> No matter how unfruitful you may possibly think our recent skirmishes at combined songwriting have been, you can be assured that for me they have been quite the opposite. You always seem to be able to add that small but important percentage of musical perspective and contribution that can make my 'almost' song into a proper one. (16 January 1985)

However, this arrangement meant that I usually never got to hear most of the really good songs until they had been recorded. It's a strange thing, but really good songs usually have a way of writing themselves, so Dave had no particular reason to play them to me. This approach had the side effect of making me a little more modest in my estimation of Dave's talent, since I got used to hearing him at his most flawed and vulnerable. It was often only when listening to the finished recording that I would remember that this was the *great* David McComb I'd been so keen to meet in the first place.

I was usually only ever given a few minutes to come up with suggestions for a particular song. I remember one sunny afternoon when Dave appeared out of a taxi outside my house in Leichhardt with a briefcase crammed full of lyrics and tapes. After running through all the new songs, one by one, he rang for a taxi and was off again. The time taken on that occasion would have been no more than two hours. Once I challenged David about this strategy, remarking that he hardly ever gave me time to get to know a song before he'd move on to the next one. Dave explained that he trusted my instincts more than my premeditation and that if I had anything to contribute I would come up with it at once. I never really agreed with this view, although, as it happens, a few times it did work out very well in the end.

The songs we worked on together that I remember most fondly are the three that appeared on *Calenture*. Of the two for which I was credited, the first, 'Save What You Can', had its genesis in Melbourne, where I was staying with Dave and Marty at Julian Wu's house. One morning, Dave showed me ten or twelve pages of lyrics, including 'Save What You Can'. It seemed a lot to take in and I didn't have time to do more than glance through them, but I do remember being instantly struck by some of the excellent lines that survived intact into the final version on *Calenture*. I don't believe there was any music for it at that stage, although I could be wrong.

Either later that same day or the next there was a gathering, probably a barbecue, in progress in Mr Wu's back yard and, hardly knowing anybody there, I stole away for a while to tinker on the piano in the living room. I came up with a delicate little piano melody, probably because the surroundings, which included precious Chinese antique vases in glass display cases, didn't invite anything more intrusive. Dave came to join me at the piano for ten minutes and I played him the tune. I knew nothing further about the song's progress until much later, when I heard the unmixed tapes for *Calenture*. As was often the case, I was stunned by what Dave had ended up doing with an idea that initially I hadn't set too much store by.

Musically, the second of the songs, 'Jerdacuttup Man', didn't seem all that interesting when Dave first sang it to me. While the lyrics were complete (I think), the music he had consisted solely of the melody for the first verse: 'I live under glass in the British museum/I am wrinkled and black, I am ten thousand years/I once lost in business, I once lost in love/I took a hard fall, I couldn't get up.' The problem was that Dave had no idea where it should go next. All he could do was sing the next verse to the same tune as the first. If you do that you'll soon realize that it's pretty flat and not obviously capable of going anywhere. But because Dave was stuck on using the song, he asked me if I could think of a way to develop it further. I replied, 'Well, what we could do is the old folk singer's trick of taking the melody up an octave and then coming back down from there.'[2] 'How do you mean?' he asked. And then I started singing the melody, pretty much as it is known now. David was stunned and shot me that 'By Jove, you've done it!' look that, I must admit, I always found extremely gratifying. After I taught him the melody — it took him a couple of tries to get the right notes for 'faces were mean' — he said we should tape it. However, we couldn't tape it without a chorus of some kind, so we hurriedly made up the chords and melody for this bit (Dave the first line, me the second): 'Old and lonely, dirty and cold/I am a Jerdacuttup man.' The idea was that while this was good enough for the purpose of making the first recording of the song we'd try to replace it with something better later. However, that part never got changed, and in the end the song's exactly the way it was put together that day. I don't think I ever heard it again between the day we worked on it and the day Dave first played me *Calenture*.

v

For me personally, the eighties was a truly depressing decade in which the ideological straitjacket of neoliberalism was fastened on the major western economies and, even more depressingly, opposition turned out to be virtually nonexistent. Although it's actually very hard for me to think about the eighties — and I've tried, fairly successfully, to ignore the fact that they happened at all — I feel certain that David McComb's songwriting represented one of the very few bright spots of the period. I consider myself incredibly fortunate to have been able to witness a major phase of his development at first hand.

As for the full-blooded collaboration which I had so ardently desired, the irony is that it didn't transpire, probably because Dave was an incredibly talented individual who needed very little help with his work at all. The puzzle is that, like Morrissey and Marr, he somehow managed to thrive creatively in dismal times, producing a vast output of often awe-inspiring songs when most other writers could scarcely manage a handful of passable ones. The era simply wasn't conducive to great songwriting and its achievements would seem, in retrospect, to have lain rather in the rapid development of computer technology. While I can say I gained valuable insights into the nature of Dave's songwriting techniques, an unresolved core of mystery remains: how he managed to flourish like a veritable hothouse plant in the bleak desert of the eighties.

Lost Chords

Julian Wu

The first time I met David McComb was back in July 1982, at the Mt Erica Hotel in Prahran, where The Triffids were supporting The Moodists. I didn't actually get to see the band play a full set that night, as I was on my way to see The Sacred Cowboys at the Post Office Hotel in Richmond. But due to the fairly small number of people — I think there were fewer than ten people at that gig — it was difficult to avoid striking up a conversation with the band. They were such a friendly bunch that I resolved to go and see them a day or two later, at a lunchtime show they were performing at Monash University, where I was studying at the time. Although The Sacred Cowboys were great, I still regret missing The Triffids that night, and I never missed another Triffids show again, whenever they were playing in the same city as I was, for the rest of my life. At the Monash University gig I was simply blown away. While the band had yet to settle on its classic line-up, it was obvious that David McComb was a talented songwriter and that The Triffids had 'it,' whatever 'it' was. I purchased a copy of *Dungeon Tape* which I listened to continually for two or three months. I sat down and learnt every one of those songs on guitar.

Apart from David's songs — which even a beginning guitarist like myself could manage to play without sounding awful — what really drew me to The Triffids was how unpretentious they were. Back in the early eighties, it seemed to be the done thing to claim to be 'working class' and disavow any middle-class origins (this was before it became widely known that The Boys Next Door/The Birthday Party were Caulfield Grammar students) but David and the rest of The Triffids made no secret that they were from happy, middle-class families, and as a result they were just easier people to hang out with compared to some of my 'too cool for school' friends.

In our first few meetings, it seemed that Alsy and Rob were the more gregarious members of the band. My first impression of Dave was that, although he was friendly, he occasionally seemed to be withdrawn and aloof. This was at odds with his position as the band's frontman, but once he got to know you and had sized you up, he would open up and reveal a wicked sense of humour and also a very vulnerable and gentle side. The path from fan to friend was rather brief.

Later that year, The Triffids signed to White Label records, a subsidiary of Mushroom Records, and relocated to Melbourne. Over those few months The Triffids played to extremely disappointing crowds. Normally there were only another five or six punters at their gigs, and so it was impossible not to get to know them well if you saw their shows regularly. It was not until the last couple of Melbourne gigs, when they played at The Tote with The Scientists and Hoodoo Gurus, that I saw them play to a crowd of more than ten people for the first time.

My fondest memories of David are probably from the early days before his health issues got the better of him. One thing which isn't readily apparent — unless you happen to read the inscriptions on the run-out grooves of The Triffids' records — is that toilet humour was a big part of the band's interpersonal dynamics.[1] I remember one evening when, sitting around in their flat — at the time, The Triffids were living in a converted warehouse on Brunswick Street, Fitzroy, and were between keyboard players; Jill Yates had recently departed and Jill Birt was yet to join the band — there suddenly erupted a round of farting which made the infamous scene in *Blazing Saddles* look tame. This prompted Dave to exclaim: 'Oh my God! It's come to this. We have to get another girl into the band.'

One of Dave's many talents was the ability to see the ridiculous in the sublime, and vice versa. In 1985, The Triffids were staying at my house, and I was watching a low-budget Italian zombie movie called *Cannibal Apocalypse*, together with Martyn and Alsy. Dave was also in the room, but sitting on the couch and writing in his notebook, not paying much attention to the movie, apparently deep in thought. There is a scene in the film in which the militia, faced with a phalanx of zombies, fires a hailstorm of bullets. Lots of shots of the zombies walking into the hail of gunfire, the rounds going off in their chests, but they keep on walking towards the gunmen until one of the protagonists runs up to a zombie and shoots it in the head, yelling: 'You can't kill them that way, you gotta shoot them in the head!' Now I'm not saying that's the only source which David drew upon when writing one of his best-known songs, but a few days later I heard him playing a new song and the opening lines seemed to draw upon that image, while evoking much more.

David was a voracious consumer of music. Although often sceptical, once he saw merit in something he was evangelical about it. On my twenty-first birthday card he inscribed '*Sister Lovers* is god!' as he was going through a big Alex Chilton and Big Star phase around the time they were recording *Born Sandy Devotional*. He also loved to compile mix tapes and give them to his friends, and in retrospect, these were great roadmaps to his musical consciousness at the time. Songs by The Beach Boys would sit alongside other acts like LL Cool J, Peter Tosh, Suicide and Monty Python. Sometimes he could be quite dismissive, but if pressed on the issue he was always willing to have a second listen and re-evaluate his position. Sometimes you just had to hook him by pointing out the connection with something he already liked, such as the Rolling Stones–Gram Parsons connection. Pretty early on in our friendship I can remember him being quite dismissive of The Rolling Stones, but a few years later you could hear The Triffids covering 'Wild Horses' and 'Sympathy for the Devil' at their shows.

Probably the biggest effect that David and The Triffids had on me was to alter the direction of my working life. I sat in on a few demo recording sessions and eventually had a stint working in their road crew, which led to a brief career as a sound engineer recording tracks for artists such as The Blackeyed Susans and The Go-Betweens, and worked in-house at the Continental Café with artists like Jimmy Webb, Ron Sexsmith and Dan Penn.

My biggest regret was that we never got to finish what was David's last record. When David approached me about working together on the costar recordings I was extremely flattered. The name of the band comes from one of David's pet dogs — Costar — who suffered an unfortunate accident to his male anatomy while getting 'fixed.' I think Dave chose the band name as a tribute to his dog, out of a sense of kinship with him due to their mutual medical misfortunes.

The first costar session went well. We managed to record 'The Good Life Never Ends' with Graham Lee and Kiernan Box (keyboard player for The Blackeyed Susans). David had based the song around a drum-machine pattern he had programmed (probably the best comparison is to 'Deep in a Dream' from *Love of Will*), but something sounded wrong about that arrangement, so we dispensed with the drum machine and recorded another version with Graham playing acoustic guitar and Kiernan a melancholy piano part. This one ended up being a keeper and so we recorded a vocal, Graham overdubbed the bass and pedal-steel parts, and finally David and Graham added some percussion with homemade shakers (pill bottles filled with rice). Listening back to the track you can hear David's voice falter a few times and while I think it shows his vulnerability in a very touching light, I know David didn't really like it and felt he was capable of giving a much better performance. I'm sure if he had been in better shape he would have nailed it, but unfortunately it was not to be. However, he seemed pleased enough with the results to organize another couple of days' recording, flying Martyn Casey over from Perth to play bass.

It was a hot summer weekend when we assembled the band in my living room and kitchen. David had recruited a full band for this session so the line-up was Graham Lee on pedal steel and guitar, Kiernan Box on keys, Martyn Casey on bass, and Stuart Soler (who had previously played with Kiernan in a band called The Disappointments) on drums. Despite the heat, we managed to lay down the basic tracks for five songs that weekend: 'I Kept My Eye on You', 'Murder in the Dark', 'Devil Please', 'Lucky for Some', and 'Everything Fixed is Killed'. Rob

McComb and Warren Ellis dropped in on the Sunday to see how the sessions were going, so Dave enlisted Rob to play guitar and Warren to play organ on 'Everything Fixed is Killed'.

Since his operation in 1996 I noticed that David tired easily. It was especially difficult for him to deal with hot weather, so he really took a beating that weekend. We didn't do any further recording for a month or two. Eventually we did some rough mixes, and David liked 'I Kept My Eye on You' enough to record a vocal. Due to his ill health we were restricted to working one day a week, so it was pretty slow going. But David was keen to begin playing live so he assembled a line-up with Will Akers on bass (Martyn was on tour with The Bad Seeds), and Matt Habben, also of The Disappointments, on saxophone. Because playing and rehearsing with the band took up a lot of David's time, it became harder to find time to work on the recordings, but we eventually managed to do rough mixes of all the songs.

After about a year or so, I figured that that was all that was going to happen to the songs. Then, out of the blue in the spring of 1998, David called me and said he wanted to put out a single and do some more recordings, and asked if Mick Harvey would be a person that I could work with. Being a long-time fan of The Bad Seeds and The Birthday Party I was thrilled. It seemed that Dave had found a new lease on life, and was pulling himself together. We decided to put out a single with 'I Kept My Eye on You' as the A-side, backed with 'Murder in the Dark' and 'Lucky for Some', and were at the point of having it mastered. I was keen to do another mix as I was aware of how 'unfinished' the record was, but Dave felt a certain urgency about releasing it. David's idea was that it would be released as an 'official bootleg' with a plain white sleeve and photocopied cover, but due to the timing of things — Christmas was fast approaching — we probably wouldn't be able to get the record pressed until the new year. In retrospect I feel that David was aware that his health was failing him; perhaps he suspected that his heart transplant was being rejected. I told him that I thought his first priority should be his health, and although Dave was considering stopping things for a while, he also felt that he might be letting down some of the band members.

The last time I saw David in person was on New Year's Eve, 1998. It was at The Standard Hotel. He was going to play with Matt Walker at the hotel's annual party, but — under circumstances strangely similar to those under which I first met him — I was on my way to another gig a few blocks away, at The Empress of India, where I was filling in on guitar with The Disappointments.

I did speak with David one more time, but it seemed that his health had taken a turn for the worse, and he sounded very ill. He was agitated because he had lost his Fender Jazzmaster and wondered if he had left it at my place.

That was pretty much the last time we spoke.

A few days later I was woken by a call from Steve Miller who informed me that David had died the previous afternoon.

Not long after that I was doing sound for another band playing at The Standard. After the gig, my hands dirty from rolling up microphone leads, packing up the PA and lugging it to the upstairs storeroom, I went into the staff toilet to wash my hands. When I closed the door behind me I was surprised to discover David's Jazzmaster leaning behind the door, where he must have left it after playing on New Year's Eve. I duly passed the guitar on to Dave's family.

Now I'm not a particularly religious or spiritual person, but that night I had a lucid dream. I was in my house, and David was knocking at my front door. He thanked me for finding his guitar, and then picked up one of my guitars and played me a song. It sounded just like one of his songs; it was great. He said: 'I know you think you're dreaming and you are, but if you can remember this one, it's yours.'

I'm still looking for those lost chords.

McComb with Fender
Jazzmaster, Hopetoun
Hotel, Sydney, early 1984.

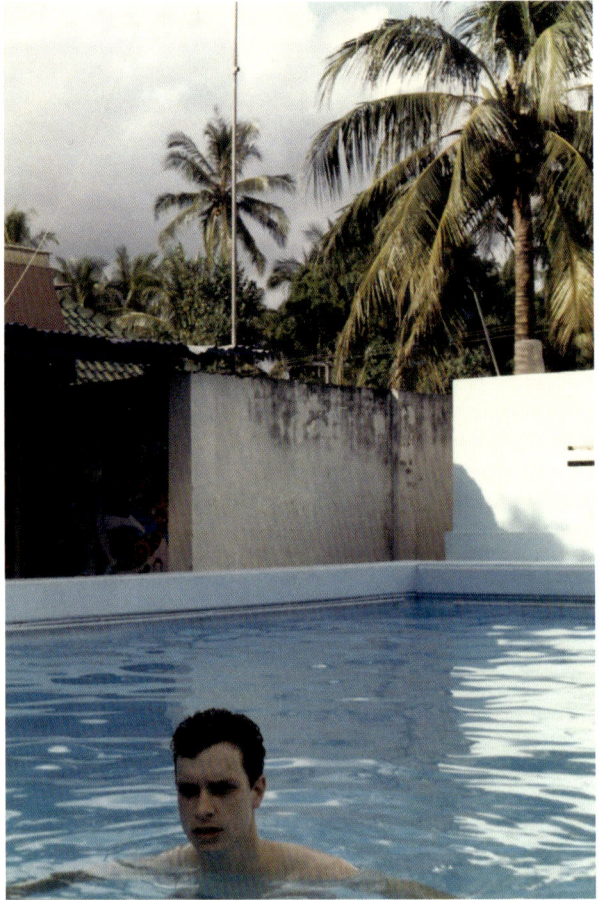

Alsy MacDonald taking a dip at a Bali hotel, April 1985, as captured by Jill Birt and featured on the inner sleeve of *Born Sandy Devotional.*

Terra Australis Incognita

Julian Tompkin

Growing up in blood-red mining country south of Kalgoorlie, I was never too sure of what it was to be 'Australian.' The standard country-town soundtrack of John Farnham, Cold Chisel and Men At Work didn't make sense to me. Surely it couldn't all be about *taking the pressure down* with *cheap wine* in *a land of chunder* — about BBQs on Sundays, mateship, and faith in an honest nation buckled down to the business of living?

David McComb, together with compatriots Nick Cave and The Go-Betweens, gave voice to a refusal of the flag-waving, working-class anthems that saturated the aural plain of this young, vast country. In an era when INXS were taking the well-packaged image of a new, FM- and US-friendly Australia to the globe, The Triffids offered something significantly different.

Above all, McComb returned a sense of *mystery* to Australia that had long been forgotten. His was a land that existed previously only in the dreams of Pythagoras, Macrobius, Isidore of Seville, Thomas More, Henry Neville, Francis Goodwin and Frenchmen Denis Vairasse and Gabriel de Foigny: *Terra Australis Incognita*, the enigmatic land of the fabled Antipodes, or the utopian paradise that possessed explorers from Marco Polo to Amerigo Vespucci. The fact that England became obsessed with The Triffids is no surprise. Here was this band from the colonies — of all places, Perth — with a sound even London hadn't yet discovered. The curiosity was overwhelming, as in the case of seventeenth-century adventurers returning from *Terra Australis* with sketches of kangaroos, Sturt's Desert Pea and great white gums shredding their bark.

McComb's music was pure and melodic, but melodramatic. It was celestial, but written in a suburban shed in Perth. It was personal, but enchanting. In the eyes of England at least, Australia was mysterious again: a land of ghosts and terror and beauty and the great unknown (Nick Cave, and later, Warren Ellis, would second that). Back home, the roads weren't so urban-planned anymore. Everything felt different.

Richard Gunning, *Crucifixion*, oil on canvas, 1992. At McComb's insistence, this image was used on the cover of The Triffids' *Australian Melodrama* CD compilation.

what I like above all in a song
is a sense of Mystery (not the modern
dictionary meaning – more a kind of
inaccessible truth, an unresolved core
of strange beauty). Are you with me?

Fragment of a post-
card sent from David
McComb to James
Paterson, postmarked
10 November 1984.

Jesus Calling: Religion in the Songs of David McComb

Andrew McGowan

At least one of David McComb's obituaries mentions that he had won a prize in 'Divinity' while at Christ Church Grammar School in Perth.[1] The statement illustrates the complexity of the man and the music, but probably scores some points for irony too. His life and death were hard, and more characterized by passion than piety.

Yet there are at least two ways in which religion appears in the body of lyrical work that David left behind. Late in 2006, Australian author Nikki Gemmel wrote of feeling her expatriate 'eyes prickle' while reading the lyrics to 'Wide Open Road' in *Meanjin* during an agnostic celebration of Christmas in London.[2] McComb's lyrics and music have that eye-prickling effect for many people, not least for Australians of a certain age but apparently for Scandinavians and Belgians too. Their evocative power is usually connected with yearning involving love, distance, or time, the capacity to open up some infinite horizon and our distance from it. These lost horizons and flashes of nostalgia always suggest transcendent questions, which if not institutionally religious are inevitably theological.

But explicitly religious symbols and language do also have a role in his songs. In its published form, 'Wide Open Road' is not an obvious case, but even that most evocative of Triffids songs had an early history involving religion; the manuscript draft shows the second stanza ending with: 'I drove out into the desert just for you/I sang the ancient Pentecostal hymns.'[3]

I confess to a complex interest in this topic. I was both with David McComb at the school where he won that Divinity prize — he actually won more prizes over the years for English, unsurprizingly — and an early contributor to the sequence of bands that later became The Triffids. For a few years, David and I walked home from school together and talked about the elements of teenage schoolboy life — people, teachers, classmates, music, art, books and even (I think) faith. The breadth and the incisive and intuitive aspects of David's observation and expression were always evident.

I did not win a Divinity prize (I did win one for Music, which does seem ironic), but I am now a priest, theologian and historian. So I come to his work with more than one reason for curiosity about David's real, if somewhat unlikely, contribution to Australian religious culture and discourse. Rather later, I became aware of an increased personal interest on his part in religious themes and issues, an impression gained more from a few conversations snatched during post-Triffids gigs, than from the lyrics themselves. It was not a connection we ever managed to pursue in depth before he died. I come again to these words with a mixture of intimacy and distance, as well as the faint despair proper to any attempt at adding to something mysterious or beautiful by mere analysis.

I will make a few fairly modest, and possibly fairly obvious, suggestions about religion and David McComb's songwriting. I have already said that the well-known capacity of his words and music to stir a sense of transcendence deserves to be viewed as 'theological' — not to the exclusion of other possible readings or understandings — regardless of the place of religion in them. I will leave that assertion largely unexplored here.

Yet overtly religious themes and images do sometimes play an important part in his construction of that 'eye-prickling' distance between the human being who is both singer and hearer, and a horizon, variously constructed geographically (infinite distance), historically (nostalgia), and at times more explicitly theologically. The specific character of that religious imagery, unsystematic and sometimes surprising, sheds some light on the curious and powerful character of his songs generally. It is this more explicit religious content I wish to describe and explore.

Occasionally, particularly in later songs, the piecemeal use of religious images and metaphors gives way to more deliberate theological exploration. There is no hard and fast line between this feature and the other two 'theological' elements — it is perhaps where they fully converge. It is the last two senses of religious or theological meaning that I will explore a little further here: the piecemeal evocative use of words and images, fragments of pious evocation, and then the full-blown and fairly late emergence of a kind of theology, albeit a *via negativa*.

Many comments about The Triffids' music and its appeal focus on its peculiarly Australian character. The specifics of David McComb's religious imagery and the very fact of his attention to such questions and symbols sit awkwardly with that assessment. Rather than showing a more typically Australian secular apathy or animus to Christian faith, he employs its trappings powerfully, if piecemeal, in his construction of a world of yearning, distance and hope. And the specific forms that faith takes in his songs are not immediately derived from the religious practices of his own Australian upbringing, but are the product both of the US-dominated popular culture of his childhood and youth, and of the reflections on faith and religion found in a literary canon of European and American, as well as Australian, authors.

Martyrs of Perth punk

Religious themes and images take time to appear in David McComb's work. The earliest Triffids lyrics reflect the experience of a group of slightly off-beat Perth schoolboys, driven by a mixture of whimsy, anger and insecurity. Feelings expressed in the first few tapes, sessions documented in standard-issue Western Australian Education Department exercise books, are universal teenage angst and awkwardness, with little interest in the transcendent.

The isolation in Western Australia, so potent in later songs as a premise of deep yearning and an ultimate horizon, was already important. The experience of being interested in and trying to play 'new wave' music in Perth was the subject of some early Triffids (and earlier McComb/MacDonald) songs. Perth was large enough to have music stores that did stock Television and The Ramones, but not to allow a sense of connection with vibrant urban culture. As punk rock appeared, its followers there felt doubly alienated; The Sex Pistols could proclaim 'Anarchy in the UK' and jeer 'we don't care' while loving the attention, but in Perth in 1977 nobody else cared either.

Even before the name 'The Triffids' was adopted, early songs like 'Take Me to Your Leader' and 'What Would the Martians Think?' suggest a sense of a bigger universe, at a strange distance. Only in 'Martyrs' does this take on anything sounding like a religious predicament, but a fairly self-serving one: 'It gets a little boring, but that/doesn't matter, because we're/martyrs, martyrs of Perth punk.' Here the plight of being a 'Perth punk' is contrasted with the mainstream culture ('Australia/a great moronic vulture') comprising school peers who thought of The Eagles as good music, and Fleetwood Mac as a little edgy.

Jesus calling

Religion makes clearer appearances in The Triffids' vinyl output. From *Treeless Plain* onward, a lyric strategy emerges where some aspect of God, the Church or its accoutrements emerges — sometimes quite in passing — to evoke a sort of religion curiously alien to the world The Triffids' music arose in.

Treeless Plain and *Raining Pleasure* speak to the baby-boomer Australians whose experience of religion is itself a wasteland. These songs have little connection with the tired suburban Protestantism of late twentieth-century Australia, but flirt with religious images drawn from American musical traditions that David had absorbed for years, and which were also a common part of his Australian contemporaries' experience. This world of chapels for crying and convents to find refuge in, of flawed priests and whooping preachers, of ecstatic prayer and grovelling penitence, waits in the background of his lyrical constructions and occasionally bursts through the lines of his writing.

On that first commercial album, 'Branded' has a hint of the Cain and Abel story (Genesis 4), but its only biblical character is the Devil: 'You were there with the Devil, you handed him the knife.'[4] The brooding atmosphere of 'Hanging Shed' involves 'a strange unholy tale,' an idiom from a past distant in space and time. The higher power does appear, along with a lighter mood, in 'Plaything'. This song has a feel of 1950s middle America about it ('Now you're wearing someone else's pin'), as does the deity, who is 'the good Lord [who] has our best interests at heart/He's making an effort and starting again.'

'Jesus Calling' is both a more whimsical and a more fulsome foray into religious language. The tongue-in-cheek mix of hot Gospel and modern love flits back and forth between the hearer's expectations and the narrator's loyalties. Its 'Jesus' embodies what is higher or better than whatever the present, and the present relationship, offer. 'Jesus Calling' uses a mid-twentieth-century Gospel music motif, of ancient message and modern technology combined (compare 'Royal Telephone', and William Spivery's 'Operator'). On the *Raining Pleasure* lyric sheet, the last lines read: 'I'm afraid I'll have to call the whole thing off now/I'm afraid I'll have to disconnect your line/I have Jesus calling me.' Here Jesus doesn't just 'call' in the classic sense, 'o'er the tumult' or 'softly and tenderly,' but actually dials — on a bakelite rotary phone, surely.

This mixture or juxtaposition of romantic and religious calls and claims becomes characteristic.[5] Sometimes, as here, the divine summons or message is an alternative to the present relationship. In other cases there are subtler and elusive shifts between the two kinds of images or loves, leaving us wondering which is which.

The power of these religious images, whether sporadic or sustained, comes in part from their own strangeness, their belonging in large part to the world of popular culture which post-war Australians had discovered, through television and radio, as a sort of wonderland. At a distance where detail was unimportant, David was even less constrained than Hollywood myth-makers from combining elements of American religiosity (or anything else) that belonged to traditions as disparate as New England Puritanism and frontier revivalism. The result is a world partly Western Australian, but with Nashville and New Orleans neighbourhoods of a former generation just around the corner.

That world — especially but not exclusively in its religious dimension — often contributes to the sense of exile or loss which McComb could conjure so effectively. Sometimes the religious horizon serves as the answer to the seeker's question, whether it is desperately sought or despairingly spurned. At other times it makes a fleeting appearance only to add an element of unsystematic pathos, or to amplify the emotive power of some other image or idea.

Bury me deep in love

David's best-known use of religious language and images is also one of his most explicit quotations from any lyrical source, the use of

'The Three Bells' in 'Bury Me Deep in Love'. The borrowing is unapologetic, and in places almost verbatim: 'and the little congregation … prays for guidance from above;/Hear our meditation;/Lead us not into temptation.'

For American and Australian listeners in the fifties and since, 'The Three Bells' evokes a whitewashed chapel set among the hills of Maine or Michigan, whereas the French original ('Les Trois Cloches') had envisaged Roman Catholic ritual and practice in rural Europe. Although the English translation is relatively faithful, the more commonly recorded and truncated version erases references to infant baptism and a priest — offences to the Congregational mindset of the New World's implied audience.[6] Yet the two versions present the same neat and cyclical view of an unchanging world, whose religious institutions exist to mark and bless the safe and secure transitions of its collective life.

McComb's use of the song drags it from the neat depiction of a life-cycle into a ragged existential quest. The chapel is now set in a valley framed by a precipice, from which a 'lonesome climbing figure, slips and loses grip.' Its spire stands not to summon a rural community, but as a guide 'for travelling strangers in distress,' embodied by that fallen unknown. The contrast between the two images, of pastoral piety and desperate searching, drives the song, and the plea of the chorus and title is then far more than that of an average love ballad.

The chorus is addressed to an unnamed ultimate reality, first called upon to take the fallen seeker and 'bury him deep in love.' The cry to 'take him in, under your wing' is a biblical allusion (see, for example, Psalms 17:8), yet at some points in the song the plea is transferred from the divine to a more immediate and human desire for love, as the singer asks 'bury *me* deep in love.' Yet a continued theological strand appears in the addition to the chorus of 'The Three Bells', where the congregation goes past its modest prayers about meditation, temptation, and celebration, to demand 'some kind of explanation.' The inhabitants of this rural religious synthesis have broken out of their caricature and improvised, a little shockingly, on their own script. As they do so, they seek a theological as well as an existential or affective response. The thick texture of symbolism manages to coexist with an element of protest, and of profound doubt.

There may be other chapels waiting in the imagination that hears 'Bury Me Deep in Love', and which add to that song's texture for many listeners. One is from Elvis Presley's (originally Artie Glenn's) 'Crying in the Chapel', whose place of prayer lies somewhere between Jimmy Brown's and David McComb's. That relatively gentle account emerges from a revivalist evangelicalism of the deep South, where the sinner is more akin to McComb's hero than to Jimmy Brown but does find his way home. These sinners or searchers are deep in need, and their chapels are sanctuaries, not merely centres for rites of passage.

Convent walls

The early McComb song 'Convent Walls' is one of a few in which the carnal desires of the singer (or his addressee) are opposed to a form of monastic religious calling or sensibility, of equal power but quite different kind to the Protestant imagery of 'Jesus Calling': 'every day you'll hear the bells that call you to his service again/You'll walk forevermore in his shadow … And with all your voice you'll adore him/ Lay yourself down there in humility before him/He'll know you oh so well.' A variation on this motif appears in 'Save What You Can', from *Calenture*, where a companion's definitive break is described as entry into the house of God: 'The final time we touch/I watch as you enter the church/You turn and you wave, then you kneel and you pray/And you save of yourself what you can save.' Like the 'little congregation,' these would-be nuns are the chorus in a tragedy of religious nostalgia. They have stepped into the songwriter's imagination from a pre-Vatican II Roman Catholic world, far from the lived experience of David McComb or most of his hearers. Traditional brides of Christ rather than modernized à la 'The Singing Nun', they play their needed part in this emotional tug-of-war precisely as bearers of nostalgia. This image is visually reprised in the artwork for McComb's solo album *Love of Will*, which features stills from the movie *Black Narcissus* (1947), a psychological drama set among a group of Anglican nuns in the Himalayan foothills.

Although not devoid of irony, these loves lost to come higher calling are envious or even thankful, more than they are bitter or dismissive. The imagery serves to create a place or choice better than the present, a place or choice ultimately inaccessible to the writer or

singer. The songs' affective power is only increased by their being pop-
ulated with characters from a world of cinema and literature of the
past, rather than 'real' figures or places.

The Lord burns every clue

David's solo album, *Love of Will*, contains his most explicit and concentrated set of lyrics involving religion. In the booklet accompanying
the CD, the nuns of *Black Narcissus* serve as quirky visual indicators
of a theological motif, and the lyrics likewise ask pressing and even
disturbing questions. Some will wonder about intimations of mortality, given David's state of health by 1993.

The imagery of *Love of Will* as a whole is not only more explicitly
religious than his earlier output, but specifically eschatological. One
song deals with resurrection, another with ascension, a third with
afterlife. Yet there is no resolution of David's or anyone else's ambivalence about faith, religion, or God. Rather, the warring demands of
honesty, doubt and hope are expressed in more powerful and disturbing terms.

'The Day of My Ascension' repeats the familiar mixed message of
human love and divine, but is distinctive in that the narrator himself now seems to be playing God ('People love me, well, people try/I
have to leave them all by and by/Some day I'll leave them high and
dry/On the day of my ascension'). 'Setting You Free' and 'Heard You
had a Bed' also involve that ambiguity of mundane and supernatu-
ral relations; in both, the singer is 'on my knees' to a woman, and the
narrator of 'Lifelike' goes further: 'fall to my knees, I look to the sky/
I'm shaking like a leaf but you gave me the second sight.' Like 'Day
of My Ascension', 'Lifelike' also involves a bolder or more desperate
conflation of the two perspectives, describing a relationship as a resurrection: 'Now I touch your body every prophecy is proven true/
MATTHEW, MARK, LUKE & JOHN, ROLLED AWAY THE STONE/BUT THE
BODY WAS GONE.'

'Leaning' is more a re-working of an existing song than mere
borrowing. It takes over the chorus, words and music, of a nineteenth-century revivalist Camp Meeting hymn by Elisha Hoffman
and Anthony Showalter, 'Everlasting Arms'—later a country gospel
favourite as well as part of the African-American gospel repertoire.

McComb's version adds a verse and expands the chorus convincingly, lyrically and musically:

> Sometimes you can't even see him but
> you know he's there beside you in the dark …
> Sometimes you can't even feel him
> but if you leave an open heart
> you know that he'll come in …

Although the theological overshadows the romantic in a characteristic back-and-forth between the two, there is still some of the familiar ambiguity. The other familiar motif of choice or conversion, from one love to a higher, also appears in a re-written line: 'I'm leaning, leaning, remote and removed from all your charms/I'm leaning, leaning, leaning on the everlasting arms'. The scene familiar from 'Convent Walls' and 'Save What You Can', of escape to a love divine, has now become the narrator's own choice, not his lover's.

Yet the most remarkable song in the whole of David McComb's work, theologically speaking, is 'The Lord Burns Every Clue'. Here he comes as close as anywhere to a critique of institutional religion: 'Some say they can name him/Some even lay a claim to him …/We bend our knees and pray each night/And curse ourselves for doubting him'. This account of failed piety and ritual is plaintive rather than dismissive; religion is understandable or natural, but cannot penetrate the divine silence. Those described here might be the congregants of 'Bury Me Deep in Love', faithfully going through the motions but erupting on occasion: 'give us some kind of explanation'!

Like 'Leaning', 'The Lord Burns Every Clue' is a sort of faithful agnostic meditation, but this song ends only by posing and re-posing its own implied question, rather than resolving it with a divine or human embrace: 'But he leaves no mark on us/We know not where he leads us …/No shred of note that bears his shaky scrawl/He leaves no trace at all'. This is a mystical reflection on a God who is absent — perhaps, David suggests, by choice. The irony of a divinity whose revelatory action consists in remaining hidden is as powerful as it is plaintive. It is an ode for Ludwig Wittgenstein, or Karl Barth.

Place in the sun

Although the set of religious symbols in David McComb's songs does not fit neatly with any one form of Christianity, it has some affinity with a trajectory of introspective and somewhat pessimistic thought that can be traced from Paul of Tarsus to Augustine of Hippo, and then through the Reformation to Kierkegaard. This is a Christianity of grace, not works, which may or may not include the trappings of symbol and ritual, but always centres on the need of a broken person for redemption.

That dynamic of grace and loss, so often present in his songs even where religious language is not, defies assimilation to the glib 'spiritual but not religious' tag that might otherwise suggest itself for McComb's ambivalent stance in relation to God and Church. There is no trace here of the banal 'spirituality' of contemporary popular thought, the benign and domesticable reality that makes all quasi-divine; David's divinity is gut-wrenching, all-absorbing, fearsome, and largely absent.

The religion of David's songs is therefore not the 'semi-Pelagianism' more or less inevitable in the kind of Anglican boys' school we went to. It is, however, unmistakeably Christian, and far more resonant with edgier forms of both Protestant and Catholic piety or faith. While it may have been influenced by some childhood familial experience of a Presbyterian Church in suburban Perth,[7] as well as informed by religious education at Christ Church Grammar School, the details of its imagery were really those of his own voracious teenage and adult absorption of an unlikely and wide-ranging canon of music and literature.

David's religion is also not much like Nick Cave's well-known love of the Old Testament. It meets the eye and ear as a pastiche of elements from the film, popular music and other media of the mid-twentieth century, but there is also an enormously sophisticated layer beneath, created from his formal and informal forays into literature such as the works of Rainer Maria Rilke and Flannery O'Connor; David's music would make an eerily apt soundtrack for any re-make of *Wise Blood* (1979), the film based on O'Connor's 1952 novel.

While eclectic, the force of American mythology in this imagery is striking. The songs, religious in symbolism or not, manage the creation of a mythic American-tinged world that perhaps was only imaginable from Perth, or at least from Australia, in the sixties. Its wild preachers in dustbowl towns are neighbours to tortured souls behind convent walls as well as salt-of-the-earth rural chapel-goers, all serving a deity mysterious, dangerous, deeply loved and often denied. Into this landscape the narrators or subjects of McComb's imagination come driving or stumbling, spires as well as saloons in the backdrop, bringing the sensibilities of their less exotic home towns and marvelling in a world writ large, more colourful than their own.

The eclectic or imported character of these religious elements need not make them less Australian. Debates about Australian values and virtues across the time this essay was written are a reminder of how banal it is to characterize Australia and its culture by what is iconic in the view of a few, rather than in terms of the real mixture of experiences and influences that actually constitute Australian cultural practice. Although David McComb's religious world seems rather American, it is a sort of America assembled in a psyche formed in suburban Perth, Melbourne pubs and London garrets, and steeped in Rilke and Thomas Mann, as well as O'Connor and John Steinbeck. And given the experiences of the people who followed The Triffids or who have found some significance in their music — the intellectuals, expats, artists and travellers — we might have to admit that this America of the mind is a very Australian sort of reality.

David's songs are a darker and more pessimistic contribution to a chorus of younger Australian artists and intellectuals who surprisingly, given the national secular self-image, find in Christianity rather more than delusion or boredom. Nick Cave, Tim Winton and Nikki Gemmell herself are among those who have publicly been connected with Christianity, if in ways somewhat oblique both to the traditional or institutional Church and to mega-Church fundamentalism. These are serious questioners, and with David McComb they are in good company. They remind us that religion, whether or not we profess it, is more than propositions or institutions but is cultural and existential, a quest that recognizes the perplexity of life and which seeks symbols and examples that make sense of suffering, loss and love.

ABOVE: Backstage at The Prince of Wales Hotel, St Kilda, 2 March 1985.

RIGHT: Martyn Casey, Megan Simpson, Alsy MacDonald and Jill Birt, as captured by David McComb in London, 1985.

Death of a Grandmother

David McComb

Enter laughing girl all bruised thighs red bra and glitter-gel hair —
Carries a death's head into the bluelight disco: A smeared green
pass-out stamp on her wrist like tubercular phlegm on her pubescence
Writhing riesling moselle rum & coke and blackberry nip Yeah boys like it
Her grandmother faints in the sexual din, turns alabaster, wheezes the
names of saints, sinks unbreathing into feathery multiple air-cushioned
layers of knitting and crochet, camphor and catnip, legwarmers and
lactose, to the fading theme from *Blue Hills*. Tears. Curtain.

Temporary
Monuments

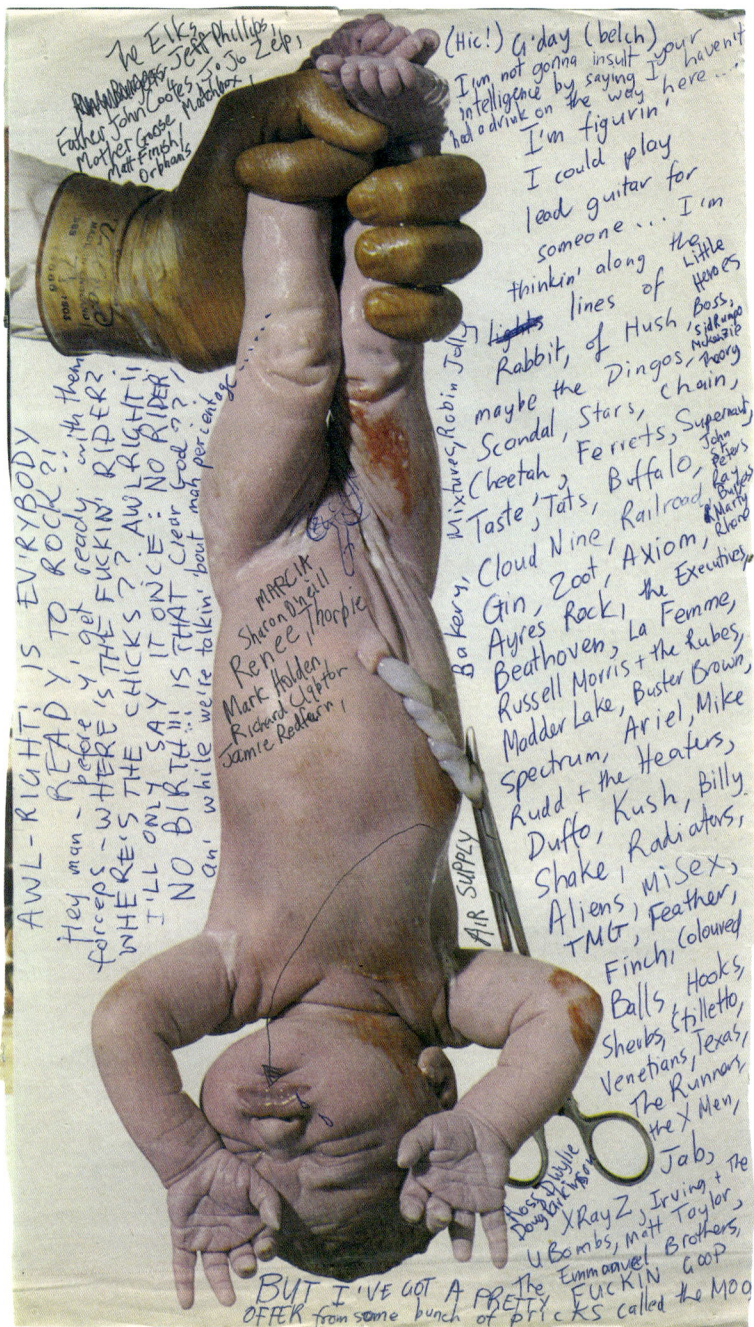

'Handsome' Steve Miller at birth: mixed media portrait by David McComb, 1987.

Still Life

Niall Lucy

I

What we need here is some good old-fashioned scene-setting stuff. To wit:

The action takes place in the coffee shop at The Art Gallery of Western Australia. It's half past two on a Sunday afternoon and there's a Hans Heysen painting on the wall. Heysen was a Dutchman. My typewriter was made in Holland.

Tom Robbins said that typewriters should be made out of balsa wood or hewn from the trunk of a cypress tree. Why not a ghost gum?

But I'd prefer them to be made out of cheesecake, with whipped cream for a ribbon, strong black coffee in the keys, and a margin alarm that plays a few bars of your favourite song.

Get the picture?

II

'You've got to have disrespect,' says David McComb. 'You can't be provocative by being in awe of the pop tradition.' Chalk up another quotable for *Spare Times*, courtesy of my National Panasonic mini-tape recorder. But there's a limit to what it can record. To wit:

A man and a woman in their early thirties at the table behind McComb have been silent ever since they realized that our conversation is in fact an interview, and therefore that one of us must be famous. They're desperately trying to figure out which one of us it is.

'But I know there's nothing new under the sun,' McComb continues. 'And maybe in ten years' time I'll recognize the futility of all this and hang up my larynx.'

— Or maybe they're missing something. Maybe they've stumbled in on an exhibition of performance art?

You can never quite tell what's going down in an art gallery.

III

After some deliberation, and with the help of a third party, McComb and I decide that the place mats in the Art Gallery coffee shop are made of vinyl. They only *look* like they're made of leather.

'Some people can carry off confessional lyrics,' McComb says later. 'You know: *My girlfriend she left me/Oh woe is me/Pour me another beer.* But you have to be a very honest and naïve sort of person not to see the irony in anything and not to see the opposite side of an argument.'

IV

The youngest of four sons, David McComb …

— grew up in Nedlands

— went to school at Christ Church Grammar

— studied journalism at WAIT.[1]

'Ideally … ideally,' he says, 'I'm totally against translating something that's supposed to work in mysterious ways.'

V

Later, the coffee almost gone:

'T.S. Eliot is a major influence on pop music. No one admits it, but so many writers of pop music have ripped him off. Like, David Bowie bases some of his whole scenes of decadence upon T.S. Eliot. Rowland S. Howard from The Birthday Party wrote a song which is just lifted, line by line, from one of Eliot's poems.[2]

'Of course, there are some who say poetry should be just kept right out of pop. Like, Nik Cohn — have you read his book, *Awopbopaloobop Alopbamboom*? — says that Bob Dylan is the central evil figure in pop music, because he destroyed it by changing the lyrics.

'But it's too late now.'

VI

And again:

'I've been influenced more by people,' McComb says, 'by a couple of friends of mine. They're a few years older than me and I met them when I first started going to pubs. They have a real hell's broth way of speaking: clichés, slang, always talking in vernacular. And I love slang.

'There have been all sorts of conspiracy theories about language. You know: it's always been in the hands of the bourgeoisie; and men have been the owners of language, traditionally; and the ruling class has always been the creator of language, via the Oxford dictionary or fine literature or whatever.

'So, pathetic as it may seem — and I'm not ascribing any enormous value to it — but slang, dirty jokes, toilet-wall graffiti ... seems about the last refuge where the tentacles of decency haven't quite crept in yet.'

VII

HEE HAW HEE HAW HEE HAW: an ambulance blares down Roe St, drowning out the voices on my National Panasonic mini-tape recorder. And my old Adler portable isn't what it used to be. There's ten years' of dirt and ash beneath the keys, and the 'L' keeps jamming.

'The ear-y songs were basica--y saying we are obnoxious, fucked-up teenagers. Every now and then there'd be a brief f-irtation with some-thing obtuse, but basica--y that was it. They were easy to understand on a -itera- -eve-.

'And I was very frustrated, because a-- I cou-d come up with were just nursery rhymes. In no way cou-d I emu-ate the groups I -oved, -ike Te-evision. So, unti- rea--y quite recent-y, I was dissatisfied with not being ab e to get any resonance or depth into The Triffids ... not being ab-e to inject any fee-ing of substance. Everything seemed to come out -ike twangy-twang. Too much whining.'

This is ridiculous.

VIII

Later:

'I always just like a real lonesome sound about a record. Like "Mystery Train" by Elvis Presley. That's a really forlorn and yet dangerous, lean-and-hungry sort of sound.

'Another great song, and I'll sound like an old hippie, but the opening verse of "Visions of Johanna" [Bob Dylan, *Blonde on Blonde*] … it's really naked and rough.'

IX

'Clever, intelligent songs just wash by me now. I'm just not that interested anymore.

'People like Elvis Costello — sure, he's intelligent and, sure, he's a hell of a craftsman — but he just seems to have replaced emotion or desperation or anything that can be good about music with all these puns and word-plays. Except for *Get Happy!* That was a good record, but apparently he was drinking very heavily at the time.

'Now he just seems to have resigned himself to being the clever elder statesman of pop, getting more meticulous and ingenious. And I was sure that sooner or later he was going to stop, and come out with an album that says something like, *I feel bad/I'm going to kill myself* — where he doesn't bother to rhyme or put in any puns.

'And I'm sure it would be his best album ever.'

X

At a dollar a cup, the coffee here isn't bad. Not very strong, but not bad for a dollar.

Outside, the sky is Spanish blue.

'I don't think we've ever been as old-fashioned as people have made us out to be,' McComb says. 'We've just done our hell's best never to be modern — because modern's always out of date.'

Ornithology

Laurie Duggan

Yeats said: a poet
'is never the bundle
of accident and incoherence
that sits down to breakfast.'

Yeats was a shit.

The Indian summer is over,
leaves of the fig only beginning to yellow.
I'm happy we don't have real seasons
— the sight of all that dead vegetation
between Washington and New York
last year's fall,

and what a relief it was
to get to San Francisco
and the green of eucalypts:
not simply a sense of being
closer to 'home'.

Groan of a tram from the Esplanade.

A dirty wind

distant radios

turpentine

the Triffids singing
'Chicken Killer'.

Tambourine Life!

I punch holes in the mystery bags
                        — in the mixed metaphor of political
                                        commentators
        'puncture a few sacred cows'

                        Buried items:
                                        my guitar
                with blackened bass strings.

    I couldn't understand why older people owned musical instruments
                        they no longer wished to play
            — were these the discarded apparatus of courtship?
                    (for me, simply the knowledge that imagination
                            exceeded physical capacity
                and I would never be able to play the tunes I 'heard'
                        — this and a hatred of the 'folkie' strum.
                I would want to make an acoustic instrument sound
                                        electric;
                        play against its limitations

                        — of a piece I guess
        with my feelings about poetry;
                        no wish to condone a limited and sectional interest
                                        in its workings.
            Works of the past remain great even if we venture elsewhere,
                    they're taken for granted if used as templates

                                    and I always suspected
                    the search for romanticism's narwhals
                            — why not the washing machine?
                the sausage?
        (The Mystery Bags of Charles Péguy!)

A Temporary Monument

Jean Bernard Koeman

An exhibition as statue.
An exhibition as monument.
For one man: David McComb.
And for all.
In veneration.[1]

For me, the capacity for veneration is a cardinal human virtue. Whether it derives from envy or love, it is a force that engenders pure energy.

While musing on a suitable starting point for a solo exhibition, I ran through each of my hundred heroes: What would Nabokov write? How would Schnittke sound? What would Broodthaers make of this? And so on, until I'd exhausted them all. Or so I thought. In the figure of David McComb — who had once reached out to me with *Born Sandy Devotional*, the LP that would become my soundtrack to a long trip through his arid and dusty continent — I encountered an arresting metaphor for an artist's love of another's artistic pursuits.

Didn't McComb's fiery energy spring from his self-proclaimed adoration of Dylan and Leadbelly and the poets Les Murray and Marina Tsvetaeva? Didn't the music of his band, The Triffids, impart an admixture of loss, rage, the empty landscape — the dustbowls of Woody Guthrie, the melodies of The Byrds and The Stooges, the poetic voice of Joseph Brodsky, the agitated, inventive energy of the 'Post' Wave?

I soon abandoned the idea of a solo exhibition. Instead, given the availability of a newly constructed exhibition space with plenty of attractive corners, unusual rooms and transit areas — highly suitable for site-specific interventions — I invited twenty artists I admired to construct a temporary memorial to someone most of them had never heard of. The artists were selected for their suspected affinity with the ideas that McComb embodied, and for their fluency in building conceptual artwork in public space. Thus a memorable series of artworks was created, and curated as the site-specific exhibition *A Temporary Monument for David McComb* (Kunstencentrum STUK, Leuven, Belgium) throughout April and May of 2004.

Beginning with the flowers gasping for sunlight on Heimir Bjorgulfsson's billboard, with a hand-drawn roadmap in our hands, we follow a pronounced route through the dips, valleys and plateaus of the STUK architecture. We wander towards Vaast Colson's sheepshearer's barn, a wonderful 'cobbled-together' shack with bright chinks of sunlight and a module where members of the public can make their own mix-tape cover. Adjoining it, in the inner courtyard, stands Sean Dower's solitary tree, hung with windswept cassette tape: 'The Music in Trees'. In the darkness of the corridors and stairways of the transit areas we become aware of Peter Stel's Las Vegas-style fluorescent lettering: DON'T LEAVE ME, it reads, and on the other side, DON'T BELIEVE ME. A bewildered McComb cries in the dark, his impassioned lyrics intermingled with an all-but whispered version of 'It's All in the Eyes of a Dreamer' — a composition by Charles Manson sung by Georgina Starr in a voice that is at once self-assured and empty, sweet and dangerous. Just as unsettling is Sean Dower's plunderphonic counterpoint: fractured elements of the 1962 film soundtrack, *The Day of the Triffids*.

Further on, descending into even deeper caverns, we encounter 'The Ring', a recording of an interminable car journey along the entire Icelandic coast by filmmaker Fridrik Thor Fridriksson. Here the rough journey sung of so often by McComb — both magisterial and frightening — comes completely to life. Hermann Maier Neustadt also provides an atmospheric image: in the setting of a lonely hotel room the sounds of multilayered voices, drum rolls and distant guitars can be heard.

We move on. Back to the heights, back to the light, to the quivering bare pines and the tarred kitchen unit of Freek Wambacq: a road movie made from the materials of an open-plan house. We survey the spectacular bustle of the STUK café, a gigantic raw diamond having been hurled there, meteor-like, by Gregor Passens. We go upstairs. With the raw sounds of noise-combo Spasm still smouldering in the broom-cupboard, we encounter Brian McKenna's 'Blinder by the Hour', an assemblage of moving pictures from *The Day of the Triffids* grafted onto one of McComb's most beautiful songs. From here we might gaze at Erik Odijk's cinemascopic vistas in charcoal and reflect that, whether we are in Wales, Perth or Buenos Aires — or Belgium — the wilderness is always treacherously close.

Witness, for example, the razor-sharp photographs of Geert Goiris: a burning man and a mountain in Azerbaijan full of eternal fire. Through the flames, on a map of Western Australia made of beer bottles, we discover the demons of the 'rock star' McComb: Stef Kamil Carlens draws him as a rag doll in the arms of a satyr. Cautiously, then, we enter the last, dark room of the STUK exhibition gallery. Maria Barnas has filtered all the objects, places and nouns from McComb's lyrics and distilled from them a series of 'after-images' with photographs, comments and slides.

At journey's end, as if coming home to our own teenage bedrooms — the source of all admiration and devotion — we encounter the HAP brothers' replica of a teenage artist's bedroom, a hallucinatory monochrome adaptation fashioned entirely — lamps, posters, cassettes, chairs, the stray twig in the jam pot — from cardboard. This, then, is where the journey ends. We may be overcome by a musty melancholy, but we pull ourselves together because the synergistic cohesion of the whole makes a vital and lasting impression.

With this elixir — art, friendship, devotion — we go forth.

Over two evenings during the STUK exhibition, songs of David McComb and The Triffids were subject to impassioned renditions by The Seabirds — a band comprising Bjorn Eriksson, Stef Kamil Carlens, Patrick Riguelle, Joost Van den Broeck, Jan Hautekiet, Werner Lauscher and Harald Vanherf, brought together specially for the occasion. It gave gooseflesh on the brain to hear their tribute numbers 'Stolen Property', 'Raining Pleasure', 'Setting You Free' and 'Save What You Can'. And it was here, during these unlikely musical collaborations, that the concept behind *A Temporary Monument*, a certain notion of wonderment and reverence for unknown heroes, finally shone majestic, true and radiant.

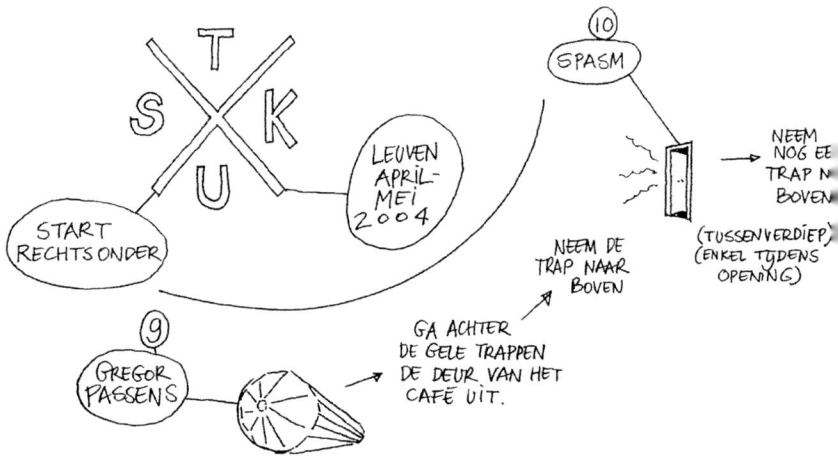

START RECHTS ONDER

LEUVEN APRIL-MEI 2004

S T K U X

(10) SPASM

NEEM NOG EE TRAP N BOVEN

(TUSSENVERDIEP) (ENKEL TIJDENS OPENING)

NEEM DE TRAP NAAR BOVEN

GA ACHTER DE GELE TRAPPEN DE DEUR VAN HET CAFÉ UIT.

(9) GREGOR PASSENS

GA BINNEN IN'T CAFÉ.

GA TERUG NAAR BENEDEN.

ROAD MAP

VOLG NAUWKEURIG DE PIJLEN EN AANWIJZINGEN OP DEZE KAART, VAN (1) TOT (18)

(8) FREEK WAMBACQ

OM DE HOEK NOG EEN TRAP NAAR BOVENTERRAS.

(4) PETER STEL

GA BIJ VUILBAK DE TRAPPEN OMHOOG.

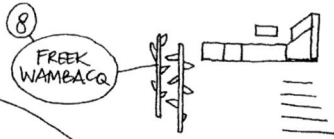

HEIMIR BJORGULFSSON
VAAST COLSON
SEAN DOWER
PETER STEL
GEORGINA STARR / SEAN DOWER
FRIDRIK THOR FRIDRIKSSON
HERMANN MAIER NEUSTADT
FREEK WAMBACQ
GREGOR PASSENS
SPASM (ENKEL TIJDENS OPENING)
ERIK ODIJK
SEAN DOWER
BRIAN McKENNA
GEERT GOIRIS
HEIMIR BJORGULFSSON
STEF KAMIL CARLENS
MARIA BARNAS
HAP

BEDACHT EN SAMENGESTELD DOOR JEAN BERNARD KOEMAN

(1) HEIMIR BJORGULFSSON

(2) VAA COL

142

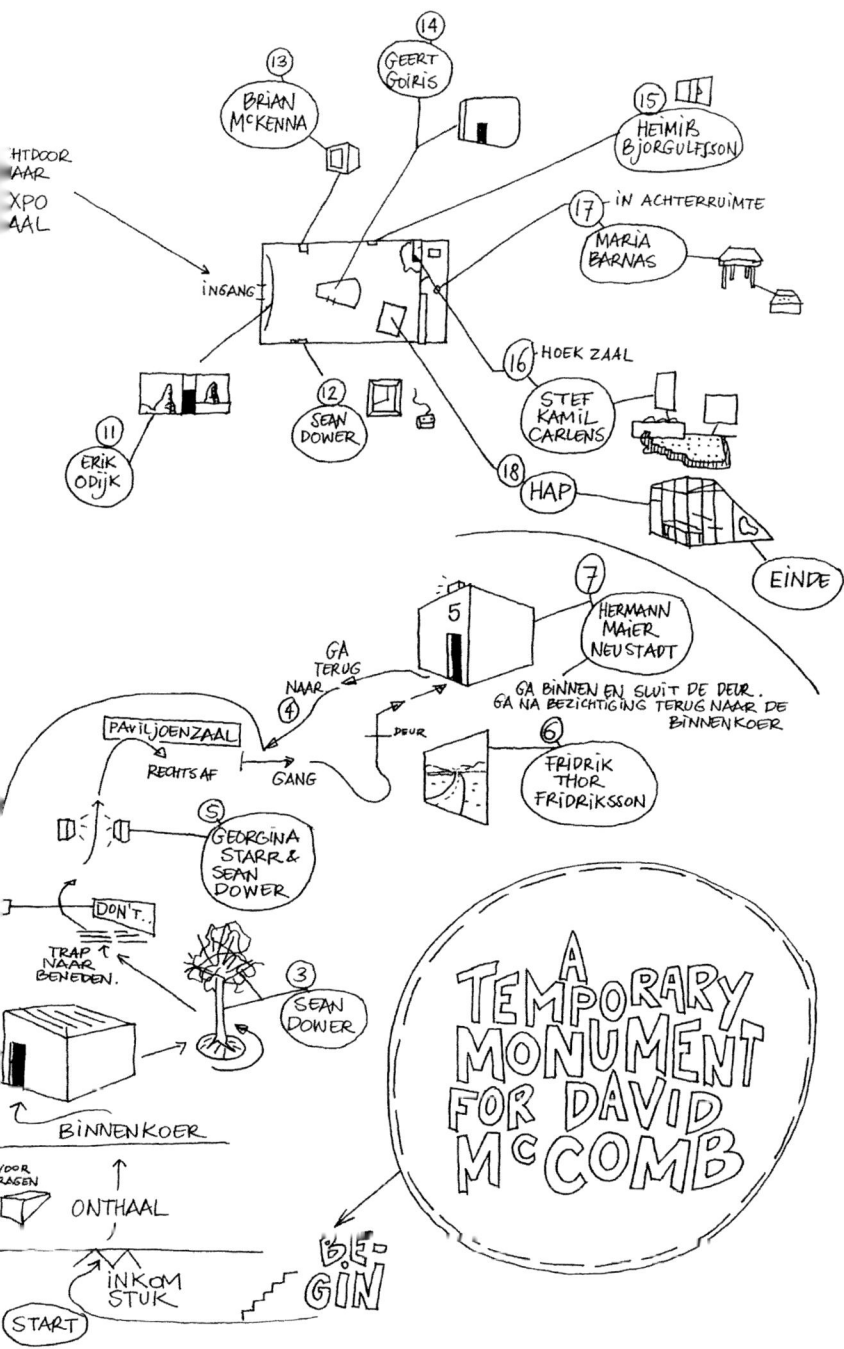

HTDOOR
VAAR
XPO
AAL

(13) BRIAN McKENNA

(14) GEERT GOIRIS

(15) HEIMIR BJORGULFSSON

(17) IN ACHTERRUIMTE
MARIA BARNAS

INGANG

(16) HOEK ZAAL
STEF KAMIL CARLENS

(11) ERIK ODIJK

(12) SEAN DOWER

(18) HAP

EINDE

5

(7) HERMANN MAIER NEUSTADT

GA TERUG NAAR (4)

GA BINNEN EN SLUIT DE DEUR.
GA NA BEZICHTIGING TERUG NAAR DE BINNENKOER

PAVILJOENZAAL

DEUR

RECHTS AF   GANG

(6) FRIDRIK THOR FRIDRIKSSON

(5) GEORGINA STARR & SEAN DOWER

DON'T.

TRAP ↑ NAAR BENEDEN.

(3) SEAN DOWER

A TEMPORARY MONUMENT FOR DAVID McCOMB

BINNENKOER

VOOR DRAGEN

ONTHAAL

INKOM STUK

BE GIN

START

143

McComb at a
London picnic,
with Bleddyn
Butcher in
background.

Extraordinary Friends

Nick Cave

At Easter in 1990, I attended a massive Aussie Diaspora picnic in Peaslake, Surrey. I don't know why. I was probably drunk. Dave McComb was there. He was definitely drunk. As Peaslake, Surrey, is in England, it rained. As it was an Australian picnic, which by definition means a lot of alcohol and no food, we got drunker. By the time we were helped into the back of the van to go back to London we were singing-drunk. Singing-drunk is midway between hugging-drunk and fighting-drunk. It is the station that the Irish and the Aussies stop at for a while and the English go screaming past. Dave and I sang to each other. These were the songs:

Maxwell's Silver Hammer
I Threw it all Away
Walk on By
This Guy's in Love
Leaving on a Jet Plane
Bridge over Troubled Water
Lemon Tree
On Top of the World
Georgie Girl
Thunder Road
Blue Moon
California Dreamin'
Calling Occupants of
   Interplanetary Craft
Say a Little Prayer

The Boxer
Suspicious Minds
Kentucky Rain
Bird on a Wire
Morningtown Ride
Cecilia
Yesterday
Anything Goes
What'll I Do?
Last Night (I Didn't Get to
   Sleep at All)
Close to You
Belle Isle
Tonight I'll be Staying Here
   with You

We know this because the next morning Dave, weirdly, made a list. Dave was a list-maker: girls I have loved, books I have read, Indian meals I have regretted. I remember marvelling, in the back of that van, at Dave's capacity, not only to remember lyrics, but to sing in tune. This was brought painfully home to me when I started up 'California Dreamin'' and Dave asked (not unkindly) what key he should sing the backing vocals in. Then an argument ensued over the line 'I got down on my knees and pretend to pray.' I was wrong. Dave was right. And then we got fighting-drunk until Dave launched into the magnificent 'Calling Occupants' and made everything all right. As I got to know him better, I realized that his abilities extended far beyond the norm. He actually did have the capacity to telepath messages through the vast unknown, if songs can be telepathy. Like many of the songs we sang that day, his own songs call from the strangest places and at the oddest hours. Whether calling from the baking salt pans of the Western Australian desert or the darks of a broken heart, whether praying or pretending to pray, their gist is hopeful and brave: 'We are your friends,' say the songs. Interplanetary, ultra-emissary and quite extraordinary friends.

Cave again availed himself of superlatives when he inducted The Triffids into the ARIA (Australian Recording Industry Association) Hall of Fame in 2008, describing the band as 'extraordinary', bass player Martyn Casey as 'mind-bendingly brilliant' and David McComb as 'a truly brilliant songwriter and great lyricist … head and shoulders above the rest of us.' — Eds

Draining Pleasure

James Cook

It was cold for September, thought Jim, as he watched Mike walk back from the bar with two pints of Guinness. The open fire was only just beginning to take the edge off a chilly autumn night.

'Got the tickets, then?'

Mike dropped the packet of crisps he had been holding in his teeth onto the table. 'Yes mate.'

'Good man!'

The Swan was a ruined barn of a boozer on the Stockwell Road. Inside it was the colour of an oven, smoke hanging in long cigar-shaped clouds beneath the high ceilings. Tonight, as most nights, it resembled an exclusive male-only drinking club. Once the only late licence around, the pub was now in decline. Ever since swanky late-night bars had opened up the road in Clapham there was no need for anyone to step voluntarily into The Swan.

Jim lit his roll-up and carried on where he had left off. 'I just went off them a bit, y'know, when you couldn't walk into a service station or a lift without hearing them.'

Mike put the pints down and unzipped the packet of salt and vin-egar crisps. 'But that's a good thing, surely? Seeing as they're one of your favourite bands.'

'I know, I know, it's just …'

'What?' smiled Mike.

'I just liked them more when only we liked them. When they were, like, our band, our discovery.'

'Here we go again,' groaned Mike. He'd heard this riff a hundred times before.

'Did you see them on the Grammys the other night?'

'Yeah, I saw that,' Mike said, pulling deeply on his Marlboro Light.

'Y'know that Elvis move that McComb does?' said Jim, screwing up his face. 'Well he never did that at The Croydon Underground in '85.'

'That's because you couldn't swing a cat in The Croydon Underground in '85.'

'I know, but do you remember that gig? We were still at school.'

'Course I do,' Mike nodded. 'One of the best gigs of my life.'

'Well do you remember when they walked on stage and we both knew we were looking at The Real Thing? And how strange they looked … you just knew they'd been on the road forever. They had the road dust on them, man. They smelt of the road!'

'Nah, that was The Croydon Underground; it always smelt like that.' Mike was joking but it was true. It was like The Swan. He just knew that when the smoking ban came into force all you were going to smell were the bogs.

'I think that fame can spoil a band sometimes,' said Jim.

'Yeah, but you can't begrudge them their fame. They *had* been on the road forever; you're right about that. They slogged it out on the live circuit. It took them years till they got that U2 support at Milton Keynes Bowl, *The Longest Day*. Remember that? And even then they had to endure meatheads throwing bottles of piss at them. Poor Alsy took a direct hit.'

'I dunno, it's like they had their eye on the main chance just like every other band,' said Jim, shaking his head.

'Of course they had their eye on the main chance! This was their job, their lives. They'd all given up their day jobs to follow the dream, mate! You know, music doesn't come for free, it doesn't grow on trees. Real people have to sacrifice their lives for it!'

'Yeah, but sacking Graham and Jill was unforgivable …' Jim said.

'They streamlined. They had to make it a gang; four horsemen! The public love that. You can't beat that format. Look at the great groups: The Beatles, The Smiths …' Mike was getting into his stride now.

'Okay, okay. Just all the rock & roll posturing. When Rob got thrown off that plane for Air Rage.'

'Classic. It doesn't hurt to be a bit rock & roll.'

'I dunno, there's just too much capering for me. And what about the make-up? The blue eye-shadow? I remember an interview when they said if an image division of a record company had to deal with them they'd probably vomit. What happened to that?'

'Yeah, but that wasn't coming from a record label. That was McComb experimenting with his image, pushing the boundaries of what could still be done with a rock star's image in the late nineties. It was as important, creatively, as the music.' Mike paused for a second and looked into his glass, swilling the contents around slowly. 'Though I draw the line at that black stripe he had across his face at the Tibet gig. Bit too Adam and the Ants for me, that.'

'Well at least we agree on something! But forty-five quid for a ticket to see them at Wembley. I'm sorry man but ...' Jim trailed off. 'Same again?'

'Please, mate.'

Moving away from the fire to the bar, Jim became aware of the cold again. Fuck, those poor bastards must have felt it coming from Perth to this. He wondered if they remembered the lean years trying to make it in London. In the corner of the pub the television was tuned to MTV. McComb and the band were blasting their way through 'Everybody Has to Eat', their encore performance at Live 8.

Jim returned from the bar with two pints. 'Guinness is off so I got you a Fosters.'

'Oh for a draught of Vintage!' Mike said, wondering if his friend would get the reference.

'You always were a pretentious git, weren't you? There's nothing wrong with a beaker full of the warm south!'

Mike just grinned and dabbed at the salt in the empty crisp packet.

'You know what's ironic?' Jim said, placing the two fresh pints on the table. 'Croydon Underground is a Walkabout Inn now. It's just wall-to-wall covers bands playing INXS or The Triffids.'

'You can't blame The Triffids for Walkabout Inns! That's fucking preposterous!' said Mike. 'They just happened to break through just as all the other major Aussie cultural exports came over here. Around '87, '88 — Kylie, *Crocodile Dundee*, Fosters. They rode that wave. All power to 'em I say. It's like you want to begrudge them their luck as well!'

Both men were quiet for a while and took sips from their pints. They'd always had the same taste in music but Jim couldn't help having a proprietorial attitude towards 'their' bands. An observer might have thought they were arguing but they weren't. Both of them secretly enjoyed these heated discussions, especially after they'd had a few beers.

'I'll tell you what finally freaked me out,' Jim continued. 'When The Triffids knocked Alanis Morissette off the top of the album charts in '96. I bought the new album in Woolies and the old dear behind the counter said to me — "It's very different to their last one!" I just thought: fuck me, it's over.'

'You know what that's called don't you?' said Mike.

'What's that?'

'Chronic Musical Snobbery. You probably hated it in '87 when everyone at school was going: "Hey! Have you heard this great new band called The Triffids?"'

It was true. Jim went off The Triffids just as the world woke up to them. It amused him, though, to see how seriously Mike was taking this. He decided to wind his friend up.

'When they used "Tender is the Night" as the theme song for the Samaritans in '92, I mean, pass the sick bag.'

'You're all heart, aren't you? That probably saved lives that did!'

'I'm winding you up!' Jim said, laughing so hard he spilt beer on the table.

'Listen', said Mike. 'Do you still like The Triffids?'

'Yeah man, course I do,' Jim said. 'Fuckin' love 'em. One of the best bands of all time.'

'Then you should be fucking grateful it's them at Number One and not Alanis Morissette. It's inevitable that when a band gets that big some of the rough edges are smoothed out. It makes them a subversive force — then they're able to *infiltrate* the mainstream. The Triffids are the only cool band with a twenty-year career and huge global sales to keep their integrity intact.' Mike finished his rant and took a gulp on his pint. 'Right, neck that, they're on in a minute.'

Jim downed the dregs of his Fosters and put the glass down on the damp flyer: *The Triffakes: A Tribute to The Triffids*.

'Come on,' said Mike, 'we could never afford to see them at Wembley so we may as well enjoy the next best thing!'

WHACK! WHACK!

Steve Kilbey

THURSDAY, 17 JANUARY 2008

killer wakes before dawn   a wild night   sydney has turned
cold and deserted   the wind bite bite bites   it comes in
unexplained   all night long   the triffids songs go round in
my troubled dreams   somethings got me so itchy   standing
in the warping auditorium   im all mixed up   its all mixed
up   im singing the wrong words   im leading the wrong
life   it almost seems right and then …   strange day the day
before   took evie starr and the woofle to the beach   the sun
is irradiating out there   oh ocean is soothing cold clear   i
catch some little waves   woofle (looking more and more like
dr seuss creature), the woofle plays in the sand on the shore in
her pink zip-up swim suit   occasionally a wave reaches her
and she breathes a long ooohhhh!   she asks lotta questions
all the time   dad whos that?   dad whats this?   dad
where ya been?   shower ok, dad?   shops, dad, back
soon?   last nite i held the woofle on the balcony   she'd
been annoying the other 3 trying to watch something   we
looked at the moonless sky   moon gone hinda clouds dad? the
woofle almost says   i start to sing moon river   she leans
back away from me   and gives me a poignant meaningful
look   like   oh that song … of all songs …!   then   she
clings on tightly tightly to me   her face pressed dramatically
into my neck   her chubby little arms squeezing for all theyre
worth   scarlet is a super senser of anything marvellous   she
acts like we're an old married couple   and moon river is 'our
song'   i must admit i do a nice croony version of it   out

there in the foggy night   wider than a mile ... im crossing you
in style, one day   something dave mccomb might have written
almost   why does the woofle carry on like this?   shes
been here before, baby   oh you cant get like that at 2   shes
sentimental n nostalgic for times long past   she still feels her
memories   buried deep deep down   she aint no first time
arounder   (none of us are presumably)   anyway we stand
on the balcony in the night   with the chalk and the little toys i
keep treading on   with the withered vegetables in planterboxes
and fleshy shrubs   towels hanging on railing   kids swimmers
carelessly hung   the beautiful white flowers in the garden next
door   the diffused lights of sydney   my little woofle childe like
a baby beethoven   her wild hair   her broad forehead   her
deep blue eyes   that look out at you so knowingly   woofle
i couldnt bear anything to happen to you   the rehearsals have
been going well   im getting on very well with everyone   ricki
says that everyones happy with me   oh i like that   oh i do
like it when everyones happy with me   oh i want to please the
triffids and the audience   mick harveys a lovely bloke and a
good singer to boot   chris abrahams on piano   what an
amazing piano player oh how i wish i could be like him   and he
is   the sweetest nicest most 'umble geezer   melanie oxley
singing beautiful versions of daves songs   sister to jeremy n peter
from sunnyboys fame   again a nother lovely person   toby
from youth group   a big triff fan   a warm mellifluous
voice   rob snarski a real singers singer a creamy voice   his
brother mark deep and resonant on bury me deep in love   the
triffs emselves are an idiosyncratic bunch   they are each perfectly
apt on their respective instruments   graham lee running the
show plays exquisite steel n lap guitar   jill on keyboards plays in
a very triffidy way   she steps out to sing occasionally   and
raining pleasure is a show stopper   'in your arms i believe
its raining pleasure'   marty on bass now in bad seeds with
mick h   wow   a propelling bassist who drives the entire
band   he just plays n plays n plays   instantly recognizable
style hes borrowing my bass cos its so good   alsy on drums
is inventive thoughtful and unique   rob mccomb is just right

on guitar violin n a mean harp   ricki is cramming cramming
cramming to learn everything   im trying to take too much in
at once he says   nonetheless hes coping well   mick harvey
jumps in on the xylophone or vibes   its a small orchestra   a
tall thin suntanned weathered looking geezer   prowls around
snapping shots   i get it in my head that its the other mccomb
brother   he checks me out occaisionally   steve miller
from the moodists is there   as an emcee i guess   a few
people at rehearsals are surprised by my dedication   and the
way im throwing myself into these songs   steve miller is one
i guess   he enthusiastically shakes my hand after i belt out
my numbers   'youre … youre … (grasping for a word) …
good!'   thanks steve i hope so   these songs are some of the
best ever written in rock   we do field of glass the ten minute
epic   including weird spoken n screamed passages   thats
right scream   i turn into joe cocker spaniel in this one   after
i finish field of glass rob jill n marty say good job   jesus … daves
were big shoes to fill and i need encouragement   when i sing the
songs however   something takes over   i get sent,   'sent'
a word my dad would use in humourous awe   when he saw a
muso or singer going off his head whilst performing   'look slim,
hes been sent' hed say n we'd have a laugh   now im getting sent
with daves songs   i walk around trying to get a look at the '3rd
mccomb'   he looks bit like rob n dave   but he looks like a
wizard too   i see him deep in conversations with various triffid
alumni   i suddenly deeply need his approval   oh i hope he
likes how im trying to do these most important songs   then
unexpectedly we're introduced   steve do you know … i
cant hear his name over music   the guy smiles his strange
smile   he makes me feel like a kid   hello he says and shakes
my hand   have you met before? says someone   how could
we? says the guy   we only just got introduced!   he walks
off   i still dont know who he is   is that another mccomb
brother? i ask   much laughter   it turns out its bleddyn
butcher   legendary   i do mean legendary photographer
for english *NME*   he was photographer du decade in the
eighties   hes writing a book on triffids   he took loads of

pix of em back in the day   when they were feted as superstars
in england   too much wild acclaim n too much record co
pressure   their calenture record an equivalent of our gaf[1]   all
drum machine souless n underdone   fighting against idiots
in record co etc   wow bleddyn butcher, huh?   gee hes an
imposing kinda lookin' character   anyway   various peoples
approving of my field of glass   including mark snarski sending
me up a little   cos i was overdoing the 'satchmo' stuff   thats
right satchmo   and if ya cant beleave yer urbane olde hero   is
singing like satchmo get yer bum down the metro   sydney, nsw
aust   thurs   fri   sat   sun   darling wife coming on
sun night   should be real good by then   oh jericho!

FRIDAY, 18 JANUARY 2008

strange days indeed mama   singing with the triffids   3
or 4 of best songs ever written   by anyone   how weird it
is   i sit backstage and wait   backstage backstage   3
different dressing rooms   the triffids sit in their room with their
families   mick harvey wanders in our room   phew! he says
as he cops a faceful of my reefer   uh oh contact high!   i
meet the real mccomb brother tonight   john mccomb oh a
lovely gentleman   he gives me seal of approval … its important
to me, understand?   i want everybodys blessing for this   as
each person reassures me further and further   i throw myself
deeper into these songs   im telling you if you aint heard born
sandy devotional …   its one of the very best   it aint glam
rock   it aint new wave or new romantic   it aint showbizzy
schmaltzy dollops neither   i dunno what is that word?   some
kinda intense authenticity   one of them old fashioned
geniuses   you know young hotblooded prolific   doomed
to die way too young   born sandy devotional   and im out
there in those landscapes   the flatlands, the pines, the lonely
stretches   anyhow   eventually my cue is given   in
which mr miller the emcee spins some yarn   hmmmm …   i
go on   and wide open road starts up   that exact drum
machine as on record   (and it doth sound good!)   the

band kick in with that first big chord   the road opens up before
me   i see it all the blue sky   the dark asphalt highway moves
away into the distance   heat shimmer   feeling of revenge
retribution   feeling of loneliness   i dont sing this one as well
as i'd like to   whats stopping me then?   its just that … well
… i dont know   nevertheless the crowd love this song   who
wouldnt?   i dont wanna draw attention to myself really   i
am there as a hired gun to do my job   which is   to sing these
fucking songs in the spirit they were intended   namely   with
passion intensity and (dare i say it) balls   balls as in no namby
pamby malarkey   better to sing wrong notes   than to sing
these numbers   with a limp wrist i guess   tho of course thats
my own take   anyway the audience seem to like w.o.r (despite
me)   next up   the band hits stolen property   the audience
gasp with pleasure as they recognize the intro   i sing this one
better   oh its a beautiful song   convoluted confused brilliant
song that it is   a dialogue with himself?   what a pleasure
to sing something like this   then lonely stretch   i go totally
'off'   better than all other road songs put together   yes you
can go to town on this   a lonely lo a lonely stretch   i exit stage
right   yeah a big rounda applause   after all these are 3 of the
best   wait around a bit more   all hot n sweaty but no where
to go go go   finally its encore time   we do field of glass   i
go totally nuts in this one   shredding my larynx   not used
to being rudely used like this   my throat sounds shot   what
the hell   i put more into it   and it rasps and splinters like an
olde time blues guy   oh   is this how its done …?   i was
just trying to sing it like dave and um …   it came out like this/
that   never mind   everyone seems to likey by crikey   seals
of approval   cool   i split immediately   lift home
with chris n ann marie   who are valve bouncing on the
show   wow they really loved it!   wow   my second hit
musical festival thingo in one week[2]   if only life was always like
this   ok   onwards   to   night   two

second night with triffids already last night   my voice going
going almost gone   there is an art to 'belting' i obviously havent
mastered   my brother jlk leaves phone message today   good
… but now yer voice is shot …   yes oh dear hes right   my
normally resonant voice reduced to a husky croak   last nite it
failed me   i would go for the big high powerful note   which
i know i can hit and …   my voice would disintegrate before
my eyes   first my ears   now my voice   i tell thee
verily my children   take nothing of thy physical body as a
given   things will and do clap out   today i will try to talk as
little as poss   but my olde larynx aint happy with me   but
i guess   i cant control myself   went for a swim today in
the foggy misty rain   its been raining nonstop for 2 or 3 days
here   its lush and green and delicious   this summer
rain   in the sauna i hear a ridiculous conversation   between
some fat hairy old git about my age   and some handsome
well toned but slightly vacuous youngman   who vaguely had
something of the faun about him   with his curly hair n pointy
beard   he was saying   'havent you ever had ecstasy oh
wow   oh everyone should have it   oh not that im advocating
it or anything'   and the old git saying 'bloody drugs whos gonna
pay for yer livers   whats wrong with a bit of booze   dont talk
to me about drugs!'   all punctuated by my sudden guffaws   as
each side trotted out its cliches   the pool was crowded   and i
got pissed off n climbed out   ive read some good reviews of triffs
n me   but now am worried bout voicey voice   tonite will be
filmed   vishnu guide us through this night

i lost my voice last night   it was cutting in and out   i
couldnt hang round and do encore   and the whole gig being
filmed …   so bitterly disappointed   only once before
have i lost it   yes   i had manuka honey   lemon
etc   no good   toby from youth group says try whiskey   i

did   nonetheless my voice clapped out   whenever i needed
it   in wide open road it would not hit the notes   instead
a woeful raggedy distorted racket   graham lee donged himself
in the mouth with a guitar   (thats rocknroll! says cheeky mick
harvey)   at the end i whisper to him   i cant sing field of
glass graham …   ok he says   go home and rest   while he
dabs at swollen mouth with hanky   today   today   will
try not to talk   almost have no voice at all right
now   why?   another couple of days it wouldnae have
mattered   ah human frailty   killer, you starting to fall
apart   and so much to do   so much left to do   praying to
roman god of voices for smooth sailing   but i fear tonite could be
more of the same   im so sad   damn it!

MONDAY, 21 JANUARY 2008

yessaday morning   me n evie go to pharmacist   he
says   i can sell ya whatever ya want   but nothing gonna
help yer throat   so you should just shut up all day   (i
have paraphrased him a little)   family has lovely swim at
bondi   natalie swimming like a dolphin   evie like an
otter   aurora wades around   the woofle eventually gets in
n she loves it   we all eat sno cones on the boardwalk   nk =
grape   ek = red raspberry   lil sk = red raspberry   ak
= fairy floss   big sk = bubblegum + pineapple   hey says
evie … howcome you get 2 flavours, dad?   me: cos i bloody
well paid for em!   meanwhile the woofle does the 'nakey' dance
at the showers   olde ladies fainting with pleasure   as the
chubby little woofle bounces around sans clothes   family stops
in to organic cafe   owner says sorry   no food for you … ive
run out!   me n nk swear we'll never go there again …   we
go instead to a lovely jewish joint   where we have felafels n
chips   all the time   i no talky talky   everyone has
advice   whisper says pharmacist   dont whisper says jlk who
comes to babysit   dont drink says some   congac or red wine
say others   finally we get to gig   nk comes backstage for a
while   talk to ricky   mick harvey etc   finally after much

anticipation   i hit the stage   i do my songs with much gusto n
little voice   yes i channelled dave mccomb   and many triffids
people   including his big brother john   say   yes yes the
passion   you had the passion   then encore   i come on
n do field of glass   ten minute doors-y epic   i go fucking
nuts   you AINT never seen me like this   i channel mccomb,
morrison n any other bloke   going nuts on a stage   DADDY
DADDY HE DONT UNDERSTAND   WHACK!   DOGGIE DOGGIE
HE DONT UNDERSTAND   WHACK! WHACK!   i finish in a
pool of sweat n shredded (wheat) voice   the normally restrained
marty casey gives me a hug   jill n graham say well done   alsy
n rob like it   ive made it   julian n james the triffs #1 fans give
blessings   nk comes backstage   wow!   i told ya darlin' you
aint never seen me sing like that   a conversation ensues   in
which nk says something like   she wants to take me home and
'discuss' my performance   all the way home in cab she holds my
hand   and giggles   looking at me all starry-eyed   ok i
gotta do more gigs like this i think   get home doodles n woofle
all safely asleep   and then nk …   and then i wake up
today   1st day of new church album   hmmmmmm   hard
to change gears   ok   onward n upward   sk

A Sea of Plastic Daffodils

Graham Lee

According to the Dave McComb school of songwriting, mystery is the most important element in a song. If it doesn't contain mystery it's not a complete song. This is why he preferred 'Would You Lay with Me (In a Field of Stone)?' to 'Waterloo Sunset'. The king of mystery left plenty behind in his songs and in the lives of those who were touched by the music or the man.

I last stood on stage with Dave at The Standard Hotel in Fitzroy on New Year's Eve, 1998. He sang 'Sweet Jane' and was very ill. That night he left his Jazzmaster guitar behind a door at the pub. It was still there three months after he died, when Julian Wu went looking for it.

One small mystery solved. Many others still remain.

Dave conducted his life (his music) clearly and thoughtfully, but with room for risk-taking, seemingly thoughtless decision-making and, yes, mystery. He chose the members of The Triffids deliberately but with no real way of knowing if those choices would prove to be wise. His aim was to write songs that were destined not just to be Australian classics but songs that could stand with the best of Dylan, Cohen, Reed and (ahem) David Allan Coe. He knew that effective musical frameworks for his songs wouldn't be got from a bunch of session players or an orthodox guitar band. So he followed some inspired hunches.

By the 'Oz Rock' standards of the day we could barely play and at least one prominent Australian rock musician told us so in no uncertain terms. But he had no appreciation of the fact that the music we made was perfectly suited to the songs that Dave wrote, and that these songs stood head and shoulders above the pub-rock drivel that most bands (including his own) were serving up in the eighties.

It was a mystery to us why we should be included on the bill for the *Australian Made* tour of '86–'87 but we were told that Michael Hutchence had insisted, as the tour was intended to showcase Australian bands that had made their mark outside the country. I can't pretend that the most common look on the faces of punters attending those stadium shows, upon encountering The Triffids, was not one of confusion and, occasionally, abject disgust. Dave put on a great show, striding about the stage in his gold waistcoat, his stagecraft having been well honed by a summer of European festivals. On at least one occasion he even joined in with 'Barnesy' (Jimmy Barnes), Michael Hutchence, Chris Bailey, Chrissy Amphlett et al. to belt out 'Good Times' at the end of the show.

The mainstream was not a place we despised but, in retrospect, it was not a place we'd have felt comfortable lounging around in. To record-company people Dave must have seemed at times to be in urgent need of therapy. When Hot Records were in the UK looking for a major label deal for *Born Sandy Devotional* and whatever was to come next, we decided to go to a woolshed to record a rough-and-ready collection of songs on an eight-track, with a young and green engineer at the controls. I suspect they may have kept this information out of any dealings with Virgin, Island and the rest.

There are many things I never got around to thanking Dave for. I'd like to formally make reparation here, in no particular order.

Thanks for rescuing me from the torpor of a failing relationship while on the dole in Sydney, and plonking me on garden furniture amidst a sea of plastic daffodils in a Belgian television studio. Turning to you, the host had said: 'So, you are the new Jim Morrison. How do you wish to die?'

Thanks for a nickname. When I told him most pedal steel play-ers had nicknames Dave felt he was being short-changed. We were watching Evil Roy Slade at the time in London. 'I've got it,' he said, and dubbed me 'Evil'. Amazingly, it stuck. He then proceeded to try to turn me into some kind of cult figure by instructing crowds to give me a wide berth.

Thanks for letting me sing a few songs with the band live. The first of these, 'Once A Day', was an old country song written by Bill Anderson that I'd heard done by Scotty Stoneman. Scotty got thrown out of the Stoneman Family band for being a drunk, and eventually died from abusing the lithium he was prescribed to help him beat alcoholism. When that song became too popular and we had crowds of drunk guys baying for it, it was mercifully retired. The next was 'Rent' by the Pet Shop Boys. This was chosen by Dave. How he knew it would work I have no idea but, incredibly, it did. After that came 'You Don't Own Me', made famous by Leslie Gore. Visionary or what, Dave? I felt empowered in an oddly feminine way when singing it.

Thanks for remembering every single birthday I had while I knew you, and for always sending nicely apt cards that arrived right on time. Thanks for all the Christmas cards and the bi-annual cassette compilations too. I sometimes wonder whether Dave would have fully adapted to the world of email and mobile phones. It would certainly have made keeping in touch with loved ones while on tour a lot easier. Who knows? We might never have retired hurt. But he would have kept sending cards and writing letters, I'm pretty sure.

Thanks for all those withering glares when I dared play a clichéd country lick, forcing me to develop my own sound on the pedal steel. When I was first asked to play with the band I'd only spent six months wrestling with the complexities of the instrument. Dave made the call and I reminded him of this fact. He responded: 'That's why I asked you.'

Thanks for taking me around the world by plane, bus (double-decker and all), train, smelly van and oversized ferry full of football hooligans, Swedish teenagers, Norwegian truckdrivers and gypsies. Thanks for all the trouble I got myself into and the joys and woes I discovered while doing so.

Thanks for lending me Flannery O'Connor's *Mystery and Manners*. I still read it every now and then and it reminds me of the rigorous approach you took to the job of writing. Thanks also for passing a very amusing hour or so in your company watching the *John and Yoko* telemovie in our hotel room in Denmark.

Thanks for your absolute dedication to the process of writing songs, prose and poetry. It seems amazing now to think that we were constantly being handed such songs to play. I'm sure we became somewhat blasé about it, curse our wooden souls. Imagine sitting in a room and hearing 'Save What You Can', 'The Seabirds', 'Lonely Stretch', 'Jerdacuttup Man', 'Blinder By The Hour', 'Hometown Farewell Kiss' for the first time, and knowing that this was our repertoire.

Thanks above all for the songs. When we played in Sydney recently I made a short list of absolutely essential Dave McComb songs. It came to fifty-four. Had I chosen the songs I'd like to have done rather than just the essential ones I'm sure it would have been well over a hundred. We ended up rehearsing forty-four to playable standard and performing thirty-three or so each night. As they rolled out like a continuous set of perfect waves, the depth of Dave's catalogue of writing became clear, and three hours passed in a heartbeat. Audience members reported the same. We had flowers on stage, a slideshow featuring the likes of a cigar shop and a TV dinner, Handsome Steve Miller as emcee, Dave's brother John showing childhood photos (Dave with two dead rabbits and a face-splitting grin; Dave sniffing flowers), all remaining Triffids, most of The Blackeyed Susans, a huge sound courtesy of ourselves and guests, a bar on stage. I know he would have loved it.

And therein lies the really difficult part about all of this. There are so many things I still have to thank Dave for and there's so much going on at the moment — the reissue of all the albums and more, a resurgence of interest in the music, books being written about the band and Dave, films, documentaries — the fact that he's not here to see it all is as bitter an irony as I would ever hope to feel.

the shape of a secret

Mick Harvey

'a secret in the shape of a song' loomed into being like a benign ship out of the fog the approach being a simple would you like to be involved an unquestioning response determining one's inclusion or otherwise it could only be speculated as to what kind of event it could be the songs of a friend a friend like so many others lost 'too early' the songs of a band who were my contemporaries in a milieu where self absorption was part of the process so much then unfamiliar in fact so many remembered scraps of songs dave graney's cassette in maida vale songs heard at concerts albums I don't have big gaps in the history not surprising really as there was berlin the city of refuge and multiple projects obsessively mine but london visits and odd shows about the place so things just came in piecemeal until late in the piece when it was suddenly over then occasionally a soirée would evolve at the corner of ladbroke grove and bassett road some years later sydney was the place I'd see the susans coming through town and they'd play the annandale then melbourne was the place and a solo album was afoot and we were in the same city somehow mysteriously and we'd fall together at various places in different connections socially out on the town at janet's house in gipps street or in the garden at bank street and late on at the front bar of the espy where costar played those unreleased morsels delivered from a bar stool and so through the other side and onward to nearly a decade later where songs the songs take precedence or so the structure would have it songs I would deliver were some I had chosen some I had not yet all carried with them an obligation in a sense at once a joy a privilege a communal celebration the sheer volume of work almost overwhelming at the same time only scratching the surface so many remembered scraps of songs as before such a total immersion a kind of adult baptism the river of songs an entire body of work flowing before us the triffids supreme comradeship respect in fact a kind of awe in practice unbearable the good life never ends the longing the absence his presence everywhere yet nowhere and mr miller and all of us just wanted to talk about love — L-U-V.

'Evil' Graham Lee on stage with The Blackeyed Susans at the Linda Gebar tribute concert, *Life's What You Make It*, Melbourne, 2008.

How to Climb Inside a Song and Disappear Completely

Sean M. Whelan

there's always a hole somewhere
you left it open for us
time and time again
Leonard Cohen built a tower of song
but you, you were always so much closer to the ground
yours was more like a barn
or a woolshed
a woolshed of song

and there's the gaps between the palings
and that's where the sun spills through
a ladder of gold
travels the length of the hay-strewn floor
one part light
one part dark

I stand inside
and watch the seagulls form a guard of honour
I sense your lips moving somewhere
your tongue
the almighty spark

how do you climb inside a song
and still remember where you live?

you made it easy
by placing a jilted lover
sitting in the corner
with a lip line the exact shape
of the West Australian coast line
and eyes
weeping white sand

I remember the Old Greek Theatre
a stage adorned with electric tulips
and a bubble machine
giggling its way through the encore
we pushed our faces up
closed our eyes for good measure
the bubbles landed like kisses
and your hands were raining treasure.

This is Not a Swan Song

Niall Lucy

It's really only as drinkers that The Triffids have found a niche in the Australian rock industry. Career-wise and musically they've always been too baroque to be accepted on any other terms.

'It's just such a big operation,' David McComb says when we meet in Sydney. 'It's really hard for anyone to see any money from it at all. I mean, I personally am okay, because of the songwriting. But it's hard for people like Graham [Lee]. More than anyone in our group, he just does not have a home. He's been sleeping on a hell of a lot of people's bedroom floors, ostensibly out of faith and devotion to The Triffids.'

Which would seem to be a very good reason for dissolving the band. No money, no regrets?

'I don't think it's anyone's fault,' McComb says in reference to why, after almost eleven years, The Triffids aren't more financially viable. 'I think it's just the fact that we've chosen to be "bi-hemispheral," and we don't work live very hard [i.e., perform live often enough]. We travel between England and Australia and Europe, and yet we don't work live very hard! It's sort of a recipe for disaster ... but I wouldn't have done it another way.'

Despite sometimes using the past tense, McComb is adamant there's life in The Triffids yet. At present, they plan to go on 'long service leave' in July (following an Australian tour which begins in June) before regrouping to record another album, probably in London, around the middle of next year. After all, they're still good friends.

'That's one thing that still completely works,' McComb says. 'I still view everyone in the band as, you know, a personal friend. But in itself that's no reason to keep on doing another album.'

Even so, it's probably the familial nature of The Triffids that's been their abiding strength and one of their most endearing charms. ('But you'd have to qualify that by saying that families can be nasty critters, too.') If they've chosen to go their separate ways for a while, this doesn't contradict their felt connection to the ties that bind.

'We're probably all only half-developed people,' McComb grins. 'But you put the six of us together and you get a fairly well-rounded, decent human being — if you take the nice bits from everyone.'

Not that the needs of the band should dominate those of the people in it. Indeed, McComb insists that 'it's more important that the people survive than The Triffids survive. If someone's going to have their life put into a bit more order by some domesticity, then that's more important than The Triffids, as a rock group, surviving.'

All of which is only hypothetical, of course, since at this stage The Triffids are planning nothing more permanent than a well-earned rest following their current world tour (Europe/Japan/Australia), which began in the UK last month.

Meanwhile, their latest album, *The Black Swan*, has just been released here and McComb is cynical about its chances of escaping from the dungeons of bad taste and ignorance in which so many opinions about pop music are forged.

'*The Triffids are eclectic. They're aimless, and they can't make up their minds what they want to do,*' he sighs, anticipating criticism of the album. 'It's got to the stage where people are so uptight and narrow-minded that they can't handle a few different types of music on the one record!'

But if *The Black Swan* does suffer for its musical diversity (there are songs here that Van Morrison, John Lennon and The Pet Shop Boys would like, as well as a tango, a bit of country gospel, a few twisted ballads and chaotic dance tracks, and an audacious number in 7/8 time), The Triffids won't be surprised or upset. It won't be the first time they've been accused of being self-indulgent for celebrating too wide a range of musical styles.

Three of the songs on the new record were written with founding member Phil Kakulas, who's remained a friend since leaving the band in 1980. Another three were co-written by McComb and Adam Peters, a Londoner who took a shining to The Triffids in 1985 when he heard the early studio cuts of *Born Sandy Devotional*. Comparing the sound to Lou Reed's *Berlin*, Peters offered to play on the album for nothing and has been a part of the UK chapter of The Triffids' extended family ever since.

'I really like collaboration these days,' McComb says, hinting at how he might spend his time when The Triffids go on vacation in July. 'It makes songwriting into something other than just me, you know, pouring out my little tiny misery or something like that. I don't know, it just makes it ... I couldn't actually say "social," but you have to go round to somebody else's house and speak to them instead of just sitting in your own room.

'Dare I say it?' he dares. 'A good form of therapy, really.'

Certainly the results of these collaborative labours have been keeping McComb very busy. He and Peters will be releasing a single in their own right in the UK later this year, 'I Don't Need You'/'Willie the Torch', which Island thinks will pick up a lot of commercial airplay. ('I think they're crazy. I hope it comes out here, but that depends on Mushroom.') Nor has McComb been idle over the summer months in Perth, having formed The Blackeyed Susans with Kakulas, Alsy MacDonald and Robert Snarski (late of Chad's Tree), with an EP due for release this coming spring.

But his first priority is still The Triffids. Having invested so much time in a band that's never enjoyed mainstream recognition in this country, McComb remains no less inspired by the future than when The Triffids (then called Blök Musik) first took to the stage in Perth, at the Leederville Punk Festival, in 1978.

'We've been lucky,' he insists. 'Brilliantly lucky.'

There have been times, too, when they've simply been brilliant — as in the case of their sprawling, degenerate live shows in Australia last year.

The Triffids are coming. Can happiness be far behind?

Deep in a dream:
demo recording
session, London,
1990.

The Black Swan

Phil Kakulas

David McComb believed that the song should come first. By the time of *The Black Swan*, The Triffids' last studio album, he had put that conviction before just about everything else. Before the band, before family, even before himself, he felt his first duty was to the song. It drove him to work hard at his art and hard at the craft. 'The worst trick God can play on you,' he would quote Bowie, 'is not to make you an artist, but to make you a mediocre artist.'

Dave imagined *The Black Swan* to be The Triffids' equivalent of The Beatles' 'White Album': a double album of songs so disparate that their very diversity becomes their collective strength. Each song arranged and played according to its own needs, complete with a growing cast of extras. I guess I was one of those extras.

I grew up with Dave and Alsy MacDonald. In our early teens they formed Dalsy; a couple of years later I joined and we named ourselves The Triffids. This was Perth, Western Australia, in the seventies. In Dave's own words: 'This was the Perth of Norman Gunston, clear blue skies, watersports, all-night TV horrorthons, Hungry Jacks, the WAFL [West Australian Football League], the P76, the Noonkanbah episode, and more watersports. Politics was a distant rumble. There were slim pickings for precocious Stooges/Velvets/Eno fans.'[1]

We used to spend our school holidays writing and recording songs in the cellar beneath Dave's house, hiding out from those clear blue skies and the summer heat. I stayed a few years before leaving to pursue my own winding path through music. The Triffids moved on to Sydney and then to London, and of course to great success throughout Europe and Britain.

The next time I worked with the band was on *The Black Swan*. The Justice Room Studios were a far cry from those early days in Perth.

Here was a band enjoying the spoils of their success—a major label deal with Island Records, a 'name' producer in Stephen Street, a residential studio in the middle of some very pretty English countryside. Care for a game of tennis before lunch, anyone?

I was there to record my parts on the four songs Dave and I had written together for the album, along with Rita Menendez, the Mexican opera singer I was playing with at the time. The songs, like 'The Clown Prince' and 'Blackeyed Susan', reflected our interest in John Zorn-like tangos and Greek time signatures. But Dave had also been writing hip-hop-inspired sequenced numbers as well as band-oriented material for the album, all equally diverse. Keyboard player Jill Birt's two contributions further expanded the selection.

The lyrics, in the main, were portraits and character studies, among them the unhinged frontman of 'The Spinning Top Song', the pastoral gent of 'New Year's Greetings', the world-weary travellers and thirsty romantics of 'Falling Over You' and 'Bottle of Love'. The rest of the songs described the landscapes they inhabited: the Australian summer of 'Too Hot To Move', the desperate isolation of 'One Mechanic Town', and a masterful haiku-like song called 'American Sailors' that manages, in less than a minute, to capture the wistful feeling of a hot Fremantle night in January when the US Navy ships are in and the women are restless.

Recording usually started late morning, finishing up around midnight. Dave and Stephen would spend long hours at the desk, with the rest of us—band and 'extras'— coming and going as required. Bass player Martyn Casey would often act as quality controller, being called on to make a ruling if needed. The songs dictated the instrumentation and approach. 'Band' songs like 'Too Hot To Move' and 'One Mechanic Town' were done as live as possible, capturing the feel of the band, the muscular precision that had been honed through years together on the road. My songs were layered, overdubs added one at a time to create the arrangements. The sequenced songs like 'Falling Over You' and 'Goodbye Little Boy' were developed with Adam Peters and then refined by Stephen, usually in the mornings while he waited for the rest of us to wake up.

Tensions were, I suppose, inevitable. The Triffids were a formidable live band, each member bringing something unique to the mix, be it

Graham Lee's evocative steel-guitar playing, Alsy's cliché-free drumming or Rob McComb's and Jill Birt's very individual and intuitive approaches to their instruments. Throw in the fact that Marty is one of the world's great bass players and it's no surprise that they may have felt a little miffed at being asked to step aside on their own album. The songs came first after all, and that sometimes meant at the expense of people's feelings. But if egos were bruised, the band was still gracious enough to make us extras feel welcome, and confident enough to follow Dave's vision. Still, it must have been confusing for them when Dave seemed unsure which direction to choose, or even if he needed to choose at all: Solo? Band? Hip-hop? Tango? Why couldn't he have it all?

Unfortunately, it was not to be. Soon after the recordings were finished it was decided that *The Black Swan* would be released as a single album only; the band was forced to drop almost a third of the songs, including 'Shell of a Man' and 'Go Home Eddie'. Without the breadth and range of the original track listing it struggled to build the 'big picture out of postcards' intended. The record confused some critics and fans. *The Black Swan*'s aesthetic was a vast departure from the polished continuity of its predecessor, *Calenture*. In fact, its bowerbird approach had more in common with that other Triffids oddity, *In the Pines*. Reviews were favourable and sales respectable, but many — myself included — were left wondering what might have been.

A tour and a live album followed before the band split in 1990. Looking back, that split seems inevitable. The threads of Dave's solo work are already present here. From his singles with Adam through to our work together in The Blackeyed Susans and on to his solo pursuits with The Red Ponies and costar, *The Black Swan*'s broad embrace well anticipates Dave's post-Triffids output.

It reminds me now of the compilation tapes Dave used to make and give away as Christmas presents. From girl groups to hip-hop, Kraftwerk to country, punk to gospel, they were crammed with the most amazing individual songs, but together they added up to something more. They built a narrative, albeit a lateral one. I think Dave was aiming for the same effect when he conceived *The Black Swan*. I think he was aiming high. And nearly twenty years on, in this age of mash-ups and mix tapes, the album's eclectic nature doesn't seem nearly so surprising. In its original format as a single LP, *The Black Swan* never stood a chance, but restored now to its original conceit, it might just be the 'sprawling, messy masterpiece' it always promised to be.

Even if Dave's not here to see it happen, I like to think so.

Jarrah staircase
descending to
limestone base-
ment, The Cliffe.

Please Take Me Home

Chris Coughran & Nathan Laurent

The history of Australian popular song abounds with 'vagabond holes' of one sort or another. In the well-known bush ballad, advertising jingle and unofficial national anthem 'Waltzing Matilda', to cite a salient example, a lyrical drama unfolds around an itinerant swagman encamped by a secluded waterhole. Far from 'jolly' in the version penned by A.B. 'Banjo' Paterson, the drowned swagman of 'Waltzing Matilda' decries the colonial system of which he is a victim with an appeal to folkloric sensibilities that echo both European balladry and a much older tradition, the oral cultures of indigenous Australia: 'And his voice can be heard as it sings in the billabongs …' The swagman's ghost, however, insofar as it may be heard at all, sings not in tune with any *genius loci* but rather, a melody based on a popular Scottish tune, 'The Bonnie Wood of Craigielea', a song derived in its turn from an old Irish ballad, 'Ga'ng to the De'il and Shake Yourself', the title of which may be translated (in accordance, one suspects, with the fateful sentiments of Paterson's beleaguered protagonist) as: 'Go to the Devil and Shake Yourself.'[1] The protagonist of 'Waltzing Matilda' disappears, then — jumbuck, tuckerbag and all — into the vagabond's hole of his own desire, his own dreaming, only to resurface, unwittingly, as the ghostly harbinger of a spurious 'Australian' identity, one that is endlessly reconstituted throughout innumerable textual variants and cultural contexts.

Vast stretches of the imagination are required in order to exhume the swagman's remains from the miry billabongs of cultural memory, in order that we might hear his melancholy voice afresh, after so much tedious repetition. But hasn't David McComb accomplished precisely this feat within the lyrical scope of 'Jerdacuttup Man'? His bog body's intimations of earthly injustice — 'no luck in business and no luck in love' — curiously echo the plight of that putative 'jolly' swagman ('Who'll come a-waltzing Matilda with me?'). Singing from beyond the grave, his 'ten-minute nap' having lapsed into an archaeological 'ten thousand years', the ghostly protagonist of McComb's ballad sings of an individual life cut brutally short, but also (to make matters considerably worse) of an interruption to that profound slumber which, quite possibly — and almost certainly, in the context of the album of songs, *Calenture* — is the best that can be hoped for in an all-too-imminent afterlife.

There is of course no explicit reference to 'Waltzing Matilda' in 'Jerdacuttup Man'. Neither, for that matter, does McComb specifically invoke Seamus Heaney's 'Bog Queen' or any number of other paeans to peatlands — although listeners are free, as always, to make such intertextual associations for themselves. From Jerdacuttup in Western Australia to the peatlands of northern Europe might seem, at first glance, an impossibly vast stretch. Yet McComb successfully bridges the pole and its antipode within the compass of his lyrical vision. Not 'Lindow Man' — discovered in August 1984, the ostensible inspiration for the song — but 'Jerdacuttup Man' is McComb's refrain. Personal and archaeological time collapse into one another; ancient dreaming and contemporary desire intermingle freely. Place-names typical of the language of the Nyungar people — 'Jerdacuttup', 'Tarrilup' — emerge unexpectedly, inflecting some of McComb's most haunting (and arguably, haunted) compositions. The harbinger of an implicit postcolonial sensibility, the speaking subject of 'Jerdacuttup Man' is at once Lindow Man, the drowned swagman of 'Waltzing Matilda', and the preserved head of Nyungar warrior Yagan, expropriated by the Liverpool Royal Institution in 1833.[2] Jerdacuttup Man is also an emblem of McComb himself, the singer-songwriter in exile: profoundly disturbed and yet hopelessly desirous of some kind of homecoming. Construed in and across these multiple contexts, the line of song with which 'Jerdacuttup Man' (and implicitly, McComb also) beseeches us — 'Won't you please take me home?' — becomes a plea for love, respect, repatriation, return. Such desiderata, while compelling, are attainable only at the expense of desire itself — a theme in which the balladeer, alas, is only too well versed. It is to Jerdacuttup, then, that McComb will return; irrevocably, and under tragic circumstances. And yet, by virtue of the faithful transcriptions of some diligent recording angel, his plangent *voice can be heard as it sings*, across an inscrutably vast and lonesome terrain.

In the context of a commercially ambitious pop music album, 'Jerdacuttup Man' strikes us as a strange choice of song title and refrain. The seeming disparity between 'Jerdacuttup'—about as obscure a geographical reference as one may find—and the rarefied ambience of 'the British Museum' (coloured by the recording's conspicuously Western, if archaic, cadences and orchestration) lends the song a certain uncanniness.[3] Initially titled 'Cry of the Peat Man', McComb's ultimate choice of title alludes not only to the Jerdacuttup Plain of Western Australia (where a family property is maintained, and The Triffids' *In the Pines* woolshed recordings were made) but to the routine practice of naming archaeological discoveries for their geographical location—thus 'Java Man', 'Lindow Man', 'Peking Man', 'Piltdown Man', etc. So that what seems, at first, so strange about 'Jerdacuttup Man' turns out to be an elucidating mirror of everyday life, reflecting firmly entrenched cultural practices and habits of mind. For isn't postcolonial experience already inscribed—so deeply that it may no longer even consciously register—with the expectation that the British Museum is, as a matter *of course*, the natural habitat for such relics of the primitive and the exotic, enshrined for perpetuity in various states of suspended putrefaction, as 'Jerdacuttup Man'? One latent effect of McComb's lyrical discourse, then, is to *re*-familiarize social and historical contexts that are all too readily taken for granted, including the practice of expropriating indigenous remains to metropolitan centres under the aegis of colonial science.

While it is tempting to conclude that 'Jerdacuttup Man' is nothing more than an arresting allegory for McComb's own (self-imposed) exile in London—an aesthetic response occasioned by a visit to the British Museum's exhibition of Lindow Man, a peat-bog body discovered in 1984—McComb's composition is nevertheless imbued with an implicit understanding that evolutionary archaeology and attendant museological practices developed within a prevailing discourse of colonialism. Indeed, insofar as the song elicits empathy for the spirit of an ancient nomad whose body has been taken from its resting place, 'Jerdacuttup Man' resonates with contemporaneous indigenous struggles such as the campaign to repatriate the head of Nyungar warrior

Yagan — an 'artefact' shipped to London in 1833 and subsequently held by the Liverpool Royal Institution until 1997 — which aroused considerable media interest in Perth and beyond in the early 1980s.

Jerdacuttup may be a Nyungar place-name, but the preserved body described in the song is more consistent with the peat-bog burials and ice-mummy fields of Europe and America than with any prehistoric remains discovered in Australia. Although the history of Australian archeology does not boast such a well-preserved specimen as Lindow Man, evidence has been unearthed of an elaborate 4000-year-old 'status burial' of a man and small child at a site known as 'Tomb 108' at Roonka Flat in the lower Murray River valley in South Australia: 'A skin cloak appears to have been wrapped tightly around the man's body and fastened with bone pins. … A double-stranded band of notched wallaby teeth encircled the forehead. … The child wore a bird skull pendant, a necklace of reptile vertebrae, and had ochre staining on its feet.'[4] In 1973 a number of spears, wooden digging sticks and returning boomerangs were discovered — preserved in a layer of peat dating to 10,000 years — at Wyrie Swamp in the Mount Gambier district, also in South Australia.[5] Closer to McComb's native Perth, exploration of the limestone cave known as Devil's Lair in the Margaret River area of Western Australia — one of the continent's most significant archaeological sites — has yielded evidence of some 33,000 years of human habitation, according to research that was published by the Western Australian Museum in 1984.[6]

The point of recounting such discoveries here is not to suggest a direct influence on McComb's songwriting, but to convey something of the broader cultural significance of indigenous remains — primitive and exotic, or 'wrinkled and black,' as McComb renders them — given the substantial colonial investments of evolutionary archaeology. Augustus Pitt-Rivers, a seminal figure, predicted in 1875 that once archaeologists had 'exhausted the antiquities of civilized countries, a wide and interesting field of research will be open to them in the study of the antiquities of savages [sic], which are doubtless to be found in their surface and drift deposits.'[7] Indeed, within two decades of this prediction, archaeologists had unearthed prehistoric human fossils of great significance in the European colonies, *Pithecanthropus erectus* ('Java Man') being the first in a series of such discoveries. In her discussion of a Dutch exhibition to mark the centenary of the public display of Java Man, Bouquet concludes that 'it was, amongst other things, an attempt to explain the motivation for removing an object such as *Pithecanthropus* from Trinil, Java and interring it in Leiden, the Netherlands. ... The point was to show the enormous drive for evidence of evolution from the nineteenth century onwards.'[8] Science, once again, comes to the aid of a perplexed colonial subjectivity — this time, in order to assuage feelings of guilt or complicity in the history of expropriation — but by the 1980s, at least in Australia, the questionable treatment of native remains and artefacts by archaeologists and museum directors had begun to decisively inform debates over heritage protection.[9]

Within this broader historical context of colonial archaeology and curatorial practice, the refrain of 'Jerdacuttup Man' — 'won't you please take me home?' — emerges as a plea for repatriation on behalf of such museum specimens as Yagan's head. This repatriation subtext is understated, to say the least, and the relevance of McComb's songwriting might easily have been overlooked, in the 1980s, by those who found greater political surety in the lyrics of Peter Garrett, Paul Kelly, Shane Howard or Neil Murray — not to mention Kev Carmody and Archie Roach, among a host of indigenous Australian songwriters.[10] Yet the manifold allusions and implications of 'Jerdacuttup Man', while complex and subtle, clearly resonate with a range of social issues and longstanding cultural disputes.[11] If nothing else, Jerdacuttup Man's lament serves as a rejoinder to that officious British Museum publication which matter-of-factly states that 'the modern literary response to the discovery of bog bodies' is only natural, given 'the sense of wonder' such specimens evoke 'combined with the feeling that they have in some way *cheated death, to live again.*'[12]

The balladeer, perchance, begs to differ. Indeed, one suspects that, like Yagan the Nyungar warrior (a memorial statue of whom, located on Heirisson Island near Perth, has been repeatedly beheaded by vandals), McComb's protagonist would rather rest in peace than face the ordeal of colonialism — the prospect of a brutally oppressive social order, replete with innumerable murders, disinterments, exiles and expropriations — all over again.

Bury him deep, then — in accordance with the wishes of another of McComb's narrative personae, certainly, but in deference also to the restless spirits of Yagan and Trugannini.[13]

Polaroid test shot, c. 1987.

Towards a Minor Music

Niall Lucy

Shakespeare wrote *King Lear*, though he himself was not a king. He wasn't a prince either, but no one's ever accused him of faking it for writing *Hamlet, Prince of Denmark*. To tell a story you don't have to have lived it: you don't have to be a criminal to write a crime novel, or a skylark to write a poem about one. And you don't ever have to have gone down to St James Infirmary to sing the 'St James Infirmary' blues.

* * *

'St James Infirmary', the song made famous by Louis Armstrong and The Hot Five's 1928 recording in Chicago, originates (without originating, as it were) in the nineteenth-century 'Rake' cycle of British and Irish folk songs, which may in turn derive from a ballad of 1790 or even earlier.[1] In one of the 'Rake' cycle versions the singer recalls 'a-walking down by St James Hospital' one fine, warm day, where he chances upon a friend 'wrapped up in flannel,' despite the weather, because he feels feverishly cold — the side effect of a mortal encounter with 'a handsome young woman' from whom he has clearly contracted syphilis. Had he known of her condition beforehand, the rake laments, 'I might have got pills and salts of white mercury' in time to prevent being 'cut down in the height of my prime.' Thus, staring at death, the rake lists his preferred funeral arrangements:

> Get six young soldiers to carry my coffin,
> Six young girls to sing me a song,
> And each of them carry a bunch of green laurel
> So they don't smell me as they bear me along.

Don't muffle your drums and play your fifes merrily,
Play a quick march as you carry me along,
And fire your bright muskets all over my coffin,
Saying: There goes an unfortunate lad to his home.[2]

Other versions in the cycle are less forthcoming on the cause of the rake's fatal illness, but most tell more or less the same story of a love-worn friend (usually a soldier or a sailor) whom the singer bumps into somewhere around a place called St James Hospital, and who, facing death, narrates an inventory of funeral requests.[3] In nearly every version, the listener's sympathy lies with the singer's friend — 'the unfortunate rake' — although in some variants, told from the woman's point of view and often called 'The Whore's Lament', it is the woman who elicits sympathy.

As for the hospital mentioned in the songs, several historical referents have been proposed. According to Kenneth S. Goldstein, in his notes for *The Unfortunate Rake* album, the earliest of these was originally a religious hospice in London where 'fourteen sisters, maidens, that were *leprous*,' lived contemplatively until, in the 1530s, Henry VIII took possession of the grounds to build St James' Palace, still the official residence of the British sovereign. A later and perhaps more plausible candidate is the Poland Street workhouse for the poor, in the London parish of St James, Westminster, built in 1725 on a site where a multi-storey car park now stands. In addition to providing rooms for work and meagre accommodation, a report in *An Account of Several Work-Houses for Employing and Maintaining the Poor, Setting forth The Rules by which they are Governed, Their great Usefulness to the Publick, And in Particular, To the Parishes where they are Erected* (1732) records that Poland Street also had rooms for the sick:

> There is one Ward for Lying-in-Women, into which many are brought out of the Streets to be deliver'd. Another Ward for an Infirmary, where, though it is generally full of Sick People, the Women that are well, are very officious to give all the Attendance they are able, under the direction of a diligent Matron, who has the care of all the Linnen and Woollen Apparel of the House, governs the Kitchen, &c. and with the Governour have their

Eyes in every corner of the House, to see that nothing be wanting that is necessary to the sick or well, and to prevent Waste.[4]

A third — in a sense, apocryphal — analogue is often given as a church in the red-light district of Storyville, New Orleans: St James' Methodist Church, which in the early decades of the last century took care of the area's poor and the infirm. But this ignores the fact that forms of the song pre-date Armstrong's 1928 recording of it by a hundred years or more.

Even so, the strong association of 'St James Infirmary' with New Orleans is hardly surprising given its status as a jazz standard in that city's bars and clubs, a status owed to the belief (which is neither exactly true nor entirely false) that the song was composed by Louis Armstrong, New Orleans' favourite son. My copy, on a collection of Armstrong's early recordings with his Hot Five and Hot Seven groups, *The Essential Louis Armstrong* (Union Square METROCD578, 2005), credits the song to 'Trad[itional]/Primrose', though it is often credited solely to Joe Primrose, the sometime pseudonym of jazz music publisher Irving Mills.[5] Whether Mills had a hand in adapting the lyrics, however, or whether he simply took advantage of the song's traditional status by lodging a copyright claim on his own behalf, it seems unlikely — since Mills was not a musician — that he had anything to do with the musical arrangement of the Armstrong version, the melody of which bears no resemblance to that of the 'Rake' cycle (the latter seeming to have become the basis of the melody for the song known today as 'The Streets of Laredo').[6] It's possible that Armstrong may have heard a melody similar to the one he uses on the 1928 Chicago recording before leaving New Orleans in 1922; it's possible, too, that he borrowed not only the music but also the lyrics of 'his' version from a version he heard back home, or even in a Chicago speakeasy. Certainly, Armstrong's is not the earliest known recording of the song, a version having been recorded as 'Gambler's Blues' in 1927 by Fess Williams and His Royal Flush Orchestra, in New York, with 'Moore–Baxter' (Carl Moore and Phil Baxter) credited as the composers, though the comic treatment given to the song in this version belies the sombre, dirge-like approach taken by Armstrong and The Hot Five. The same year (1927), moreover, saw the publication of poet Carl Sandburg's *The American Songbag*, a collection of mostly 'traditional' US folk songs that includes what we now call 'St James Infirmary', albeit under the title of 'Those Gambler's Blues'.[7] Clearly, then, the Armstrong version can't be understood as original in any absolute or straightforward sense — and yet it remains exceptional for several reasons, not least for putting the lyrics directly into the first person and dispensing with the frame narrator.

'I went down to the St James Infirmary,' Armstrong sings, immediately adopting the rake's persona, so that in this version the singer's story is his own. In 'Those Gambler's Blues', however, the basic structure of the 'Rake' cycle is retained, with the singer setting the scene for another's story to be told:

> It was down in old Joe's bar-room.
> On a corner by the square,
> The drinks were served as usual,
> And a goodly crowd was there.
>
> On my left stood Joe McKenny,
> His eyes bloodshot and red,
> He gazed at the crowd around him,
> And these are the words he said:

Whereupon the McKenny character (who in other versions is sometimes called 'McKinny' or 'McKennedy') confides to his fellow drinkers that — recently, we may presume — he saw his sweetheart stretched out on a mortuary table, and follows this with a list of his preferred funeral arrangements ('Six crap shooters as pall bearers,/Let a chorus girl sing me a song …'). When McKenny's tale has finished being 'quoted' in the first person, the song ends with the singer declaring, in the final quatrain, that he'll 'take another shot of booze' because he's 'got those gambler's blues.' In the Armstrong version, though, which compresses the story into just three quatrains, not only is the rake's or the McKenny character's narrative not given a context in which to be told, but this version's departure from realism is reinforced by a seeming lack of character motivation. Beginning *in medias res*, with the announcement that he saw his sweetheart 'stretched out on a long white table' at St James Infirmary, the narrator of the Armstrong version calls for her — spirit, perhaps — to be released: 'Let her go, let her go, God bless her,/Wherever she may be,' he sings. Without saying how she died, he gives but a brief impression (partly detached, partly sentimental) of her corpse: 'So cold, so sweet, so fair.' Then come the killer lines — the ones that draw everyone who's ever heard them, back to the song countless times:

> She can search this wide world over,
> She'll never find another sweet man like me.

Finally, in the third and last verse, we get the preferred funeral arrangements: 'When I die I want you to dress me in straight-lace shoes,/I want a box-back coat and a Stetson hat …'

Now, despite what might be called empirical evidence to the contrary, there may be good reasons for thinking that Armstrong turns 'St James Infirmary' into *his* song.[8] The version of the 'Rake' cycle that seems to have been popular before Armstrong's 1928 recording, after all, was called 'Gambler's Blues', in which there is no reference to a 'St James' hospital; so it's possible that, in New Orleans or even throughout Louisiana, 'St James Infirmary' was the more popular version and Armstrong knew it well, or that Armstrong chose to record 'St James Infirmary' — rather than 'Gambler's Blues' — in deference to St James' Methodist Church from his home town, effectively making it the referent of the hospital in the 1928 recording. Nor does 'Gambler's Blues' contain what I have called the killer lines in the Armstrong version, although (again) it would be impossible to say whether Armstrong or Irving Mills, or someone else, wrote them.

Because, though, Armstrong is not quite the song's lyricist or composer in the way we think of Shakespeare as the author of *Hamlet*, it may be only for the sake of shorthand that we might refer to 'St James Infirmary' as a song by Louis Armstrong. But this assumes that what we mean by an author is someone who is the sole originator of a text, which (as a brief aside) would not have accorded with Shakespeare's understanding of authorship.[9] In turn, the idea of the proprietary author leads us to suppose that textual meaning is a product of authorial intention   this is the cornerstone of discourses on popular music, for example, accounting for the prevalence of interpreting song lyrics (by critics, fans and songwriters alike) in terms of songwriters' lived experiences. And, by this logic, not just anyone can sing 'St James Infirmary' after Louis Armstrong … at least not without running the risk of being called an impostor.

For example: David McComb.

* * *

By current standards of 'authenticity' in popular music, McComb had no right to sing 'St James Infirmary' on The Triffids' 1984 recording of the song for the *Raining Pleasure* 12" EP (Hot MX204517). His home life in the genteel suburb of Perth's Peppermint Grove (so named for the peppermint trees which are native to the area) was comfortably well-to-do and could scarcely have been further removed from that of an old rag-timer like Armstrong, who grew up in poverty in a seedy neighbourhood of New Orleans after his father abandoned the family when Armstrong was still a child. What was McComb doing appropriating an experience that Armstrong's life, but not McComb's, gave him the authority to represent?

Such thinking makes it possible to accuse someone like Bon Scott, for example, of being a class traitor for having gone glam with The Valentines and again in his early days with AC/DC, while ignoring the fact that former art-school student David Bowie has pretty much based his whole career on camping it up. According to this way of thinking, authenticity can be read off from a strict correspondence between identity types and textual forms or performances. The authenticity of Beck's work, say, isn't compromised by his experimentation with techno music, since his subjectivity (middle class, young-ish arty West-Coast type) grants him a creative licence to be 'postmodern'; but of course if Bruce Springsteen were to set a song about the working-class oppressed to a techno beat, he'd be roundly ridiculed. So, too, the authenticity of The Sex Pistols is often invoked to the detriment of The Clash, because, by comparison to members of The Pistols, Joe Strummer grew up relatively posh.

Put like that, the reliance on identity markers to establish authenticity — or 'credibility' — in music may seem more than faintly ridiculous. Yet even in its subtler variations this formula has a stranglehold on pop aesthetics. When the markers are not broadly pre-given (class, age, gender, ethnicity) but romantically transcendental ('soul,' 'passion,' 'feeling'), the assumption remains that authenticity derives from an essential relation between a performer's inner life and his or her expression of it through music. The more that relation is seen as *singular* ('personal,' 'honest,' 'truthful'), the greater the critical approval. What I'm calling singularity, then, stands opposed, ideally, to repetition — to mere mechanical reproduction. But the problem with this is that such an opposition is always less than total except as an ideal.

Take tomorrow's sunrise. When it happens it will be a singular event: *tomorrow's* sunrise will not have happened before. Yet, as an event, tomorrow's sunrise will be a repetition of every sunrise that has ever been. It will be indivisibly singular *and* repetitive at the same time. In this way, singularity — absolute singularity understood in absolute opposition to repetition — is impossible, since nothing could be said to be so irreplaceably 'itself' that wasn't also an effect of repetition and therefore *not* itself.[10] 'St James Infirmary', for instance, in a sense belongs to Louis Armstrong and *at the same time* does not belong to him, since his version repeats — not identically, but certainly in substantive ways — a series of repetitions going back at least to 1790. In a similar fashion, part of the reason I can say who I am, or simply that I can *say* 'I am,' has to do with the fact that my language gives me — and every other member of my linguistic community — a first-person pronoun to use which of course is not mine alone, but belongs (without belonging) to my fellow language-users.

This neither means that we're condemned to repeat the past nor that we're imprisoned within language. It suggests rather that what we think of as singularity isn't so much a condition as an aspiration, an ideal; and to the extent that we self-represent as 'different,' in resistance to pre-given markers of identity, it could be said that we express our affinity with that ideal. Derrida would say that by doing so we express (though not necessarily self-consciously) an affinity with notions of democracy and justice, which are irreducible to systems of repetition in the form of politics and the law.[11] Briefly: we can't afford to think of justice being done on the basis of courtroom decisions founded on legal precedents, since we know that such decisions are often wrong. Justice, then, always *remains* to be done. Similarly, as an idea and an ideal, democracy could not be thought to be achieved, or to have arrived, with the introduction of a system of parliamentary representation, since there could never come a time when there was no more liberty, equality and friendship to be extended.[12] Democracy, then, always remains *to come*. While indeed it may be necessary for there to be official institutional (political and legal) forms of democracy and justice, these alone are insufficient, as *systems* of repetition, to affirm the impossible singularity of democracy or justice as an idea and an ideal. It follows from this that such affirmation occurs not at the spectacular, public level (so much for the 'politics' of Bono and Bob Geldof), but at the level of the micro-social everyday. It might even be said (and again I am drawing broadly on Derrida's work here) that such affirmation takes the form of a certain kind of reading practice or attitude, a certain form of relation to texts and textuality that insists on keeping open the possibility of further interpretation rather than seeking to disclose an underlying truth.

This may account for David McComb's preference for songs he regarded as harbouring an essential *mystery*, leading to the paradox that these would be irreducible to anything like an essence in a positive sense. Small wonder, then, that he should have been drawn to 'St James Infirmary' (albeit The Triffids' version reinstates the frame narrator while incorporating — repeating — the 'killer' lines from the Armstrong version), given that the song refuses to relinquish its mystery to all but the most unimaginatively literal-minded of listeners. The McKenny (or, in The Triffids' version, the McKennedy) character's boast — 'She'll never find another sweet man like me' — can be made to make sense, in other words, only at the cost of demystifying its essentially indeterminate and imponderably suggestive nature. To argue that, in the context of the song's history, say, the boast represents some kind of gruesome comeuppance for the dead whore from whom the rake contracted syphilis, would be to reduce every version of the song, from Armstrong's to The Triffids' and beyond, to the status of a pure repetition without any semblance of singularity or 'personality' — the mere mechanical reproduction of a putative original. To inscribe the boast within the unifying and determined form of a certain history would be to lend the McKenny/McKennedy character all the psychological roundedness of a realist figure, turning the sublime into the mundane. Any attempt, then, to reduce the song's mystery to some underlying historical, psychological or other unifying 'truth' would be a refusal of that mystery.

Whether or not McComb intended any of this, however, is largely beside the point. Certainly I'm not suggesting that The Triffids recorded 'St James Infirmary' as a self-conscious affirmation of democracy and justice, let alone of deconstruction. They recorded it, I dare say, for the perfectly unremarkable reason that the song's melody and sense of mystery appealed to them; and I suspect they might have done so also because the song struck them as traditionally if not vernacularly 'American.' The fact that, in a sense, it's *not* a traditional American ballad is neither here nor there: the history of the song's performances and variations makes it over into one.[13] Such a history is not determining, of course, as though only a certain type of subject should be permitted to perform the song, but even so that history is inseparable from whatever might be regarded *as* the song called 'St James Infirmary', which is irreducible to an archetype or original. Every version of the song is an original performance in its own right, helping not to resolve but to repeat and reinterpret (and therefore to reveal again, for another first time) its essential mystery.

By choosing to sing 'St James Infirmary', then, McComb could be said to have expressed his identity in 'personal' terms — in terms other than those constructed for him by his age, nationality, social background and the like. He expressed himself, as did The Triffids, by association with a certain kind of musical tradition that, in 1984, was incompatible with commercial rock and pop. Whoever associates — or 'identifies' — with that tradition, which is still a kind of secret within official, mainstream culture, belongs (without belonging) to a virtual community made up not of social beings, but of kindred spirits. McComb *chose* to sing 'St James Infirmary', as we may choose to affirm that choice in responding to the mystery of The Triffids' version of the song; and in this it could be said that something like an ethics appears in the barely discernible form of an affinity with whatever — a song, an event, a stranger — refuses to reveal 'itself' to us in familiar, repetitive terms.

This would be a far cry from saying that McComb expressed *himself*, his interiority, by singing 'St James Infirmary'. What can be said instead is that McComb's identity — like every identity — was not something to be expressed, but invented. Rather than being fixed and stable, or having an underlying essence, what we think of as our identity is an ongoing, creative work in progress — but without a necessary purpose. Our 'becoming' is discontinuous, because it isn't directed at any inevitable endpoint. This, with a nod to French philosopher Gilles Deleuze and psychoanalyst Félix Guattari, is to acknowledge that our identity isn't given to us by, say, the universal essence of human 'being', since being or life doesn't have an essence.[14] 'Life', as Claire Colebrook (herself drawing on Deleuze and Guattari's work) puts it neatly, 'just *is* the power to create, differentiate and further itself'.[15] Partly, then, who we are is an effect of who and what we differentiate ourselves from, and define ourselves against. So by choosing to cover what was an obscure and quirky song in the context of the rock scene at the time, The Triffids differentiated themselves from the identity of a mainstream rock band — and they did so, too, in defiance of an idea of 'Australian' identity. Australian 'being' and being 'Australian', they helped to show, doesn't have an essence and isn't tied to clichés. To 'be' Australian doesn't mean having to overcome life's desire 'to create, differentiate and further itself'.

Such desire flows most noticeably through songs and other works of art that might be called 'mysterious'. A song like 'St James Infirmary', say, creates affects that are not pre-given, insofar as we can't quite account for the narrative according to standard sense-making protocols.[16] The song doesn't work as a representation of something other than itself, or as a communication of some pre-existing truth; and in this it works to disturb a sense that the world 'is' in certain essential, pre-given ways. A literary equivalent would be Kafka's writing, which counts as a prime example of what Deleuze and Guattari call a 'minor' literature: a literature that seeks not to represent or repeat familiar states of affairs, but to create new ones.[17] All great literature is minor in this respect, on Deleuze and Guattari's account, since it creates an opening to unexpected or hitherto unforeseen possibilities. Unlike other discourses — science, say — a minor literature is primarily affective rather than communicative or referential: it *affects* us before and beyond any cognitive or referential sense we might try to make of it, and such an affect remains a kind of secret that can never be brought into the language of science or philosophy. This, too, we might say, is how 'St James Infirmary' works — affectingly.

It may also help to explain the 'alternative' nature of The Triffids' music, which, in the context of the corporate rock mainstream, could only ever be understood as 'minor' in a pejorative sense. Deleuze and Guattari, though, might say that such minority status is at odds with the longevity of the affecting power of that music — a minor music that despite its lack of commercial impact continues to work its affects (though not necessarily forever). In this way, whatever gave prominence to features regarded as secondary or occasional elements of commercially successful pop songs — lyrical or narrative ambiguity, perhaps; non-standard instrumentation; a 'warm,' lo-fi production sound — might qualify as minor. But these would not be fixed and permanent, such that today The Ronettes' 'Baby, I Love You' might count as an example of a minor music. The point is that a song or a record would not be minoritarian *in essence*, but rather only in a context or according to a certain way or attitude of response.

Again, the example of Kafka is illuminating. Kafka himself was not an insect or a mole, yet he wrote stories from those creatures' points of view. The world as we think we know it, indeed, is barely recognizable from Kafka's writing, which isn't representative of pre-existing states of affairs but rather inventive of new ones. Although Kafka was a Czech, moreover, he wasn't a 'Czech writer' but simply a Czech (and a Jew) who wrote: his writing doesn't represent the 'experience' of the Czech people, which is not to say it represents universal humanity either. It doesn't 'represent' or 'express' at all; it *invents*. Kafka didn't write as a fully unified, sovereign subject in complete conscious control of language, but rather gave himself up to the intensities and affects that language enables and from which new possibilities — new ways of understanding or relating to identity, reality and the world — may emerge. His writing counts as a minor literature, then, to the extent that each time we read one of Kafka's works we are left with new questions to ask, precisely because his writing is not representative or expressive of pre-existing states of affairs, of the world as we think we know it to be. It is only through institutions like the Kafka Museum in Prague — which narrates, however fascinatingly, a story of his life and explains his writing as an expression of it — that Kafka is turned into a 'major' writer whose work is all too familiarly representational. As a major writer, Kafka becomes a type of 'the' writer in general, the singularity of whose writing is lost to the all-encompassing idea of writing understood in terms of representation and expression.

Such is the fate of all art — that of The Triffids, for example — when reduced to the expression of an intending, fully unified consciousness. This is not to say, of course, that David McComb didn't mean something by singing 'St James Infirmary', or that he didn't intend his own similarly mysterious songs — 'The Seabirds', say, or 'Kathy Knows' — to 'have' certain meanings. But to respond to those songs simply as determined effects of McComb's intentions, or as somehow grounded in his identity or subjectivity, would be to deny their potential *affects*. It would be to turn them into major works, condemning them to repeat a certain idea of what music 'is' at the expense of considering what it can 'do'. The problem here lies with the interpretative task of demystification, such that a song must be taken as a sign *of* something that precedes it; as a sign of something *else* — a true feeling, a real-life recollection, an actual experience. But as the mere repetition of something that already 'is', a song is lost to all possibility of engaging with what it might be said to 'do' as pure, affecting sound. If music affects us at all, in other words, it does so at the level of the body, which is not to discount its potential cognitive or intellectual effects but simply to acknowledge that these are never exclusive. It is the body that responds to music, and jazz was the first popular music of the modern age to create new possibilities for what people might *do* with their bodies. When Armstrong and The Hot Five took an old song and made it *swing*, then, they actualized what in a sense was always already immanent within the 'Rake' cycle — just as jazz (especially before it had a name) was an expression of potentialities that were immanent in music.

The resonant percussion and reverberating piano sounds of The Triffids' version of 'St James Infirmary' bring out certain other sonorous qualities of the song, heightened by McComb's impassioned vocal. We are not listening to the song if we are trying to make sense of The Triffids' arrangement in terms of what it might be a 'representation' *of*. Indeed, we are not listening to any version of the song — or any song — if we're trying to understand it as the expression of an actual experience. Songs are not virtual forms of actual life, since actual life does not preclude the virtual in the form of ideas, desires, projections, imaginings and other affective responses.[18] (Dragons, for instance, are no less a part of actual life than other animals.) If The Triffids' version of 'St James Infirmary' has something like a ground or an antecedent, then, it is not to be found in the life-world understood as different from the world of texts, but rather (and rather obviously) in other versions of the song: including Armstrong's, even if they never heard it.

* * *

Shakespeare was neither a king nor a prince, but he wrote *King Lear* and *Hamlet, Prince of Denmark*. While he may not have had personal experience of regency in some naïvely actual sense, he knew all about it theatrically — textually — from the plays of Marlowe, Nashe and Greene. The sources of Shakespeare's plays (rather obviously) were other plays, and not his life in Stratford-upon-Avon. But that's not to say his sources were virtual in the sense of not being real.

If, in short, you want to be a playwright, first you need to see some plays; and if you want to be a songwriter you had better listen to a lot of songs. It's in this way that a work of art does not derive from a single, authorial consciousness, or from the inner life of a producer, and doesn't represent an aspect of the real world defined in terms of the opposition of the actual and the virtual. A song like 'St James Infirmary' doesn't tell us 'about' the world as we suppose it to exist already, although it may affect us in a way that causes us to question our everyday assumptions about the nature of subjectivity, for example, which we tend to think of according to an ideal of absolute self-consistency. Such thinking predicates a common world of universal experiences for unified subjects to 'have' and thereafter, if they so wish, to communicate to themselves or other subjects through language. The McKennedy character's boast doesn't fit this way of thinking, leaving the options of rejecting it for being 'unrealistic' or of responding openly to its mystery or affects. The conditions of those affects are not reliant on deciding whether or not there was ever an actual St James hospital, and they aren't dependent either on tracing the song's mutations back to an original source in eighteenth-century England or

Ireland. The point of describing the song's history would be simply to investigate the candidate grounds of its ultimate meaning, in order to see that each of these fails to account for its affects.

As an example of a minor music, then, 'St James Infirmary' is a song without a definitive composer, a meaning or a place of origin. Its affects are not attributable to the representation or expression of a transcendental source. But in this it is not essentially different from, say, McComb's 'Estuary Bed', a seemingly 'personal' song based on memories of childhood family holidays in the seaside town of Mandurah, Western Australia. For music to be responded to as music, for it to be allowed to be something more and other than the expression of an actual experience, it has to be dissociated from critical markers of authenticity in the form of ultimate grounds. Only then might we accept that The Triffids' cover of 'St James Infirmary' — a seemingly minor or supplementary example of their body of work — tells us everything we need to know about them.

Bladder Wrack

Gavin Martin

Ahh David, bonnie lad, I hardly knew ye.

Actually I know more about you, about a version of you, than I do about most. It's all there in the swirl and sweep of your music. It's there and I hear it now, coming strong and clear on Track 8 of *Born Sandy Devotional.* Closing in on the section between 1:48 and 1:52, and the vocal performance … the measure of it, get the weight of it, the raw gargle at the peak, the sense of withering disgust and sheer elation, all knotted in there, tight like a tourniquet.

Delicious, David, delicious — there you are captured in the ever-present now through the miracle of technology.

There you are, Dave, getting into the grain of them thar 'Personal Things', getting into the mind of the character, the characters even; all the senses are alive and they pulsate and reverberate and they ache and they shudder against the walls of heartache. Rattling and roaring back and forth between you and the band.

And it's coming again now at the end of minute one of 'Kelly's Blues' on *Calenture.* So clean, so precise, so sure; a valiant swagger; your wracked and bloody slashing guitar — swift, keen, and decisively electrifying. That's David there like some vanquishing angel, breathing fire, ardour and (com)passion. And there he is again, coming back in circa 1:30, the voice crying out, all lost and lonely, curdling out of a Roy Orbison-edged darkness sending tremors deep into the song.

Your voice David, your artistic voice, it's still very strong. Strong and mighty, more so every time I get to hear it. *Mighty, mighty … for a spade or a whitey*, as Curtis Mayfield once said.

It really is a deathless thing the finery of the art, David.

That's what you left innit?

The masterful sweep that, in the period I'm dwelling on, took in Marty's subtle punch and canny depth charges, 'Evil' Graham, Jill, Alsy, brother Robert, Adam Peters and 'thousands of others, too gifted to mention' as the sleeve note of *Calenture* has it.

David got off on the scintillation of collaboration, no doubt about that.

Collaboration with mates making music, and something else, something more profound for a man who was, it seems, a lonely-hearted hunter. He got off on collaboration in life, too.

Oh that may have changed later, maybe David McComb succumbed to the Scotch-Irish Planter self-destruct gene that was displayed time and again through the lives and careers of the Belfast three — Van Morrison, George Best and Alex Higgins.

Maybe he went to some dark lonely place in his heart and couldn't get back out. I mean hell, shit, fuck — where was his heart, he'd had it replaced, hadn't he? The Planter offspring with the transplant. For a man who thought so deeply, who felt so profoundly, who was all *head, heart and soul* in his work, losing that organ, to be replaced with another, must have been a mindfuck.

But of my time with David in Perth there was something I could be sure of. David was proud of those mates of his, no doubt about that. Proud of the world they'd all created in the stultifying surrounds of the most remote city on the whole damned planet. That's the sense I got when he held court, introduced me around, black-swanned me about, after getting me over to Perth in nineteen hundred and eighty-nine.

Such generosity had he shown in getting me there. It was David and his London-based mates, see, mates at the record label, Mick the PR, Bleddyn (snapper, friend, future biographer) — who helped spirit me ahoy on the big silver bird from London to Perth, David's birthplace. I believe it was, for all concerned, but in particular for The Triffids, who were never slow to throw a party, a case of get in and spend the budget while you can. Because even then the tightening of the belt round the stomach, the pull of the noose round the neck of the record industry money-pot, was abroad.

What a gift for me though, even in the days of 'living off the pig's back' — of being an indentured servant to the old *NME* (boozy lunches, long nights drinking the long draught, grooving and musing, blah, blah, blah). Getting to the continent 'back of beyond' was surely something out of the ordinary.

Childhood dream come true: going to Oz.

In days back there in the before time — growing up in Ulster where I'd lived eighteen years, the last sixteen of them by the sea — going to Australia was something of a fantasy. The lolling by the surf. The heady sun. The ripening. The warmth. It played a symphony in my head, the thought of going there, it really did. There were always plans and dreams and 'if we win the pools'-type conversations in our house. My parents got out of Belfast before the 1960s–70s war kicked in; Bangor was another world but not so far away as to be immune. So they always wanted for something better, a distant dream but one to hold onto, one to pass on maybe. I mean other people were doing it, the £10 Pom thing. If it wasn't for Paul, the brother up there in the Downs Syndrome institution, some sixty miles away, Mum and Dad unable to look after him in the family home, unable to tear themselves from the regular visits by planting themselves far away, over the ocean … well, we might've been there. Everything would have been different. I could have been living in Perth. We could have been £10 Poms! I have to believe we'd have made a better fist of it than the Bells, who went and then came back after a few years. Or the friend's stepbrother who went with his wife sometime in the early eighties — sold up lock, stock and barrel — and came back after just two weeks because Perth was 'so unfashionable'!

Oh, you don't know how much that made me laugh. Someone from Bangor calling somewhere else, somewhere at the other end of the earth, 'unfashionable'!

Small town attitudes? Bangor majored in them.

Y'see Bangor, where I grew up, where I drank beer, had my first awakenings, heard about Elvis dying, experienced — ahh, the heady thrill — The Sex Pistols' 'God Save the Queen' go to Number One. Where I saw my Aunt with tears in her eyes when she greeted me at the breakfast table after chancing a peep of The Sex Pistols' Jamie Reid 'Queen with the safety pin through the lip' poster above my bed. Bangor. Bangor. Bangor. Not Bangor in Wales, Bangor in Norn Ireland. Like Neil Young sang, *all my changes were there* — and I guess a part of me will always be there.

It was there, many years later, in February 2007 — eighteen years after my Perth sojourn — that I was asked to contribute to this very collection. Oh it was apt, f'sure, that I should be back there for the first time in ages when I got the email. Poetic, even.

Bangor: the closed minds, the cultural drought in a seaside town presided over by the blue-nosed city fathers, intent on fucking everything up, or so it seemed, for everyone.

Bangor, I was to find — its climatic lack aside[1] — had much in common with the Perth David knew and even described in his music.

So why me? Why had David (and co.) chosen me to take the trip? It wasn't as if I'd been especially kind to The Triffids.

'Bomb Australia now' was how I'd ended the review of their mini-album in the *NME* a few years before.

Cute, huh?

Not to mention somewhat injudicious coming from someone who had been raised in a time and place where getting bombed was a risk taken daily, by braver and/or less fortunate folk than I.

'Course I'd since seen the error of my pigheaded ways.

Now I know folk who still say it's a little overcooked, Gil Norton let far too loose with the gilding, but *Calenture*, that was the one for me.

Oh I'm happy to be persuaded otherwise, happy to hear that it's *Born Sandy Devotional* that represents the peak, or that actually it's *In the Pines*. I just don't want to hear the argument put forth when I'm lost in the warm, impossibly velvety caress of 'Bury Me Deep In Love', or when I'm caught in the cauldron, the hot storm, the dust-catching-in-the-parched-throat drive — and anguish — of 'Vagabond Holes'. I certainly don't want to hear about it when I'm dazzled by the miraculous shimmer, the choice wonderment of 'A Trick of the Light', or the churning wrath of ages pulsing through, into and around 'Jerdacuttup Man'. Just to feel him there, then and now, that was the thing with David — the way he let you feel him. The heart wrapt in a brain, the brain wrapped in a heart.

And *Calenture* came upon me again, all newly packaged and expanded just before I was approached to write something for this book. Marty Casey supping beer in his Grinderman incarnation (with that other Oz rock giant, Nick Cave) was so cool, so modest and polite after all these years, thanking me when I told him I'd managed to scrape a few lines into a national daily about it being a lost master-piece of eighties rock.

When really what it is like, is this: The Triffids were sainted warriors. Collectively to a man and woman they meant something, laid some-thing down for the ages. What sonic pronouncement has Australia (or anywhere from back then, in that time) got that still stands up today? Music for the ages.

I ask myself: how many of the bands from back in those days do I still play for pleasure?

Not many.

How many do I play for illumination?

Fewer still.

Yet The Triffids, steered by David — the tall, louche, gallant, envi-ably pencil-thin frontman — fall into both categories.

So this was the scheme, y'see, back there when I went out to cover The Triffids on the eve of the release of their *Black Swan* swansong. I'd never had a crack at interviewing The Triffids. I was, or was con-sidered, I guess, in the milieu in which I toiled, to be something of a writer with — what is it called? Gravitas?

Perhaps.

I also had a wish to appear a dutiful and gracious guest. So when I arrived through immigration at Perth to find — unusual in my experi-ence — a fully stocked duty-free liquor store, I bought bottles of whis-key and champagne for my hosts.

Foolish me: thinking we might sip lightly at the champers before bedding down after twenty-four hours on the jetlag machine, the whiskey to be produced later, perhaps a few drams near the end of my stay.

Come the early hours of the next morning, endless slabs of Black Swan Lager had been downed along with the whisky, champagne, and copious quantities of the local weed.

The 'legendary' Irish taste for alcohol? Pshaw and fiddlesticks! It was nothing compared to what these guys — and gals — could sink. By the end of the evening I had lost a wallet filled with hundreds of dol-lars (only to have it miraculously returned the next day), and my cen-tre of gravitas well and truly altered. It was never quite the same again the whole time I stayed there.

Memories of Perth? The beach as impossibly wondrous and warm as I had imagined it. The mystical shipwreck on the beach at Fremantle, as if planted there to make David appear the dazed, washed-ashore minstrel from afar. I didn't ever want to leave the surf; purest cleanest ecstasy it gave. Still, there was something damnably clubbable and attractive about sharing a few mid-afternoon beakers of suds from the communal jug in a cooling tavern. And the weird cultural mirror that was thrown up by the London-themed shopping centre situated beside my hotel was, uncannily, like a taste of home.[2]

Bangor: the Unionist stronghold of North Down more snobbishly, proudly British/English in attitude and outlook, when I had been growing up, than almost anywhere in the so-called United Kingdom. In Triffids songs the narrator's home town was variously pined for, despised and set alight — feelings I could relate to.

And what do I remember of David back then on that trip? That he was gracious, attentive, always wanting to be sure I had amusement and company during my stay.

The sit-down interview, when it came, after all the easygoing, oh-so-natural hospitality, seemed forced, strained even. He got desperately drunk — I did my bit but nothing like he did and when it was over I only had to crawl into bed. He had to drive home!

I don't have the tapes now, having lent them to someone more diligent in their research, more painstaking in their appraisal of David than I. But when I think back, it seems we were battling a mutual ache, the dark black dog gene. David was laying it on the line and I was the waspish interrogator, wheedling it out of him to make 'good copy.'

I know that the next time I saw him — after I got back from Australia and the article had been printed — David said something about it being 'easy to get someone drunk and make them look a fool in print.' I don't think he was immoderately upset when he said that. But it exposed the raw sensitivity of an acutely defined artistic temperament.

One of the last times I saw David in the flesh was at a homecoming — or was it a farewell? — party at The Triffids' London headquarters. The convivial sort of get-together they did so well. And then, in the middle of the bluff revelry, an odd moment. Opening the toilet door to find David sitting glumly, trews round the ankles, on the can. Seemingly settled into long, unproductive labour.

Sheeit! I couldn't leave him there stranded in my memory, up shit creek without even a turd for a paddle, so to speak.

So in 2007, when I was asked to write this, I got to hear David again in Northern Ireland — as I walked along the Orlock headland between Groomsport and Donaghadee in the County of Down — on a gloriously rare 'throne of Ulster' day.[3]

The weather seems changed. I don't think that twenty years ago I'd have seen a pond full of fattened frogs or spent a week there in Bangor, in February, with so much sunshine.

Great Triffids territory, that sweeping Orlock landscape, the sensual, curved hills ending in rocky outcroppings and deserted bays. And I got to hear David — not through an iPod, a Walkman or anything like that, but through the songs of his that I carried in my mind.

I had this feeling (call it a fantasy if you like), that David, the dazed, ravaged sailor-captain of *Calenture*, was somehow cast adrift from this land in the before time. That David was — in simple or complex terms — a reincarnated Celtic Warrior Poet King. A son of the soil, one of Van's voyagers born before the wind, set to sail into the mystic.

Scotch-Irish: that was his lineage, for sure, on the paternal side. This same County of Down where I now tread, had bred his forefathers. This strong sense of David, and of the mark that he had left in the world, just would not quit as I continued on the walk.

A glorious day but nobody around. Out there, away from shore, the water windblown, whipped to occasional white peaks, but not stormy.

The bay I then encountered was like something magical or sacred, enclosed on either side by craggy bladderwrack-strewn rocks. The rusted wrought-iron remnant of a long-gone jetty on the flat sand, inlaid with shingle where the tide had rolled in, was a haven for gulls, curlews, herons and sandpipers.

Looking out across the sea, there were the uninhabited Copeland Islands, and further on the distant blue hills of Scotland. Of course! This was it, the sacred realm, the ancient kingdom of Dalriada, birthplace of Van's *Caledonia Soul Music*, as sung of on the unforgettable 1970 bootleg and improvisational masterpiece of the same name. There was some sort of thrall set up there by Van, a web of wonder, a challenge thrown down to all the artists that have or would try to know 'true Gods of sound and time.'[4]

David was certainly one such: brave and bold, reckless and foolhardy, dedicated enough to the call, to take up the challenge and seek out the artistic homeland of the heart.

Where do you find it, this homeland of the heart, the telltale wounded heart, the organ that holds all the pain, the excitement, the scars of your life? Even on land, so inviting when viewed from afar, it can be hard to negotiate the path to the heartbeat.

It's all a question of balance. When you are younger, you clamber over the rocks, easily confident, gambolling freely. Going down there now — twenty-five, thirty years on — I realize that when you are older and the body has sustained knocks, you are aware of the fragility of bones and self.

Balance, that was the key: finding the balance between the abundance and abandonment of youth, and the care and experience of age.

I felt old, scared of falling on the rocks, scared of losing balance.

Balance — getting the weight and measure of the words, chords, phrasing, the poised interaction of the musicians around him — was something David persistently sought. And, more often than not, he struck that balance in his work.

In Perth he had told me that work was the key; the old Protestant work ethic perhaps gnawing at his core. That was why he'd formed The Blackeyed Susans during the holiday respite in 1989: 'Life's directionless enough as it is without getting up in the morning and having nothing to do,' he told me.

That whole Protestant / Catholic / Loyalist / nationalist / republican face-off in Ireland is crumbling or reconfiguring now. Permanence as an ideal is snuffed out in the light of new dispensations, ruling bodies and the input of foreign power and money.

David described himself as a lapsed Protestant, and in his short life saw a considerable change in his parents. From the Bible-toting religious types who sent him to Sunday School as a child, they became scientists who believed, he told me, that people live on through their genes.

Maybe that's so, but down there on the deserted bay at Orlock I had another feeling of what people did and how they left themselves behind. David would probably laugh or recoil from my cosmic blether, but it was born on the soft wind, whipped up on the waves, coming in on the susurrant ebb and flow of the tide. In my head and in my heart I could feel and hear David's music, curled up, bathed and sanctified — buried deep in love or gnarled and wracked by the salty savagery of the sea.

So yeah I think I knew him, much as you could know anyone. His was a rare blessing — to be able to transmit personal thoughts and feelings through song, character and voice. And those that listened were blessed to be able to hear and feel him.

As time slips away, that blessing just gets deeper.

Blessed Be

David McComb

1.   Blessed be
all smudge, lag and excrement found in me.
I'm grateful should my small deposit
of shed-skin and tumour-worn cells
achieve grace through anonymity;
washed up as detritus grit,
mingled among beach sand,
toddlers' shit
and the bone-granules of dead sea life.

2.   Blessed be
sea urchin, starfish, anemone.
Glory to saltwater that stung.
Honour to pigface, praise to
triumph of tidal residue,
to all drift-scrap dashed by spray.
All hail protean blue.

Tasmania, mid-1990s.

Sean Dower's preliminary sketch for a rainwater-dissolved watercolour, showing Welbeck Court, West London, where several members of The Triffids lived in the 1980s. The artist has rechristened the building 'Triffid Court' and hung unspooled cassette tape in a nearby tree 'as a kind of memorial offering.' For the exhibition *A Temporary Monument for David McComb* (STUK, Leuven, Belgium, 2004), Dower 'transferred all known recordings of David McComb onto cassette tape and suspended the unwound, loose tape in the trees around the venue. The tape fluttered, rustled and glistened in the wind. It hung there as potential — the plight of the romantic being whether anyone notices or listens. There are still probably weather-worn remnants of these tapes drifting around Leuven.'

206

Dressed to kill:
McComb with
costar crony Will
Akers, at a subur-
ban photo shoot,
Melbourne,
April 1998.

Edwardian couple
in the garden
at The Cliffe,
Peppermint Grove.

The Cliffe

Bleddyn Butcher

I have more than the usual amount of money to insulate me against the slings and arrows of outrageous fortune that the Heritage Council might throw at me. I understand there is a sense of nostalgia here, but it is not heritage. Does anyone know who Neil McNeil, Hugh Lance Brisbane, or Harold McComb were? If John Lennon had lived here, or even [Australian wartime Prime Minister] John Curtin, I'd understand that.[1]

In the Passey collection of photographs at the Battye Library of Western Australia, there is a glass plate of an unidentified Edwardian couple 'sitting in the garden of The Cliffe, 2 The Esplanade, Peppermint Grove, overlooking the Swan River.' They're seated some distance from the camera, at the edge of a raised concrete pond. Behind them, the river reaches across Freshwater Bay to Claremont and Dalkeith. At the far horizon, beyond Point Resolution, there's a vague suggestion of Como, or Applecross. To the couple's left and looming above them is a statue of Venus riding her clamshell along the crest of a giant iron-and-brickwork wave … or maybe that's a pedestal. To their right, pampas grass flutters, masking the high fence of what might be a tennis court. The foreground is lawn, bordered with zamia palm. Both parties are formally dressed. The woman is buttoned neck-to-wrist — neck-to-ankle — in white. Her face is concealed by a lace veil, her hands by a muff. A small white flying saucer has crash-landed on top of her head. The man is middle-aged, high-collared, cloth-capped and moustachioed. He's wearing a dark suit and boots, with his arms and legs crossed and a pen or maybe a pipe in his right hand. He's keen-eyed, almost jaunty and looks completely at home. Although the Battye doesn't identify the sitters, it's reasonable to suppose from their attitude and location that they are the owners of the house, Neil

McNeil and his wife Jessie Alexandra Lawrie. McNeil built The Cliffe in 1894, two years after buying the plot, and extended the building in 1898. By 1905, the era of the Passey photograph, he'd no doubt already begun clearing the ten acres of parklands, 'tastefully laid out with lawns and flower-beds, and further beautified by the introduction of decorative statuary in bronze, collected by Mr McNeil on various trips to England and the Continent,' as *The Cyclopedia of Western Australia* admiringly noted in 1913.

McNeil was born in Dingwall, in Ross, in the north-east of Scotland, in 1855, the second son of railway contractor Neil and Elizabeth (née Urquhart) MacNeil [sic]. In 1860, the family moved to Australia, settling in Ballarat, epicentre of the Victorian gold rush and site of the Eureka Stockade rebellion. Ballarat was a much bigger deal than Melbourne in those days, reaching city-size by 1871. After completing his education at Ballarat College, McNeil followed his father's trade. He joined the family firm as a superintendent but soon set up on his own, winning government contracts to build railways in South Australia, Victoria and Tasmania. He arrived in Western Australia in 1882 to supervise construction of the Jarrahdale–Bunbury line.

Jarrahdale was then a mill town, thirty miles south-east of Perth, named for the tall eucalypt which abounded locally. Jarrah, as the first settlers found, is an unusually hard wood, as strong as mahogany and no less weather resistant, making it especially suitable for use in large-scale public works such as bridges, wharves and railways, as well as shipbuilding. For the cash-strapped young colony, jarrah was a valuable resource. When Governor Weld began granting loggers longer leases in the late 1860s, there was an immediate and international demand. By the time McNeil arrived, Jarrahdale had its own rail link to the coast at Rockingham. Extending the public line south to Bunbury would improve general access to the forests, farms, mills and mines of the greater South-West.

McNeil soon acquired timber interests of his own. He began exporting wood to England (where much of it was used to pave London streets) and, demonstrating his confidence in the material, used jarrah throughout when building The Cliffe. In 1897, four years after the Bunbury rail link was completed, he bought the mill at Jarrahdale; in 1902, having obtained a forty-year extension on the timber lease, he joined his holdings to the Millar Brothers' karri concessions. His interests, meanwhile, had begun to diversify: when gold was discovered in Coolgardie in 1892 and then Kalgoorlie in 1893, he invested. He also invested in real estate, buying office buildings in Perth and Fremantle and further lots in Peppermint Grove. Not long after the Passey photograph was taken, he bought 9000 acres on the Blackwood River and an orchard in Mount Barker, just north of Albany. He grew apples and pears in export quantities, and took a keen interest in plums. In 1915, he divided the parklands at the western end of his estate into nineteen residential lots. He died childless in 1927.

Jessie went to live with her sisters, selling The Cliffe and the remains of the estate to Hugh Lance (for Lancelot) Brisbane, who'd come to Western Australia with his Victorian-born Presbyterian parents in 1894. At the time, Brisbane was a thirty-four-year-old sales manager for Wunderlich's clay roofing tiles. In 1933 he passed The Cliffe with its freakish jarrah shingles on to his elder brother David William, a railway engineer and businessman. Within five years, Wunderlich — renamed H.L. Brisbane and Wunderlich Ltd in WA — had become the largest producer of clay tiles in the state. David Brisbane worked in the Federated Malay States until 1942, when he returned to Perth as managing director of the Midland Railway Company, also chairing the board of West Australian Newspapers Ltd, and helping to develop the Kwinana oil refinery. When he died in 1960, his riverside holdings were purchased by Cotswold Investments and subdivided. Five of the six lots were put up for auction in April 1962. The three lots containing The Cliffe, its outbuildings and vegetable gardens, were passed in. Dr Harold McComb, who'd been falsely outbid at the auction, was approached by the agents and gladly agreed to a sale.

Harold McComb was born in Brisbane in 1924, son of Rowland McComb and Kathleen Earnshaw. He studied medicine at Queens College, Melbourne University, and married fellow graduate Dr Athel Hockey in 1947. Athel was born the youngest daughter of Frank Höche, a metallurgist working for BHP, and Kathleen Butler. Athel grew up in Whyalla, South Australia, and Newcastle, New South Wales, before settling in Melbourne. The newlyweds lived in England while Harold studied plastic surgery at Oxford, gaining his fellowship in 1952. Athel, meanwhile, worked as a locum in England and Wales. In 1955, they moved to Western Australia with their young sons, Peter and John, settling in Claremont. Harold was the state's first qualified plastic surgeon and very much in demand. He developed a Surgery and Burns unit at Royal Perth Hospital with Leslie Le Soeuf, and ran similar units at Princess Margaret, Charles Gairdner and Fremantle hospitals. His time was hardly his own. Athel was also working whenever she could. A third son, Robert, was born in 1957. When a fourth boy, David, arrived in February 1962, Harold and Athel knew they'd have to move. Their two-bedroom house in Victoria Avenue was too small for four boisterous boys. The Cliffe had (and, for now, still has) twenty-eight rooms and a large, sheltered garden. Plenty of space to play. Room enough, inside, for a bedroom each. Dining rooms, music rooms, a *scullery*. Wide central hallway. Brass bell to summon the clan to supper. When the McCombs arrived to take possession of their rambling mansion-cum-playground, a bulldozer sat primed in the driveway. The agent thought for sure they'd want to knock the house down and rebuild. After all, it's the Western Australian way.

David absorbed this legend early. His home was old, outdated even. It was made entirely from timber! He heard all about the 'great faith' McNeil had placed in jarrah, and the role the house played in showing off its 'tremendous endurance.' He heard, too, that the local shire council had not been convinced: the Road Board, as it was then called, introduced a 'limestone and/or brick only' building code in 1897: no more all-timber houses. His home had history!

In 1973, as an eleven-year-old, he tried to make sense of it in a school history project on 'The Cliffe and Peppermint Grove'.[2] He traced the story back to the first years of settlement. In 1832 (David gives the date as both 1835 and 1837), the Crown had awarded 256 acres of Swan River frontage to John Butler, an innkeeper who'd established a halfway house on the Perth–Fremantle road. The plot, Swan Location 84, corresponds almost exactly to present-day Peppermint Grove. Butler left the colony in 1836 after a rumoured dispute, but the property remained in his family until his wife's death in 1887. A syndicate joined by the explorer Alexander Forrest then petitioned Governor Broome for permission to survey the estate and divide it into residential plots. The petition was granted and the Butler estate duly surveyed, and the first plot sold at the end of 1891. Among the first residents, David notes, were Edward Keane, former Lord Mayor of Perth, and Sir John Forrest, Alexander's brother, fellow explorer and the newly self-governing colony's first Premier. Other early investors included syndicate members George Leake and Alexander Forrest, D'Arcy Irvine, the syndicate's surveyor, and Neil McNeil. All six built riverside mansions. All six had streets named after them.[3]

Peppermint Grove is Australia's smallest municipality, an exclusive enclave of prime real estate bounded by Freshwater Bay in the east and the Stirling Highway a kilometre or so to the west. This hundred-hectare haven first won municipal status in 1895 when residents led by Shelley Barker petitioned the Premier (Barker's near neighbour) to appoint a Road Board for the locality. The Premier apparently took some convincing but was at length won over. The Board, with Barker at the helm, set about its appointed business, the paving of roads. Leake Street was surfaced first, 'closely followed by the metalling of McNeil Street, View Street' (running north-northeast along the old Perth–Fremantle track), 'and Keane Street.' At this point, before completing what David describes as 'a very necessary work, the metalling of Forrest Street,' the Board ran out of money. A fresh delegation attended the Premier. Reluctantly, once more, the Premier agreed.

'There have been four attempts,' David continues in his next paragraph, 'to amalgamate the various local authorities': 1903, 1912, 1955 and 1973 all saw attempts to merge Peppermint Grove with Buckland Hill (now Mosman Park) and North Fremantle or Cottesloe. All four attempts failed. 'Yet again,' David says of the most recent proposal, 'it was rejected by the Peppermint Grove ratepayers who, evidently for historic and domestic reasons, did not wish to see their identity disappear.'

Wry understatement or recycled platitude? The comment could be either, neither or both. The essay in question was written by a conscientious schoolboy on routine assignment. It's thorough — including house and street plans, and running to over 3000 words but leans too heavily on its sources to reveal much of its author's formative thought or opinion. David sticks, so far as he's able, to the facts. There's no doubt he knows his family's pretty well fixed. He lives in a mansion, with stables servants' quarters and 'an assortion [sic] of sheds' on a massive, rambling block. He quotes appreciatively the *West*

Australian's assessment (dated 15 January 1929) of Peppermint Grove as 'a quiet haven.' Yet, even at the tender age of eleven, David seems to have been uncomfortable with this knowledge, subtly unsure of his ground. He's not even sure, he admits at the outset, that he's chosen a suitable subject: 'although it is 79 years old, [The Cliffe] is not a very historic landmark.' Its history is not very well known — is perhaps not worth knowing. Unlike, say, the Barracks Arch in front of Parliament House in Perth, it's neither tourist attraction nor *cause célèbre*: it's a wooden bungalow tucked away behind a limestone cliff, barely visible from the road. Its position in the everyday life of the shire is similarly inconspicuous, not to say marginal: 'The house is only just in Peppermint Grove,' David worries; 'in fact the borderline runs along our fence.'[4]

Perhaps his research has unnerved him, given him his first glimpse of history's rapacious face. Certainly, listening to his next-door neighbour Tom Bunning — son of Robert Bunning, one of McNeil's fiercest competitors and a Peppermint Grove resident since 1906 — has made a vivid impression on David:

> Sixty years ago fish and crabs were able to be caught in great numbers along the shores of Freshwater Bay. Boys speared flounder in considerable numbers in the early winter. In season they trawled for tailer when the gulls gave unmistakable signs of their presence. Black bream also were caught in the early winter and prawns abounded in season.

These are Arcadian scenes, vivid glimpses of plenty steeped in pellucid nostalgia. David knows he won't see their like. His essay reports an ecological mistake of 1905 — 'Colonel le Souef [le Soeuf, in fact] (the curator of the South Perth Zoo) released a set of twelve kookaburras in the vicinity; these were carnivorous, and soon the native bird population had diminished considerably' — and lists the species lost (robins, blue wrens and kingfishers).[5] It also points out that brumbies, the wild horses which would of a bygone evening appear among the peppermints, are no longer seen. Legend has it they would dig in the sand for fresh water whenever the swamps were dry. David misses those pawky horses. He sees them in his mind's eye.

He remembers the bulldozer, waiting in the driveway: chugging, impatient for change. No sense postponing the inevitable: the house has long since served its purpose. The showpiece has seen better days. Its history is written; over and done. David appears to concur. At least, the essay ends bleakly, on an all-but-hopeless note: 'The Cliffe is an old house, soon to die, as it is becoming weak and is being continually threatened by termites. The once strong roof is rotting away, and there will probably never be another owner, and there is no hope of its being preserved. Nothing is heard of McNeil except, of course, McNeil street, which will be the only memory of the dying face of The Cliffe.' McNeil was the last of the West-Coast Mohicans, a gentle adventurer, 'always willing to help a friend.' The Cliffe is his memorial, an elegant expression of his fading estate, as of the passing of a Golden Age.

David says nothing about his own family nor can he foresee the large part the house will play in the course of his life. He concludes his notes on The Cliffe's history at the point where the McCombs arrive to take possession: 'After [her husband] died, Mrs. Brisbane divided the property, and sold the actual house area to us in 1961' — full stop (except there isn't one). No further detail adduced.

In fact, according to Harold McComb, Mrs Brisbane sold the property to David's sentimental friend Tom Bunning, the power behind Cotswold Investments. 'It was he who planned the subdivision, keeping the choice corner block for himself. The other front block was sold to Sir Frank Ledger (major engineering) and a block on McNeil St was sold to Plunkett (I think).'[6] The front blocks were the site of the tennis courts, east of the house, overlooking the bright panorama of Freshwater Bay: the tennis courts which McNeil had 'stubbornly,' in David's account, refused to surrender when the Road Board sought to extend the Esplanade from the foreshore at Keane Street straight through to Bindaring Parade, and around which, therefore, had been constructed a treacherous slalom, known locally as 'Devil's Elbow'. But the tennis courts, too, were history. The Ledgers dug them up and built an eyesore in cream stucco and orange-clay tile, blocking The Cliffe's views of the bay.

The horizon was shrinking. The bulldozer was closing in.

* * *

Protected for many years by a heritage listing, The Cliffe is owned at present by Mark Creasy, who has often publicly stated his desire to demolish it. On 5 June 2008, in an unprecedented move, the WA Parliament rescinded The Cliffe's heritage listing, against the advice of the State Heritage Council. While the house remains standing for now (albeit, in a state of considerable disrepair after more than a decade of neglect), it appears to be surviving on borrowed time. — Eds

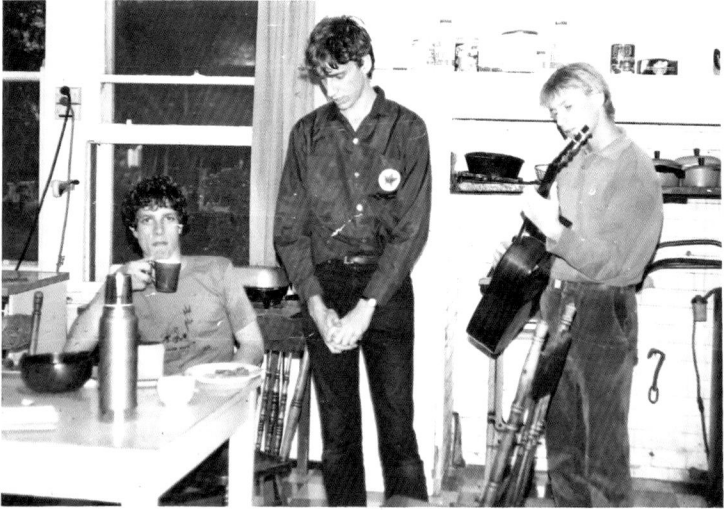

ABOVE: Kids in the kitchen (from left): Alsy MacDonald, David and Robert McComb at The Cliffe, c. 1979.

The Cliffe

Our house
is really quite extraordinary
I think it is a person
Or at least a character, a personality
it is big
& watching
silent, understanding
wise but not an outspoken genius.
It is dark
& calm
smooth, thoughtful
intricate but not rash or sharp.
It is faithful
& omnipresent
in a nice way
seeing all but not being a sticky-beak.
It is a good house
I shall have to talk to it
someday.

By the Thames, early 1990s.

Elegy For

John Kinsella

in memoriam, Dave McComb

Concurrent, we fill the city.
Without, the air is too full
though we break out, as dull
as cotton wool, as sharp as tacks.

A visceral beauty, lipstick
smudge on a glass, knit
as close as shorelight,
dry rasp of wheat-ears.

Heart devout as our sleeves,
flat-out art to taste
the salt of Prevelly Park, laced
with shells that echo.

That's the lyric warped
around the river, higher
function to pleasure,
serenade the sun that grows

on you. We open your eyes
and hear the swell surge
upwards, an urge
to open nocturnes.

It's reputation. The songs
we spool from partial
info. Penitential
rumours, shadows of vocals.

You can't guard flames
in elegies of those you don't
know, of those you can't
pull up on the screen of memory:

which audience we're part of,
which elegy selects success
on the jukebox: a recess
of scores. Freo Doctor

smooths heat, contracts
lengths of summer.
I hear the Prime Minister
defend the Klu Klux Klan

behaviour of his army:
this 'letting off steam'
to melt the dream,
we dance in propaganda.

This is how I relate to you:
'relate', a dirty word
that's grown, a sword
of grammar and syntax.

I passed a house I lived
in — once — yesterday —
cleared away:
development.

I was arrested by a tune
playing over in my head:
obsessive to the point of dead-
head contretemps, living dead

scratching, soon-to-be-dead
tossed about the Freo lock-up,
rag doll aliens, refrain
like sand, bloodstain

in custody; I tell you I witnessed
death washed down the drain;
we cross the Pont, the Seine
with its life-love, its disdain.

Backdrops to write against.
In the cast of space we scored
again. In the cast of space
we hummed the pace

of boomtown and corporate
take-overs, starlings shot down
over the Nullarbor — heading our way,
away, this the end of our stay

as blessed time passes
with each key, in key, a passenger
liner at the quay; who will listen,
fund our croonings again?

Blue verticals, horizontals.
Those double triple quadruple blocks
to join in mansion, a prayer
of rose gardens and river

views, mausoleums and analogies
of travel — locals out — locals
opening night. Up to Four Squares, wander
North, open out. Friends defer

like hauntings, like fashion:
performance: each of us
in each other's pockets
our sleeves, your hearts.

Staving off inevitables,
we watch from ashen tables,
sing higher than Norfolk Pines,
this gifting us, this turning

inside out, an aubade
to sunset, horizon's loud
cicatrice, as soothing as a road
torn wide open:

travel jars the mind
and that's the sign
of the times, the crowd
standing still in flight,

to look out on morning:
good morning, good morning,
and I am reminded
how to know, to listen.

Production still, 'Save What You Can' video shoot, 2006, showing New York artist Steve Keene at work on a wall of paintings inspired by the lyrics and music of The Triffids.

225

Thomas Hoareau, *Lovers (Business as Usual)*, oil on linen, 1988.

Western Australian artist Thomas Hoareau provided artwork for The Triffids' early records 'Spanish Blue' and *Reverie*, and is credited with introducing the term 'calenture' to David McComb. According to the artist: 'David at one time wanted to use this painting for the cover of an album, and kept a reproduction of it framed when he was living in London.'

HOW TO GET TO THE WOOLSHED AT "WOODSTOCK":

① Take Albany highway out of town to Williams.

② After Williams, and after Arthur River take left turn off highway towards Wagin, Newdegate, etc.

③ Pass thru Lake Grace, Lake King, Ravensthorpe.

④ At Ravensthorpe take road to Hopetoun (NOT Esperance).

⑤ About 20 miles after Ravensthorpe turn left at a road, funnily enough, called Lee Rd. It also might say "Woodstock" Lee Rd is a gravel road.

⑥ Three miles down turn right through the white posts to "Woodstock" The woolshed is in the scrub in front of you.

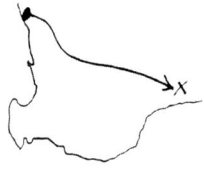

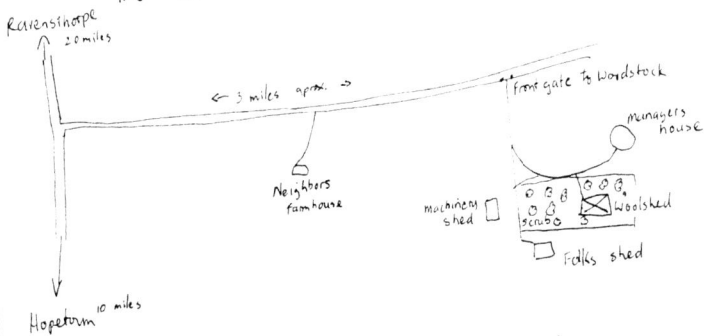

Ravensthorpe
20 miles

← 3 miles aprox. →

front gate to Woodstock

managers house

Neighbors farmhouse

machinery shed

scrub

Woolshed

Folks shed

Hopetown 10 miles

⑦ Welcome. We hope you had a pleasant journey.

David McComb, 'mud map' providing fellow Triffids with directions to the woolshed near Jerdacuttup where *In the Pines* was recorded in 1986.

Unmarked Tracks

The Triffids at WAIT
film and TV studio,
24 January 1983.
One of a series of
shots by future
band member, Jill
Birt.

Happy Wheels

Robert McComb

Although we were very different I always felt close to Dave. We always got on well and never fought, physically at least. Being third and fourth in a family of four boys involved a certain dynamic. Pete, the eldest, forged all the rites of passage with our parents, despite actually going on to study medicine just like them. John followed up with a greater level of freedom and rebellion. I had a relatively easy path and Dave had the trappings of being the youngest. He had a different relationship with Dad than the rest of us, less involved with sporting activities like sailing, which was (and still is) a great passion of Harold's. Dave was closer to Mum. At school he regularly won prizes for English and Religious Studies, but also played hockey. He body-surfed at North Cottesloe Beach, where we spent long summer holidays in the late sixties. He also enjoyed spear-fishing on the reefs off Hopetoun near the family farm.

Our eldest brother Pete was a big Rolling Stones fan, and their early records, along with Eric Burdon and The Animals, were played in the big old wooden house we grew up in: The Cliffe, in Peppermint Grove. By the age of twenty, when Dave was ten and I was fourteen, Peter had married and moved out with his Canadian wife. He finished medical school and took off for the UK and then Canada.

The first single I bought was the double A-sided 'ABC'/'I Want You Back' by The Jackson Five, followed by The Rolling Stones' 'Honky Tonk Women' backed with 'You Can't Always Get What You Want'. Dave and I played these on an old mono record player in a big white cabinet along with other great music like *Cosmo's Factory*, The Beatles' 'White Album', and even some Burl Ives!

I remember on one occasion miming to *Sgt. Pepper's* with Alsy and Dave in one of many rooms at The Cliffe, although this one was specifically a music room at the time. We had Pete's electric guitar and some biscuit tins and chopsticks for a drum kit. I recollect having a tantrum and throwing the drum cymbals (biscuit tin lids) at them for getting out of time. Older brothers will tend to dominate and I did care that we did it right!

Our elder brother John was a big Dylan fan so we had a good dose of that in the seventies, together with his collection of records by Black Sabbath and Rory Gallagher. After John moved out of home, I soon followed and Dave had the place to himself for most of his time at WAIT (Western Australian Institute of Technology, now Curtin University).

The Cliffe was a great house to grow up in. It's an enormous jarrah house of about seventeen rooms with a large cellar and a granny flat, both of which were used for Triffids' rehearsals. We were able to set up our gear with a little vocal PA and have long, productive sessions with tea breaks in the kitchen. We used to get complaints from Mr Carrew-Reid next door when we practised in the cellar, as the noise would pass out through a big ventilation grille. The second song on The Triffids' 5th cassette is titled 'My Next Door Neighbour', something of a dedication to him, in which he's described as a burdened man.

Our father, Harold, is an enthusiastic fan of music, especially Dixieland jazz, classical, and old musicals. He would play tapes like *High Society* or Gilbert & Sullivan operas down at the farm, singing along in full voice and encouraging us to join in. But he was hardly enamoured of our intention to make The Triffids our career. As we were about to leave our jobs and studies in Perth for our first trip to Sydney I remember him saying, 'You'll never be The Beatles.' Later he would give us credit, after hearing positive accounts from the children of his fellow surgeons in the operating theatre. It was, and probably still is, hard for Dad to relate to Dave's artistic creativity. He told me only recently that he thought Dave was ahead of his time.

Dad had a great hi-fi set up in the lounge room, although his Quad electrostatic speakers could not handle the powerful bass and drums of rock music, and would discharge with sparks flying. His Revox tape recorder was used to record all six of The Triffids' early cassette albums, proving to be a valuable piece of equipment.

I was not part of the earliest incarnation of The Triffids. I'd left home and Dave was still at school, hanging around with Alsy and Phil Kakulas as teenage punks, in the most creative ways. I was getting involved with Tiger Mountain Band, a group I met through new friends at college and had joined as a violinist. We did covers and a few of local 'roots' singer Bruce Gilbert's songs. Bruce went on to form many good reggae bands around Perth, and I must say that TMB were not solely a reggae outfit. We did Jackson Browne, Bob Dylan and even some Lou Reed! I quickly moved on to guitar as well as violin when Dennis Byrne left the group and sold me his Hofner semi-acoustic for $100, on the condition that if I ever sold it again it must be to him. I still have it. I played it on The Triffids' 4th and 5th before buying the Fender Telecaster Thinline. About this time, Dave and Phil Kakulas came down to one of our gigs at The Albion in Cottesloe and made polite comments on the set. But I could see that their band with its outright punk stance as well as witty and profound lyrics had so much more to offer. I got The Triffids to play at a couple of parties I held with my girlfriend at the time, Jill Yates. They wore slippers and hung Chinese communist posters behind themselves, playing songs like 'Mark' and 'New Vision', off The Triffids' 1st and 2nd cassette albums.

When Phil Kakulas left The Triffids I offered my services, and Dave accepted but initially only on a 'temporary' basis. I did not mind this stipulation, as I was happy to be involved with what was so obviously, to me, the most creative band in the world. My technical abilities (although I only got to fifth-grade violin and taught myself guitar) were seen as a distinct risk in light of the 'punk' sensibilities of the time. Dave would keep a very tight rein on any clichés, disparaging anything that vaguely resembled The Eagles or Eric Clapton, and I would be given strict instructions for almost every song. Dave clearly enjoyed having the violin to carry some melodic lines. My ability to arrange gigs also helped to establish my role. Before I joined The Triffids they had played lunchtime gigs at Christ Church Grammar School chapel, friends' parties, and a Victims' benefit gig in Leederville — The Victims, featuring Dave Faulkner, being Perth's leading punk outfit in those days — but never pub gigs. Dad undertook parental taxi duties at Leederville. The first gig I remember playing with The Triffids was Hernando's Hideaway, with The Scientists. Kim Salmon was very supportive and I knew Ben Juniper who was playing with them at the time. The other very early gig we did was at The Stoned Crow in Fremantle. I knew some people who were working behind the bar and managed to score us a residency. The management paid us fifty dollars and we charged fifty cents on the door, a cover charge which soon rocketed to a dollar.

I remember our rehearsals as being quiet and productive, but Marty has reminded me that when he joined the band he could not believe how rudely we spoke to each other during the arrangement and rehearsal of songs. Being brothers, and Alsy a virtual brother, we didn't stand on ceremony when it came to discussing what was good or bad in our playing, and Marty was astounded at the forthrightness of our interaction. For instance, I was quite used to Dave telling me, in no uncertain terms, not to dare try any tasteless guitar licks. This dynamic is surely part of what helps good bands develop, and to have a clear, shared objective.

Dave was always amazing to work with. He had a totally inspiring vision of each song, whether fully realized or not, and would always have new material to work on, as well as a current set list. Some songs would be presented as completed works, with all parts quickly demonstrated and others as either partially complete or tentatively arranged. Dave always sought a faithful interpretation of his ideas, but also encouraged group involvement in the final solution of a song, without ever losing sight of that original vision. This was particularly true with rhythms, and Alsy would often try a variety of beats until one emerged to suit a song. Dave managed to develop a real 'group' ethos and to project everyone's talent, despite his clear leadership role.

We were all totally committed to the band. We survived off a minimum allowance and part-time jobs. When we left Perth the band wage started at fifty dollars a week and stayed that way until we went overseas. Eventually, in the last few years of the eighties, we achieved a whopping $200 weekly allowance. All the rest of the money we made was poured into recording, equipment, bus fares, airfares and accommodation.

During the early years in Perth, Dave was studying at WAIT while I worked for the Division for the Intellectually Handicapped as a social trainer. We mainly performed shows on the weekend at places like Alberts' Tavern in Nedlands or Adrian's nightclub in Northbridge. The band line-up changed a lot, with Alsy deciding at one point to leave for study at university. This was a real shock and I almost expected Dave not to go on without his childhood friend and musical sounding board. Instead, he was quite businesslike and we found a replacement drummer, Mark Peters. Mark was a jazz fanatic and after a short while we made plans to replace him. He insisted on fifty dollars a week, which was more than an even division of our modest profits at the time. Luckily, Alsy gave word to Dave that he had changed his mind, resuming his place after a suitable time without any dramas. I know that Dave was very pleased to get Alsy back. We also acquired Margaret Gillard on keyboards, all due to Dave's planning.

Dave always viewed the band from a global perspective and had an awareness of our broader significance. There were frustrating moments of synchronicity too. I remember Dave being annoyed when he listened to The Only Ones and heard in one of their songs the exact same chord progression that he had used for one of his.

The fans we attracted at those early gigs were incredibly important. We would know, or get to know, just about everybody in the room, often no more than fifty people. It was as much a social scene as a musical one. There were many parties associated with WAIT people. We operated outside of what music industry there was at the time, getting our own gigs, doing handbills. There were other bands doing much the same, such as The Scientists and The Manikins, although we didn't often do gigs together.

After playing in Perth for three years and saving as much money as we could, we headed for Sydney. It could have been Melbourne, but Jill Yates had set up home in Sydney and I could stay with her, and that was a start. When we got to Sydney, Margaret and our sound guy Jason decided they had fallen in love and wanted to go back to Perth. This was just before our very first Sydney gig. We enlisted the help of Jill Yates on keyboards, and she accompanied us on a tour of Melbourne. In Sydney we were lucky to meet Sally Collins, who was managing The Sunnyboys at the time and gave us supports at big underage shows. We did our own poster runs and stepped on a few toes of the local promoters by covering theirs with ours. We either didn't know what a cut-throat industry pub-rock advertising was, or more likely did it to get attention.

After the first trip to Sydney — which had been made in my Kombi van, which could not make the journey again — we bought 'Happy Wheels', a second-hand Toyota Hi-Ace van named after a silly television commercial. I remember one occasion when Alsy used Happy Wheels to help a friend move house in Sydney. At that time we kept all of our effects pedals, leads and electric gadgets in a big plastic rubbish bin. Alsy had unloaded some of the gear from the van and absentmindedly left the bin by the side of the road. He soon realized and drove back to find the street full of empty bins; the garbage truck had just made its round. The Triffids headed out to Lucas Heights rubbish dump on the outskirts of Sydney, a massive landscape of stinking mountains, to search for our equipment. We consulted with the staff and waded through the most likely pile for a bit before accepting the needle-in-a-haystack reality. Another little blow to our cause.

We would return to Perth periodically from here on, but largely to rest and do profitable shows. Now with an established following and low overhead costs we would save up for our next venture, which would be Europe. We crossed the nation by road too many times to remember; two or three of us in Happy Wheels and others taking their turn on the killer bus trip.

The focus for the band was always the next record. Playing and touring were obviously important, but our hard work and thriftiness were directed towards the goal of self-funded recording. Apart from our first single, 'Stand Up' — the result of studio time won in a 6NR radio competition — we paid for all our recordings (hence the numerous midnight-to-dawn sessions, when studio time is cheaper). Dave was incredibly prepared for all sessions. He would have track lists and production notes in one of his many notebooks. I remember one of these notebooks, containing all the work for *Treeless Plain*, had a narrow escape on a trip from Frankston to St Kilda, in Melbourne. We had just got back from playing with The Uncanny X-Men at The Pier Hotel (a Premier Agency gig) when Dave, panic-stricken, realized he had left his notebook on the roof of Happy Wheels after we'd loaded the gear in Frankston. He rushed out to find his notes scattered around The Prince of Wales Hotel car park, a speed-bump having finally dislodged the notebook from the roof of the van. Dave was lucky that day!

When he was nine years old, I tried to explain to my son Max about a band I was in back in the eighties. He asked, 'What happened to all the money?' — which I thought very insightful, even if he was only quoting Bart Simpson (from the episode in which Homer joins The B-Sharps). I tried to explain that it wasn't about the money, that it was more of a quest or something like a fellowship.

That was when he understood: it was like Frodo and his band of friends.

In the pines: The Triffids on campus at WAIT, January 1983.

Everybody has to eat: Robert McComb preparing a band meal, The Prince of Wales Hotel, St Kilda, late 1982.

Noise Works

Niall Lucy

This piece is based on an interview I did with David McComb and Alsy MacDonald in about 1988. Twice it was due to be published in Sydney music magazines of the time, only for the magazines to go bust, one after the other, before the issue it was scheduled to appear in came out. It was then set to appear in a Melbourne music paper, which also folded suddenly prior to publication; so I gave up trying. Although, mysteriously, a version has been available on the Internet for several years, the piece is published here officially for the first time.—NL

We are what we consume. Our pleasures speak for us. Out of everything we choose some things: to get married, to be a yuppie, to never grow up.

'It's like dancing about architecture,' says David McComb. 'Have you heard that phrase? If possible, it's best to keep your terminology reasonably under control.'

Just keep the message simple and factor out the contradictions: don't confuse advertising with art …

But it's hard to keep even your patience under control against the clamour coming from outside a grimy coffee shop in the heart of Sydney's inner-city Newtown on a busy Friday afternoon. An endless stream of trucks and buses changing gears at the traffic lights on King Street sets up a powerful interference pattern in the process that changes thoughts into words. McComb and his close friend Alsy MacDonald, who together formed The Triffids over a decade ago in their home town of Perth, have to struggle to be heard.

'We've never tried to present ourselves as something that's very graceful or has, you know, a beautiful form,' MacDonald explains. 'It's just not really our way. We realized quite soon on that we were never going to excel like that.'

'Right. I think you can be specific about it,' McComb agrees from behind very dark sunglasses as the traffic surges by outside. 'I mean, ungainly rhythms are a part of it, of what The Triffids are about. Ninety-nine percent of pop music these days is about having absolute regularity of rhythm, having a metronomic beat.' His eyes are hidden but his voice just rises above the raucous symphony of cars braking and accelerating in the street, asserting itself over the clatter of coffee cups and chatter of other voices in the café.

'Whereas The Triffids might occasionally glance into that, basically I think our music is about surges, is about crescendo, is about beats which resemble spasms. It's immediately why we gravitated towards 3/4 time, why we have this long bunch of songs starting with "Too Hot to Move" and "Red Pony" and going right the way through to "Jerdacuttup Man" which are in 3/4 time or 6/8 time.

'That's been really important to The Triffids: it's an anti-streamlining thing which heightens the storytelling effect of the lyric.'

The danger, of course, is that these songs might be dismissed as overwrought with passion. 'Well, it does get read that way by our detractors,' McComb nods. 'Often, to be quite racist, often English people have an inability to cope with emotion, the display of emotion in music. I've really noticed it when we — and I hope this won't seem patronizing — but when we went to Greece and Italy, you know, it's just taken much more naturally that you would create music that way: it seems completely natural to be really open and dramatic. What English people might call melodramatic, that sort of passion.

'I mean, after all, that's the most effective thing that music is for, really, as a vehicle for passion.'

McComb picks up his coffee cup and stares off into the street, leaving MacDonald to parry the question of how The Triffids see themselves in relation to what the media calls Oz Rock.

'Well, it's extremely marketable, but what it actually is I don't think anyone really knows. It's something that's almost created artificially to deliver overseas.

'I think Australia is finding out very quickly, very shrewdly, that things Australian have to be marketed: they don't generate their own interest. To most of the rest of the world things from Australia have to be sold to them, they don't go out of their way to find out about it. It's handed to them on a platter.

'And I think we have managed to avoid selling the idea that we're Australian.'

'I think it's the great challenge of the moment,' McComb resumes, 'to reflect the location where you come from without degenerating into clichés. It's quite different if you come from America where you're just tapping into whatever Chuck Berry wrote, whereas in Australia you've got this very daunting, but very inspiring, impossible task: to create a new vernacular. Or create something without degenerating into caricature that can reflect, you know, a sense of place.'

Therein lies the rub: how to lower your voice and still be heard above the noise?

'The whole thing with music of the last six years, I suppose, is the idea of the group shedding members to become a two-person Eurythmics-type, you know, a dual-haircut band,' McComb argues. 'And they record albums with samplers and stuff and then go on tour with session musicians. That's a definite sort of pressure on all groups these days because you've got the technology which means that you only need two people.

'But any band that can survive this process — a large band like The Triffids with six members — and manage to adapt to technology in the way that we are only beginning to, and yet not become an anachronism … if we can do that then I think we'll be in a very special position. Because we'll be one of the few bands that have sort of stuck around and haven't been repackaged, and yet aren't playing sixties music.

'I think it's important that someone does that.'

We are what we consume.

Our pleasures speak for us.

'I don't think we'll ever get to the stage where The Triffids can use technology expertly,' MacDonald says while the other is throwing back the last of his long black. 'I mean, we don't really have the knowledge and the skill to make it sound as smooth and acceptable as people are used to hearing it nowadays. So in a way that works for us because we

Jill — hope you like our parcel of junk — I thought you deserved something a bit more interesting than just a standard letter.
Speaking of which, I think my last actual letter to you was fairly dreadful. We had just moved in and I was very tired and looking on the black side of things. Feeling much better now, although I certainly don't possess a special affection for Sydney
It has many drawbacks as a place. Anyway, this is not a letter, it's a junk-parcel
Keep laughing, Dave. xxxooo

PS— we are making Triffids hankies and T-shirts (like the cover of the record) so if anyone wants them, let us know.

PPS— Niall Lucy may be writing an article about us for the National Times. Whoopee!

PPPS — We are watching a Clark Gable movie on TV right now, it is raining but not yet cold (although I'd like it to be). We are headlining in Newcastle this weekend, for god's sake. why.

David McComb, tidings from Sydney, 1983.

Alsy and Dave, Marlborough Street, Surry Hills, 1983.

sort of stumble in the dark a lot of the time, and can come up with some really good sounding things.'

'Everything that you like that comes out', McComb adds, 'you can't just change the band to adapt to that. You just have to realize your limitations.'

Which is not to say The Triffids are deaf to the virtues of contemporary dance music because of any piety for the past. As always, their live set takes in a cover version of The Velvet Underground's 'Pale Blue Eyes'. But it also currently includes Madonna's 'Into the Groove', cutting against the grain of what an audience expects will be a shared experience.

Madonna and The Velvet Underground are too many worlds apart to be contained by the reassuring notion that The Triffids have a unified vision in any sense which doesn't turn that notion into a problem.

'Yeah. Well, that's like it's a vision which encompasses aggression and tenderness', McComb says. 'If it has those two things does that mean it's not one vision? I find no emotion real, in any art form, unless it's present with its opposite. I mean, that's why you don't get many great love songs which are just completely saccharine: there's often a tinge of hatred or bitterness to, ah, make things pop into relief.'

McComb leans back in his chair, still wearing the dark glasses that give him the power to see without being seen. They reveal only what he wants to show, and that's anybody's guess. But despite the noise, the impertinence of being interviewed, the fear of not having anything to say, he's firmly in control.

'We have more power to do what we want now than, say, seven years ago', he stresses, as if addressing a shareholders' meeting. 'We have more power to move around the world and we have more power over our sound. You know, simple as that.

'The ultimate sort of goal, really, is to have that sort of power.'

Ten years could seem like forever to be playing in the same band and still making records. But McComb and Alsy MacDonald are too impatient to reflect on the past for long, since the future is so full of promise.

As the noise continues unabated, it's a wide open road …

iTunes eat
your heart out.
Promotional
artwork by
Martyn P. Casey.

McComb's Ambivalent Romanticism

Wilson Neate

Over the years, critics and fans have tended to frame David McComb's work with The Triffids by drawing on aesthetics associated with an idea of romanticism: an oversimplified privileging of sensibility over intellect, emotion over reason, together with significant investments in such notions as self-expression, artistic originality, spontaneity, authenticity and transcendence. In fact, McComb's artistic accomplishment displays a complex, ambivalent relationship with what might be called the tenets of romantic ideology. That is to say, certain aspects of romantic aesthetics are useful for approaching McComb's work, not simply because of the ways in which it embodies them but, more importantly, because of how it departs from them.

One of the few book-length studies to trace rock music's connections to these aesthetics is Robert Pattison's *The Triumph of Vulgarity: Rock Music in the Mirror of Romanticism* (1987). According to Pattison, rock's blend of African-American blues with a celebration of youth, energy and authenticity recycles motifs found in the work of Wordsworth, Rousseau and Whitman, albeit in a mass-cultural context. As an American cultural form, however, Pattison contends that rock is more intimately linked to Whitman's populist pantheism, which locates the divine in the here and now of the physical world in contrast to the English romantics' affirmation of transcendence. In rock's 'vulgar' version of this pantheism, the celebration of all aspects of our environment as manifestations of the divine succumbs to an egocentric impulse that reduces everything to the purpose of fulfilling the desires of the self. While Pattison could be accused of over-generalizing here, his study is useful all the same for accentuating what I see as a key dynamic in McComb's work. Doubtless Pattison would view McComb as a stereotypical, narcissistic 'rocker,' driven by the desire for gratification and pleasure, but McComb's music isn't a purely sensual celebration and satisfaction of the self. Rather, it attempts to achieve some form of transcendence in the English romantic sense even as it displays an awareness of failing to achieve that state. McComb's music occupies the uneasy space between the recognition that the here and now is all there is and a constant striving for something more. That tension between a desire for transcendence and a feeling of being bounded by an embodied, material existence is far from a shallow delight in the physical, as envisaged by Pattison, and indeed this aspect of McComb's work is something that Pattison's aesthetics of rock don't adequately accommodate or explain.

Authenticity and cultural identity

> Australia's finest export since Swan Lager …[1]

In Anglophone popular music, authenticity is inextricably linked, at some level, to a performer's origins and background. In the most obvious cases of contemporary urban British and American music, such as rap and grime, the relationship is arguably transparent. Barring the possibility of a highly calculated and cynical performance, the identity and the appeal of artists like 50 Cent, Eminem, Dizzee Rascal and Lady Sovereign are constructed around the notion that the real person and his or her artistic persona are one and the same. That connection is cemented by the artist's constant reference to his or her lived experience and ongoing self-identification in terms of ethnicity and class. This articulation of identity in and around the work of certain artists provides critics and fans with a readymade narrative of authenticity, a statement of who the artist is and — quite literally — where they're coming from and where they're at. While the most obvious examples of an appeal to authenticity as a criterion of artistic value occur in predominantly black urban musics, a similar dynamic plays out in staunchly white contexts, as the nineties' Blur/Oasis rivalry demonstrated. The response of the fiercely working-class Gallagher brothers to Blur's *Parklife* was to accuse Damon Albarn and his band of being Southern 'middle-class wankers' who were slumming it. Albarn responded with a jibe that reframed authenticity in exclusively musical terms, comparing Oasis to Britain's dullest blues-rock regurgitators,

Status Quo — perhaps the worst insult that can be levelled against a group.[2]

In these terms, authenticity would seem to have little relevance to The Triffids, whose founding members came from privileged, white, middle-class, suburban backgrounds which they neither concealed nor foregrounded. The politics of identity were not an issue for McComb, whose sense of self was not at stake in the same way that it might be for a black, inner-city artist, and The Triffids' music displayed no instantly obvious link with any one region or nation. In fact, the band's music largely drew from an eclectic range of foreign influences: American blues, folk and country; fifties girl groups; sixties psychedelia; Dylan and The Velvet Underground; seventies New York punk; and even eighties rap and hip-hop at the end of the group's career. However, if The Triffids did not make a specific identity central to their music, one was quickly constructed for them, most clearly in the British music press, which shaped the narrative of who The Triffids were and where they were from. Although neither the band nor their music manifested any deep sense of cultural difference, the media narrative often sought to focus on precisely that dimension, identifying The Triffids as Australian in lazy and superficial ways. Articles published in the UK music weeklies frequently incorporated a generalized statement on the band's origins that amounted to little more than a recycling of clichés exposing limited Northern Hemisphere knowledge and attitudes: references to flora, fauna, barbecues, beer, ocker stereotypes and a handful of the usual Antipodean pop-culture suspects. As late as 1989, the *NME*'s Gavin Martin described The Triffids as 'an Australian export to match Fosters, XXXX and Dame Edna Ever[a]ge.'[3]

If the British music press wanted to situate The Triffids as Australian, then *Born Sandy Devotional* appeared to make that task somewhat straightforward. Immediately striking is the jacket photograph, an aerial shot of a coastal inlet and its small shoreline community, framed by blue sea, white sand, arid fields and dark green bush. Few cover images resonate so strongly with a record's lyrics and sound as the expansive, light-filled environment captured on this sleeve. Indeed, in one of the most eloquent and perceptive pieces written on The Triffids, Bleddyn Butcher characterizes the album as 'tangibly indigenous, evoking both the look and the mood of the Lucky Country.'[4] Interestingly, however, an entry in a notebook kept by McComb during the preparation of the record reveals that while he had an idea of the image he wanted for the cover, he did not have a concrete location in mind: 'Cover of "Devotional", he wrote, 'postcard-type (aerial?) picture of a beach — blue water, white sand (deserted) covering whole cover …'[5] Despite this initial non-specificity, a note on the album sleeve links that image to a very particular place: 'The cover photo shows the West Australian township of Mandurah in 1961.' Such a connection between The Triffids' music and their homeland was nothing new, of course. The title of the band's debut album, *Treeless Plain*, transliterates the Nullarbor Plain, the 7200-square mile expanse of desert with which The Triffids developed familiarity in the early years as they trekked east in search of broader exposure. That landscape would play a prominent role in the band's history and mythology and, as Butcher notes, its presence is certainly felt on *Born Sandy Devotional*.

Not surprisingly then, at the time of *Born Sandy Devotional*'s release (and through its reissues), Australian and non-Australian critics alike often associated the album with The Triffids' homeland, in terms of both music and lyrics. In a 1986 *Sounds* article, Jonh Wilde commented that 'The Triffids are more Australian than most, in their sound as well as their outlook.'[6] The *NME*'s Dele Fadele called *Born Sandy Devotional* 'an indirect lovesong of an album to [The Triffids'] native Australia.'[7] For the *Irish Times*, Sinéad Gleeson described the record as 'filled with parched images of the late David McComb's rural Australia; landscapes that are reflected in songs of isolation, love and despair.'[8] Writing in the *West Australian*, Ray Purvis said: 'Many of the songs … have the same light, space, suffocation, languidness and ennui of the WA coast during the long summer months.'[9] In the British webzine *GodisintheTV.com*, Jenna Leonard articulates how many non-Australian critics approach the album: '*Born Sandy Devotional* … is similar to how *we imagine* the landscape of Australia: nothing for miles, sparse, empty and lonely.'[10]

When discussing his work with UK journalists in the mid-eighties, McComb did occasionally underscore the importance of The Triffids' cultural identity, contrasting his attitude with that of other recent Australian imports: 'When the Birthday Party came to England,' he told Jonh Wilde, 'it was as though they rejected everything about

Australia and that's still quite an Australian thing to do. We've actually been eager to talk about Australia, we're not going to pretend we've come from Mars.'[11] Comparing *Born Sandy Devotional* with *Calenture* in an interview with Paul Mathur, McComb was even more emphatic about the band's identity and the ways it manifested itself: '*Born Sandy Devotional* ... was much more to do with West Australian imagery and had a much stronger sense of place. A picture of the place [is] on the cover saying "*This* is a record concerning *this* area of the world." '[12] However, it's important to note that although McComb's songs may often appear to be grounded in the geography of his homeland, the latter is also a context amid which greater dramas play out, dramas that have a broader reach. There is no reason that these two levels of meaning should not coexist, and in interviews McComb accommodated that possibility. For instance, in his *Sounds* interview with Wilde, while insisting on his Australianness, he also maintained that *Born Sandy Devotional* was about 'Anywhereland.'[13]

If critics have sought to highlight the band's authenticity by pursuing the links between The Triffids' music and Australianness, a tendency among fans has occasionally bristled at such an approach, as if any attention to geographical specificity undermines a true appreciation of the universal greatness of McComb's work. Both positions remain within the parameters of romantic discourse. The fans' response (to which I'll return momentarily) is interesting in that it uncovers a more acute anxiety about the worth of the music, an anxiety that seeks to raise it above the vulgar realm of popular culture and to consider it in the transcendent context of its greater artistic value, spiritual resonance or emotional power. Dave Simpson's review of the 2006 *Born Sandy Devotional* reissue triggered such a reaction when he commented that McComb's 'lyrics seem rooted in the Australian outback.'[14] Triffids fans, as represented by participants in the forum on the band's website, disagreed with Simpson's observation. In their view, he and other critics are mistaken when they connect the band's sound with a particular context because such a perspective overlooks the transcendent quality of McComb's work. Forum member Urpal posts: 'This repeated linking of *BSD* to the Australian outback like it's some sort of aural geography lesson ... really gets on my tits. The songs are no more about the Australian outback than "By the Time I

Get to Phoenix" is about a road journey across America.'[15] In a similar vein, Urpal suggests: 'The album may have come from a particular place but it deals with moments we all have stored somewhere in our memory — and it taps into them through a force of imagery and emotional depth lacking in most literary art.'[16]

Such appeals to universality notwithstanding, 'Wide Open Road' — one of the 'ultimate Australian' songs, according to a 2001 Australasian Performing Right Association poll — is described in the Australian ABC-TV documentary *Long Way to the Top* as both 'a subtle search for national identity' and 'the moody music of authentic experience.'[17] In an *Option* magazine interview, McComb himself seems to concur: 'It was written on the road in Australia so it's 100% real experience.'[18] Moreover, anticipating the master narrative of *Long Way to the Top*, the intention behind 'Wide Open Road' was to 'evoke Australia without all these clichés and Men At Work-isms.'[19] In deference to the cult of authenticity: 'You have to battle between the caricature and the truth all the time, and sometimes it's very tempting to settle for the caricature.'[20] McComb was keen to articulate what he felt to be genuinely authentic, essential identity, and the pursuit of that identity led him to an exploration of Australianness on a deeper level. As Butcher writes: 'The stories [McComb] tells disturb the Ocker image and contemplate the desolate soul within.'[21]

If *Born Sandy Devotional* was grounded in a recognizable part of the world, then *Calenture* — partly due to the band's own growing experience of rootlessness — deals with what McComb calls 'an absence of a sense of place.'[22] It's this absence, paradoxically, that lies at the heart of his concern with identity and fuels his desire to represent it. Beneath the clichés often trotted out by other artists, there is an anxiety about the lack of a national identity and it's that deep-rooted unease which, for McComb, is characteristically Australian. He discussed this in several interviews, commenting to Jonh Wilde, for example, that Australians were 'hung up about not having an identity, not having a culture as such.'[23] More bluntly, he told Adam Sweeting: 'In Australia, you honestly get a complete sense of just nothingness.'[24] Again, Butcher offers the most articulate account of McComb's relationship with Australianness: 'I recognise the landscape, and not just that. David has also begun to examine a peculiarly Australian malaise, the hedonist's hangover. His songs offer disturbing glimpses into the national psyche, finding an *emptiness*. … Abandoning received images of Ocker culture suggests a search for a more complex understanding of national culture … [and] the vision that emerges is unsettling.'[25]

Although McComb rues the paucity of cultural images, his primary objective is not so much to propose an identity or even to offer authentic representations to challenge popular stereotypes such as those informing the musings of journalists in the British music press. Rather, his work comprises something of a metadiscourse, concentrated on the difficulty of representing that perceived absence. As he mentioned to the *NME*'s Gavin Martin: 'It's something that's very inspiring and infuriating about this place — there's nothing to write about and yet nothing's been written about it.'[26] Aware as McComb is of the problems involved in articulating an essential identity, he is nevertheless drawn back to a sense of there actually being a pure, traditional identity that can be expressed. He wants to believe in the possibility of representing a national self but feels he doesn't have the cultural credentials to do so. For example, he recognizes that there is a Western Australian identity to be articulated and he mentions novelist Tim Winton as someone who does this well, expressly because of his first-hand experience of that culture: '[Winton]'s lived here longer than I have and hung around the beaches and the bush so he can write *authentically* about what it's like to be amongst all this. But I can't go on writing about "Wide Open Roads" because I only occasionally go down one.'[27] This points to a fundamental ambivalence on McComb's part as, elsewhere, he deplores that 'myth of honesty' by which certain artists are accorded 'some special status' within the rock formation; adding, in terms of his own career as a writer, performer and recording artist, that 'it's not enough just to knock it out in the bogus name of spontaneity.'[28]

The Triffids' final studio album, *The Black Swan*, underscores the ambivalence at play here as McComb goes back and forth, embracing and rejecting essentialist discourse. The album's title refers to the state emblem of Western Australia, but in interviews McComb also links it to the Thomas Mann novel of the same name.[29] The album's title is thus emblematic of the tension between a desire for rootedness and a simultaneous rejection of an essential identity. The diverse sound of *The Black Swan* conveys this tension. McComb explained the record's sonic eclecticism as a reaction against what he saw as rock's trend towards homogeneity: 'I think we were totally despondent that pop music didn't evoke a place, a spirit or an atmosphere anymore. Whether it came from Sydney or San Francisco it seemed to have a very common guideline, working to a strict equation.'[30] Ironically, McComb appeared to be suggesting that music *should* have an essential, individual identity, one that is linked to its place of origin. On *The Black Swan*, though, The Triffids don't construct *one* sonic persona that connects the band with a particular place but, instead, rehearse and perform a number of different cultural identities. The record is postmodern in its mix-and-match of styles and traditions: there are numerous non-indigenous elements, such as tango, opera, hip-hop, rap and thirties European cabaret, alongside songs like 'Too Hot to Move, Too Hot to Think' that critics and fans have described as being evocative of Perth.[31] In this way, the record embodies an ongoing contradiction as McComb apparently criticizes contemporary music's depthlessness or lack of rootedness in the context of globalization, but conversely, his music displays so much cultural cross-dressing that it denies the possibility of stable identities or origins.

Amid this free play of identities, ambivalence persists. McComb believed he was no longer equipped to write convincingly about aspects of his own culture, and yet *The Black Swan* is brimming with music from traditions with which McComb certainly had no native familiarity. In interviews at the time of the record's release, he baulks at what he feels to be the spurious idea that one must be part of a culture to create art about it. He wants to have it both ways: he claims he's not qualified to write about aspects of contemporary Western Australia and yet he happily incorporates elements from African-American and Latin traditions, where the stakes for authenticity are considerably higher and the politics of identity far more rigorous.

In an interview with Jon Casimir, McComb addresses these issues, referring explicitly to the notion of an essential identity and the idea of authenticity as it pertains to performing music that is part of one's tradition: 'OK, so we don't have the right to do Spanish music or music with a hip-hop drum program because we're from Perth and we don't have the cultural credentials. Fuck it! We do it. That's how the best music works, by people who aren't qualified just getting out there and doing it. Of course, there's some brilliant stuff which is genuinely pure too.'[32] Ultimately, McComb is arguing for a more progressive model of culture — 'I'm a great believer in one form of music infecting another and revitalising it' he submits, in defence of *The Black Swan*'s eclecticism[33] — but at the same time he reinscribes familiar old terms such as 'genuinely pure', 'emotional' and 'real.'

While *The Black Swan* foregrounds McComb's appropriation of non-native musical forms, previous Triffids records displayed a similar tendency, albeit in less boldly adventurous terms. Almost from the outset, The Triffids looked to American music for inspiration. Inevitably, even when McComb contemplated the Australian psyche, he was doing so through the lens of another culture's music — or as Mat Snow put it, The Triffids 'prob[ed] … deeper into American roots music as a way to say something about their own turf.'[34] This is, of course, the practice of almost every band to have worked in the rock idiom; populist narratives of authenticity place great stock in artists whose music purportedly remains closer to what are deemed rock's original roots. Ironically, that judgement overlooks such artists' distant, heavily mediated relationship with that supposedly original tradition. As Gracyk points out, it's historically inaccurate to claim even that the majority of black American artists in the fifties enjoyed an unmediated relationship with a source tradition.[35] Even so, McComb's music was always closely aligned with American artists. While British punk originally galvanized The Triffids into action, the band was listening more closely to US groups such as The Velvet Underground, Dylan and New York punk rock of the mid-seventies. By the time of *The Black Swan*, as well as dabbling in Latin American and European styles, McComb was immersed in contemporary African-American urban music.

Although American influences are always at the root of any rock band's sound, McComb's lyrics also looked in that direction for literary models. He spoke of his fondness for contemporary Australian poets and prose writers, but his work also exhibited an interest in American literature, gravitating, like Nick Cave's, towards a Southern 'gothic' imaginary. In McComb's songs, this comes across not only in the physical landscape but in the characters who inhabit it and the mood that colours it; he combines something of Carson McCullers' focus on marginal figures, isolated within their communities, and Flannery

O'Connor's grotesque sensibility, sense of menace and thematization of spiritual crisis. This influence is apparent in a song like 'Chicken Killer', with its intimations of madness, violence and ostracism.

The negotiation of national and cultural identities in McComb's music is by no means unique to his work. Rather, it attests to the power of the ideology of authenticity that has permeated the culture of rock music, influencing the assumptions of performers, critics and fans alike. Wittingly or unwittingly, McComb is operating under impossible romantic assumptions and his work is unable either to live up to them or to reject them completely. This anxiety further manifests itself in McComb's thinking about the creative process itself and in critics' and fans' discussions of his artistic identity. These are the topics to which I turn in the following section, examining how McComb's music calls into question romantic notions of authorship and creative identity.

Authorship and creative identity

> The biggest joy/spur is the perverse question hanging over my head 24 hours per day — am I of the stuff of greatness, or am I just another of the thousands of ugly, despicable beings in their bedrooms clutching glasses of vodka, with a bunch of filthy exercise books …[36]

Invariably, the romantic artist is cast as a solitary visionary whose work represents a spontaneous outpouring of the emotions following an encounter with the sublime. In his preface to *Lyrical Ballads*, Wordsworth developed one of the best-known accounts of romantic creativity. According to his formulation, the artist's experience of the sublime inspires poetry, but the subsequent creative act is intensely meditative and reflective as the artist, after the fact, articulates the emotions prompted by that transcendental encounter: 'Poetry is the spontaneous overflow of powerful feelings: it takes its origin from emotion recollected in tranquillity.'[37] Just as academics and rock critics have often appropriated a romantic myth of the artistic genius and his heroic creative process, Triffids fans likewise embrace that ideology quite fervently in their discussion of McComb's work.

With regard to the emotional dimension of his work, McComb himself was typically ambivalent. While all evidence points to a meticulous, crafted and cultured songwriting process, he told Jonh Wilde:

'I don't rate intelligence as top of the hierarchy of what music should be; I rate physically violent emotion as the highest thing.'[38] Moreover, talking about 'Wide Open Road', he contended, 'you can have 17 billion hours of semiotic argument about the metaphorical content of a song, but if it doesn't make you cry into [your drink], it isn't worth anything.'[39] Triffids forum members echo these sentiments, frequently appealing to his work's emotional aspect in their commentary. For instance, forum member vpsaarinen writes: 'The thing that makes [*Born Sandy Devotional*] so special to me is that it is just so full of recognisable emotions, emotions that ring true, not mere playacting as often is the case with popular music.'[40] According to the logic of this statement, McComb — an artist working in the medium of popular music — is distinguished from other popular musicians because of the authentic emotional tenor of his work. In a subsequent post, vpsaarinen goes further, connecting what he sees as The Triffids' *real*, *emotional* gravitas with the idea of true artistic achievement: 'The fact that Dave's songs can convey such strong feelings and interpretations is a testimony to the greatness of his art.'[41]

The notion that artistic greatness hinges on triggering extreme emotions and feelings in one's audience is problematic. There are myriad examples of pop and rock musicians whose work connects with audiences in ways that arouse the emotions and elicit strong affective responses, but that does not automatically qualify their work as art. The records and performances of artists as diverse as Whitney Houston, Skrewdriver, 'N Sync and GG Allin might convey feelings and prompt intense emotional reactions, but that doesn't translate into instant artistic worth.

Beyond the sort of generalized, spontaneous emotion mentioned by vpsaarinen, for some Triffids fans emotional transcendence takes on a distinctly spiritual character. Forum member Snowy, for instance, muses that 'expansive, grand music … gives me a feeling that there's something bigger, greater and more important than day to day problems. Not wanting to sound too wanky, but it's something almost religious.'[42] Along the same lines, Urpal ventures: 'Music can definitely be something to lean on for comfort in a time when your mind is troubled and life looks bleak. The Triffids are certainly one of the better places of last resort.'[43]

Although these extreme emotional and spiritual responses to The Triffids' work attest to some of the ways that romantic ideology colours fans' thinking about rock music, McComb's untimely death has furthermore encouraged Triffids aficionados to develop an almost parodic romantic narrative around the band. McComb's demise at a relatively young age, following a period of chronic ill health aggravated by alcohol and drug consumption, frames him as the stereotypical creative genius who died young, never receiving the recognition he deserved. This tendency is underlined by the decision by forum members to organize and fund the placement of a commemorative plaque on the London building where *Born Sandy Devotional* was recorded. This was a wonderful gesture, but not without a morbid undertone. While the plaque ostensibly celebrates The Triffids' finest record, its installation was clearly about commemorating McComb. It's impossible not to connect the (green) plaque with the famous blue plaques dotted all over London, plaques that are generally linked in the popular imagination with artists, particularly writers like Chatterton, Keats, Shelley and Coleridge. One of the guidelines posted by Graham Lee on The Triffids forum is 'Above all please don't dwell on Dave's death.'[44] But although rarely mentioned directly, his death does loom large across the discussion boards. An occasionally cult-like aura surrounds McComb's life and death, the prism through which many fans apparently view The Triffids' records.

Press coverage has displayed a similar inclination, which has become more and more pronounced in post-mortem reappraisals of McComb. Writers have taken McComb's death seemingly as a justification for imposing on his music a simplistic framework derived mainly from the more melodramatic clichés of romanticism, presenting him as a tragic, ill-fated, self-destructive artist. Discussing the *Born Sandy Devotional* reissue in *Mojo*, Martin Aston describes McComb as 'a *sensitive bard* in a culture defined by AC/DC'; Dave Simpson calls him a 'doomed Romantic.'[45] François Gorin's *Télérama* feature on *Calenture* and *In the Pines* carried a photograph of McComb captioned with the words 'David McComb, leader dandy et junky est mort en 1999' and the review itself characterized him as 'escogriffe ombrageux aux moues de dandy sous influence.'[46] In a review of the same reissues for *Magic* magazine, Christophe Basterra refers to McComb as 'tourmenté.'[47]

If the emotional and spiritual dimensions of McComb's songwriting endow it with a transcendent aesthetic identity, for many critics and fans the apotheosis of such an identity is the work of literature. Consequently, McComb's songs are frequently considered to be the work of an 'author' or 'poet,' as opposed to a mere songwriter. This is evident in press coverage stressing McComb's literary talents. In his appraisal of *Calenture*, Jonathan Romney cites McComb's 'richly dramatic poetry of the sort that owes nothing to conventional pop imagery.'[48] Lauren Zoric, reviewing *Calenture* and *In the Pines*, contends that 'the glorious romantic poetry of this grand gesture is still unparalleled in Australian music history. … McComb's voice is overwhelming, a terrifying embodiment of ruinous emotions reined into literary form.'[49]

A focus on The Triffids' lyrical content is most pronounced among fans. Speaking about *Born Sandy Devotional*, a record boasting a remarkably rich and varied musical palette, Urpal states: 'the album's greatest strength is the literacy of the *author*.'[50] Elsewhere within the forum, having quoted a section of 'Jesus Calling', the same poster observes: 'So snappy, engagingly straightforward yet both redolent of childhood experiences and suggestive of a secondary "higher" meaning. The condensed language of a true poet.'[51] Commenting on *Calenture*'s 'Jerdacuttup Man', mtrain's primary frame of reference is literature, not music: 'The first time I heard this song the poem "the Tollund Man" by Seamus Heaney sprang to mind, I think that's one of the reasons I admired the band so much — so many of the songs had such an incredible quality to the lyrics. I don't know of many other bands that could do this without coming off as completely pretentious. I wonder if there is any prose/poetry of Dave's out there that we have yet to see?'[52]

Although some fans view McComb's work as a manifestation of a romantic aesthetic, closer scrutiny of his creative process, as documented in his notebooks, suggests otherwise. That's not to disparage his accomplishments as a songwriter and performer but, rather, to emphasize that some of his personal writings concerning The Triffids' records problematize the popular view that McComb was a romantic. These materials undermine notions that he was a tormented, isolated soul, spontaneously pouring out his emotions and making authentic art under the influence of transcendental encounters with the sublime.

Early on, McComb set a pattern of documenting his thinking about his work. Like generations of teenagers, he appeared to put as much stock in the *idea* of being in a band as in the actuality. As one of his earliest notebooks (titled 'Triffids') shows, it wasn't enough for The Triffids just to self-release their first eponymous tape in 1978 — McComb needed to provide accompanying materials asserting their identity as a rock band. The notebook (a Western Australian standard-issue exercise tablet bearing the state seal of a black swan) contains the following: McComb's diligently handwritten and sometimes brilliantly inane lyrics for the songs, annotated with times (all in blue ink) and writing credits (in red ink); photographs of the band members posing awkwardly in their suburban neighbourhood; photos of their instruments and equipment; and faux press-release Q&A sheets for each band member.[53] These meticulously prepared materials leave no doubt as to the absolute importance and seriousness that forming and playing in a group carry in the teenage imagination; they also attest to a sense of irony and a certain distance from the endeavour. A similar impression is given by 'History of The Triffids', a third-person narrative charting the band's emergence, handwritten by McComb in late 1979.[54] These documents read almost as parodies of what it means to be in a band, with their attention to detail, their gleeful recycling of rock cliché and their elevation of a suburban teenage hobby to the level of great importance.

While McComb's early writings about The Triffids make for entertaining juvenilia, they are noteworthy in that they anticipate the degree of planning and deliberation — also recorded in handwritten booklets — that would accompany his work when The Triffids became a more serious proposition. Crucially, these subsequent notebooks reveal a creative process that has very little to do with a romantic imagination: they underscore the extent to which McComb's work was carefully calculated and consciously situated within a rock music tradition of endlessly borrowing from and emulating others. This in no way diminishes the significance of McComb's achievement. Rather, his detailed personal commentaries simply undermine clichéd notions of authenticity and spontaneity that fans and critics might wish to attribute to his work. The excerpts from McComb's notebooks included with the *Born Sandy Devotional* reissues are illuminating in this regard, demonstrating the considerable amount of thought, preparation and conceptualization that went into the writing and the recording.

On a simple level, the degree of calculation extends even to the apparently straightforward process of naming the record: McComb lists twenty-three possible titles for *Born Sandy Devotional*, while notebook excerpts accompanying the reissue of *Calenture* list twenty-seven alternative titles. More significant, however, are McComb's copious notes covering the sonic elements that he intended to incorporate into songs, from 'Thousands of dischordant [sic] recorders wailing, screaming, wildly fluctuating, like a plague of hummingbirds' to 'Lots of "found" background noise and non-musical sounds.'[55] The latter is especially interesting in that it runs counter to a romantic ideal of creativity, with such elements creating an *illusion* of immediacy, authenticity and spontaneity. McComb also compiled — in advance of the recording — a thorough list featuring the tracks slated for the album, followed by the sonic references and allusions to other songs that he wanted each of those tracks to make. In typically meticulous fashion, McComb broke these references down into discrete components. For 'Tarrilup Bridge', for example, he named seven songs and noted the exact noises and instrumental components that he wanted to emulate: from the 'selection of noises' on Tom Waits' 'Shore Leave', to the 'rhythm' of The Birthday Party's 'Jennifer's Veil', to the 'crowd noises' on Gram Parsons' 'Hickory Wind'. As for the much-vaunted literary dimension of his work, as expressed here it has little to do with a supposedly pure romantic aesthetic identified by critics and fans: McComb stressed a desire to imbue his work with a writerly, 'VERY LITERARY' touch, but only 'to prevent [it] from being soppy.'[56]

Further selections from McComb's notes are included with the 2007 reissue of *In the Pines*. These also demystify McComb's creative process, particularly on a record that's something of a red herring in the popular narrative of The Triffids' oeuvre. Much has been made of this album as a return to the band's roots, eschewing Northern Hemisphere recording-studio gloss in favour of a back-to-basics DIY approach in the group's homeland. On the surface, there is some truth to that assessment. It was recorded over five days in April 1986, 400 miles from a city already the most isolated in the world. To outsiders, the actual location for the recording was quintessentially Australian: not only were the band in the middle of nowhere, but they were ensconced in a woolshed, fuelled by copious amounts of alcohol (the sleeve notes famously detail a budget in which $340 went on drink). Even so, *In the Pines* was not a return to the band's roots. The Triffids were largely suburban kids and this was no random desolate location on which they had stumbled — it was actually a property owned by McComb's parents. In fact, this unorthodox recording was far from spontaneous. According to the liner notes, the album's original concept came from a friend, Paul Bolger, in 1982. The careful planning for the sessions is immortalized as item #7 in minutes from a band meeting held on 29 January 1986. These are reproduced with the 2007 reissue and comprise an interesting document that shows McComb not only profoundly engaged in the artistic process, but also well aware of the band's place in commercial terms: 'The resulting LP of course *might* not be suitable for the likes of Virgin, but we still plan to make it a bloody good record.'[57]

Much of the mythology surrounding this record centres on its back-to-basics approach, with the emphasis on lo-fi recording and the use of 'found' sounds and instruments. However, this was not a case of a band arriving at a remote woolshed and making use of what they encountered. In the same minutes cited above, McComb gives an indication of how far ahead he was planning. Aware of what he would 'find', he mentions the projected use of 'readymade instruments, water tanks, wind, etc.' (indeed, 'water tank' is credited on the album, along with 'floorboards,' 'broom' and 'metal percussion'). Notwithstanding this idea of making do with what's at hand and including communal sing-alongs featuring visiting friends (the Graham Lee-led 'Once a Day'), the informal atmosphere of the record is, in fact, carefully orchestrated.

The faux authenticity of *In the Pines* is articulated by McComb in a letter to co-producer Bruce Callaway after the recording was complete. McComb wanted the record to sound spontaneous and relaxed and, with that in mind, had intended for the tracks to be bookended by the band members' in-studio chat. However, the recording engineer stopped them talking. McComb asks Callaway to 'reconstruct the atmosphere,' that is, to recreate the originally desired sound that never actually happened. He instructs his co-producer to take the few segments of chatter that did make it onto the tape and to cut and paste them around the songs because it will 'add a lot more feeling to the record. … We're not worrying about AM radio play — it's important instead to make a record which has a sense of character or warmth that is not found on today's studio records.'[58]

Bearing in mind this illusory spontaneity and crafted authenticity, it's worth returning briefly to The Triffids' final studio album. As noted, the diverse stylistic reach of *The Black Swan* problematizes traditional constructions of authenticity and cultural identity; it furthermore undermines romantic notions of the creative process. Several of these numbers are so self-conscious in their stylistic appropriations that they come across as pastiche, or even parody: musically, 'One Mechanic Town' is a parody of the rambling rock outlaw sensibility, complete with Morricone-esque flourishes, and McComb's braggadocio on 'The Spinning Top Song' seems like a wry take on exaggerated rock masculinity. Amid such thoroughly crafted stylistic surfaces is one of McComb's most beautiful and moving songs, 'New Year's Greetings'. The track appears to embody romantic ideology in its portrayal of the individual pitted against a materialistic society and in its emotional range, which resonates in the grand musical arrangement. But while some might see this as the apotheosis of McComb's unique artistic spirit finding expression in song, that's not entirely the case. In addition to the music's Van Morrison pastiche, the song, as McComb told Jon Casimir, is based on someone else's poem: Les Murray's 'The Widower in the Country'.[59]

Transcendence and narrative

This is your first taste of mystery …[60]

Further complicating such notions as authenticity and transcendence, McComb's songs frequently eschew the well-wrought lyrical urn in favour of fragmented, less immediately accessible structures. Not only does the semantic fragmentation in McComb's lyrics work against the kind of pure emotionality that some Triffids fans seek as the critical element in a transcendental listening experience, but it also places responsibility on the listener. It positions him or her as a producer of meaning, undermining the traditional concept of authenticity according to which the author is the sole originator of signification.

Many of McComb's most memorable songs are akin to short stories in that they give listeners a sense of place, elements of chronology, action and characters (or at least a narrative consciousness). Crucially, though, these components rarely coalesce in such a way that listeners are able to assemble a closed system of meaning. To some critics, this is a flaw. Reviewing the *Born Sandy Devotional* reissues, Owen Jones complains: 'The lyrics are a bit weak … they don't seem to refer to anything.'[61] Bleddyn Butcher makes essentially the same point, considering McComb's weaker songs 'obtuse' and 'allusive.'[62] McComb and the voices in his songs rarely give a complete picture, instead offering partial narratives that suggest and hint rather than disclose. In several cases, this dynamic is present both at the lyrical and the musical levels: the lyrics are elliptical and oblique, whereas the sound subverts listeners' traditional experience of narrative development and fulfilment. One of the most notable examples is 'Field of Glass'. This nine-minute psychodrama is, seemingly, a tale of doomed, class-crossed lovers, recounted in a fractured, expressionistic manner. Mirroring the narrative fragmentation and the violent shifts in focus, the music is alternately menacing and explosive, frustrating conventional expectations of song structure. With similarly dark, brooding lyrics, 'Lonely Stretch' hints at extreme violence but without any final clarification of the protagonist's circumstances and, in musical terms, there's no narrative release or resolution for the listener.

This coincidence of lyrical and musical fragmentation is not in fact typical of McComb's work with The Triffids. More common are those songs in which the oblique lyrics and conventional musical narratives function in opposition to one another. Musically, 'Tarrilup Bridge' has a naïf simplicity that's emphasized by Jill Birt's childlike vocal. Rather than challenging the listener, the song insinuates itself effortlessly, its basic melodic figure almost instantly imprinting itself in the memory. This quality contrasts starkly with the puzzling, incomplete narrative centred on the mysterious death of the song's narrator. Likewise, 'Chicken Killer' hooks the listener with its banal but catchy sing-along refrain, whereas the lyrics, although vividly evoking madness, loss and violence, never coalesce to offer a clear account of the protagonist's situation.

Most striking are the songs in which the tension is more acute, compounded by a stark contrast between unresolved narratives and seamless musical arrangements. This tendency is particularly note-worthy on *Born Sandy Devotional*, for which McComb crafted what he called a 'widescreen' sound, distinguished by its lush, expansive quality.[63] On 'The Seabirds' and 'Wide Open Road', for example, the sonic framework is grand, anthemic and full of longing, as is the vocal delivery; the lyrics, on the other hand, distil autobiographical experi-ence into incomplete vignettes of dislocation, psychological turmoil and, principally, loss — absence again is the yawning hole at the cen-tre of these narratives. The listener is pulled by the drama and the epic drive of the music towards a transcendent experience; yet that prom-ised fulfilment is never attained as the lyrical narrative resists closure and keeps the listener engaged in the process of constructing meaning.

Transcendence and the inescapable body

I'm shrivelled and black and my bandage is torn …[64]

McComb's work often dramatizes the denial of transcendence, not only in the form of his lyrics but also in their content. This can be seen in a recurring emphasis on the earthbound, embodied realm, which thwarts a generalized romanticism's transcendental impulse.

Musically, 'Jerdacuttup Man' begins on a hauntingly beautiful note. The yearning, lofty register created by the opening uillean pipes and harmonica transports listeners to a timeless space; yet the lyrics — a mundane, somewhat grotesque first-person tale of a bog man in the British Museum — underscore an inescapable rootedness in the cor-poreal realm. McComb's bog man chronicles his failed attempts at salvation through the pursuit of love and money before succumbing to his own mortality. McComb playfully exaggerates this dimension, placing Jerdacuttup Man on display at the museum, his anatomi-cal details and his decay foregrounded throughout. 'Bury Me Deep in Love', on the other hand, addresses the gulf between the promise of transcendence offered by religious belief and the individual's suspicion that he is condemned to a material existence in a Godless world, with-out hope of salvation. McComb's extensive use of religious imagery affirms, as he once commented to Mat Snow, 'the scar that God has left on humanity.'[65] Indeed, many of his characters have fallen from grace and are doomed, from the outset, by some original sin. 'Hanging Shed',

'Life of Crime' and 'Estuary Bed' appear to return to a primal scene, which is the root of the alienation expressed in the songs and often intimately linked to the threat of violence.

Occasionally, this sense of corporeality thwarting the possibility of transcendence comes more explicitly from an encounter with the sublime in nature. Rather than serving as the impetus for the transcendental experience as it would in the canonical romantic text, nature underlines McComb's characters' feelings of abandonment in the world. On 'Wide Open Road', the landscape's awesome majesty highlights the frustration and isolation of the protagonist. The protagonist of 'The Seabirds' attempts to surrender to nature — to the sea and the flock of gulls. At the conclusion of the song, though, he remains trapped in his embodied state, neither consumed by the ocean nor taken by the seabirds, their impassive black-eyed gaze signalling their indifference to him.

Ultimately, whereas popular and critical responses to The Triffids reveal a strong investment in romantic ideology, McComb's relationship with romanticism is marked by ambivalence and an emphasis on corporeality that resonate with recent, innovative work in romantic studies.[66] By recuperating an embodied, materialist sensibility traditionally suppressed within romantic scholarship, such studies have yielded a deeper, more variegated account of the romantic ethos. McComb's latter-day romanticism performs a similar task in the face of the traditionalist discourses of fandom and rock criticism, which impose a narrow view of his work, one that is unable to accommodate the more elaborate and dynamic processes in his writing and performance.

Against the grain of some critics' and fans' perceptions, McComb's work doesn't allow for a simplistic construction of authenticity but instead suggests a profound ambivalence in that regard. Only by stepping outside of a reductive romantic paradigm that privileges authenticity can we begin to grasp his work's nuances and complexities.

By the same token, McComb's music comprises an attempted transcendence (in the English romantic sense) even while displaying an awareness that such attempts are doomed to fail. Indeed, it's this unresolved tension underlying McComb's creativity that accounts for much of his work's power and endurance.

ABOVE: Walking the dog.
McComb with family pet,
Daisy, Perth, early 1990s.

OVERLEAF: Live at the
University of Melbourne
Student Union, 7 January
1984,

Return to the Sea

David McComb

Return to the sea,
Hoping to recognize
The wide smiles of tidal debris,
To greet beaming clusters of
Thorny saltbush and pigface,
To say, this is where
I helped you over the final sandhill,
This is where ice-cream
Stuck to your sandy fingers,
And where flies pestered
The sore on your knee.

But we can't hear the shell's innards
For the din of the surf.
And direct sunlight
Has exposed our skeletons
As outcrops of pockmarked, unwanted reef,
Bleached away of all reason of flesh
On this gleaming shore.

McComb with canine com-
panion, on the flatlands of
the family farm, c. 1991.

Love in Bright Landscapes: McComb's Lyricism

Chris Coughran

Desire is the struggle to not always look behind, at what is gone, at what will be gone. But desire is memory, the memory of first love, gone. Desire is poetry, the first language, stark and pained, coming out from the desert. Desire is imagining you have really left that first love, that old language, back out there, more or less buried in the desert, to be scorched by the desert sun, perhaps it will leave some traces, some sun-whitened bones, but not many. And you, you can start all over again, you can write the story from the beginning.[1]

In *Shards of Love: Exile and the Origins of the Lyric*, María Rosa Menocal traces the history of the lyric, with its perennial theme of unrequited or otherwise ill-fated love, back (by way of Jim Morrison and others) to the ancient deserts of the Middle East. For Menocal, the voice of the poet, like that of the prophet, emerges from the twinning of memory and desire within the specific context of an arid, desolate wasteland. It is not just the content of Menocal's thesis — the idea that contemporary rock lyricists share with poets of antiquity a certain 'fascination with the generative power of unhappy love' — but the evocative form of her argument that seems highly apposite to the case of David McComb.[2] The ideal condition of Menocal's lyric poet is one of *exile* from the object of his (or her) devotion — 'placed on probation from your limbs' as McComb expresses this in 'Unmade Love' on *Calenture*. Accordingly, the uninhabited desert or *wilderness* becomes an ideal backdrop from which the lyric, comprising the poet's delicate 'shards of love', emerges into being — the same 'wilderness,' arguably, of which McComb sings in 'Wide Open Road'; the 'unmarked track' of 'Lonely Stretch', etc.

In a handwritten note to himself that was published only post-humously, some twenty years after the first pressing of *Born Sandy Devotional*, McComb wrote that the theme of the forthcoming album would be 'Unrequited Love. But the language will reach way above and beyond that: VERY LITERARY to prevent from being sappy.'[3] This pencilled fragment is of a piece with Menocal's understanding of lyric poetry. By virtue of the note's privacy, however, it can hardly be thought to exemplify that 'recherché gesture' described by Menocal, 'the conscious attempt' on the part of a select few rock musicians 'to inscribe themselves into the annals of high literature.' Rather, McComb would seem to have intuitively sought out, during a time of emotional upheaval brought about by the disintegration of an intimate relationship, 'the consolation of the classical model that he needed to create poetry from his pain.'[4]

On record, McComb's literary aspirations are subtle and allusive, a song title such as 'Tender is the Night', for example, evoking F. Scott Fitzgerald's novel of the same name. Indeed, it is only in posthumous paraphernalia, such as the forty-two page, perfect-bound book-let accompanying the twentieth-anniversary reissue of *Born Sandy Devotional*, that McComb's literary credentials are directly invoked.[5] McComb himself, although an avid writer of fiction and verse in addi-tion to lyrics, appears to have been highly ambivalent about a literary career, and wary of rock pretenders to the mantle of poetry.[6] He seems to have been mindful, in particular, of the popular song as a 'composi-tion keyed to and written for an aesthetic, that of music, that is dra-matically different from the aesthetics of writing which is meant to be read.'[7] Presumably because fiction and poetry rank 'higher' than rock or pop music in the orthodox hierarchy of cultural values, McComb occasionally confessed to harbouring feelings of 'inadequacy' for not having been 'involved in some more serious artform.' And yet in the same breath, as it were, McComb seems to have recognized, or at the very least suspected, the ultimate merit of his vocation: 'although pop music is supposedly frivolous, I have a sneaking feeling that it's very honourable and noble to be able to sing in a group.'[8]

McComb elaborated on the intimate relationship between the singer of popular music, the song's lyrics, and the listener, as follows: 'the voice is the magic charm, and ... the storyteller and the dweller in language, the ones who live by and for language, occupy sacred territory.'[9] Lofty sentiments, perhaps; but McComb articulates them in defence of insurgent hip-hop and rap music, which he perceived, in the early 1990s — in contrast to the hysterical biases of commercial FM broadcasters in Australia at the time — to be as valid as forms of contemporary poetry as they were permutations of rock & roll's irrepressible ethos.

The somewhat vexed relationship of popular music to 'more serious artforms' is fruitfully discussed by Antoine Hennion, who observes that the genre of the pop song 'borrows from a wide variety of other genres,' including poetry and the lyric theatre. As Hennion conceives of it, the pop song 'owes most to the novelette' — that is, to narrative fiction — 'in the way that it almost invariably tells a story, set out in a few words, concerning the relationship between two or three individuals.'[10] This narrative function is certainly not lost on McComb, whose finely wrought, ironical vignettes of 'Love in Bright Landscapes' — to cite one of several prospective titles for the album that would be released as *Born Sandy Devotional* — involve the transposition of a perennial theme (unrequited love) to localized, particular and contemporary, semi-fictional contexts; *semi-fictional* because, in the final analysis, the singer himself becomes 'part and parcel of the song he sings, in the form of the "character" he impersonates ... The singer has to become a character in whom are confused the singer's own life history and those life histories of which he sings.'[11]

Waxing lyrical

In 'Wide Open Road', McComb sings with a bittersweet irony: 'now you can go any place/that you want to go' — the irony being that McComb's narrative persona appears not to relish the prospect of unfettered roaming. The narrative voice 'crying in the wilderness,' conveying a sense of emotional pain intensified by geographic isolation, makes a mockery of that expansive sense of optimism enshrined in seminal American texts such as Whitman's 'Song of the Open Road' or Kerouac's *On the Road*. In stark contrast to those ebullient paeans, 'Wide Open Road' evokes Australia's notorious 'tyranny of distance,' effectively transposing it into the private and utterly personal contours of an inner, emotional landscape. These inner and outer topographies alike exude forsakenness; consolation neither pours forth from on high, nor may be located within: 'The sky was big and empty/My chest filled to explode/I yelled my insides out at the sun,/At the wide open road.'[12]

As opposed to the easygoing, touristic pleasures offered by Australia's freeways and highways, McComb's characters are impelled to explore more circuitous approaches, more tortuous paths to the objects of their desire. The notion of tracks and tracking — of finding oneself 'off the beaten track' or 'on the wrong track' altogether — is a recurrent theme of *Born Sandy Devotional* (indeed, 'Unmarked Track' appears on McComb's list of prospective album titles).[13] If the singer of 'Wide Open Road' has 'lost track' of his friends, family and lover, then the implications of such a loss are taken to an extreme in 'Lonely Stretch'. The song chronicles a kind of 'dark night of the soul,' a moment of profound spiritual disorientation, a negative epiphany in the context of outback isolation:

> I took a wrong turn off of an unmarked track
> I did seven miles I couldn't find my way back
> Hit a lonely stretch, must be losing my touch,
> I was out of my depth
> Land was so flat, could well have been ocean
> No distinguishing feature in any direction

An apparition of the narrator's beloved — 'Could have sworn you were shining right there on the verge' — prompts a fervent confession: 'I was wrong, wrong from the start/You could die out here from a broken heart.' Absolution, however, is forbidden in this bleak, nocturnal landscape. Far from being reunited with his beloved, the narrator concedes that he will miss his mark, that special 'spot on a map, … just a tiny dot' where his lover may be found. Instead of arriving at this destination, he 'could be driving in circles till the end of the week.' In desperation, he turns to another faltering illusion, the *ne plus ultra* of the idea of connubial fidelity, an omnipresent God's love being compared with the nocturnal landscape now threatening to engulf him: 'Rock my soul in the bosom of Abraham … So high can't get over it, so low can't get under it, … I took a wrong turn,' etc. Indeed, the narrative thread linking one 'track' to another on *Born Sandy Devotional* is an obsession with the idea of faithfulness. Charting a path through the emotional wilderness of a painful breakup, McComb confesses that in writing the album, 'I found myself almost following the idea of fidelity as a complete all-consuming faith, to give … some sort of direction.'[14] 'Lonely Stretch' provides the perfect vehicle for this *idée fixe*. Arguably, the song is infused with a few drops of the same kind of intoxicating romanticism as, say, Berlioz's *Symphonie Fantastique*. Although the latter's kaleidoscopic chromaticism, sumptuous orchestration and prolonged duration are sharply at odds with the lean, bluesy structure of 'Lonely Stretch', the *themes* of the two compositions are remarkably congruent.[15]

The setting of 'Life of Crime' is a small outback township, 'miles from nowhere, just a little dot on the map.' The object of the narrator's desire cannot be pinpointed with cartographic precision, however, since (as with 'Lonely Stretch') the metaphor of the 'dot on the map' suggests, at once, the idea of geographic isolation, an elusive lost object (the *objet petit a* of Lacanian discourse?) and erogenous zones of his love's body, from which he has been driven into exile. Relentlessly, obsessively, the song's narrator leaves no stone unturned as he attempts to track down his absent love:

> I followed the tracks that you left behind
> I followed the rail and the curve of your spine
> And the grass still grows on the side of the road
> Sun still burns
> Rain still falls
> Sin still burns little fiery holes
> I hold on tight now to nothing at all

The diffuse spirit of European romanticism animates this albeit sketchy and imprecise plotting of exterior landscape in terms of the human body, psyche, and desire. There is an almost metaphysical correspondence between the narrator's 'chest burning, rising falling' and his subsequent observations on the growing grass, burning sun and falling rain. These are signatures of the one constancy remaining to him now, cold comfort that it is. The terse image of the song's narrator 'holding on tight … to nothing at all' captures the manner in which cathexis (the retentive obsession over an ideal form of relationship) even more so than catharsis (the putative, purgative aesthetics of rock music) informs the lyricism of *Born Sandy Devotional*. A somewhat cryptic remark in one of McComb's exercise books lends support to this view of his writing process: 'End of B.S.D./Twice as devoted to you.'[16]

In 'Estuary Bed', memories of childhood are stirred by an observation, common enough along the Australian coast in summertime, of 'children … walking back from the beach/Sun on the sidewalk is burning their feet/Washing the salt off under the shower/And just wasting away … the hours and hours and hours.'[17] Almost immediately, this opening scene begins to drift, away from a rendering in terms of 'eyesight' and toward the private, inner folds of the narrator's 'memory.' By the start of the second verse, the singer has strayed altogether from the field of visual perception into the realm of a distinct — that is to say, none the less vivid — personal reminiscence:

> Come on, climb over your father's back fence
> For the very last time we'll take the shortcut across his lawn
> Then lie together on the estuary bed
> Perfectly still, perfectly warm

This 'estuary bed' — an ideal or delightful place, the *locus amoenus* of pastoral convention — demonstrates McComb's penchant for wordplay. For, apart from denoting the bottom of a large body of water, a 'bed' is also an ideal place for both sleep and sexual intimacy. And, to be sure — the fences of patriarchy, the lawns of suburbia notwithstanding — the narrator and his companion find themselves immersed in a semblance, or presentiment, of 'oceanic feeling.' An 'estuary' is literally the place 'where the tide meets the stream'; metaphorically, it is that ambiguous zone, altogether fluid, in which memory and desire commingle freely. The fantasy element no doubt increases, retrospectively, in order to compensate for the narrator's ultimate eviction from this seaward 'garden of earthly delights':

> Silt returns along the passage of flesh
> I hear your voice
> I taste the salt
> I bear the stain, it won't wash off

I hold you not
But I see you still
What use eyesight if it should melt?
What use memory covered in estuary silt?

This failure of memory, as of eyesight, is regrettable; yet the narrative and instrumental cadences of 'Estuary Bed' desist from lamenting an irreversible and unavoidable 'fall' from childhood innocence (the pleasure principle) into the world of adult experience (reality). Recorded and written during McComb's first London sojourn, 'Estuary Bed' is optimistic about *leaving*, not returning, home.[18] The listener is left with the joyful, almost jubilant refrain—an allusion to Shakespeare, or perhaps Wordsworth: 'Sleep no more … Old skin is shed/Sleep no more on the estuary bed.'[19]

Shards of love (reprise)

McComb's ambition of making recordings with 'atmosphere' attests to the persistence of romanticist aesthetics, in the guise of an 'ambient poetics' concerned with 'conjuring up a sense of a surrounding atmosphere or world.'[20] On an album such as *Born Sandy Devotional*, this ambience is not merely the effect of creative recording and mixing techniques, an aura emanating from the synthetic reverb plate or digital delay line. An equally palpable sense of atmosphere is evoked by McComb's lyrics themselves: a surrounding world that serves as a counterpoise to the personal concerns and predicaments of the songs' respective narrative personae. A good many of the songs on *Born Sandy Devotional* thus approach the ideal condition of lyric poetry as theorized by Schopenhauer:

> It is the subject of will, i.e., his own volition, which the consciousness of the singer feels; often as a released and satisfied desire (joy), but still oftener as a restricted desire (grief), always as an emotion, a passion, a moved frame of mind. … Besides this, however, and along with it, by the sight of surrounding nature, the singer becomes conscious of himself as the subject of pure, will-less knowing, whose unbroken blissful peace now appears, in contrast to the stress of desire which is always restricted and always needy. The feeling of this contrast, this alternation, is really what

the lyric as a whole expresses, and what principally constitutes the lyrical state of mind. In it pure knowing comes to us, as it were, to deliver us from desire and its stain; we follow, but only for an instant; desire, the remembrance of our own personal ends, tears us anew from peaceful contemplation; yet ever again the next beautiful surrounding in which the pure will-less knowledge presents itself to us, allures us away from desire. Therefore, in the lyric and the lyrical mood, desire (the personal interest of the ends), and pure perception of the surrounding presented, are wonderfully mingled with each other; the subjective disposition, the affection of the will, imparts its own hue to the perceived surrounding, and conversely, the surroundings communicate the reflex of their colour to the will. The true lyric is the expression of the whole of this mingled and divided state of mind.[21]

What emerges over the course of listening to *Born Sandy Devotional* is a lyrical cum narrative vision of bewilderment, in which strands of love, loss and landscape are inextricably intertwined. Across various tracks of the album, a pattern emerges: in the absence of the narrator's (human) beloved, the landscape becomes more prominent, its features all the more pronounced. Uncannily familiar, and by turns womb-like and reassuring, hostile, or indifferent, the features of the landscape seem to bear a strong resemblance to the narrator's beloved, in the absence of whom no merely human companionship will suffice. Throughout *Born Sandy Devotional*, a traumatic separation is replayed over and over again, with the landscape itself coming to assume the characteristics of a second persona. As one privy to the intimate details of the lovers' affair, it stands in for the absent beloved, commanding the narrator's attention but not, ultimately, his loyalties or affection.

Much more than a backdrop, then, to the lives of McComb's semi-fictional, semi-autobiographical characters, features of the physical environment emerge as displaced objects of the narrative persona's wayward desire. A few further illustrations will suffice to demonstrate that this is true not only of *Born Sandy Devotional*, but of McComb's work as a whole.

'In the Pines', McComb's paean to a 'very fine and private place', portrays a secluded forest situated 'in the shadow of a hill' — that is to say, planted and nourished by a veritable stream of feminine imagery.[22]

As with McComb's 'estuary bed', this pine forest affords womb-like protection from harsher elements ('No place is darker/And no place more still'). But the primal innocence of this scene is offset by a kind of 'Weird Melancholy', in the form of the song's minor-pentatonic mandolin riff. Redolent of Australia's colonial past, the tune's arrangement speaks, perhaps, to novelist Marcus Clarke's grim assessment of Australian forests as 'funereal, secret, stern. Their solitude is desolation. They seem to stifle, in their black gorges, a story of sullen despair. No tender sentiment is nourished in their shade.'[23] And indeed, as sung by McComb on The Triffids' woolshed recording, it remains unclear (at least on my well-worn vinyl copy) whether it is the narrator's 'bride' or his — slightly more sinister — 'pride' that is the centrepiece of this sylvan scene. That plosive ambiguity, coupled with the aforementioned minor tonality and the deviation of a lilting, 6/8 timing into a frenetic waltz, allows ample space for the blossoming of a dark secret — a sense of mystery — appropriate to the ballad form.

The vanished idyll, never to be relived except through the unreliable faculty of memory, informs the closing track of The Triffids' final studio album, *The Black Swan*. With its lingering fade-out — instruments first, followed by McComb's plaintive vocals — 'Fairytale Love' indeed sounds like the kind of song fabled to be sung by a dying swan. The song's lyrics recapitulate the pastoral tradition from the Old Testament book of Isaiah ('even the wild dog lies down with the lamb')[24] — to nineteenth-century nostalgia for a pre-industrial past ('In an earlier time, in a green land above/By the mill and the willows we made fairytale love'). The song's dying refrain evokes an erstwhile 'golden age' of childlike innocence: 'No blemish of lust, flesh unfreckled by sin … We thought that our pleasure would always remain.'[25] Unmatched in McComb's repertoire, the sentimental nostalgia of 'Fairytale Love' is complemented by 'toy piano' timbres and the gentle cello- and flute-like envelopes of electronically bowed guitar.

Elsewhere on *The Black Swan*, more complex pastoral spaces emerge. In 'New Year's Greetings' — a song loosely based on Les Murray's poem 'Widower in the Country' — McComb draws a clear distinction between the city and the country. As opposed to 'those Sydney shoeshine boys' euphemistically plying their trade, McComb's widower boasts:

a little place to myself up on Stony Ridge
I got it made in the shade
I sleep in the afternoon
Leave my bed unmade
No-one breathing down my neck, black coffee and a shave
I whistle a little of whatever AM radio plays

Yet the country widower's apparent nonchalance — 'it's a long walk to the corner shop/In the January heat, it's a big decision/To either think of you, or not' — is a confidence trick which convinces nobody, least of all himself. His rosy picture of rural tranquillity, privacy and self-sufficiency is shattered by a nocturnal 'return of the repressed':

And in the evening when the skyline is cut in two
By a figure resembling you
Wet matches won't light, and I double take
Wind shudders to a halt, main roads are washed out

At this moment, the narrator's isolated vantage point — far removed from the tawdry attractions, sexual entanglements and, if truth be told, undeniable conveniences of city life — turns in on itself, and 'all around, as far as the night can see/Is just the gaping lack of you and me.' Here lies the dead centre of the narrator's world, a void eerily echoed by The Triffids' circumambient instrumentation — an aurally rich rejoinder to the dry understatement of Les Murray's poem. A day in the life of Murray's country widower, by way of comparison, lacks even a semblance of spontaneity, wonder, or surprise. The 'I' of the poem who narrates (from his 'bed unmade') will chop wood, boil water, eat supper — going through the various motions of a relaxed rural lifestyle — but remains devoid of the feeling he evidently once had for his deceased spouse. Not even dreams, the only possible hint or proof of an extramundane reality, will punctuate his predetermined routine: 'Last night I thought I dreamt — but when I woke/The scream-ing was only a possum skiing down/The iron roof on little moonlit claws.' The constancy of rural life is but a mockery of the love he has irretrievably lost, an unfathomable absence which emerges only now and then, as an emotional scar or symptom: in the guise of the wid-ower's 'dark … thoughts,' or else a nightmarish 'screaming.'[26] Perhaps

McComb's most surprising embellishment of Murray's image of the country widower is that catalogue of consumer products and services which the narrator of 'New Year's Greetings' can proudly claim to live without: 'I don't need no Eyewitness News, no Seven Eleven/No Southern Fried Chicken, no Man from Prudential/To give me good times on easy terms.' It is difficult to conceive of Murray's narrator as caring very much, one way or another, about such fleeting impressions of global capitalism.[27] Given the ultimate irony of McComb's narrator's situation, such tokens serve to remind us just how double-minded, vis-à-vis the life of the city and conventional 'pastoral' distinctions, McComb's country widower really is.

Several of McComb's unpublished songs yield further traces of shattered 'love in bright landscapes,' lyrical topographies in which elements of 'rock', 'stone', 'ironstone' and 'sand' prevail. In 'The Mistake of Returning', such features become symbols of both alienation from the narrator's erstwhile home and estrangement from a former lover. The bitterness with which McComb's native landscape is rendered — 'a threadbare land/Where no green buds are formed and nothing new gets born' — suggests that it may have outworn its fruitfulness as a source of lyrical invention.[28] In just eight sparse lines, 'The Mistake of Returning' sketches a bleak, barren and unforgiving environment, one that forbids its weary narrator's return from exile. The fantasy of return — to one's homeland, as to one's cherished beloved — proves to have been a delusion of bewildered memory, a mirage born of nostalgic desperation. In 'Song of No Return', by way of comparison, the fall from innocence into experience is rendered with poignancy rather than bitterness: 'Once you leave you can't go home/There's something stronger/Takes you where you wish you'd never gone.'[29]

Invariably, McComb's vignettes of ill-fated love in bright landscapes bring a subtle and complex irony to bear on the 'simple wish-image of bucolic pleasure' — that cloying 'shrine of the pleasure principle' in which Leo Marx, among other theorists, discerns a poor travesty of pastoral literature.[30] At its most luminous, McComb's body of work limns the murky distinction between literary and popular culture, suggesting as it does the plight of a wayfarer who must endlessly negotiate an uncertain terrain, the perfidious interstices between 'rock' and a hard place.

McComb in a sea of kangaroo paws, cn route to Gingin, Western Australia, early 1990s.

Red Ponies European tour,
1995, with Warren Ellis in
foreground.

Vivid Fragments

Megan Heyward

I knew David a little, just a little. I knew him in vivid fragments, made sharp through the cold, bleak lens of London, and exile. It was late 1989 to 1991, mostly, when Dave stepped through my life. This is what I recall.

Sydney in the 1980s, first of all, to set the scene. Most of us under thirty, those who were worth knowing at least, seemed to swirl in packs. We swirled from pub to pub, band to band, from Hopetoun to The Trade Union Club, Harold Park to The Annandale, and beyond. Everybody was in a band, or several bands, or you had friends who were in bands. Failing that, you went to see bands anyway. It was simply what you did, if you were young, and it signalled a serious personality problem not to be involved somehow in music culture. This was the time when it seemed every pub on every corner in Sydney, from Sutherland to the Northern Beaches, Bondi to Parramatta, had live bands playing, often four or five nights a week.

Back then, in that indie music flowering, we were oblivious to the rarity of the situation: that perfect combustion of time, place, isolation, confidence, post-punk DIY and rebellious elements that allowed such a glorious array of bands to emerge, all over the country, almost at once: from The Birthday Party, Go-Betweens, Died Pretty, Triffids, Scientists, Hoodoo Gurus all the way to The Particles, Lighthouse Keepers, John Kennedy, Cruel Sea, Chad's Tree, and a thousand in between.

Sydney was much smaller then, in population, sprawl, sense of itself. A city perched on the edge of the Pacific, yes, but if you lived in Glebe or Newtown or Surry Hills, in rundown, greyish houses you rented for $120 a week, Sydney was a place that you liked, but it seemed … well … not quite real. Not as real or valid as perhaps

London, or New York, where you were planning to head off to in the near future. As we swirled from venue to venue, from The Annandale to The Harold Park, The Sandringham, 'The Hoey' (The Hopetoun), lugging gear, performing, seeing friends play, greeting familiar faces, we were blind to the beauty of the time.

I first met Dave in 1989, at a dinner party at the Enmore home of my friend Julia Butler, an ex-pat from Perth who had trekked east to Sydney earlier in the decade. The Triffids were in the middle of their last Australian tour, and we'd seen them play a night or two before. On stage they had been astounding, Dave swaying and swooping over the stage, tall, lean, strikingly handsome, voice rich and deep. Flop of thick hair, dark, beautiful sad eyes. Jill Birt raining pleasure in her halting, uncertain voice. The band strong, fierce at times, but never with that macho pub rock swagger of some other Australian bands.

I recall a wild dinner party with details blurred by way too much alcohol. Dave was a great raconteur, funny, extremely intelligent, as anyone who knew him would attest. I shared a cab with him back to Glebe, both of us the worse for wear. Somehow he'd given me his London contact details, as I was soon to be leaving Sydney on that dread sojourn, the European trip. Final destination: London.

This was life before the Internet and the mobile phone. There was no email, no travel blogs to keep in contact with family and friends as you journeyed; no global roaming. When you travelled, low budget, you were essentially cut adrift. The main method of communication? Airmail letters, pale blue, inked with longing. And the occasional very expensive phone call, made in times of desperation from the Central Post Office in Florence or Rome or Madrid, and later, from bleak flats in London, always at nightmarish times, like 6.00 a.m. or midnight. Hoping, hoping, that the person you'd left behind was home. So you could talk, just for a few minutes, perhaps every few weeks. It was hellish on the heart.

I travelled alone from Sydney through Europe for four months, leaving my heart behind. I contacted Dave sometime after arriving in London — early 1990, late winter. London was freezing, so cold it seemed to turn your blood to lead. So cold that your breath would hang in the air as you lay in bed at night. Dave had recently returned and was living with his new love, Joanne Alach, in a little flat in West

London that had been provided to him by Island Records, for whom Dave was working on a solo album. His flat was glamorous in comparison to my own squat in South London — hell, at least Dave's place had central heating — but it was tiny just the same. Importantly, though, Joanne was with him. I think Dave was determined that London would not wreak havoc on his personal life again, after the difficulties of the Triffids years.

Dave was my friend in exile. He looked out for me, one exile to another. Often I would visit on a Saturday afternoon, when he would enact an odd little ritual to help keep the homesick at bay. Someone from home regularly sent him cassettes of Roy and HG's *This Sporting Life*, which went to air on weekends on JJJ in Australia. Dave would play these tapes on a Saturday afternoon, mirroring the time of the original broadcast in his little flat in the middle of cold, grey London — savouring, as did we all, each vicious nickname, slur, snide remark and outrageous lie they would call upon in their commentary.

Dave was friend to many exiles. There was a whole bunch of them, either based in London or dropping in from Europe, who would call upon him and Joanne in their West London flat. Dave loved to talk. He was bright, opinionated and extremely charming, the antithesis of the stereotypically uncommunicative Australian male. It was as if he were threading us all together, trying to shape some tiny model of what we'd all left behind.

This was the time that Dave was negotiating the terms of his solo album, and there seemed to be a series of delays and problems emerging with Island. I recall Dave recording demos with Rob Snarski and Kenny Davis Jr (the latter, at the time, from The Jackson Code) during the summer of 1990 when Rob and Ken were briefly in London, Ken staying at my place in Stockwell. Dave had written 'Ocean of You' specifically for Rob, to bring attention to his glorious voice. Dave was never precious about his music, and would share it with friends — demo versions, rough mixes, spare copies of older work. Knowing I was strapped for cash, and that music helped with the homesickness, he gave me a batch of cassettes: *Stockholm*, *The Black Swan*, the demo cassette of what was to become *Depends on What You Mean by Love*. (Recently I found them, with their rough typing and homemade covers, sitting in a forgotten drawer, as I moved house.)

Tortuously for David, delay after demoralizing delay meant that the solo album he was trying to record and release with Island would not be released until the end of 1993, through Mushroom, as *Love of Will*.

As for me? I had tried to keep in contact with my love, back in Sydney, but the gods toyed with us as they'd toy with a fly. A pile of blue love letters lay testament to the agony — letters come late, letters gone missing, letters out of sync. Letters would arrive in Innsbruck when I was in Rome. A letter written in November would arrive in Feb., while a later one might arrive in January. And all the time, the cold working its way into your heart, making your blood run slow, chilling you from the outside, till it went all the way in.

David and Joanne were exceptionally kind to me during that period, and for the time that followed. They invited me over, hung out, encouraged me to get out again. I remember it in blurs: a Notting Hill Carnival, drinks at the pub, visits to their apartment, lots of Roy and HG. According to a friend, Dave came to a party at my squat with Shane MacGowan of The Pogues in tow. It may have happened, but I'd had too many cocktails by that time of the night to notice. Blurring was common, then.

The last time I saw Dave was in 1994, when The Blackeyed Susans came to Sydney to promote *All Souls Alive*. It was an astonishing line up at The Annandale — Dave, Rob Snarski, Phil Kakulas, Graham Lee, along with Warren Ellis and Jim White, who gave an incredible, almost possessed performance, the sheer joy of all these friends on stage together spiked with the frenzy of Warren Ellis's violin, and a room high on camaraderie, nostalgia and beer. Dave sang lead vocal on a few songs, including a swaying, inspired rendition of Leonard Cohen and Phil Spector's anthemic 'Memories', and his voice, fired up, cut like steel. It was one of those nights when the roof seemed to lift slightly off The Annandale, through heat, excitement and joy, and the crowd demanded a raft of encores, so delighted to be seeing Dave back on stage again. Afterwards we all trawled over to Newtown to continue the celebrations long into the night.

Earlier in the evening, before the show, the band had been selling and signing copies of the new album. I still have my copy, with its bizarre range of personal messages from the nice to the indecipherable. Dave, in his self-deprecating, sarcastic way, had simply signed his glamour photo on the CD by inking '666' squarely on his forehead.

That night was about as far as you could get from the whole London experience, the grey, the cold, the longing. And though I only knew him a little (just a little), of all the things I recall about Dave — his intelligence, his physical presence, his humour, the ever-so-slight wheeziness of his speaking voice — it's the kindness and generosity I remember most. The thing about Dave is that he understood distance and isolation, the slow unravelling of even the most potent relationships under those grey English skies. He understood exile, living as he did in the lively confines of his little West London apartment, so remote from the treeless plains and wide expanses of his art.

London, early 1990s.

Into the snake pit:
McComb on the
family farm near
Ravensthorpe in
southwest Western
Australia, early
1990s.

precious spirit escapes

Steve Kilbey

sometimes i get kinda confused
between stories paintings songs
old rumours
or things i heard just the other day …
david mccomb looks out from the pastel and gouache
sitting on my easel in a spare room where i'm painting him
painting him for a book
david mccomb next to a lake 200 kilometres south of perth
heat haze days
everything shimmering
davids tracking someone down
looking through the ashes of a campfire
squatting by the side of the road
he pokes the grey ash with a stick
he strides off through the bush
he drives away and hits a long and lonely stretch
i follow on
i drift to a car
a car parked in the shade of a cooly-bar tree
the bonnets up
theres a guy with his head down in the engine
a girl sits in the car
a kinda imaginary girlfriend
a sulky blonde listening to a distant fm station
a theoretical woman
she sits there smoking impatiently
the bloke comes out from under the bonnet
broad shouldered

slender wristed
thinning sandy hair
why its …
grant mclennan
steven?
grant says
steven i think my fan belts busted
he looks thoughtful
steven, what are you doing here?
a cloud passes over head
and the bush turns monochrome
he lights a peter stuyvesant
and puffs thoughtfully
he squints into the early afternoon
i took the wrong road round steven he says eventually
birds call in the trees
the cloud dissipates in blueness
dont ask me what i think of your painting …
grant exhales in a puff of lilac smoke
i prefer it when theyre a bit more … abstract
but grant i say
i thought it was just one of your stories
the stories you used to tell
grant stubbed out the cigarette in the sandy soil
i better go he said
how far away is he?
but grant your fanbelts busted i said
but he smiled and said
a painting is like a dream is like a song
and the car started up
and he drove away with a toot toot on the horn
and a laugh which made him cough
yes grant had told me
when he was alive
grant had said oh i like paul kellys randwick bells
grant had said oh i like mr someone and neil finn
i said what about wide open road grant?

and grant said well thats strange you should mention it
cos that song is about me …
and that made me laugh
grant was serious though
listen to the end of it then
at the end of wide open road
youll find cattle and cane
but grant, i listened and i couldnt find it …
meanwhile dave mccomb is writing a song
hes chasing a man who stole his baby
hes in a painting in a book
hes made that wrong turn
its getting dark out there
he can almost smell the sea
he does up the windows in his car
his high beam digs deep into the black
he keeps thinking he can see her
he keeps thinking he can hear this melody
he keeps thinking he can find his way back
grants checking into some small motel
the girl sits in the doorway as the night air turns cold
grant smiles as i walk up to the desk
no one here can see you steven he says with a grin
youre a ghost in your own painting
youre a fugitive in the song arent you? i say
how far away is he do you think? grant asked
we both looked out
down the long dark wide open road
the night was calm and serene
no loud sounds disturbed its serene hum
its hard to believe hes out there … i say
how would he know where to find us? grant asked
the next morning its still 1984
grant wakes up next to the sleeping girl
he looks at the time and goes back to sleep
mccomb wonders what he'll do when he catches up with them
hes parked opposite another lake

in the early morning air he stands there eternally
his blue black hair like a wild elvis
his long tall physique
his op shop clothes like a baroque and broke preacher
he looks into the rising sun
the sky looked big and empty
for a second he looks up and sees me
kilbey! he laughs derisively
and shakes his head
but dave but dave i say
he starts up the car
soon all trace of him is gone
but dust
grant is filling his car up at a servo somewhere
wheres the girl? i ask
he shrugs ... flighty he says
do she go back to him? i ask
nah! he never found us ... grant smiled his wandering eye smile
the one that reminded me of jesus and bernie in powderfinger
she met some other man he said sadly then
but the song ...? i say
yes why dont you sing that song then steven?
like you always wanted to ...
mccomb cruises along in his old car
he jams a cassette in the player
he lights another cig
he strums another chord
he writes down another line
he drives down this desolate highway
this lost and found highway
memory of girl smoulders in his heart
desire for revenge
shes stolen property he says to mclennan in his mind
in the painting hes still looking eastward and outward
his eyes are unfocussed
the pupils are blurred
he is onstage

Portrait of David McComb by Steve Kilbey; pastel and
gouache on acid-free paper (2007).

he is in the wilderness
he is in the act of creation
the silver lake behind
the acacia trees with magic bark
the birdsong and cicadas
forever looking out at the horizon
its nineteen eighty-nine for a moment
me n mclennan sitting in his flat at bondi junction
in some dark n leaky room
we're writing some songs
grants playing wide open road and laughing about it
he turns the riff into cattle and cane and back out again
lets go to the enmore he says
next minute we're watching the triffids playing
its the enmore theatre in sydney
the triffids are promoting the black swan
theyre playing wide open road at this moment
unbeknownst to them
this will be last gig in sydney for a long long lifetime
as phantoms grant and i watch from the balcony
at the end of the song
instead of ending in the usual place
the band jam on a little
dave and rob mccombs guitars answer each other
and THERE!
grant grabs my arm
sure enough for a split second
there it was the clue
and the proof
grant and i were back in bondi junction again
you never believed me did you? he asks triumphantly
a song within a song
is any of this really true? i asked out loud
is it ever
he said

The Listening Boy

Sam Twyford-Moore

For a moment there it seemed that the entire Australian underground simply packed up and left for Britain — starting perhaps with The Saints, who found themselves just as stranded overseas as they did at home — and although it's interesting to watch the birds migrate, you have to wonder what shook them out of the tree, what sound or fright. Australia was seen as culturally barren for bands of this sort. Exiles then, in the classic literary sense, like a generation of fine Russian writers, dressed as expatriates. It's a lark to imagine these bands as the Nabokovs and Sorokins of their day — Russian writers as American academics, not quite fitting in at home or abroad, heavy accents, ill-fitting overcoats. Rather: Australian singer-songwriters as London's rejects, freezing in flats, recording tracks near railway lines, rehearsing albums in the south of France, performing live on Spanish television programs, giving bemused answers to Japanese translators in tired telephone interviews.

David McComb belonged to a generation of (anti-)antipodean songwriters who found confidence in the interior even as they fled it. Young artists with heads full of books (and steam), carrying around ideas of Europe without knowing the soil — and in their suitcases, reams of lyrics, a few scribbled suggestions worked over and over, first sketched and finally etched into the 'Australian' self-consciousness.

The Triffids were named after a 1951 post-apocalyptic novel, *The Day of the Triffids*, by British writer John Wyndham: respectable pulp, a staple of the school curriculum. The Birthday Party derived its name from the bleak, black Harold Pinter play. The Go-Betweens, slightly sweeter souls, took their name from L.P. (Long Player?) Hartley's lyrical, nostalgic novel *The Go-Between*, published in 1953. Each of these books was turned into a film or television play, and it is little secret that each of these bands was cinema-literate. The Triffids, though, whose cultural reference point is unashamedly lowbrow, have perhaps the most appropriate namesake. The eponymous characters in Wyndham's nasty little novel are plants driven by an insatiable hunger, able to uproot themselves, raging against a purblind human race. Among the noxious weeds that ravage the Australian coastal landscape (bitou bush taking over the beaches, lantana devouring the suburban fringe) these alien life-forms with gnashing teeth and powers of locomotion must have seemed a fitting emblem of the multifarious process of colonization. Ever in search of greener pastures, these nomadic Triffids must have laughed — or else cringed — to have their music characterised as being rooted in the Australian landscape.

* * *

The Go-Betweens wanted to capture that 'striped sunlight sound' — a reference to pop sounds, probably Californian, though it makes me think about the Heidelberg School in Australian art, about art in light, and then my head goes back to the music, and tries to find the light in the music. And then back to McComb — who may be perceived by some as a dark figure, but there is so much light in his imagery — and the thought that perhaps the sun, the light, can be a threatening thing too. It's almost as if this generation of songwriters had studied at the Heidelberg School, Arthur Streeton protégés. Australian light, indelible — and here, look how important it is to McComb. The cover of his solo record, *Love of Will*, features a washed-out photograph of McComb, his hands shielding his eyes from the sunlight — it's easy to imagine him placed on the very beach from the cover of *Born Sandy Devotional*, come full circle.

I'd love a photograph of the two, Robert Forster and David McComb, perhaps back-to-back, to see who is the taller.[1] Both men remind me of Russell Drysdale's broomstick-limbed figures (the inspiration for John Brack's long-limbed ballet dancers and office workers). McComb could be a figure in one of those desolate, ochre portraits. I feel like that was the life he lived, inside someone else's painting.

'Wide Open Road' was the track that led me to thinking about McComb in painterly terms. It is, I imagine, the sort of song Russell Drysdale would have listened to while driving into the outback — red dust trailing behind the spinning rear wheels of a Morris Minor, boot filled with paint-tins and boxes of brushes — had the song existed in the 1930s and 1940s, when Drysdale went out there. McComb looked to the landscape for inspiration with that song, surely, like the artist. Then again, it is just as easy to conceive of McComb using a Drysdale painting as the starting point for a song, a rendition of something dry, dusty, melancholic, Australian. Think of Murray Bail's short story 'The Drover's Wife' (1975), which uses the Drysdale painting of the same name as the basis of a paranoid fable about the woman in the centre of the picture. I like the idea of McComb standing in front of the mid-period Drysdale, thinking up a song, inspired by the brushstrokes.

Going through Drysdale's paintings online, in their grainy, scanned mutilations: I had begun to think the exercise futile until I came across an image with a title which struck me as one that could have been penned by McComb, *The Listening Boy* (1949). A young boy in a ragged white shirt and frayed khaki slacks looks to his left, alone in the ochre landscape save for a large metal outpost and a cluster of houses (or fences?). The Boy looks like I felt when listening to *Born Sandy Devotional* — head one way, left lean, trying to get the music in the ear, head the other way, right lean, trying to read the lyrics — only there's nothing else around.

* * *

The request came through, printed down the length of one of Drysdale's dead brushes. They wanted us to play at Drysdale's wake, so we got tickets to the funeral more or less, not that they were skinning them off or nothing, and Dave showed up, suit tattered like his note-books; perhaps the suit was pin-striped, like lines in those books too. Dad and Dave drove out there, to the Drysdale house, and it was an open-plan sort of place, with plenty of space for the sound, but then N. Mort sidled up and said they really wanted to hold it out in the desert, and that would have made more sense. We would have made more sense out there. So we were there early, and we sat out the front, and wondered what Drysdale thought of his lawn while he was still alive. It was well-kept, and we wondered what brand of mower he used. The funeral was over, and the people were back, and they started to funnel into the house. We were let in, through the back door, the carpet was dappled with paint, looked like someone had been spitting gum all over the place, but it was paint, and D. said something like, 'Imagine the unholy mess we would leave behind if the guitars spat out gunk,' and that humbled us, for our notes just carried through the air, and though they stuck in the brain, they never stained the carpets. It was the last time we'd play in a house, that's what we swore to though, and maybe it was because the place was filled with people but we wanted out. 'Red Pony' was the only song they really wanted us to play, and we did, it suited the mood, burned up the carpet, and the wallpaper. Dave was none too happy with the performance though. The whole gig was painful, dead and dusty. Dusty Drysdale. Dead in the ground. Then John O. asked about the amp, but we told him he was a screwy image-maker, with nothing more than graphic design qualifications, but Dave told us to leave him alone, that he was all right. Then we played 'Beautiful Waste', which really broke up the old widow, who sat beneath the window, and we knew then it was she who had invited us.

*   *   *

David McComb could be an Australian in Paris, in some far-off, important year. He could be Colin McCahon on a lonely, cold New Zealand day, the low grey clouds drifting like faceless sheep. He could be Drysdale, red dust covering his work boots. Or a fifteen-year-old Fred Williams, coming home late from art class, collapsing into a teenage bed. McComb paints from the same scenery, only with lyrics and music instead of oils and canvas. McComb can be imagined working in any medium, placed at any time; he will always speak in the same damned, damning voice. Looking at *The Listening Boy* then, there is only one thing you can see for what it is, when you do, his voice — travelling, speaking.

Hyde Park, London, early 1990.

South by South-West

Jonathan Alley

After two decades in the world of radio and magazines, I've never encountered anyone — either in person, performance or via their work — who has inspired me to delve into their dark corners and brilliant dreams to the extent that David McComb has. Permeating his lyrical reflections of outback Australia, his aural paintings of cities — imagined characters, lovers, journeys — is McComb's uncanny ability to place himself in song, situating himself within the tale he is narrating. He establishes setting, develops character, creates conflict, atmosphere and story within a verse. He drops himself in and out of stories, blurring fiction and autobiography, life and imagination.

Film was one of many different strands of popular culture McComb drew inspiration from. Evidently he understood the affective power of the iconic images that cinema could generate. The liner notes to the reissued *Calenture* album include McComb's handwritten memo ensuring Gil Norton had heard the soundtrack to David Lynch's *Blue Velvet* — McComb having apparently crossed out a reference to the soundtrack of Jean Jacques Beineix's *Betty Blue*. Among noteworthy producers, McComb lists Jim Dickinson with reference to Wim Wenders' *Paris, Texas*, a film in which, tellingly, Ry Cooder's ghostly score almost represents an extra character in the film, like the landscape in which it's set.

Apparently McComb wished to put The Triffids on-screen in a way that bypassed what he called 'anonymous promo clips' and the 'deadlock of international AM radio.' Among Sally Collins' personal collection of material from her days as manager of The Triffids, is a treatment for something McComb had planned to call *South by South-West*. Neither a fictional feature film nor documentary, it planned to use the language of cinema to communicate what The Triffids were

LEFT: Framing
device. David
McComb with
camera, outside
Bridgetown
in south-west
Western Australia,
September 1982.

OVERLEAF:
McComb sporting
'Amish' beard,
London, c. 1991. In
the background,
stills from the
movie *Black
Narcissus*, as
featured in the
booklet accom-
panying McComb's
solo album, *Love
of Will*.

all about. The basic premise of *South by South-West* is to 'show The
Triffids on their home turf ... defining their style, identity and personality through the extraordinary geographic locations of the wilderness areas of south-west Western Australia ... combining elements
of documentary, music video, home movie (footage) with ... surreal
landscape shots.' McComb insists that the film be informed by a 'sense
of irreverence, informality and surreal humour.'

When we've asked interviewees if they'd care to speculate on what
McComb might have achieved had he lived, responses point almost
exclusively to the realms of academia and literature. But given the

perspicacity of his mind's eye, his zest for characters, stories and setting, I wonder if he might have written a screenplay in time.

McComb's images and stories, all painted in song, have become entwined with the motley fabric of Australian culture. Beckoning, they loom large and ever mysterious.

In attempting to paint David's story on screen, the deeper you go, the more daunting the task reveals itself to be. But in a way, he's laid a path for anyone who wants to use the language of the screen to tell his story. Each bar of his major works will effortlessly suggest a myriad of images — visual impressions that evolve as you immerse yourself in the songs.

When it's reaching 2.00 a.m. (again), the wine bottle is empty (again) and my bones ache for bed and I shudder at the prospect of the next day (again), I often wonder why I'm doing this; and wonder if I'm taking liberties to which I'm not entitled, touching on stories that aren't mine to tell. Then I go back to the songs. The songs don't go away, they stay, they are here, left for us, and for the subsequent generations. And the songs go on spinning and turning, fusing the human spirit with the everyday life we see around us in a place we struggle to understand.

The Singularity of The Triffids

Claire Colebrook

One way of thinking about a band like The Triffids, is that a certain sense and value, a certain *élan*, accrues to the fan of this edgy eighties West Australian band, known at once for their deviation from convention and for their capacity to employ and vary a wide range of conventional musical styles. To think of the band in this way — as having a meaning for us, today, because they mark a certain moment of the past — is to place the force of music in second place to relations of convention and reception. The music's power would then lie both in its marking of time and place (eighties west-coast Australia/urban London and Europe) and in a certain reaction to the music industry: not yet highly synthesized and rendered suitable for mass marketing, but not entirely resistant to the quite sincere adoption of musical traditions and norms, such as folk (the ballad narrative of 'Tarrilup Bridge'), pop (the eighties synthesizer and lyrical harmonies of 'Goodbye Little Boy'), blues (the chord progression, brushed drum kit and acoustic bass in the jazz style of 'Butterflies into Worms'), rock (the frequent use of ranging guitar breaks) and country ('Estuary Bed' and its use of pedal steel guitar). But I would suggest that the essence of this band's work lies in its remarkable capacity to alter how we think about the time and value of popular music, precisely because of the simultaneous deployment and deterritorialization of established forms: that is, it was precisely because the music was neither a full identification with a certain musical norm, nor a complete negation of that norm, that The Triffids enabled new types of listening publics, new types of listening and — more radically — a new relation between time and work.[1] One often treats musical styles, motifs or even bands as having a certain specificity that marks time — the sound of the sixties, eighties trance or seventies punk. On such an understanding there is an act of musical creation or *work* that then allows for a certain musical time or history. Later bands can 'quote' earlier sounds (so that, today, The View are inflected by The Libertines, who in turn are indebted to The Clash), and this creates a lineage or genealogy whereby listening publics at once recognize an earlier style and allow their own listening histories to be marked out by the trajectory of pop history. One defines oneself either by listening to the music of one's youth — remaining in a certain time — or one allows one's present and future to be given by that past, by listening first to Joy Division, then New Order and so on. The Triffids, though, complicate this notion of a musical work that exists *in* time, and a notion of music history whereby works allow us to mark time (punk after prog rock, electro hip-hop after house). Instead, they deploy a series of traditional and nostalgic devices (such as folk and country) alongside electronic, urban and synthesized motifs. Rather than creating works *in time*, or quoting and framing motifs from time past, the music of The Triffids creates a time of inclusive disjunction: it is not the case that one chooses electronic *or* acoustic (and one can think here of the near riot that occurred when Bob Dylan chose to use electronic amplification in a folk genre). Rather, the music of The Triffids 'is' folk/country/traditional *and* electronic/urban/synthesized, and it thereby displays the range of affects and sound potentials from which different musical styles and different musical times are composed.

Far from situating themselves within music history, The Triffids deployed a mode of 'stratigraphic time,' where all styles and possibilities were co-present (electronic and acoustic, harmonic and discordant, narrative and lyric, stylized and improvized). It is not surprising, when we think of their music in this way — as 'minor' or 'minoritarian' in its refusal of recognition — that they took their band's title from John Wyndham's fiction about inhuman mutation and variation, as though they explored musically a new type of future in which the good subject of common sense and judgement was not simply obliterated but confronted with its own potential for metamorphosis beyond recognition.

Here I argue that the music of The Triffids challenges our usual conception of the relation between popular taste and pop history. It is not just the case that this band could be regarded as singular in its unique combination of styles — drawing on folk, country, acoustic, electronic, alternative and punk progressions and motifs — it also took those styles and submitted them to internal variation. This occurs most explicitly in the vocals which oscillate between highly melodic and spoken forms, displaying at one and the same time the speaking or lyrical voice's capacity to become pure sound, and the musical or melodic voice's capacity to be punctuated by inharmonious or dissonant elements (consider the 'Holy Roller' section of 'Stolen Property', for example). Or, we could see such variation in the two tracks I will be focussing on here: the popular 'Wide Open Road' on *Born Sandy Devotional*, with its standard chord progression, verse-chorus structure and apparent reference to place; and the less mainstream 'When a Man Turns Bad' (one of the bonus tracks on the *Born Sandy* reissue), that is marked by a bass line remaining on the same note (of the tonic) and same pulsating rhythm throughout, over which non-melodic and non-harmonic electric guitar effects accompany sung/spoken vocals. There are also such juxtapositions or internal variations within certain tracks, such that a track can begin with folk or country themes and progressions only to be disrupted by dissonant and arrhythmic effects: what happens, then, is that the distinction between the formal and the singular becomes indiscernible. Those structures we recognize in advance and that determine our mode of listening and enjoyment are placed alongside non-idiomatic variations and transformations. Highly coded ballad forms are crossed with electronic harmonics and synthesized percussive effects, while seemingly alternative tracks that open with punk or 'indie' motifs of simple bass lines and technically simple melodic variants develop through the use of synthesizers and drum machines. Such a description could apply to the music of certain other bands of the time, of course, which is to acknowledge that the 'singularity' of The Triffids or any band (or indeed of any instance of a type) cannot be understood as *absolute* — as absolutely singular in the sense of having no relations whatsoever to general, pre-existing forms of (in the present case) blues, rock, indie and the like. While undeniably distinctive, The Triffids' music is not so absolutely singular or 'unique' that we don't recognize in it quotations and reworkings of more or less familiar aural and lyrical structures. The Triffids' 'singularity', in other words, cannot be understood as belonging to the band on its own, exclusively, uniquely and absolutely. Again, the same argument could be made of a band like Air Supply, say, but the question here might have to do with the ways in which a band like The Triffids seems to tease us with a sense of its singularity, whereas 'the singularity of Air Supply' would seem oxymoronic.

If arguments regarding art's value or sense have been poised between essentialist and sociological accounts, the former arguing for the formal qualities of a work, the latter for its meaning in relation to reception, then the peculiar and radical eclecticism of The Triffids forces us to find a way beyond such oppositions. Their music is at one and the same time deeply embedded in a series of historically and culturally recognizable forms (including contemporary postmodernism, the recycling of inherited forms, nostalgia, hybridization, etc.), indicating that part of its sense and audibility is grounded in tradition and listening publics; at the same time, their mixing and de-formation of those recognizable modes tears sound away from any already existing, recognizable or unified population. Their work is, I would argue, 'minoritarian': not the music of an existing minority (West Australian subculture of the 1980s), but a work that tears its listener apart in what Deleuze and Guattari refer to as 'inclusive disjunction.'[2] Whereas art populations tend to operate by exclusive disjunction — I like punk, not jazz; bebop not trad; Christina Aguilera not Britney — thereby allowing formed identities and allegiances, The Triffids combine terms in inclusive disjunction: punk *and* country *and* electronic *and* folk *and* acoustic *and* dissonant *and* narrative *and* elegiac and … More importantly, such combinations bring the very matter of music to the fore: what we hear at one and the same time are 'formed matters' (recognizable motifs, progressions and rhythms) and the de-formation of those matters into a 'generalized chromaticism.'[3]

Since art's inception as a modern discipline there has been an intimate, if problematic, relation between populations and taste. If one assumes that the value or beauty of a work of art is based on what we (as human beings possessed of a certain nature) find pleasing, then we can say that the existence of a population is prior to a work's possible popularity; something would be judged to be valuable because it is in accord with our capacities for reception. When Immanuel Kant wrote his *Critique of Judgement* (1790) he was reacting against the assumption that art's value lay in the degree to which it met with human enjoyment. Kant made a similar argument regarding ethics: an act is good not because it flows from a general moral sense or human tendency to do good. On the contrary, we behave morally and recognize our truly *ethical* or super-sensible nature when we act *despite* our feeling or natural humanity. I have no sympathy for you, cannot really recognize you as one of my kind, and I may not even recognize you as human; but even so I extend help towards you. Such, for Kant, is a truly moral act because it does not rely on what we naturally are, but on how we might imagine ourselves to be. Consider a similar opposition in terms of music and taste: a song that was heard and immediately recognized by a populace as 'just what we like to hear' — another aggressive thrash tune, another summer anthem, another trad ballad — appeals to already given criteria and relations. But if what we hear is not yet discernible as music or of our kind, and perhaps compels us both to question what music is, or what *this* music is, then we are invited to listen to what is played as a possible instance of what might count as music for a listening populace not yet in existence. Kant described this virtual populace as a *sensus communis*, or the experience — in listening — of what others *would* recognize as being of value. Such a theory of judgement was directly political, for it relied upon imagining a community of consumers that was not already in existence and could be imagined — ideally — as a populace different from contingent and competing fans (the word 'fan' being a late-nineteenth century US abbreviation of 'fanatic') of various tastes. Instead, one could imagine what *would be valued* if we could abstract from our already determined and particular likings. Not only did such a theory intimate a 'higher' taste not based on fashion and populism, and not only did such a distinction lead towards a privileging of avant-garde forms that destroyed or negated populism, it also suggested that art was at its most valuable in its capacity to create (rather than please) seemingly unified publics. The aesthetic and moral theories against which Kant was reacting assumed a humanity or population already in existence: a moral feeling we could all rely upon, a taste that all decent folk 'like us' already recognized.

Despite first appearances it is the populist ordering of the relation between popularity and value that Kant overturns in his theory of judgement. Kant defines beauty and the proper judgement of the work of art as distinct from any form of enjoyment that would be based on our bodily, human or supposedly general nature. What we *feel* in the enjoyment of a work of art is not any aspect of physical (or as Kant would refer to it, 'pathological') affect, though it should be remembered that Kant was never placed in front of a Marshall stack. Instead, the relation between the self who enjoys and the object enjoyed is purely formal: in everyday experience I have to synthesize the material I receive into recognizable concepts, but in the work of art it is not the recognition of an object but form — *regardless of any specified object* — that enables me to feel myself as a forming power. This is why art is not so much disinterested but before or beyond interests: before I can recognize an object as useful for me I must have some concept of it and refer it to my life as an individuated and meaningful whole. Aesthetic enjoyment occurs before (or outside of) such ordering; indeed, it is the feeling of ordering, synthesizing or allowing to come into form that characterizes the work of art. One of the words used by Kant and his commentators to describe this relation between a self who orders and material ordered is 'harmony', but this must be distinguished from harmony in its literal musical sense. What is felt as perfectly married or synchronized is the mind's capacity for bringing material into a relation ready for recognition, and the received data's apparent suitability for subjective reception, *as if* the world we viewed were made in accord with our capacity for knowledge and reception. What follows, for Kantian aesthetics, is a direct but inverse relation between populations and popularity: a work of art that was widely enjoyed or effortlessly popular, readily consumable and requiring little or no effort, would be of no aesthetic value precisely because it was easily recognized, not allowing us to exercise our forming powers, not allowing us to feel ourselves synthesizing the work of art. It would appeal to what we already are — the general populace of consumers — rather than what we *might be*. So, it is not the case that something is good because it is popular; nor is it the case, as Pierre Bourdieu would have it, that some works of art (such as those of high modernism) establish themselves as good insofar as they are not popular.[4]

Both of the anti-Kantian (or empirical) ways of thinking about value — the dependence on a human nature, or the sociology of created publics — establish the existence of a population (either the general public and their established tastes, or the elite and their distance from that taste) and then measure artistic worth according to the degree to which it answers that population's self-defining interests. The general populace (however contentious or illusory this notion might be) is what it is by liking and listening to the same material: youth groups define themselves by listening to certain forms of music, for example, while subcultures define themselves by taking those forms of recognition and enacting a de-formation (in turn creating new definitions and recognitions). If being an adolescent of the 1970s was largely achieved by listening to prog rock, being a punk was enabled by taking the very features of the latter — large forms, high technical complexity and competence, sophisticated chord progressions with complex modulations, extended instrumental solos — and inverting those values; punk was marked by a lack of instrumental skill, simple chord progressions without key changes or complex modulations, non-narrative lyrics and small ensembles. A sociological approach to taste, music and popularity would assume neither that a population has an intrinsic nature, nor that its defining or constituting tastes were established by anything other than contingent connections. Instead, for such an approach, populations are created through the mutual recognition and enjoyment of certain forms, and in doing so they enable other populations to be defined in opposition. On this account relations would be *internal* to the structure of an opposition: punk is what it is only in opposition to prog rock, for example. What something *is* is determined by its relations.

Such an account of art and populations might seem to be offered by Deleuze and Guattari's theory of territorialization and assemblages: a body (such as a social body or even an organism) comes into being only through processes that establish a territory, or a relation among terms.[5] It is not the case that there are identities, such as human subjects, who then enter into society; on the contrary, a certain relation among bodies is produced (what they refer to as the social machine), and this then establishes each body as having a recognizable stability or individual form.[6] Deleuze and Guattari's examples are frequently musical, in describing both the origin of art and the origin of social forms. Art begins with the refrain: a body can mark itself off and give itself a locale — creating a space between and among bodies — through a refrain. Further, such refrains are themselves established not by taking an already given system of relations and terms (such as Western harmony) but by a process that forms matters, or that creates distinctions and differences in sonorous material. Deleuze and Guattari were not alone in regarding the production of individuation and relations as occurring primarily through sonorous material, and were also seemingly in accord with a post-Romantic conception of music and art that insisted that the being and sense of a work could only be apprehended from its relation to other works.[7] What something *is* can only be discerned by the relation it bears to other terms, to networks of consumption and to other possible sign systems.

What makes Deleuze and Guattari's work interesting, however, is precisely its resistance to this too easy reduction of the sense of a work of art to its possible networks of recognition, taste and consumption. Indeed, like Kant, Deleuze and Guattari are insistent that relations are external to terms: this means that however it is that matter is formed, synthesized or assembled (or brought into relation), there is also a potentiality for that material to be configured otherwise. This has two major consequences, both of which — I would argue — allow us to discern, today, the singularity of a musical corpus such as that of The Triffids. First, again like Kant, Deleuze and Guattari do not see taste and aesthetic sense as defined through populations; on the contrary, two modes of population — what they refer to as 'major' and 'minor' — are made possible through aesthetic modes.[8] Second, such aesthetic modes are not contingent but have to do with matter itself. One way of assembling material is majoritarian, allowing for a certain type of population: one of ready consumption, or 'easy listening,' drawing upon already formed relations. Another is minoritarian, a mode which does not possess a population and which is not defined *against* already existing forms and modes of consumption; it draws upon the potentialities of matter itself and can be described as a generalized chromaticism. To refer to music as minoritarian is to identify two features: it releases sonorous material from already established relations *and* creates a possible or *virtual* population that could not be created as an organized body. Such a mode of music allows us to consider three key features of the music associated with The Triffids: its eclecticism, its singularity and its mode of temporality. What needs to be noted is that such a 'minoritarian' mode is neither avant-garde — a simple destruction or negation of forms established already as popular — nor explicable by already existing tastes and relations. Instead, one takes formed matters, such as existing styles, motifs, progressions, forms and tonalities, and places those matters into variation. Two features mark The Triffids in this regard: they could combine some of the most highly coded and already formed modes of music — such as folk and country — with free variation; the simplest bass lines and melodies were coupled with complex electronic effects, non-harmonic vocal doubling and non-metrical percussive intrusions (albeit, again, such features could also be said to describe, say, certain aspects of 'techno' music). Whereas complete deterritorializations — such as the atonal compositions of a Webern — operate as complete and cerebral negations of a music grounded in Western harmony and counterpoint, The Triffids would take those forms most associated with the organization of the body — such as the dance form of the tango — and combine that with material that would preclude the easy movement of the body ('The Clown Prince' on *The Black Swan*, for instance, with its use of a tango beat and instrumentation combined with background quasi-psychedelic effects).

Why, today, might one want to listen to The Triffids? Given the rate of production of popular music, and the ways in which one's choice of music places oneself, for others, in time, does the nostalgic enjoyment of this pre-digital and rather naïve sound of The Triffids merely mark one out as a musical Luddite? And does the choice of The Triffids, as opposed to any number of more widely circulated — or popular — eighties bands set oneself apart as a pretentious try-hard? Do we choose this sound, rather than another, to signal at one and the same time a difference from what would now be determined as popular, and a distance from those other eighties bands such as Duran Duran (self-described as aiming to amalgamate Le Chic and The Sex Pistols!) who would render one's taste and nostalgia all too ready-made?[9] One way of thinking about music, taste, value and what it means to listen to a corpus again can be found in the sociology of aesthetic judgement.

According to Pierre Bourdieu, those cultural objects that present themselves as dissonant or as defined against the popular are really consecrations of different types of population. So if I want to define myself against the synthesized new romantic of the eighties (too marketed, too readily available, too similar in all of its supposedly different manifestations) and the equally highly coded versions of punk (too reactive, too much a form of gesture and theatre rather than a commitment to music as such) then I would need to find music that did not yet have a broad marketing base, but that could also present itself as more than an act of noisy refusal: The Triffids. If we were to render such an argument more specific to music, and to popular music, we might also want to draw on the work of Simon Frith who, like Bourdieu, argues that music populations are formed in the selection of materials: we become who we are by assembling around certain recognized sound forms.[10] It is this commitment to the formation of oneself through the socio-cultural relations of music forms that allows Frith to go on to argue that music is essentially nostalgic: if music is the experience of time passing, then to listen again to a piece of music is to listen again to the time passed in one's youth. Now, The Triffids would seem to provide evidence for such a claim. If to listen to that music now is to hear a mode of sound no longer possible, precisely because of the digitalized, post-pop-idol manufacture of the 2000s, it is also to hear a form that in its inception was already quotational: not only did the chord progressions of The Triffids draw on existent forms ranging from country and folk to the Latin American tango, they also deployed lyrics that were highly specific in terms of historical and spatial locale, and expressive of experiences of loss, pain, mourning and absence. What I would like to suggest, though, is that the mode of time enabled by this music is less nostalgic — looking back to a present that is defined as a specific point in relation to a history laid out as a series — than it is expressive of time in its pure state. That is, what is given is not a demarcated mode of sound that could be located either as eighties music, or as retro or putatively timeless (as in those 'easy listening' modes that aim to be sufficiently generic as to come from 'any time whatsoever'); rather, we are presented with temporally marked forms — the country or folk ballad — and then the de-formation and variation. We hear the capacity for *extended time* — the time of pop music history, or recognizable forms — in transformation; time is heard as intensive. That is, rather than hearing sounds as already formed and recognizable, sounds that would mark out times and populations — 'this is a sixties folk tune' — we hear sound materials in their capacity to create time. Consider, for example, a tune such as 'When a Man Turns Bad'. This song assembles a bass line consisting of the same (tonic) note repeated with the same rhythm, while the lead vocal is then occasionally doubled by a non-harmonic falsetto 'backing' singer, whose intonation is less than perfect: not only are the lyrics of human nihilism directly resonant with the bass line's refusal to modulate or develop into a more complex progression; the accompanying guitar noises extend the voice's departure from the song lyric to a confrontation with sound's capacity to disrupt melody and harmonic progression.

Let me conclude by suggesting that this track represents an intrinsic potentiality of The Triffids' music — its orientation towards a 'haptic' aesthetic — and that once we recognize this potentiality in tracks such as 'When a Man Turns Bad' and 'The 107' (also on the reissue of *Born Sandy Devotional*), we can see that the coupling of these styles with the more popular (because more in accord with existing conventions) 'Wide Open Road' allows for the creation or deterritorialization of listening publics; it has the force of slipping some Ornette Coleman into a Benny Goodman album. In his book on the painting of Francis Bacon, Gilles Deleuze argues that art's confrontation with material — in the case of painting, colour and canvas — yields three possibilities in the twentieth century: digital, manual and haptic.[11] We experience the digital most clearly when the matter of art is completely subordinated to pure formal relations: that is, the hand becomes a way of thinking about matter as manipulable units (the 'digit'). Before digital music in its strict sense, a digital, abstract or cerebral mode is given in pure formalisms, where matter is completely mastered by relations: in 'high' culture one could think of tone-row music, in 'pop' culture the formed and technically masterful sounds of prog rock. In the other mode, the manual, the brain abandons its mastery of the body and matter, allowing for insubordination: music becomes the chance of noise or clashing sounds, the performance events of avant-garde music that take axes to pianos, or the stereotypical rock displays of smashing guitars and drum-kits on stage. The problem with these two extremes, according to Deleuze, is their negation or simple opposition between matter on the one hand, and the relations formed by bodies in order to negotiate matter; what such forms fail to confront is the way in which our bodies — who we are — are given orientation in relation to matter. The other form of art, the haptic, confronts our body's capacity to feel matter in its process of forming, to feel the tendencies of sound itself. This is given when the ear can hear the hand moving across the keyboard or guitar fretboard, when the ear is assaulted by the instrument's resistance to the voice and mastery. The combinations, variations and de-formations of The Triffids' music use the voice as more than an instrument for 'singing,' use the guitar as a way of taking formed scales and introducing a microtonal variation: what we hear is not a negation of formed matters but the musical body's capacity to create a new sound, not for a given population of organized bodies, but for a 'people to come.' And, of course, not for the first time, since what I have just described as The Triffids' use of the guitar, for example, could also describe Jimi Hendrix's guitar use (or that of Kevin Shields, Robert Fripp, Thurston Moore and others). This doesn't mean that we are condemned only to repeat the past, but simply that our forays into the 'singularity' of a band like the Triffids cannot help but spiral ever outwards — away, seemingly, from the 'essence' of that singularity. But again, perhaps, it is only bands like The Triffids that could compel us to chase after such an essence; and it may be that the very act of doing so is what constitutes us as a 'people to come.'

Out to Lunch

Tracee Hutchison

The following interview with Dave McComb was originally recorded for a ten-part radio series I presented on JJJ in January 1990. Dave was one of about thirty musicians I talked to during November/December 1989 for the series on Australian music in the 1980s. I subsequently turned these interviews into a book, *Your Name's on the Door* (ABC Books, 1992).

This was a telephone interview — I think from his parents' place in Perth. Dave and I had met briefly at 2SER (where I was doing an Australian music show) in Sydney when the band first relocated from Perth in the early 1980s, but because they had spent much of the 1980s in London they weren't a group of people I really got to know, despite being a big fan.

So, like so many people who fell in love with The Triffids in the band's absence, I had grown to know Dave through the raw humility and heart-aching desolation of his songs. Dave always seemed more comfortable when his songs did the talking for him but this was actually a most revealing and engaging conversation. It was as though he felt honoured to have the opportunity to reflect on The Triffids' considerable achievements — to be given a rightful historical place.

Reading back over these transcripts I can actually hear Dave's voice in his words. Humble, yet sharply observant, insightful and considered — and perhaps even more relevant today than they were almost twenty years ago.

* * *

David McComb, Alsy MacDonald and Phil Kakulas were still at high school when they formed The Triffids in 1978. They released six or seven cassette albums, sold them at sympathetic record stores and then won a song contest at a local radio station called 6NR in Perth. The prize was some recording time and the release of a single. The outcome, 'Stand Up'/'Farmers Never Visit Nightclubs', seemed polarized. The A-side was a bubblegum record that sounded a bit like The Dugites, while the flip-side gave some indication of how The Triffids would progress through the eighties.

David McComb: Most people preferred 'Farmers'. I guess people find that sort of thing zany. To this day we get people screaming out for that song when we play live. We felt a strong bonding with the New York bands that came out at the end of the seventies, people like Television and Talking Heads, who played guitar music in a totally 'un-' rock & roll way. They just went about things as though the whole history of rock music hadn't existed, so they could do songs about buildings on fire and doing their cleaning, or whatever. We did a song about farmers not being socially accepted at nightclubs.

The limited number of live venues in Perth in 1981 made it difficult for a band playing original music: Perth became famous in the eighties as 'cover-band city.' Despite that, The Triffids managed to carve out a unique sound in an almost hostile environment. Audiences wantonly accused the band of wilful amateurism in their live performances.

McComb: Like a lot of bands inspired by punks we were never intimidated by the fact that we couldn't play like Eric Clapton. We never fought to try to be technically proficient. I think it was something inherent in our generation. The generation above us probably thought we were ridiculous because we hadn't learned our J.J. Cale guitar licks. If that sort of thing was high on your list of criteria I think we would have been really horrible, not a very enjoyable evening out.

We actually thought that the independent music industry in Perth was terrible then, but we didn't realize what was going to happen in the next ten years. I mean, we look back on it now and it was just a golden era. There were many more interesting bands then, the punk bands like The Victims and The Scientists were a great inspiration and just went about things in a unique fashion. It seemed difficult at the time, but we'd always be getting big crowds, I think it was easier then to tempt people to go out and see original bands in Perth than it is now.

The tyranny of distance forced most Western Australian bands east, where Sydney and Melbourne continued to dominate both the live and recorded aspects of the industry. Among Hot Records' 1983 discography was The Triffids' first album, Treeless Plain, *and a single, 'Beautiful Waste'. With these records came the startling revelation that there was a Perth sound and The Triffids were it. Critics were beside themselves, major record companies got excited. The band was nonplussed …*

McComb: It didn't occur to us to align ourselves with a major label. We were making a living doing things the way we wanted to, and, unless someone's got a gun to your head, you don't see any reason to jump into bed with a bunch of people that you don't respect very much. That feeling remained, in one form or another, all the time with The Triffids. I think we were just starting to become more ambitious in terms of what we put on our records in 1983. We had this song 'Red Pony', and we wanted to have a string quartet or something on it and it just wasn't the done thing back then. That was quite a big step for us. So that was more the type of ambition that we had then, rather than just wanting to be part of the industry.

We didn't want to be a standard guitar-pop band, we wanted to branch out and do what a band from New York might be doing on their records. There still seems to be a thing in Australia — sort of a principle that people view as honesty — to do your live set basically on record, and it's important to capture the live sound of the band on record and do nothing more. We just threw that idea out the window.

Together with The Go Betweens, The Triffids had an evocative quaintness in their music that seemed intrinsically Australian …

McComb: I think it's important that bands try and address what makes them Australian, or why they should be different from a band from LA or from Venezuela or from Norway, because rock music has become such an international commodity. I think we just thought it would be good to try and have some Australianness in the geography or the climate that comes into the lyrics, that sort of stuff, just nitty-gritty really, the setting of the songs. But as far as being patriotic about the industry or feeling that you're part of the Australian scene, no, not very much. There's a certain lack of respect that a lot of Australian bands, like The Go-Betweens and The Birthday Party, had for the international scene and the critics, and I felt we identified with that.

The Triffids were at the forefront of the second wave of Australian bands who went to London in the eighties. The Birthday Party, The Go-Betweens and The Laughing Clowns had demonstrated that it was possible to base yourself on the other side of the world and survive … just. When The Triffids arrived in London midway through 1984, the English press fell over themselves to be on the guest list. The new darlings from Australia had arrived. The Raining Pleasure *EP and the* Treeless Plain *LP had both been released in the UK and the* New Musical Express *declared 1985 would be 'The Year of The Triffids.'*

McComb: It wasn't that different from going to Sydney. It was a matter of playing in small clubs and pubs around the country and just building up the grassroots following. Sure, a journalist can write about you, but it's not really going to last if you don't get people who actually have to pay to get into concerts and pay for their own records. There's a big difference. I know it's a cliché, but I think it's true about people paying for their own music.

When we got to London I think we sort of felt we had to make a kind of statement. We recorded the *Field of Glass* EP just when we got there, which is still I guess the most aggressive and violent record that we have done. It gave us heaps of confidence. I think that a lot of bands from backwaters and provincial little towns like Perth have to overcome a lack of confidence and believe that they can do something as good as anyone from anywhere in a more credible part of the world. With *Field of Glass* we'd got rid of all that aggression and violence.

As the 1987 Richard Lowenstein movie Dogs in Space *fought for an audience, Lowenstein's film-making talents were enlisted to document the largest touring showcase of Australian bands ever embarked upon in the country. The* Australian Made *tour featured some of the major acts in the country and was an ambitious attempt at a travelling mini-Woodstock to celebrate Australia's 'arrival' onto the international music map. INXS, Jimmy Barnes, The Divinyls, Models, Do-Re-Mi and I'm Talking made for a hefty line-up. But The Triffids, a band who were spending more time in England than at home and who were still enjoying the infatuation of the English music press, were by far the least likely inclusion. None were more surprised than the band when their services were requested to be a part of the biggest collective tour of Australian bands ever.*

McComb: How it came about was that INXS at that stage hadn't had that much effect in London — they were going fine in America — and I think Chris Murphy, their manager, was going around and kept saying 'Triffids' everywhere in London and in Europe, and it was obvious that we were having some sort of effect over there and they, with much more recording company backing, were having big trouble. But since, of course, they've become bigger than God everywhere! And I also think that some members of INXS felt enthusiastic about having us on the tour and that sort of clinched it. We were as shocked as anyone — we thought it was a typo error when we saw our name listed! We were only paid a nominal amount for each show. We should have gone into debt and got proper road crew, but we just had one person setting up the amps, so consequently we were probably always running into problems. We always do make those sort of short-term errors. But I must say that all the other bands were incredibly gracious to us, considering they were probably confused as to why we were there too.

In a sense The Triffids' inclusion on the Australian Made *tour had more to do with their success overseas than it did here. Historically, The Triffids were part of a genre of rock music that included The Birthday Party, The Laughing Clowns, The Moodists and The Scientists, bands that only found widespread acclaim in Australia after receiving grand overtures from the influential English press. It seemed to smack of tokenism.*

McComb: Well, I don't think it's limited to rock music by any stretch. It just seems to be a perennial thing that Australians have had to go. People like Bruce Beresford, Barry Humphries and Clive James, that generation, going to the UK in the forties, fifties, whenever it was, and the painters before that. Sometimes I think it's changing ... I think when there's some more broad-minded radio stations and the media are prepared to give some serious credibility to Australian bands or Australian musicians or artists. That might be changing. It's more that you need American approval these days, which I find is more depressing. You know, there is an anti-American feeling in Australia but it really is the ultimate thing that if an Australian band does well in America, that's it — or a movie, or a book. We really need that seal of approval. Once we get that it'll be great.

The glitter and glam of Australian Made *over,* The Triffids *returned to England and recorded* Calenture, *a more polished album that seemed more indicative of a style that began with* Born Sandy Devotional. *It was a big, resounding, orchestral sound reminiscent of the forties, blended with an eighties-style pop.*

McComb: I guess I've a longstanding admiration and fascination with Phil Spector, Shadow Morton and all the people, both male and female, who were involved in all the girl-group records, the really orchestrated girl-group records with sound effects. The whole record was done with a view to making it incredibly lush and incredibly listenable.

To me it's a really seasick record, though, compared to *Born Sandy Devotional* which was rooted in a sense of place. It was just very alienated. Out to lunch.

* * *

This was one of only two interviews I had with Dave McComb. The second was in 1994 for the SBS television program *nomad*. I often think about that 'nomad' day with David — it was the last time I saw him and I asked him if he was happy. He snapped back that it was an appalling question. It absolutely was — particularly in an interview situation — but there was just something about him that day that made me ask. In retrospect the most regrettable part of the exchange was the question itself. By asking it I was also telling him that I'd seen his fragility. I guess I'd recognized what it looked like, and I empathized. But I didn't really articulate it very well. It just came out in a clumsy question. I know that David left that day feeling exposed. I could see it in the way he looked at me when he left — an imploring look to take care with what I did with the interview. In the end very little of it went to air. It was just too revealing.

The Reissues

John Dyer

Welcome. My name is John Dyer. I work for Domino Recordings in the UK. Strangely, I'm sat in a bathroom in the middle of the night in Singapore to talk about David McComb, a man who departed this world in 1999, and his band The Triffids.

I first saw the band in 1984. I think it was at a South London college, possibly Egham College. The band had just come in from Australia; it was one of the first dates they'd played within the London area. They were supporting a band I was working for, a very incongruous band, not at all similar musically, called The Farmer's Boys. I stood at the side of the stage keeping an eye on foot pedals or something like that, pretending I knew what I was doing. I came and I saw The Triffids playing in front of me and I thought they were a fantastic band. I think I was twenty at the time, still in that moment when you're just excited about everything. But there was still something exceptional about watching them from the side of that stage. At that time I was a fan of a band called Echo and the Bunnymen, and one of the characters — it might have been Les Pattinson — drove on his motorbike all the way down from Liverpool and stood at the side of the stage as well, watching. I thought that was odd, and interesting, and at that point I duly registered 'The Triffids' and tried to find out what albums they had available.

The albums I found came out shortly after that live show. There were two albums that came out very close together, one called *Treeless Plain*, one called *Raining Pleasure*. I bought them on vinyl, and they were near the top of my tree of excitement, particularly *Raining Pleasure*, the mini-album. (To this day, twenty years on, I think I must play the self-titled track at least once a year.) Over the next few years, I saw them play another couple of times. So I've never had a deep, passionate relationship with The Triffids' music. It's just that I've always really enjoyed them. There's nothing weird about it. Nothing obsessional. Although, something happened when they released *Born Sandy Devotional* — a great album, a fantastic album which was only available on vinyl (or cassette) when it first came out. That record had a big effect on me; I guess I must have played that at home quite a lot.

As my life and career progressed, I moved to London. I went to work for Mute Records as a marketing person. The first Nick Cave album I worked on was *Tender Prey*, and I would see Dave McComb pop in to the offices now and again (he was close by to some members of The Bad Seeds). The Triffids had signed to Island Records by then. When *Calenture* came out, it was a big hope for them, and a big push. As a marketing person, I was watching closely the way Island were campaigning and working that band, trying so hard. I mean, they really chucked the kitchen sink at that band to try and make them succeed. And it was always slightly clumsy in a way, and slightly at odds with the time, the band starting to drift away from the *NME*-applauded mainstream. I think that threw the record label, it probably threw the band as well, away and off-course and off-beam from the mainstream or whatever everyone aspires to have a mainstream band to be. And essentially that was it. After that they recorded their last album, *The Black Swan*, which I wasn't a particular fan of, although I know a fair few folks who are very fond of that recording. Maybe, unbeknown to us at that time, it was all disintegrating or the aspirations of David and the band members were not being matched by the label they were working with, or with the audience they were trying to reach.

All throughout this period, I started to develop my CD collection and there was a little gap under 'T'. I was waiting for someone to release *Born Sandy Devotional* on CD. But that never happened. *Treeless Plain* and *Raining Pleasure*, those never came out; they just disappeared. In fact, Rough Trade — label, distribution, the whole lot — was on the verge of bankruptcy, and they owned the rights to those first three Triffids records. It came to the point where all of Rough Trade's debts were being called in; the warehouse was being shut down. I happened to know there was a shed at the back of their main building which stored all of the production — all the metal works, or 'plates' as they're called — for a load of seminal Rough Trade releases. I seem to recall that I nipped in, and took a few of the metal works, some of the artworks out of there. I took these masters back to Mute, so that they wouldn't fall into uncaring, unknowing hands. We made a few phone calls to some of the bands and repatriated some of the sleeves and artwork, and of course I repatriated all of The Triffids' stuff. We got hold of Dave, and we gave him all the parts and masters back.

Now I didn't know my commercial business affairs too much — that's an area I work in a lot more these days, now that I'm senior management, or whatever you call it. What I didn't realize back then was that the band had signed to an Australian label, and so actually what I was doing was giving the metal works and manufacturing parts back to Dave, but not the ownership of all the recordings. In my naïvety I waited to see if these recordings would ever see the light of day again. I think it's that frustration, that sense of waiting, that's fuelled my interest to do a reissue campaign really well, because they dropped off the map for such a long time. It was almost criminal, in a way.

Born Sandy eventually came out on CD through Mushroom, who are the owners or licensees of the band's recordings in Australia. It's great to get it on CD, I pick it up in the shop but I don't like the cover, it's just thrown together carelessly (sorry Mushroom, but it was) and it's like a riot to the senses: there's that album that I always liked, there's this band that I always liked, not being treated properly, just a little disregarded. There's no feel for it, just a lack of understanding for how important the album was.

If you talk to the band members today I think they understate, and don't quite understand, because they've probably never really looked at the accounting or the sales figures. I'm pretty sure that The Triffids sold many tens of thousands of records in the mid-eighties, and you'll hear people saying, 'Well, you know, they sold very little, they didn't really hit all the numbers.' But they were a significant band. If you're on the front cover of magazines like the *NME* you're a significant band in the mid-eighties, you mean something to people. I guess someone like me who's forty-four, people my age, we're kind of running media at the moment, not just in the UK but all over the world. And if you cast back to our musical loves and our musical influences, the mid-eighties are our formative period, the time when we got excited about new stuff. You know, there'll be bands here, in the mid-noughties, that will get celebrated in twenty years' time. You've got to be a fantastic band, you've got to be a fantastic musician or a writer, to be remembered twenty years on.

I think that's why the reissue program at this moment is just perfect, because the timing is right. So much has irritated me in that it's been done poorly, that it's not been up to the mark of where it deserves to be. And so rather than just release all the albums — six albums all in one go — we decided to stagger the release, so that we can have a chance to introduce all the musical themes, all the changes in direction that the band had throughout their career, throughout David's life. And also the chance not just to sell to old farts like me — remembering their past in some strange Singapore bathroom — but to turn on new bands, turn on new kids to this amazing writer, and just get into the music.

the Triffids

Debut Album

treeless
PLAIN

Vanishing Point

Megan Simpson Huberman

David McComb was a complicated man. His nature was both shy and extroverted, generous and ruthless, dark with sudden flashes of extreme sweetness. These competing forces within him were refereed by a fierce intellect. His evocative lyrics sprang from a passionate love of writing in all forms. A prodigious correspondent, in a time before email, he sent letters winging their way to friends around the world on an almost daily basis. He wrote to me for nearly twenty years, most often including poems that he had read and loved, which reflected some aspect of our relationship, or were just simply beautiful.

The following poem, written by Osip Mandelstam in 1913, is one he sent to me in the last ten years of his life. It seemed to me that in it he glanced some insight into his own motivation for songwriting and singing, as a way to exorcise melancholy, sorrow, love both cruel and kind, and the self. And, gratefully, blissfully, to vanish.

Poison in the bread, the air drunk dry.
Hard to doctor the wounds.
Joseph sold into Egypt
grieved no more bitterly for home.

Bedouins under the stars
close their eyes, sitting their horses,
and improvise songs
out of the troubles of the day.

No lack of subject:
one lost a quiver in the sand,
one bartered away a stallion …
the mist of events drifts away.

And if the song is sung truly,
from the whole heart, everything
at last vanishes: nothing is left
but space, the stars, the singer.[1]

Queenscliff,
Victoria, c. 1991.

Farewell from the Wharf of Innocence

DBC Pierre

Very few artworks haunt me. Our culture itself haunts me, haunts the fuck out of me. Art, music, literature, in that they reflect, in that they sometimes glance ahead of a culture, might get a stranglehold on a mood, a day, a season — but they rarely haunt me.

The music of The Triffids haunts me.

I am a musical pantheist — I love good examples of all music. Still, large-scale orchestral works, symphonic pieces from the late-classical through romantic periods, tend to speak most to me, and it's because they are sophisticated works that address the soul in great detail. Their themes are timeless, they paint struggles, pains, and longings that are human workloads at all times. Yet for me no expression of any age or complexity more evokes our culture's hell-bent departure from innocence than the careless genius of David McComb and The Triffids.

I will try to explain why.

Beneath the sequinned stage where we spent the 1980s, there lay a darker space, empty of shoulder pads and mascara. A real place, but experienced as if through a dream. Perhaps picture a desert, with a gutted stately home, buffalo roaming in perspective around it; and inside, the remains of a grand ballroom lit with neon and flame — and there a band, laughing and jamming. I mean the kind of place that wouldn't be there if you returned the next day.

Just as, in fact, it wasn't.

The 1980s had such a place. It was a music scene curiously epicentred in Australia, where Gordon Gecko's ideology, pastel interiors, and MTV were slower to arrive — they were distant promises of change seen from a desert, almost another planet, where girls still tasted salty, where widowed parents stayed single rather than admit to their kids they might shag. Around the edges of this Southern desert the real soul of an age was beating, and admitting things weren't that clear or hunky dory anymore. We were departing from a known reality into an age where you could make things up as you went along, anything at all, as long as you kept a straight face.

For me it is impossible to overestimate the extent to which certain Australian bands were in synch with that frontier time, had just the right distance from that true border between *The Good Life* and *Big Brother*. And snap: it happened around 1984. Under the noses of fluffy New Romantics, of gender benders, even of a wider alternative music scene, the likes of The Birthday Party, later Nick Cave and the Bad Seeds, and The Go-Betweens overspilled from the punk era to darken and dry around the stove of the eighties, a rich counter-argument to the age's froth.

Some of this was very dark music, gloriously so, and some of its melancholy soaked into The Triffids, who were unashamed to paint with all shades of music, even from generations before them, and places far away. But for me there was light around the band that set it apart from the scene. The Triffids weren't dark for the sake of darkness or style. They weren't sordid, or gloomy. They took no delight in countering jollity. Rather, they played familiar jolly comforts, used familiar jolly tricks, knowing they were devices from an innocence ebbed away; and it's that knowing that gives the work its bittersweet depth.

This powerful, sometimes devastating music isn't static nostalgia; it peers across the sea we're adrift on and sings knowing we're here; not capturing an age and its values, but the sound of their Doppler shift receding. As affable, light, and ingenuous as these songs get, they never fail to find us in our time and leave it rusty with yearning and dismay. I was prepared at the time of The Triffids' outbreak to call them art. Twenty years later I call them true and great art because the haunting grows, culture drags their relevance with it day by day, and I am now certain this brief eruption of songs is a farewell waved and sung from the shore of a friendly and innocent past. Don't be fooled by the whiff of high-school band, the hit-and-miss of sweet cliché, the stock vehicle of lost love: the wistful soul of The Triffids was a painful knowing that innocent times were gone for ever.

Their music is a celebration of that knowing.

That the band survived its brief time on critical acclaim and not commercial success confirms to me that culture flowed away past them as they sang to a culture flowing away past.

Now stop and listen.

They're still there, waving — and knowing where we are.

On the beach: near
Esperance, not far
from the McComb
family farm.

McComb in the leafy surrounds of his
Northcote, Melbourne home, June 1997.

Unquiet

Matt Merritt

Forget the verdict, speculation in the gutter press,
a service for family and close friends, or the tight
clusters of pilgrims round the spot where they found the car
and the condo he left unlocked and lit up like Christmas.

Once or twice, late night, the phone rang
and I answered to find the unfinished business
strung silently between us in that heartbeat before the click

and purr. And twice, in later years, I saw him out there.
First, in the migraine-light of mid-morning,
blinking back an evening of cheap local wine
in a town not twenty miles beyond the border.

He was wearing his hair longer, and his face was leaner,
harder, but even as I reached to smooth away inconsistencies
he was gone into the colour and sway of the market. Then

again in buzzard weather, way out on the flats, when our bus
slowed for some wreck, and he was driving an oncoming truck.
And, of course, this time eyes met. His rewrote the story so far
for me, while mine reflected back his original edit.

Notes

Stratton, *Suburban Stories*

1. 'Serial killer commits suicide in WA jail', ABC Online, 7 October 2005: <http://www.abc.net.au/news/newsitems/200510/s1476861.htm>.

2. For a discussion of Perth as a suburban city see Jenny Gregory, *City of Light: A History of Perth Since the 1950s* (Perth: City of Perth, 2003).

3. Veronica Brady, 'Place, Taste and the Making of a Tradition: Western Australian Writing Today', *Westerly* 4 (1982): 107.

4. Dorothy Hewett, 'The Garden and the City', *Westerly* 4 (1982): 99.

5. Fred Botting, *Gothic* (London: Routledge, 1996), 1.

6. Bruce Bennett, *Homing In: Essays on Australian Literature and Selfhood* (Perth: API-Network, 2006), 67.

7. Botting, *Gothic*, 7.

8. Estelle Blackburn, *Broken Lives* (Mosman Park, WA: Stellar Publishing, 1998), 12.

9. ibid., 43.

10. ibid., 305.

11. David Punter, *The Literature of Terror: A History of Gothic Fictions from 1765 to the Present Day* (London: Longman, 1979), 241.

12. Blackburn, *Broken Lives*, 305.

13. Margot Luke, 'All the Lonely People: Peter Cowan's Early Fiction', in *Peter Cowan: New Critical Essays*, eds Bruce Bennett and Susan Miller (Nedlands, WA: University of Western Australia Press, 1992), 85; and Dorothy Hewett, 'Empty Streets and Lonely Beaches: Peter Cowan's Moral Universe', in *Peter Cowan*, 4.

14. See Deborah Chambers, 'A Stake in the Country: Women's Experience of Suburban Development', in *Visions of Suburbia*, ed. Roger Silverstone (London: Routledge, 1997), 88.

15. Liner notes, *Born Sandy Devotional* (Domino REWIGCD24, 2006).

16   Wilson Neate, 'Born Sandy Devotional', *All Music Guide*: <http://www.allmusic.com/cg/amg.dll?p=amg&sql=10:ut7uak8khm3p>.

17   The term 'girl groups' refers to all-female singing groups from the first half of the 1960s such as The Crystals, The Ronettes, The Chiffons, The Supremes, The Shangri-Las and The Shirelles. See John Clemente, *Girl Groups: Fabulous Females That Rocked the World* (Iola, WI: Krause Publications, 2000).

18   On the Brill Building composers see Ken Emerson, *Always Magic in the Air: The Bomp and Brilliance of the Brill Building Era* (New York: Viking, 2005).

19   I cannot resist noting that the same motif is present in Stella Gibbons' parodic portrayal of the Gothic farm-life of the Starkadders in *Cold Comfort Farm* (1932). There, Aunt Ada Doom saw 'something nasty in the woodshed' when she was young and has never recovered. She never tells and neither the other characters nor the reader ever find out what the awful thing she saw was.

20   Jon Stratton, 'The Triffids: The Sense of a Place', *Popular Music and Society* 30, 3 (2007): 377–99.

21   Michael Sutton, '*Calenture*', *All Music Guide*: <http://www.allmusic.com/cg/amg.dll?p=amg&sql=10:6kd3vwrva9yk>.

Snarski, *Memories*

1   Accordion and keyboard player with Rabbit's Wedding and The Jackson Code. — Eds

Nichols, *Wow and Flutter*

1   B. George and Martha Defoe, eds, *International Discography of the New Wave Volume 1982/83* (New York and Sydney: Omnibus Press/One Ten Records, 1982), 433. Note: {++} is the *Discography's* shorthand for 'pre-recorded cassettes.'

2   David McComb cited in Clinton Walker, 'Irony and Distance', in *Inner City Sound*, ed. Clinton Walker (Portland: Verse Chorus Press, 1982; rev. 2005), 161.

3   'The Triffids', *Distant Violins* 8 (1983), n.p.

4   Jon Stratton, 'The Triffids: The Sense of a Place', *Popular Music and Society* 30, 3 (2007): 378.

5   ibid, 379.

6   David McComb, 'Letter from Sydney', *Pelican* 1 (1982), n.p.

7   Alsy MacDonald, interviewed in Larry Meltzer, dir., 'The Triffids: *Born Sandy Devotional*', *Great Australian Albums* (SBS Television, 2007).

8   David McComb, 'History of The Triffids, Part One', *The Triffids*, viewed 24 July 2008: <http://thetriffids.com/sitefiles/extrasa_2.shtml>.

9   'The Triffids', *Distant Violins* 7 (1983), n.p.

10   David McComb, 'History of The Triffids, Part One'.

11   David McComb, 'History of The Triffids, Part Three', *The Triffids*, viewed 24 July 2008: <http://thetriffids.com/sitefiles/extrasa_8.shtml>.

12   See Paul McHenry and Chris Spencer, *The Australian Various Artist on Cassette 1978–96* (Golden Square: Moonlight, 1996), 19–23; and Tyrone Flex, 'C-30, C-60, C-90 Go! Go!! Go!!!', *Roadrunner* 4, 11–12 (1981), 8.

13   Andrea Jones, '"Fast Forward" Fills the Gap Between Magazine and LP', Australian *Rolling Stone* 340 (1981), 18.

14   David McComb interviewed by Count Anthrax von Sinucide, 'Triffids', *Party Fears* 3 (1986), n.p.

15   Dave Warner quoted in Sandra Roe, 'The Original Dave Warner', *Pelican* 48, 3, 31 March 1977, 8.

16   'The Geeks Story', viewed 13 June 2007: <http://www.perthpunk.com/Geeks%20Story.htm>.

17   'The Coits: Punk Rock Hits Perth', *Pelican* 6 (1979), 16.

18   Anonymous Manikins member quoted in Peter Reeves, 'The Manikins: An Interview', *Pelican* 6 (1979), 16.

19   McComb quoted in Tracee Hutchison, *Your Name's on the Door* (Sydney: ABC Books, 1992), 19.

20   'The Triffids', *Distant Violins* 8 (1983), n.p.

21   Robert Wallace, 'Independents Struggle for Survival', *Rolling Stone*, 14 June 1979, 11.

22   As with The Triffids' 4th, an unauthorized sketch of Bemelmans' Madeline graces the cover of *Dungeon Tape*, on which a recorded version of the McComb song 'Madeline' first appears. — Eds

23   Rob Young, *Rough Trade* (London: Black Dog, 2006), 48.

24   David McComb quoted in Toby Creswell, 'The Triffids: A Shot in the Arm and a New EP', Australian *Rolling Stone* 384 (1985), 27.

25   David McComb interviewed by Count Anthrax von Sinucide, 'Triffids', n.p.

26   Later surfacing as 'Not the Marrying Kind' on the self-titled EP *Lawson Square Infirmary* (1984), a one-off collaboration between The Triffids, Graham Lee (at that time not yet a member of the band) and James Paterson. — Eds

27   'The Triffids' *Distant Violins* 8 (1983), n.p.

28   ibid.

29   David McComb, 'Biography', Mushroom Music Publishing, 1994, viewed 24 July 2008: <http://www.mushroommusic.com.au/songwriters/songwriter.asp?id=191>.

30   McComb quoted in Walker, 'Irony and Distance', 162.

31   Toby Cluechaz, 'The Triffids', *Roadrunner* 5, 2 (March, 1982), 29.

32   See sleeve notes, *In the Pines* (Liberation BLUE136.2, 2007).

33   David McComb interviewed by Count Anthrax von Sinucide, 'Triffids', n.p.

Paterson, *Hooked on McComb*

1   This practice may be more widespread than commonly acknowledged. John Lennon, for instance, is known to have often used another song as a template while composing. Thus, 'Come Together' is based on Chuck Berry's 'You Can't Catch Me', with a fragment of the latter's lyric inevitably finding its way (unconsciously, perhaps) into The Beatles' song. Threatened with legal action by Berry's publisher, Lennon managed to resolve the matter by agreeing to record versions of several songs from the publisher's catalogue, including 'You Can't Catch Me', on his 1975 *Rock'n'Roll* album. — Eds

2   I should mention the role of serendipity here. The only reason I knew what to do was because the previous night I had been listening to a bootleg of a Dylan concert from the mid-1960s, which includes a song that makes the same leap up an octave.

Wu, *Lost Chords*

1   While perhaps some of the inscriptions on the run-out grooves of The Triffids' records could be described as lavatorial, certainly they are not all of a piece. For those interested: 'PRENATAL HARD-ONS' appears on the A-side of the 'Beautiful Waste' single; 'SMEGMA' on the B-side of *Treeless Plain;* ' "HOLY HORN FOR THE PIOUS PORN" ' on the A-side of *Raining Pleasure;* 'THANKS BLEDDYN AND JUDE' on the B-side of *Born Sandy Devotional;* 'PAPAL SEMEN IDENTIFIED' on the A-side, and 'POPE HELD ON INFANT RAPE CHARGE' on the B-side, of a promotional copy of *Field of Glass;* 'Thanks to Sally … Love The Triffids …' on the A-side of *Stockholm;* and, on the A-side of The Blackeyed Susans' debut 12" EP, *Some Births are Worse than Murders,* featuring David McComb, Alsy MacDonald and Martyn Casey, 'FREE THE TORCH'. — Eds

McGowan, *Jesus Calling*

1   Pierre Perrone, 'Obituary: David McComb', *The Independent* (London), 13 February 1999. A CCGS directory of the class of 1978, published for the twenty-fifth anniversary of David's class leaving, presents the topic as 'Religious Studies' but memory suggests otherwise.

2   Nikki Gemmel, 'Opening our Hearts to Christmas', the *Age,* 23 December 2006. David McComb's draft of 'Wide Open Road' is published as a facsimile in *Meanjin* 65 (2006): 188.

3   *Meanjin* 65 (2006): 188. The published version reads: 'I drove out over the flatlands/Hunting down you and him.'

4   Album lyric sheet, *Treeless Plain*, 1983. All subsequent quotations have been sourced from the equivalent sleeves, or from the online collection maintained by Graham Lee, viewed Dec. 2006: <http://thetriffids.com/sitefiles/lyricsa.shtml>.

5   See further, for instance, 'Hometown Farewell Kiss' or 'Holy Water', both on *Calenture.*

6   Interestingly there was a more Roman Catholic but less faithful rendition into English, 'While the Angelus was Ringing', recorded by Frank Sinatra and others (As performed and recorded by The Browns, 'The Three Bells' reached number one on the US country and pop charts in

1959. The song has been recorded by, among others, Les Compagnons de la Chanson, the group featuring Edith Piaf which popularized the French original, 'Les Trois Cloches', in 1946; Nana Mouskouri; Ray Charles; Roy Orbison; Chet Atkins; Elaine Paige; Alison Krauss & Union Station; and Tina Arena. — Eds)

7   A point made by Jon Stratton, 'The Triffids: The Sense of a Place', in *Popular Music and Society* 30.3 (2007): 383, 387–95. Stratton correctly identifies a certain dualism and emphasis on divine grace and sovereignty in the Christianity of songs such as 'Bury Me Deep in Love'. To render this view 'Presbyterian' however, or to attribute it largely to the influence of this early experience, confuses an ideal type (better termed 'Calvinism') with the more liberal realities of Australian Presbyterianism of the 1960s.

Lucy, *Still Life*

1   The Western Australian Institute of Technology, now Curtin University of Technology.

2   Such claims are probably best attributed to the bravado of youth than to musicology. Although several commentators have posited a tenuous connection between Bowie's lyrics and Eliot's poetry, there appears to be scant evidence in support of McComb's suggestion that Rowland S. Howard plagiarized an Eliot poem.

Koeman, *A Temporary Monument*

1   Steven Vandervelden, STUK Co-director.

Kilbey, *WHACK! WHACK!*

1   *Gold Afternoon Fix* (1990), an album by The Church. — Eds

2   Kilbey performed in *Cannot Buy My Soul*, a tribute to Kev Carmody, a few days prior to *A Secret in the Shape of a Song*, the Sydney Festival event recounted here. — Eds

Kakulas, *The Black Swan*

1   David McComb, 'Biography', Mushroom Music Publishing, 1994, viewed 24 July 2008: <http://www.mushroommusic.com.au/song-writers/songwriter.asp?id=191>. The Noonkanbah land-rights dispute erupted in 1980 when a US oil company, with the backing of the WA government but to the outrage of Indigenous people, the unions and many other Western Australians, announced its intention to drill for oil on Noonkanbah cattle station in the state's north, located in a region sacred to the Yungngora people. At the time, local and national media coverage of the event was fuelled by the government's inflammatory use of police, and a convoy of non-union truck drivers, to break picket lines around Noonkanbah. In 2007, the Federal Court found in favour of the Yungngora people's Native Title claim. — Eds

Coughran & Laurent, *Please Take Me Home*

1   'Origins of the Christina Macpherson Tune, *Who'll Come a Waltzing Matilda with Me?*' National Library of Australia, viewed 25 August 2008: <http://www.nla.gov.au/epubs/waltzingmatilda/1-Orig-Christina.html>.

2   Yagan led strong Indigenous resistance to white authority in the early Swan River colony around Perth, and eventually a bounty was put on him for death or capture. He was killed by a young settler on 11 July 1833 and two months later his decapitated head was taken to England for phrenological examination, after which it was kept in storage at the Liverpool Museum until, in 1964, having deteriorated beyond further 'scientific' value, it was buried in a wooden box along with the head of a Maori and a mummified Peruvian. Following many years of lobbying from Nyungar elders, Yagan's remains were handed back to a delegation of his people at the Liverpool Town Hall on 31 August 1997, the day Princess Diana died. His head is now in Perth, unburied.

3   As James Paterson recalls: 'the first I ever heard about [Jerdacuttup Man] was when Dave sent me a postcard of the peat bog man at the British Museum. It was pretty enigmatic, because the postcard just

contained the message "Jerdacuttup Man" on the reverse, and I personally couldn't see the connection between the peat bog man in the British Museum and the location in [Western Australia]!' Even so, Paterson 'identified with the song' because of a prior visit to the British Museum during which he 'spent a long time looking at the mummified body of a man found in the desert in Egypt, dating ... to about 3000 BC! We weren't looking at the same mummy, but it was nonetheless a parallel experience.' 'James Paterson', *The Triffids*, <http://thetriffids.com/forum/index.php?topic=1605.75>.

4 Josephine Flood, *Archaeology of the Dreamtime: The Story of Prehistoric Australia and Her People* (Sydney: Collins, 1983), 119, 177.

5 Josephine Flood, *The Riches of Ancient Australia: An Indispensable Guide for Exploring Prehistoric Australia* (Brisbane: University of Queensland Press, 1999), 24, 207. Peat is also found north of Perth in Western Australia: see A.J. McComb and P.S. Lake, *Australian Wetlands* (Sydney: Angus & Robertson, 1990); Elizabeth Bilney, 'Australian Peatlands', *Wetlands Australia* 6 (July 1997): 6–7.

6 Charles Dortch, *Devil's Lair: A Study in Prehistory* (Perth: Western Australian Museum, 1984). Bone tools at the site include 22,000-year-old bone points, many with a telltale glossy sheen on their tips. According to Flood, microscopic analysis suggests that 'some of these were probably used for sewing skins together to make cloaks to ward off the glacial cold' (*Riches of Ancient Australia*, 39–40).

7 Augustus Pitt-Rivers quoted in Tony Bennett, *Pasts Beyond Memory: Evolution, Museums, Colonialism* (London: Routledge, 2004), 136.

8 Mary Bouquet, 'Thinking and Doing Otherwise: Anthropological Theory in Exhibitionary Practice', in *Museum Studies: An Anthology of Contexts*, ed. Bettina Messias Carbonell (Oxford: Blackwell, 2004), 200.

9 See Cressida Fforde, Jane Hubert and Paul Turnbull, *The Dead and their Possessions: Repatriation in Principle, Policy and Practice* (London: Routledge, 2002); Derek John Mulvaney and Johan Kamminga, *Prehistory of Australia* (Sydney: Allen & Unwin, 1999), 8–11; Moira G.

Simpson, *Making Representations: Museums in the Post-Colonial Era* (London: Routledge, 2001); and Tom Flynn, 'The Sacred in Secular Societies', *The Spectator*, 5 July 2003, 42.

10   Both Carmody and Roach, although musically active in the 1980s, would come to prominence only in the following decade, with the release of their respective debut albums *Pillars of Society* (1989) and *Charcoal Lane* (1990).

11   By the same token, 'Native Bride' — a relatively obscure track relegated to the B-side of 'Wide Open Road' — appears to disparage European forms of longing even as it reinscribes the evolutionary assumptions of colonial anthropology: 'Going back to the stone age/You're going to take a native bride.' McComb's narrative persona effectively contributes to a broader cultural debate by insinuating that imperialist nostalgia is an insufficient basis for a politics of Indigenous reconciliation — venturing, rather, an oblique admonition of white Australia for the hollowness and self-deceptiveness of its reconciliatory gestures: 'I fell into the hole that was left where your heart was … when you kissed the native bride.'

12   R.C. Turner, 'The Lindow Man Phenomenon: Ancient and Modern', in *Bog Bodies: New Discoveries and Perspectives*, eds R.C. Turner and R.G. Scaife (London: British Museum Press, 1995), 204.

13   Trugannini, fearing she might be dismembered for scientific purposes like so many other nineteenth-century Tasmanian Aborigines, is said to have pleaded with a friend as they boated on a river: 'Bury me here, it's the deepest place … Don't let them cut me, but bury me behind the mountains' (quoted in 'Her Will to Survive', *First Australians*, SBS Television, 2008). Within two years of her death in 1876, Trugannini's skeleton was exhumed by the Royal Society of Tasmania and placed on display in the Tasmanian Museum. Not until 1976 were her remains cremated and scattered in accordance with her wishes — although specimens of Trugannini's hair and skin were discovered in the collection of the Royal College of Surgeons of England, Oxford, as late as 2002.

Lucy, *Towards a Minor Music*

1   See *The Unfortunate Rake: A Study in the Evolution of a Ballad*, notes by Kenneth S. Goldstein (Folkways FS 3805, 1960).

2   See 'Folk & Traditional Song Lyrics', *A Traditional Music Library*, for the full version: <http://www.traditionalmusic.co.uk/folk-song-lyrics/Unfortunate_Rake.htm>.

3   Here and below I'm relying principally on Rob Walker's archive of research on the song at his website, *No Notes*: <http://nonotes.wordpress.com/about/>. See also Walker's essay on the song's history, 'Name That Tune', in *Gambit Weekly*, 14 June 2005: <http://www.bestofneworleans.com/dispatch/2005-06-14/cover_story.php>.

4   'St James, Middlesex, London: The Poland Street Workhouse', *The Workhouse*, 2 May 2008, viewed 25 August 2008: <http://www.workhouses.org.uk/index.html?StJames/StJames.shtml>.

5   A twelve-page score by 'Composer: Joe Primrose' is available at the website, *Musicnotes*: <http://search.musicnotes.com/?q=st+james+infirmary&search_id=Top&hl=n>.

6   Mills did sing occasionally, though, especially with Duke Ellington for whom he is credited as writing the lyrics for such tunes as 'Mood Indigo' and 'It Don't Mean a Thing (If It Ain't Got That Swing)'. In a 1930 recording with Ellington's Harlem Hot Chocolates band, Mills (using the pseudonym 'Sunny Smith') sings a version of 'St James Infirmary'. For a tenuous Triffids connection to 'The Streets of Laredo', see Conway Savage's live cut, featuring ex-Triffid and fellow Bad Seed Martyn P. Casey playing bass, on Savage's *Rare Songs and Performances 1989–2004* (Beheaded, 2005).

7   For the lyrics and guitar tabs, see *ezfolk.com*: <http://www.ezfolk.com/guitar/tab/qrst/stjames/stjames.html>.

8   As US composer Ezra Sims tells Rob Walker at the latter's *No Notes* website, what makes Armstrong's 'St James Infirmary' distinctively 'his' is the microtonal playing: 'to really write down' Armstrong's version of the song, and to 'be able to reproduce it, you must be able to indicate much smaller intervals than the half-steps that are on the piano, much smaller increments' (see the section, 'Q&A: Ezra Sims'). It should

be acknowledged, too, that part of the mystery of the Armstrong version has to do with the lo-fi quality of the recording, due to the rudimentary studio technology of the time, which lends the record a certain ghostly effect.

9   On the question of authorship (Shakespeare's included) see Niall Lucy, 'Introduction: The Source of Plagiarism', in *Plagiarism!*, eds John Kinsella and Niall Lucy, special issue of *Angelaki: Journal of Theoretical Humanities* 14.1 (in press).

10   I'm drawing here on some of the ideas of French (Algerian born) philosopher Jacques Derrida: see for example his *Limited Inc*, trans. Samuel Weber (Illinois: Northwestern University Press, 1988).

11   See Jacques Derrida, *Specters of Marx: The State of the Debt, the Work of Mourning, and the New International*, trans. Peggy Kamuf (New York and London: Routledge, 1994); and Niall Lucy, *A Derrida Dictionary* (Oxford: Blackwell, 2004), 14–25 and 111–18.

12   See Niall Lucy and Steve Mickler, *The War on Democracy: Conservative Opinion in the Australian Press* (Nedlands: University of Western Australia Press, 2006).

13   There are countless versions by American blues, jazz and country artists, sometimes under the title of 'St James Infirmary' and sometimes not. Cab Calloway and The Hall Johnson Negro Choir, for instance, both recorded versions of 'St James Infirmary' in 1931, while others to record it under the same title include Hot Lips Page (1941), Josh White (1944), Billie Holiday (1947), Bobby Bland (1961) and Lou Rawls (1963). There are variations by Jimmie Rodgers ('Those Gambler's Blues', c. 1930), Blind Willie McTell ('The Dyin' Crapshooter's Blues', 1940) and, more recently, by Dr John ('Touro Infirmary', 1982). Rock artists to cover the song include The Doors (who play a fragment of 'St James Infirmary' as part of a medley featuring 'Fever' and 'Light My Fire' on their 1970 live album), Janis Joplin (1971) and, lately, The White Stripes (1999), Van Morrison (2003) and Tom Jones (with Jools Holland, 2004). You can hear 121 versions of the song (including The Triffids' version) at the blues site, *Honey, Where You Been So Long?*: <http://prewarblues.org/category/prewarbluesorg/>.

14   See Gilles Deleuze and Félix Guattari, *Anti-Oedipus: Capitalism and Schizophrenia*, trans. Robert Hurley, Mark Seem and Helen R. Lane (Minneapolis: University of Minnesota Press, 1983).

15   Claire Colebrook, *Gender* (Basingstoke: Palgrave Macmillan, 2004), 180; emphasis added.

16   Deleuze borrows the notion of 'affects' from seventeenth-century Dutch philosopher Benedict de Spinoza's *Ethics*, using it to refer to a form of response (not quite a 'feeling') that isn't caused by a system of representation and which can't quite be registered in language. Affects are pre-personal, corporeal responses to what Deleuze calls 'intensities' (which might be glossed as 'energies' or 'forces'), taking such forms as an apprehension of fear or an experience of joy.

17   See Gilles Deleuze and Félix Guattari, *Kafka: Towards a Minor Literature*, trans. Dana Polan (Minneapolis: University of Minnesota Press, 1986).

18   See Gilles Deleuze, *Bergsonism*, trans. Hugh Tomlinson and Barbara Habberjam (New York: Zone, 1990).

Martin, *Bladder Wrack*

1   What climatic lack? Now I'm old and grey there is nothing better than standing there on the headland being showered, bathed, sanctified by the wind and the rain.

2   Built in the 1930s, London Court arcade in the heart of Perth city's shopping precinct is modelled on Elizabethan-style architecture. For Perth kids of generations past, the arcade's exoticism, in a cityscape that otherwise resembled a wasteland, seemed to outweigh any inkling of its incongruity. — Eds

3   A term coined by Van Morrison on the song 'Orangefield'.

4   Patrick Kavanagh, from his poem 'On Raglan Road', originally published as 'Dark Haired Miriam Ran Away' (1946).

Butcher, *The Cliffe*

1   Property developer Mark Creasy quoted in Romy Ranalli, 'Grand Mansion Now a Rotting Wreck', *The Post*, 29 September 2007, viewed 1

August 2008: <http://www.postnewspapers.com.au/20070929/news/012. shtml>

2   Kindly supplied to the author by Athel McComb.

3   In Peppermint Grove, there are only six streets running from east to west: McNeil, Forrest, Leake, Irvine, Keane and Johnston (Harry Frederick Johnston, another of the young colony's surveyors, led an expedition to the Kimberleys in 1884, and was appointed Surveyor General in 1896.)

4   Later in life, David would consistently situate The Cliffe in Cottesloe, a suburb which shares the same postcode (6011) as Peppermint Grove. However, directly across its northern borderline, just on the other side of the drive, is the suburb of Claremont (6010).

5   The kookaburra is not native to Western Australia; it's an introduced species, an interloper from the eastern states.

6   Letter from Harold McComb to the author, 13 December 2007.

Neate, *Ambivalent Romanticism*

1   David Giles, 'T'riffic', *Record Mirror*, 3 June 1989, 17.

2   David Tiltman, 'It Was 5 Years Ago Today: Oasis and Blur Went Head to Head', *The Independent*, 13 August 2000, 8.

3   Gavin Martin, 'Beach to Their Own', *New Musical Express*, 15 April 1989, 14.

4   Bleddyn Butcher, 'Return to Oz', *New Musical Express*, 28 June 1986, 26.

5   David McComb, liner notes, *Born Sandy Devotional* (Domino REWIGCD24, 2006).

6   Jonh Wilde, 'The Outer Limits', *Sounds*, 20 September 1986, 37.

7   Dele Fadele, 'Triffic!', *Triffids Clippings*, viewed 12 January 2007: <http://homepage.ntlworld.com/peter.herron/paper%20clip%20article%20scans/NMEreissues_review.jpg>.

8   Sinéad Gleeson, 'The Triffids: Born Sandy Devotional', *Irish Times*, 16 June 2006, viewed 2 January 2007: <http://web.lexis-nexis.com/universe>.

9   Ray Purvis, 'Year of The Triffids', *The West Australian*, 15 June 2006, 8.

10   Jenna Leonard, 'The Triffids: Calenture/In the Pines', *God is in the TV: An Online Cultural Fanzine*, 1 March 2007, viewed 7 March 2007: <http://www.godisinthetvzine.co.uk/content/content_detail.php?id=1441&type=Albums>; emphasis added.

11   Jonh Wilde, 'The Outer Limits', 37.

12   Paul Mathur, 'High Plains Drifters', *Rock Australia Magazine*, 10 February 1988, 16.

13   Jonh Wilde, 'The Outer Limits', 37.

14   Dave Simpson, 'The Triffids: Born Sandy Devotional', *Guardian,* 9 June 2006, viewed 6 January 2007: <http://arts.guardian.co.uk/filmandmusic/story/0,,1792852,00.html>.

15   Urpal, 'Re: BSD in the Guardian', The Triffids Forums, 10 June 2006, viewed 10 February 2007: <http://thetriffids.com/forum/index.php/topic,1035.msg16299.html#msg16299>.

16   Urpal, 'Re: BSD in the Guardian', The Triffids Forums, 11 June 2006, viewed 10 February 2007: <http://thetriffids.com/forum/index.php/topic,1035.msg16315.html#msg16315>.

17   *Long Way to the Top*, ABC-TV (Australia), 5 September 2001.

18   'The Trouble with Triffids', *Option*, July–August 1987, *Triffids Clippings*, viewed 15 January 2007: <http://homepage.ntlworld.com/peter.herron/triffids_clippings.htm>.

19   ibid.

20   Ann Scanlon, 'Hometown Farewell Bliss', *Sounds*, 9 January 1988, 18.

21   Bleddyn Butcher, 'Return to Oz', 27.

22   Paul Mathur, 'High Plains Drifters', 16.

23   Jonh Wilde, 'The Outer Limits', 37.

24   Adam Sweeting, 'Desert Songs', *Melody Maker*, 2 August 1986, 14.

25   Bleddyn Butcher, 'Return to Oz', 26–7; emphasis added.

26   Gavin Martin, 'Doom and McComb', *New Musical Express*, 22 April 1989, 17.

27   ibid; emphasis added.

28   Paul Mathur, 'High Plains Drifters', 15.

29   David Cavanagh, 'Fishing on Swan Lake', *Sounds*, 15 April 1989, 11.

30   Gavin Martin, 'Doom and McComb', 17.

31   According to Triffids forum member kate, the song 'captures the hot humid summer nights we get [in Perth], when in the middle of the night you lie awake in bed, sweaty and unable to move except perhaps to the verandah to try and get some breeze'. 'Too hot to move, Too hot to think/Jerdacuttup Man', The Triffids Forums, 28 May 2006, viewed 10 February 2007: <http://thetriffids.com/forum/index.php/topic,992.msg15798.html#msg15798>.

32   Jon Casimir, 'The Black Swan', *Rock Australia Magazine*, 17 May 1989, *Triffids Clippings*, viewed 17 January 2007: <http://homepage.ntlworld.com/peter.herron/triffids_clippings.htm>.

33   Gavin Martin, 'Doom and McComb', 17.

34   Mat Snow, 'Blinded by the Light', *Sounds*, 10 October 1987, 41.

35   Theodore Gracyk, 'Romanticizing Rock Music', *Journal of Aesthetic Education* 27, 2 (1993): 47–8.

36   David McComb, liner notes, *Born Sandy Devotional*.

37   William Wordsworth, 'Preface to *Lyrical Ballads*, 1802', in *William Wordsworth: A Critical Edition of the Major Works*, ed. Stephen Gill (Oxford and New York: Oxford University Press, 1984), 611.

38   Jonh Wilde, 'The Outer Limits', 37.

39   Dave Swift, 'Delirium Days', *Melody Maker*, 14 November 1987, 26.

40   vpsaarinen, 'Re: make you cry, so moving boo hoo', The Triffids Forums, 29 June 2006, viewed 10 February 2007: <http://thetriffids.com/forum/index.php/topic,918.msg17098.html#msg17098>.

41   vpsaarinen, 'Re: FOG, "lost indie classic"', The Triffids Forums, 26 January 2007, viewed 10 February 2007: <http://thetriffids.com/forum/index.php/topic,1437.msg22261.html#msg22261>.

42   Snowy, 'Re: My first Triffids hearing', The Triffids Forums, 25 November 2005, viewed 10 February 2007: <http://thetriffids.com/forum/index.php/topic,615.msg9793.html#msg9793>.

43   Urpal, 'Re: My first Triffids Hearing', The Triffids Forums, 24 November 2005, viewed 10 February 2007: <http://thetriffids.com/forum/index.php/topic,615.msg9750.html#msg9750>.

44 Graham Lee, 'Welcome To The Forums', The Triffids Forums, 14 January 2004, viewed 10 February 2007: <http://thetriffids.com/forum/index.php/topic,4.msg7.html#msg7>.

45 Cited in Urpal, 'Re: Born Sandy Devotional', The Triffids Forums, 31 May 2006, viewed 10 February 2007: <http://thetriffids.com/forum/index.php/topic,1010.msg15881.html#msg15881>.

46 François Gorin, 'Musique: The Triffids. Calenture', *Télérama*, 27 January 2007, viewed 10 February 2007: <http://www.telerama.fr/musique/M0701231130500.html>. ('A moody beanpole of a man, with the expression of an inebriated dandy' — trans. Margaret Sankey).

47 Christophe Basterra, 'The Triffids: Calenture', *Magic: Revue de Pop Moderne*, February 2007, 83.

48 Jonathan Romney, 'The Triffids: Calenture', *Triffids Clippings*, viewed 17 January 2007: <http://homepage.ntlworld.com/peter.herron/paper%20clip%20article%20scans/unknown_calenturereview.jpg>.

49 Lauren Zoric, 'The Triffids: In the Pines/Calenture', *Mess and Noise*, viewed 20 March 2007: <http://www.messandnoise.com/releases/5592>.

50 Urpal, 'Re: BSD' (msg16299); emphasis added.

51 Urpal, 'I had an itch I had to scratch', The Triffids Forums, 14 March 2006, viewed 10 February 2007: <http://thetriffids.com/forum/index.php/topic,876.msg13481.html#msg13481>.

52 mtrain, 'old And Lonely, Dirty And Cold', The Triffids Forums, 5 October 2005, viewed 10 February 2007: <http://thetriffids.com/forum/index.php/topic,112.msg504.html#msg504>.

53 The notebooks are digitized under 'Teenage Hits' under the 'Lyrics' menu at *The Triffids*, viewed 2 January 2007: <http://thetriffids.com/sitefiles/extrasbk1_1.shtml>.

54 See 'Early History' under the 'Biographical' menu at *The Triffids*, viewed 2 January 2007: <http://thetriffids.com/sitefiles/extrasa.shtml>.

55 David McComb, liner notes, *Born Sandy Devotional*.

56 ibid.

57 David McComb, liner notes, *In the Pines* (Domino REWIGCD25, 2007).

58 ibid.

59 Casimir, 'The Black Swan'.

60 David McComb, 'Field of Glass', The Triffids, *Field of Glass* (Hot 1207, 1985).

61 Owen Jones, 'The Triffids: Born Sandy Devotional', *Make Noise and Dance*, 19 June 2006, viewed 7 March 2007: <http://makenoiseanddance. com/2006/359>.

62 Bleddyn Butcher, 'Return to Oz', 27.

63 David McComb, 'Biography', *The Triffids*, viewed 2 January 2007: <http://thetriffids.com/sitefiles/HMbio.shtml>.

64 David McComb, 'Jerdacuttup Man', The Triffids, *Calenture* (Domino REWIGCD26, 2007).

65 Mat Snow, 'Blinded By the Light', 41.

66 See Alan Richardson, 'Romanticism and the Body', *Literature Compass* 1 (2004): 1–14, for an overview of such work. — Eds

Coughran, *Love in Bright Landscapes*

1 María Rosa Menocal, *Shards of Love: Exile and the Origins of the Lyric* (Durham and London: Duke University Press, 1994), 186.

2 María Rosa Menocal, 'We Can't Dance Together', *Profession* 88 (1987): 54–5.

3 Liner notes, *Born Sandy Devotional* (Domino REWIGCD24, 2006).

4 Menocal, *Shards of Love*, 144. She is referring not to McComb, of course, but to Eric Clapton's then-unrequited love for Pattie Boyd, the wife of his close friend George Harrison, a relationship which informed the composition of *Layla and Other Assorted Love Songs*. Clapton was evidently inspired by 'Layla and Majnun', a love story written by classical Persian poet Nezami.

5 The booklet includes, among other artefacts, a reproduction of a bookshelf containing tomes by the likes of Fitzgerald, Flannery O'Connor, Dylan Thomas, Heinrich Böll, Donald Newlove, Rafael Alberti, and contemporary Western Australian novelist Tim Winton.

6 '"Rock Star Publishes Slim Volume of Poetry" has such a shitty ring to it', McComb is reported to have said in an interview with Jon Casimir, 'The Black Swan', *Rock Australia Magazine*, 17 May 1989.

7   Menocal, *Shards of Love*, 152–3.

8   Casimir, 'The Black Swan'. In support of McComb's guardedly optimistic view, novelist Thomas Pynchon writes that 'rock and roll remains one of the last honorable callings, and a working band is a miracle of everyday life' (liner notes, Lotion, *Nobody's Cool*, spinART SPART46, 1996).

9   David McComb, ' "When I Die I'll Be Worshipped Like an Old Battleship": An Appreciation of Those Who Made the Hard Yards for Hip-Hop', *The Good Fight*, n.d., 7.

10   Antoine Hennion, 'The Production of Success: An Antimusicology of the Pop Song', in *On Record: Rock, Pop and the Written Word*, eds Simon Frith and Andrew Goodwin (New York: Pantheon, 1990), 188.

11   Hennion, 189. In a post-Triffids interview McComb emphatically stated that 'there's a big distance between my life and any of the characters in the songs' (Toby Creswell, 'The Triffids' David McComb', *Juice*, March 1994, 63).

12   All references in this chapter to the lyrics of *Born Sandy Devotional* are taken from the original Mushroom CD (MUSH32417.2, 1986).

13   Liner notes, *Born Sandy Devotional* (Domino, 2006).

14   Quoted in Adam Sweeting, 'Desert Songs', *Melody Maker*, 2 August 1986, 14–15.

15   Based on Berlioz's ill-fated love for Irish actress Harriet Smithson, *An Episode in the Life of the Artist* — generally referred to by its subtitle, *Symphonie Fantastique* — uses the symphonic form to tell the story of 'a young musician of morbid sensitivity and fiery imagination' who 'in an excess of amorous despair … tries to poison himself with opium. The drug, too weak to kill, plunges him into a heavy sleep with strange fantasies in which all experience is transformed into music and even the image of his beloved becomes an obsessive melody which he sees and hears everywhere.' In the symphony's first movement, the artist 'remembers the contrary moods, fits of melancholy or unreasonable joy, that he felt before he met his loved one. Then he recalls the violent passion which she inspired in him, his anguish and jealous furies, and, at last, his return to tenderness and the consolation of religion' (liner

notes, *Berlioz: Symphony Fantastique*, London Symphony Orchestra conducted by Carlos Païta, Lodia LOD 777, 1978). The symphony's final movement, 'Dream of a Witches' Sabbath', parodies the *Dies Irae* and other liturgical materials, such as plainchant; McComb, for his part, invokes Peter Paul & Mary's 'Oh, Rock My Soul' — among other versions of an African-American spiritual popularized in the 1960s, including Elvis Presley's 'Bosom of Abraham'.

16   The entry is dated October 6, the recording of *Born Sandy Devotional* having been completed in August 1985 (liner notes, Domino, 2006). Apparently for McComb neither songwriting nor live performance delivered on rock's spurious promise of catharsis: 'You can scream till you're blue in the face and throw your body around in contorted ways, but you'll still have the same problems you started with. But somehow you can transmit your *failure* to get rid of these things in a very extreme way' (cited in Mat Snow, 'Roses, Knives, Dead Bodies', *New Musical Express*, 5 January 1985, 6).

17   'Sidewalk' is of course an American term, equivalent to the British and Australian 'footpath' — suggesting, perhaps, that 'indigeneity' in pop music is always already compromised by the globalizing nature of the medium.

18   Evidence from his exercise books suggests that McComb wrote 'Estuary Bed' 'in Nottingham,   in the van & the hotel near the train station' (liner notes, *Born Sandy Devotional*, Domino, 2006).

19   'Methought I heard a voice cry, "Sleep no more!/Macbeth does murder sleep," — the innocent sleep;/Sleep that knits up the ravell'd sleave of care,/The death of each day's life, sore labour's bath,/Balm of hurt minds, great nature's second course,/Chief nourisher in life's feast' (*Macbeth*, II.ii.32–7). Cf. lines 86–7 of the tenth book of Wordsworth's *Prelude*: 'I seemed to hear a voice that cried,/To the whole city, "Sleep no more"'; William Wordsworth, *The Prelude, or Growth of a Poet's Mind: An Autobiographical Poem*.

20   Timothy Morton, *Ecology without Nature: Rethinking Environmental Aesthetics* (Cambridge: Harvard University Press, 2007), 22.

21   Arthur Schopenhauer, *The World as Will and Idea*, Volume I, trans. R.B. Haldane and J. Kemp (London: Routledge & Kegan Paul, 1943), 322–3.

22   'Yin,' the feminine principle of Taoist philosophy, refers literally to the shadow side of a hill or mountain. McComb's narrator delves deeply into this secluded domain, 'Away from the sky, away from the light/ where the overgrown branches conceal what's inside.'

23   Quoted in John Kinsella, 'Landscape Poetry?', viewed 25 July 2006: <http://www.johnkinsella.org/essays/landscapepoetry.html>. This is not to discount the significance of the American folk song from which McComb borrows the title and the refrain, 'In the pines, in the pines, where the sun never shines.'

24   Cf. Isaiah: 'The wolf shall live with the lamb, the leopard shall lie down with the kid' (11:6); 'The wolf and the lamb shall feed together' (65:25), *The New Revised Standard Version of the Bible*.

25   Lyrics to 'Fairytale Love' and 'New Year's Greetings' are taken from *The Black Swan* (White Hot/Mushroom D30057, 1989).

26   Les Murray, *The Vernacular Republic: Poems 1961–1981* (Sydney: Angus & Robertson, 1982), 2.

27   For McComb, Murray's poem 'suggested a sort of character I've met … someone who really rails against the corporate world. I had this big list of things that he rails against, pages and pages of them, but I could only choose three or four products' (quoted in Casimir, 'The Black Swan'). McComb's recourse to the conventional pastoral distinction (city vs country), with its implicit critique of sophisticated vices, is thus tempered with an awareness of the politics of globalization.

28   Not to be confused with McComb's poem of the same name, these lines were retrieved from what Graham Lee describes as 'a swag of lyrics Dave had no home for.' 'Unfinished Lyrics', *The Triffids*, viewed 22 July 2005: <http://www.thetriffids.com/unfinished.shtml#mistake>.

29   David McComb, 'Song of No Return', *The Triffids Official Lyrics Page*, viewed 1 July 2008: <http://thetriffids.com/sitefiles/lyricsa.shtml>.

30   Leo Marx, *The Machine in the Garden: Technology and the Pastoral Ideal in America* (Oxford and New York: Oxford University Press, 1964), 21, 28.

Twyford-Moore, *The Listening Boy*

1   Would McComb scare Forster if left alone in a room? Would Forster run from McComb like William Faulkner ran from James Joyce outside of a Parisian café? It is hard to say.

Colebrook, *The Singularity of The Triffids*

1   The notion of deterritorialization is used throughout Deleuze and Guattari's work to refer to the idea that things are not fixed in themselves, rooted to a homeland or natural territory, but rather are involved in processes of becoming 'other' than themselves. The emphasis here is on the transformative dynamics of *becoming* (or the force of desire), in keeping with the political, philosophical and other non-essentialist aspects of Deleuze and Guattari's work. To give an example that in its brevity may risk seeming trite: in their non-conformity with essential concepts of a rock band and rock music, The Triffids could be said to deterritorialize those concepts in a process of becoming other than themselves defined as 'rock' musicians (and especially as 'Oz' rock musicians). — Eds

2   Gilles Deleuze and Félix Guattari, *Anti-Oedipus: Capitalism and Schizophrenia,* trans. Robert Hurley, Mark Seem, and Helen R. Lane (New York: Viking Press, 1977).

3   Gilles Deleuze and Félix Guattari, *A Thousand Plateaus: Capitalism and Schizophrenia,* trans. Brian Massumi (Minneapolis: University of Minnesota Press, 1987).

4   Pierre Bourdieu, *Distinction: A Social Critique of the Judgement of Taste,* trans. Richard Nice (Cambridge, Mass.: Harvard University Press, 1984).

5   Gilles Deleuze and Félix Guattari, *A Thousand Plateaus.*

6   Gilles Deleuze and Félix Guattari, *Anti-Oedipus.*

7   See also Jean-François Lyotard, *Postmodern Fables,* trans. Georges Van Den Abbeele (Minneapolis: University of Minnesota Press, 1997)

8   Gilles Deleuze and Félix Guattari, *Kafka: Toward a Minor Literature,* trans. Dana Polan (Minneapolis: University of Minnesota Press, 1986).

9   For Duran Duran's self-description, see the band's biography at the archive of *liveDaily*, viewed 28 July 2008: <http://www.livedaily.com/artists/246.html>.

10   Simon Frith, 'The Good, the Bad, and the Indifferent: Defending Popular Culture from the Populists', *Diacritics* 21, 4 (Winter, 1991): 102–15.

11   Gilles Deleuze, *Francis Bacon: The Logic of Sensation*, trans. Daniel W. Smith (Minneapolis: University of Minnesota Press, 2004).

Simpson Huberman, *Vanishing Point*

1   In his handwritten letter, McComb evidently draws from *The Selected Poems of Osip Mandelstam*, trans. Clarence Brown and W.S. Merwin (London: Oxford University Press, 1973). — Eds

Notes on Contributors

Joanne Alach is a Melbourne-based television producer who sang backing vocals on some of David McComb's London recordings and his solo album, *Love of Will*.

Jonathan Alley is a Melbourne-based writer and broadcaster. His film on the life of David McComb, with the working title of 'Love in Bright Landscapes', is currently in production.

Jill Birt is a freelance architect based in Perth. She played keyboards and sang with The Triffids.

Bleddyn Butcher is a Sydney-based photographer and writer, recently relocated from London, who was the unofficial photographer for The Triffids in Europe. His biography of David McComb, *Save What You Can*, will appear shortly with Helter Skelter in the UK.

Martyn Casey played bass with The Triffids and currently performs with Nick Cave and The Bad Seeds. His latest project, also featuring Nick Cave and other members of The Bad Seeds, is Grinderman.

David Cavanagh is the author of several books including *The World's Greatest Rock'n'Roll Scandals* (1997), *The Creation Records Story: My Magpie Eyes are Hungry for the Prize* (2000), and a first novel, *Music for Boys* (2003). His feature writing has appeared in *Q*, *Select* and *Mojo*.

Nick Cave is an accomplished musician, writer and actor, fronting seminal bands The Bad Seeds, The Birthday Party and The Boys Next Door. His prolific output includes plays, lectures, a novel (*And the Ass Saw the Angel*, 1985) and a screenplay (*The Proposition*, 2005), in addition to film scores and lyrics. In 2008 he was awarded an honorary doctorate of laws by Monash University, in recognition of his cultural significance.

Claire Colebrook is Professor of English at Pennsylvania State University. Her most recent books are *Deleuze: A Guide for the Perplexed* (2006), *Irony* (2007) and *Milton, Evil and Literary History* (2008).

James Cook is singer/songwriter for UK band Flamingoes. He formed the band in London in 1993 with his twin brother, Jude. They resumed recording after an eleven-year hiatus and released their latest album, *Street Noise Invades the House*, in 2007.

Chris Coughran is an Honorary Research Fellow in the School of Culture and Communication at The University of Melbourne. His work has appeared in *Reading America: New Perspectives on the American Novel* (Cambridge Scholars Publishing, 2008) and in journals such as *Symbolism, ISLE,* and *Angelaki.* He is co-editor, with Niall Lucy, of *Beautiful Waste: Poems by David McComb* (Fremantle Press, 2009).

Sean Dower is a London artist employing a range of practices, including sculpture, photography, film and sound. His works have been performed and exhibited in the UK, Europe, the US and Australia.

Laurie Duggan is an award-winning poet and cultural historian whose books include *Ghost Nation: Imagined Space and Australian Visual Culture, 1901–1939* (2001), *The Ash Range* (2005) and *The Passenger* (2006).

John Dyer is Director of Domino Recording Company in the UK.

Robert Forster is best known for his work with songwriting partner Grant McLennan, with whom he founded The Go-Betweens in Brisbane in 1977. He writes a regular column for Australian magazine *The Monthly,* and was awarded the Pascall Prize for Critical Writing in 2006. The latest of his five solo albums is *The Evangelist* (2008).

Richard Gunning is an award-winning artist based in Perth, whose work features in major public collections throughout Western Australia.

Mick Harvey played guitar, drums and other instruments with Nick Cave in The Boys Next Door, The Birthday Party and The Bad Seeds. His solo albums include *Intoxicated Man* (1995), *One Man's Treasure* (2005) and, most recently, *Three Sisters — Live at Bush*

Hall (2008). He has produced albums for (among others) Robert Forster, PJ Harvey and Anita Lane, and written soundtracks for movies including *Chopper* (2000) and *Deliver Us from Evil* (2006). His film score for *Australian Rules* won Best Original Soundtrack at the 2004 Australian Recording Industry Awards, and his *Suburban Mayhem* soundtrack was judged Best Original Music at the 2005 Australian Film Industry awards.

Megan Heyward is a multimedia artist and lecturer who teaches at The University of Technology, Sydney. She is the author of a critically acclaimed hypertext novel, *of day, of night* (Eastgate Systems, 2005).

Thomas Hoareau is a prize-winning painter who has exhibited regularly in Perth since 1981 and is represented in the National Gallery, the WA State Gallery, and various public and private collections. Credited with introducing the term 'calenture' to David McComb, he also illustrated the cover of The Triffids' early single, 'Spanish Blue/Twisted Brain', and the 7" *Reverie* E.P.

Tracee Hutchison is a broadcast journalist, presenter and producer with twenty years' experience in radio and television. She is the author of *Your Name's on the Door: Ten Years of Australian Music* (1992), and *Rock Chefs for Mirabel* (2002), a fundraising cookbook for The Mirabel Foundation featuring over thirty musicians and their recipes.

Phil Kakulas plays bass with The Blackeyed Susans. He played with The Triffids in the 1970s and rejoined them for their final studio album, *The Black Swan*.

Steve Kilbey was born in England in 1954, and moved to Australian in 1957, a 'ten-pound Pom'. He has recorded over twenty albums with his band The Church and two 'Jack Frost' albums with the late Grant McLennan. He has written three books of poetry and lives in North Bondi with his three daughters and no cat.

John Kinsella is a Fellow of Churchill College, Cambridge University, and Professor of English at the University of Western Australia. He is the author of more than thirty books of poetry, fiction, essays and memoirs, including most recently *The New Arcadia: Poems* (2007), *Disclosed Poetics: Beyond Landscape and Lyricism* (2008) and *Divine Comedy: Journeys Through a Regional Geography* (2008).

Jean Bernard Koeman is an artist and curator of the exhibition *A Temporary Monument for David McComb* (STUK, Leuven, Belgium, 2004).

Nathan Laurent is a freelance welder (second class) and independent scholar.

Graham Lee is a Melbourne musician and producer, and co-manager (with Steve Miller) of W. Minc Productions. He played pedal-steel and other guitars with The Triffids after joining the band in 1985. He plays dobro on Eric Bogle's 'And the Band Played Waltzing Matilda' and has featured as a guest musician with Paul Kelly, The Paradise Vendors, The Blackeyed Susans and The KLF (among other artists).

Judith Lucy is a Melbourne comic and writer. Her latest book is *The Lucy Family Alphabet* (2008).

Niall Lucy is a Research Fellow in the Humanities at Curtin University of Technology. His books include *Postmodern Literary Theory: An Introduction* (1997), *A Derrida Dictionary* (2004) and, with Steve Mickler, *The War on Democracy: Conservative Opinion in the Australian Press* (2006). His *Tabloid Deconstruction: Essays on Australian Culture, Now!* is forthcoming with Fremantle Press.

Alsy MacDonald is a lawyer with the Equal Opportunity Commission in Perth. He played drums and occasionally sang with The Triffids.

Robert McComb is a Melbourne high-school teacher. He played violin and guitar with The Triffids.

Andrew McGowan is an Anglican priest and Warden of Trinity College at The University of Melbourne. He played bass in an early incarnation of The Triffids, and is the author of numerous scholarly publications, including *Ascetic Eucharists: Food and Drink in Early Christian Ritual Meals* (1999).

Dom Mariani is a Perth singer, guitarist and songwriter whose bands include The Stems, The Someloves, DM3 and The Majestic Kelp.

Gavin Martin was born in Belfast and has written for *NME, Uncut, The Times* and *The Independent*. Currently music critic at *The Daily Mirror*, he has previously contributed to UK collection *The Faber Book of Pop* and US collection *Rock'n'Roll is Here to Stay*. A founding member of The Family of Rock, he currently lives in London.

Matt Merritt is a journalist and poet in Leicester, England, who has published two poetry collections including, most recently, *Troy Town* (Arrowhead Press, 2008).

Steve Miller played with The Moodists and was the UK and European tour manager for The Triffids and The Go-Betweens. He is co-manager (with Graham Lee) of W. Minc Productions, releasing albums by Mark C. Halstead, David Chesworth, Essendon Airport and many others. He lives in Melbourne.

Wilson Neate is a British freelance writer based in New York. He is the author of *Tolerating Ambiguity: Ethnicity and Community in Chicano/a Writing* (1998) and, for Continuum's 331/3 series, *Wire's Pink Flag* (2009). He holds a PhD from the University of California, Irvine, and has written for *AllMusic*, *Trouser Press*, *Perfect Sound Forever*, *Amplifier*, *PopMatters*, *Dusted* and *Pop Culture Press*.

David Nichols is the author of *The Go-Betweens* (1997, 2006) and a forthcoming history of Australian rock and pop music. He became a fan of The Triffids in the early 1980s on the recommendation of a Sydney friend. He lectures in urban planning at The University of Melbourne, and writes on urban and regional cultures, community history, and the arts.

James Paterson grew up in Brisbane during the Joh Bjelke-Petersen years and moved to Sydney with his band JFK and the Cuban Crisis in early 1982. Disillusioned with the state of music during the eighties, he dropped out of playing in bands and spent the nineties studying history at the University of Sydney, where he was awarded a PhD in 2001. He currently teaches English for a living.

DBC Pierre is an Australian-born novelist whose works include *Vernon God Little* (2003), for which he was awarded the Man Booker Prize for Fiction, and *Ludmila's Broken English* (2006).

Megan Simpson Huberman is a film writer, director, and development executive. She has directed feature films, including *Dating The Enemy* with Guy Pearce and Claudia Karvan, TV drama, and documentary. She lives in Sydney with her husband, a radio producer and former tank commander, and one very tall daughter.

Rob Snarski sings and plays guitar with The Blackeyed Susans.

Jon Stratton is Professor of Cultural Studies at Curtin University of Technology. His books include *Race Daze: Australia in Identity Crisis* (1998), *Coming Out Jewish* (2007) and *Jewish Identity in Western Popular Culture: The Holocaust and Trauma Through Modernity* (2008).

Julian Tompkin is an award-winning journalist specializing in music and culture. He has been a regular contributor to (among others) *The Australian* and *The West Australian* newspapers, and is a former music editor for *X-Press* magazine. He currently organizes music festivals (including Southbound and West Coast Blues'n'Roots) in Western Australia.

Sam Twyford-Moore is a music critic for *The Big Issue*. He has been published in *Meanjin*, and currently serves as editor for *Cutwater Literary Journal*.

Sean M. Whelan hails from Northcote, Victoria, where he writes prose, poetry and performance works. His latest book of poetry is *Tattooing the Surface of the Moon* (Small Change Press, 2008).

Julian Wu is Melbourne's number one Triffids fan. He plays guitar on some of David McComb's unreleased final recordings.

Acknowledgements

Lyrics by David McComb are reproduced with permission of Mushroom Music Publishing.

Poems by David McComb are reproduced from manuscripts kindly provided by Joanne Alach and Robert McComb.

'Hell of a Summer' by David Cavanagh first appeared in John Aizlewood's collection, *Love is the Drug: Living as a Pop Fan* (London: Penguin, 1994), reprinted here with the author's permission.

'Still Life' by Niall Lucy originally appeared as 'Still Life in the Gallery: Blue Poles or Spanish Blue?' in *Spare Times 7* (1982), 8.

'Ornithology' by Laurie Duggan is excerpted from a poem of the same name originally published in *Memorials* (Adelaide: Little Esther Books, 1996), reprinted with permission.

'A Temporary Monument' by Jean Bernard Koeman is adapted from materials supplied by the author, including STUK *Boek Beeldende Kunst 2000–2005*/STUK *Book Visual Arts 2000–2005* (Leuven: STUK, 2006).

'Extraordinary Friends' by Nick Cave first appeared in 2006 as 'Nick Cave on Dave McComb' at the Domino Recording Company (UK) website, reproduced with permission.

'WHACK! WHACK!' by Steve Kilbey is reproduced in a print-friendly format from the Internet web log *The Time Being (Being the Diary of a Certain Mr Kilbey),* by permission of the author.

'This is Not a Swan Song' by Niall Lucy is an edited version of a piece that appeared in *Countdown* magazine, c. April 1989.

A version of 'The Black Swan' by Phil Kakulas was included in the liner notes to *The Black Swan* (Domino/Liberation Blue, 2008).

'St James Infirmary' (Niall Lucy, 'Towards a Minor Music') Traditional, arranged by IRVING MILLS, © 1929 (renewed) EMI MILLS MUSIC, INC. All rights reserved. Used by permission of ALFRED PUBLISH ING CO. INC. and J ALBERT & SON PTY LTD.

'The Cliffe' by Bleddyn Butcher is an edited excerpt from the author's forthcoming biography of David McComb, *Save What You Can* (London: Helter Skelter).

'The Reissues' by John Dyer is an edited transcript of a podcast formerly hosted at the Domino Recording Company (UK) website, published by permission of the author.

'Farewell from the Wharf of Innocence' by DBC Pierre first appeared at the Domino Recording Company (UK) website, reproduced with permission.

Picture Credits

Joanne Alach: 144, 170, 205, 220, 266, 268, 280–1, 282, 287, 288, 299, 302, 328, 331. **Jill Birt:** 72, 76, 78, 112, 230, 237. **Martyn P. Casey:** 44, 45, 47, 130–1, 194, 244, 325. **Sean Dower:** 207. **Richard Gunning:** 115. **Thomas Hoareau:** 18, 226–7. **Steve Kilbey:** 293. **John Kinsella:** 174. **Jean Bernard Koeman:** 142–3. **David McComb:** 31, 129 (courtesy of Megan Simpson Huberman), 132 (courtesy of Steve Miller); 116 (courtesy of James Paterson); 219 (courtesy of Robert McComb); 228, 242 [top page] (courtesy of Jill Birt). **Denise Nestor:** 208–9, 332. **Steven Pam:** 164 (courtesy of SmartShots). **Megan Simpson Huberman:** 71, 242 [bottom page]. **Rob Snarski:** 75. **Katie Stern:** 225 (courtesy of Truckstop Media). **Unknown photographer:** 20, 24, 32, 48, 218, 301 (courtesy of Alsy MacDonald); 180 (courtesy of Graham Lee); 210 (courtesy of J.S. Battye Library of West Australian History, State Library of Western Australia). **Julian Wu:** 111, 128, 265.

All reasonable efforts have been made to trace the copyright holders of the visual material reproduced herein. The publishers and editors apologize to anyone who has not been reached.

Index

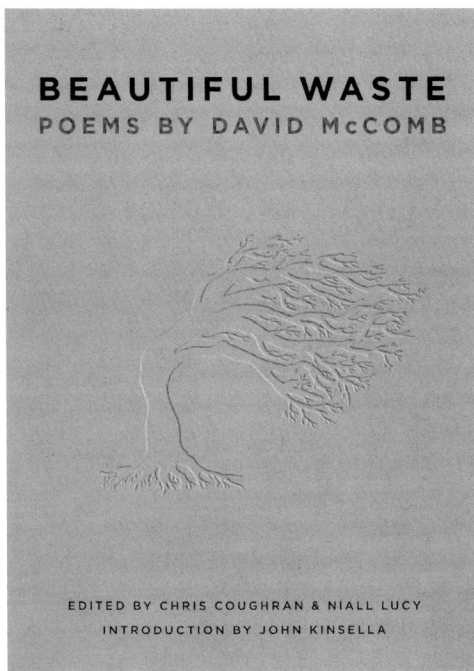

BEAUTIFUL WASTE
POEMS BY DAVID McCOMB

EDITED BY CHRIS COUGHRAN & NIALL LUCY
INTRODUCTION BY JOHN KINSELLA

David McComb, lead singer and songwriter of the Triffids - the remarkable Australian rock group of the the late '70s and '80s - died in 1999, aged just 36.
This extraordinary book of poems by McComb, hitherto unseen, displays a different facet of the songwriter's brilliance.

FREMANTLE PRESS

First published in 2009 by
FREMANTLE PRESS
25 Quarry Street, Fremantle
(PO Box 158, North Fremantle, 6159)
Western Australia
www.fremantlepress.com.au

Editors Chris Coughran and Niall Lucy
Consultant editor Georgia Richter
Cover design Allyson Crimp
Cover image Martyn P. Casey
Typography Chris Coughran

Printed by Everbest Printing Company, China

Papers used by Fremantle Press are natural, recyclable products made from wood
 grown in sustainable forests; the manufacturing processes conform to the
 environmental regulations of the country of origin.

National Library of Australia
Cataloguing-in-publication data

Vagabond holes: David McComb and the Triffids / Chris Coughran, Niall Lucy
1st ed.
9781921361623 (pbk)
Includes index
McComb, David Richard, 1962–1999
Triffids (Musical group)
Rock Groups — Australia — Biography
A781.66094